Chancellorsville
James Reason

The narrative of *Chancellorsville* begins in Missi̲̲̲̲ ̲̲̲̲ ̲̲̲̲
the western front. Before reaching Vicksburg, Cory ̲̲̲̲̲̲̲̲̲ stumbles into a
campsite where all is not well and briefly encounters a cautious Confederate
patrol. A veteran of the battles of Forts Henry and Donelson and Shiloh, but
not a soldier in the Confederate army, h continues to search for Lucille Farrell,
the daughter of his late employer. When he finds her, he also discovers that he
may have a role to play in supplying the South with the food, weapons, and
ammunition being brought in through Texas by blockade-runners. The path,
however, is strewn with renegades and outlaws, and on the horizon there may
be a rival for Lucille's affections.

Meanwhile, Cory's brothers, Will and Mac, enjoy a brief visit with the
family members still in Culpeper. Will is greatly relieved that his mother,
Abigail, who had banished him from the farm in the weeks before the war,
now welcomes him with open arms. Brother Titus's marriage to Polly Ebersole
comes as a surprise to the two brothers in gray, but their presence stirs a sense
of obligation and duty in the hotheaded Titus. Shortly after the two return to
their units—Will to the Shenandoah with Jackson and Mac with Stuart near
Richmond—the Confederate cause claims another Brannon, this one a gifted
rifleman.

In December 1862 a new Union commander launches another campaign
to claim the Southern capital, and Ambrose Burnside brings the Federal
army to Fredericksburg. With him marches the conscience-driven Nathan
Hatcher. When the battle breaks loose, Will and Mac are on the right side of
the Confederate line, and Titus is on the left. After the terrible bloodletting of
the Federal defeat, news comes that Titus has been lost. The brothers carry the
information back to Culpeper, where the aloof Polly surprisingly grieves over
the loss of Titus, her husband. She reaches out to the Brannon family and finds
a comforting response from the people she has tried to keep at arm's length.

In early 1863 a fitful calm pervades the Virginia front until yet another
Union commander is named. Joe Hooker leads his army into the wooded
wilderness of the Rappahannock again and confidently stakes his fortunes to
an encounter with Robert E. Lee near the roadside inn at Chancellorsville. As
the battle rushes toward them, Will and Mac witness the boldest move a field
commander can make and the greatest loss the Confederacy can struggle to
bear.

Chancellorsville is the fourth book in a series of historical novels spanning
the Civil War.

CHANCELLORSVILLE

The Civil War Battles Series
by James Reasoner

Manassas
Shiloh
Antietam

CHANCELLORSVILLE

James Reasoner

CUMBERLAND HOUSE
NASHVILLE, TENNESSEE

Published by
CUMBERLAND HOUSE PUBLISHING, INC.
431 Harding Industrial Drive
Nashville, Tennessee 37211
www.CumberlandHouse.com

This novel is a work of fiction. Names, characters, places, and incidents either
are the product of the author's imagination or are used fictitiously. Any resemblance to persons, living or dead, events, or locales is entirely coincidental.

Cover design by Bob Bubkis, Nashville, Tennessee.

Library of Congress Cataloging-in-Publication Data

Reasoner, James.
  Chancellorsville / James Reasoner.
    p. cm. — (The Civil War battle series ; 4)
  ISBN 1-58182-130-1 (alk. paper)
    1. Chancellorsville (Va.), Battle of, 1863—Fiction. 2. United
States—History—Civil War, 1861–1865—Fiction. I. Title.
PS3568.E2685 C47 2000
813'.54—dc21   00-055471

ISBN 978-1-58182-300-4 (pbk.)

For Scott Cupp and Willie Siros—
gentlemen, booksellers, and friends

CHANCELLORSVILLE

Chapter One

A T FIRST, CORY BRANNON thought he heard phantom voices carried toward him on the night wind. As far as he knew, he was in these Mississippi woods by himself, wrapped in a threadbare blanket and trying to get a little sleep. As the shouting continued and he realized it was real, he sat up and peered into the darkness in the direction of the unfamiliar voices.

A moment later the sharp tang of woodsmoke came drifting through the trees, accompanied almost immediately by another smell that made Cory lift his head and inhale deeply.

Meat cooking.

His empty stomach cramped. He had eaten his last piece of hardtack at midday, and stale and unappetizing though it had been, he had taken his time while chewing each bite, knowing that he might not get anything else for a while. Sure enough, by nighttime he hadn't come across a settlement or even a farm where he might have been able to trade some labor for something to eat. So he had bedded down hungry.

He pushed the blanket aside and stood up, a young man in his early twenties with a broad, friendly face and tightly curled brown hair. He had grown skinny during his long tramp across Mississippi this summer of 1862. Food was already growing scarce in these parts due to the stranglehold the Northern invaders were trying to put on the Confederacy. During his travels, Cory had heard talk that some Yankee admiral had brought a fleet of warships into New Orleans and captured the city, cutting off much of the traffic up the Mississippi River. The Union controlled Cairo, Illinois, too, as Cory had good reason to know, so they had both ends of the South's major trade route bottled up.

Cory didn't have any great fondness for New Orleans—he had nearly lost his life there—but he hated to think about that lively, colorful city being in the hands of the Yankees. That just wasn't right.

At the moment, however, he wasn't thinking about the war. His thoughts were centered on his belly. He had known hunger before. A few times during his months as a wharf rat in New Madrid, Missouri, he had thought that he was going to starve to death. An empty gut was something a fellow never really got used to.

But now, somewhere nearby, somebody was cooking supper. Maybe, if they had a little to spare, they would be willing to share it with another traveler.

Cory picked up his blanket, stuffed it into the rough canvas pouch in which he carried his few belongings, and put on his old, battered, floppy-brimmed hat. He started walking, following the sound of the voices, and only muttered a few curses when he stumbled into branches and tree trunks in the darkness.

The smell of food grew stronger, causing Cory's stomach to complain even more. Up ahead, someone laughed raucously. A man's voice called out what sounded like a question, but Cory couldn't make out the words. He spotted a faint red glow filtering through the trees and altered his direction a little so that he was headed right toward it.

Suddenly someone screamed, and a shot split the night. The screaming grew louder.

Cory halted in his tracks. Whatever was going on, it wasn't nearly as innocent as he had hoped it would be. In fact, it sounded like trouble, and if there was one thing Coriolanus Troilus Brannon avoided like the plague, if at all possible, it was trouble. After fighting at Fort Henry and Fort Donelson and Shiloh, he'd had more than his share.

He could turn around and fade back into the woods right now, he told himself. That would mean staying hungry all night, but he could stand a few hunger pangs. In the morning, he could move on toward Vicksburg and surely find something to eat somewhere. Whatever was going on in that camp up ahead, the people involved would never know he was anywhere around. There was no good reason he could see for getting himself involved in it. Besides, while he was standing there, pondering on it, the screaming had stopped.

Of course, that might not be a *good* thing . . .

He made it as far as actually turning around, then he stopped and stood there for a long moment before sighing heavily. He opened his pouch and took out the pistol that had been given him before he left Corinth. Given to him by Col. Nathan Bedford Forrest. Cory confirmed that it was loaded and tucked it behind his belt. He turned toward the glow of the campfire once again.

As he got closer, he began to hear something like whimpering. For a moment he thought it might be an animal, then he realized that a person was making that wretched sound. When he could make out the actual flames of the campfire through the trees, he stopped and allowed his eyes to adjust to the glare. Crouching in the brush, he peered through the branches and tried to see what was going on.

The first thing he was able to make out was a pair of feet in some worn-out boots, the toes pointing up. The feet didn't move. Cory shifted slightly, moving carefully and quietly, and his eyes followed the legs to the feet. They ended at a man's body, but Cory couldn't make out much of his torso because a woman was draped over him, her back shuddering as she sobbed. Her fearful sobs filled the air.

"Get all that damned cryin' out now, gal," a harsh voice commanded. "I ain't goin' to be in no mood to listen to it later."

Another man laughed. "I didn't think you cared how a gal was carryin' on, Enoch."

A third man spoke. "You always said a little fightin' made the lovin' sweeter. Ain't that right?"

"Shut up!" Enoch ordered. "You shot him 'fore I told you to, so all that caterwaulin' is your fault, Jarvis."

"He had a gun! You seen it yourself."

"That ol' horse pistol probably ain't been fired in twenty years. It'd likely blowed up in his hand had he tried to shoot you."

"Well, I didn't have no way of knowin' that, did I?" whined the third man—Jarvis.

The second man interrupted, "We gonna eat fust or what?"

"If you don't let that rabbit burn," Enoch said. "Best turn it."

"I think I know how to cook a damn rabbit."

"Just don't burn it. I don't like burned meat."

Cory's mouth tightened grimly. The three men had just killed a man and planned to rape the woman who was crying over his body, and they were arguing about how to cook a rabbit! He wished he could charge into the camp and gun down all three of them.

But that would probably just get him killed, and that wouldn't help the woman at all. Reviewing his options, Corey realized that he could not be sure there were only three men at the camp. There could be others who hadn't spoken yet, or who were off tending to horses or standing guard. He just didn't know.

As far as he could see, there was only one way to find out.

He stood up and started toward the camp, this time pushing through the brush and branches and making quite a racket. That would warn the men that someone was coming, and when he had gone a few feet he made sure of it by calling out, "Hello, the camp!" He didn't want to surprise the trio.

"Who's out there?" Enoch shouted. "Answer me, damn it! We got guns!"

"Stand easy, mister!" Cory called back. "Just a lost, hungry pilgrim." He came to the edge of the clearing where the camp had been made. "I smelled your fire and was hoping you might have a bite to share," he said as he emerged into the open, moving slowly with his hands half-lifted to show that he was no threat.

"You alone?" The question lashed at him from a short, thick-bodied man with bristly brown whiskers. That was Enoch, Cory thought, matching the voice with the name he had heard earlier.

Enoch seemed to be the leader of this group. He had a pistol in his hand.

Two more men stood next to the fire, to Cory's right. One was tall and slender and had nervous hands and eyes. He was carrying a gun, and he made Cory nervous, too. "We better shoot him, Enoch," he said. Jarvis, Cory decided. The one who had been quick on the trigger before, resulting in the body sprawled almost at Cory's feet.

The third man was short like Enoch but slender and rather mild-looking. He had lank fair hair, and like the other two, he wore a ragged butternut-colored Confederate tunic. They all wore civilian trousers, likely stolen. Cory pegged the three as deserters as soon as he'd gotten a good look at them.

He managed to smile, despite the presence of the dead man and the grieving woman. "No call for trouble, gents," he said. "All I'm interested in is maybe a haunch off that rabbit." Cory gestured toward the fire. "It's starting to burn, by the way."

"Damn it, Darby, I told you—" Enoch began angrily.

"I'm turnin' it, I'm turnin' it," the fair-haired man said as he knelt by the fire and adjusted the spit on which the skinned carcass of the rabbit had been impaled.

Enoch turned his attention back to Cory, and Jarvis asked, "You want me to shoot him?"

"Put that gun up, you idiot. This boy's no threat to us." Enoch lowered his own weapon, but he didn't holster it. "What are you doin' out here in the woods by yourself, boy? You are by yourself, ain't you? You didn't answer me before."

Cory nodded. "Yes sir, I sure am. I'm bound for Vicksburg. Got kin there." That was a lie, but only a small one. He fully intended to marry Lucille Farrell when he found her, and that would make them related.

And he *would* find her. Cory never let himself doubt that, not for a second.

"You ain't a deserter, are you? Bein' good Confederate troopers, we'd have to turn you in."

Cory didn't mention the civilian trousers they were wearing, or the fact that they were obviously not attached to any Confederate unit out here in the middle of these lonely woods. "No sir, I'm not a soldier," he answered. "Never enlisted."

That was true enough. He had fought the Yankees in three battles and ridden alongside Forrest, but he had never officially been a part of the Confederate army.

Jarvis lowered his gun, but like Enoch, he did not holster it. He said, "This fella's got a gun. I don't trust him."

Enoch snorted. "Only a damned fool'd go unarmed the way things are now. What's your name, boy?"

"Cory. Cory Brannon."

"Light and sit a spell, Mr. Brannon," The big man invited. "Rabbit's sort of small to be split up four ways, but I reckon we can manage."

Cory moved to the left so that he could step around the woman and the dead man. As he did so, the woman lifted her head and stared up at him with a twisted, tear-streaked, hollow-eyed face. She begged in a soft, tearful whisper, "Help me!"

Cory said, "There's not a thing I can do, ma'am," and stepped past her, turning his back toward her. He could hear her sobs as she collapsed on the body again.

"You're a smart lad, knowin' when not to mix in with something that ain't none of your business," Enoch said. He sat down on one end of a deadfall and motioned Cory onto the other end. Across the fire, Jarvis finally slid his pistol into its holster. Darby still fussed over the rabbit. Juices fell into the fire from the carcass, making the flames hiss and spit.

"Just out of curiosity, what happened here?" Cory asked. He inclined his head toward the woman and the dead man without looking at them.

Enoch sighed heavily. "Those folks been travelin' with us today. They were bound for Vicksburg, too, like you and us. Just met up with 'em this mornin' on the road. But tonight, once we'd made camp the fella decided he was goin' to rob us. Wouldn't be surprised if they'd pulled that on other innocent folks before. But we managed to shoot him before he could hurt anybody."

Cory tried to control his expression at the obvious lie. The dead man was no more a robber than he was. Chances were that Enoch and his companions, as soon as they encountered the couple, had planned to kill the man and molest the woman. Jarvis might have acted a little sooner than what Enoch had in mind, but he hadn't changed the eventual outcome.

"That's a damned shame," Cory said with a shake of his head. "Can't trust anybody these days, can you?"

"Not many," Enoch said. "You're lucky you fell in with us, young fella. We'll do right by you."

"I appreciate that." Cory had seen the greedy way they were eyeing his boots and his gun. He supposed they figured that letting him eat a hot meal before they gunned him down or cut his throat was doing right by him. He pushed his luck a little further by asking, "What about the lady?"

"Well, now . . . ," Enoch grinned and licked his lips. "I reckon she owes us somethin', considerin' what her man tried to do, don't you?"

Cory held up both hands, palms out. "I was just curious. I wasn't here when it happened, so I got no part in it."

"That's right," said Jarvis. "You got no part."

"Fine by me," Cory declared.

Darby took the rabbit off the fire. "Let it cool for a minute, then we'll eat."

"Save a good piece for our young friend," Enoch instructed.

Cory wasn't sure that he could eat anything. He tasted bile in his mouth. His belly might be empty, but what he had seen and heard had pretty well killed his appetite. It was bad enough that scavengers such as these men were roaming the countryside, but it made him sick to think that once they had fought for the same cause as he.

He was confident now that there were only three of them. He hadn't seen any sign of any other men, nor had anyone else been mentioned. Three-to-one odds were bad enough, though. He wasn't sure what he could do. A part of him wished he had gone back and curled up under that tree where he had been earlier.

It was too late for that now. Before the night was over, he would have to do *something,* or his own life would be forfeit.

Darby cut off a haunch from the cooling rabbit and handed it to Enoch. He gave the other one to Cory, then started cutting up the rest of the rabbit for himself and Jarvis. Cory didn't think the woman would eat, but the men made no move to offer her anything. That convinced him as much as anything that they planned to kill her when they were finished with her.

He forced himself to eat, trying to appear enthusiastic as he used his teeth to tear off strips of the tough, stringy meat. Under other circumstances, the rabbit might have tasted good, but not tonight. Even now, though, the food gave him some strength after doing without for so many hours. He wound up gnawing the haunch down to the bone.

By that time the woman had stopped crying. She was lying over the body of the dead man, almost as motionless as he was. Cory decided she had passed out from shock and grief. If not for the faintly discernible rise and fall of her back as she breathed, he might have taken her for dead, too.

Cory wasn't the only one who noticed. Jarvis pointed at her and laughed. "Look at that, would you? She's done dozed off."

Sleep had nothing to do with it, Cory thought. The woman's mind just couldn't handle any more terror, so it had retreated into insensibility. He had known such moments himself.

Enoch belched and announced, "Well, now, we'll just have to wake her up, won't we?"

"You goin' first, Enoch?" Darby asked.

"Damn right." Enoch stood up, gave his trousers a hitch, and stepped toward the woman.

Cory came off the log, slamming into the back of Enoch's legs and dumping him face first in the fire. Sparks flew everywhere, arcing brightly through the air as the big man screamed.

Cory landed on his hands and knees. He grabbed desperately for his gun as Jarvis and Darby both yelled in surprise. Jarvis's gun came up, and Cory went to the side in a rolling dive. A shot blasted loudly. Cory wound up on his stomach, unhit, and used both hands to steady the pistol as he fired across the top of Enoch, who was trying to writhe out of the scattered fire. Cory's shot hit Jarvis high on the right thigh and knocked him down. Jarvis dropped the gun, and Darby scrambled for it.

Forgetting in the heat of the moment what he had learned from Bedford Forrest about firing a handgun, Cory pulled back the hammer and jerked the trigger as he pointed the barrel toward Darby. He missed, but he came close enough to make the man jump back, away from the fallen gun. "Don't kill me!" Darby screeched as he lost his balance and sat down hard. He tried to scuttle away. "Please don't kill me!"

Cory rose to his knees, cocking the pistol again as he did so. That made him a bigger target, and Darby suddenly whipped his arm back and then forward. The knife he had used to cut up the rabbit flickered across the clearing and hit Cory in the left arm, cutting a painful gash as it glanced off his arm just below the shoulder. Instinctively, Cory pulled the trigger, and a bullet smashed into Darby's chest, driving him over backward.

With a roar of rage, Enoch finally got his hands and knees under him and pushed himself out of the fire. He came at Cory, his face a mass of burned, raw tissue, but his feet got tangled in the legs of the unconscious woman, and he fell, toppling to the side like a tree. That gave Cory the time he needed to aim his weapon. The pistol bucked against his hand as it sent a bullet into Enoch's head. The big man groaned and rolled over onto his back. His arms fell loosely out on either side of him. One hand landed in a pile of twigs from the fire that was still burning. The hand didn't move, didn't even twitch, as the flames licked hungrily at it.

Cory got shakily to his feet. His ears ached from the gunfire. He was sure Enoch was dead, and one look at the glassy-eyed expression on Darby's face told him the fair-haired man was dead, too. That left Jarvis.

The remaining marauder was lying on his back in what looked like a large puddle of black ink. It took Cory a moment to realize it was a pool of blood. His shot must have hit an artery, and Jarvis's blood had pumped out steadily until the man's face was colorless in the uncertain light from the scattered fire. He was still moving a little and mumbling incoherently, but as Cory watched, the movement stopped and a harsh, rattling gurgle came from his throat. After that, silence.

Three men, Cory considered. He had just killed three men in a matter of a minute or less.

He had killed men in battle before, and always when he was pushed hard enough he would fight back. But he had never fought like this, savagely, three against one in close quarters. He didn't know whether to feel proud of what he had done or sick. Numbly, he broke open the revolver and reloaded the cylinder.

The woman stirred as he closed the gun.

Cory tucked the weapon behind his belt again. He knelt beside her and reached out, saying quietly, "Let me help you, ma'am. It's all over now."

As her eyes opened, she screamed and jerked away from him. Cory backed off in a hurry, his hands held up so that she could see they were empty.

"Those men who were going to hurt you are dead," he told her. "They can't do anything to you now."

The woman covered her face with her hands and shook for a long moment. Then she clenched her fists and began to pound the body of the man lying dead beside her. "No! No!" she screamed over and over.

When she finally fell silent, Cory ventured, "Was . . . was he your husband, ma'am?"

She answered with a fresh round of wailing sobs, and Cory wished he hadn't said anything. He busied himself gathering Enoch's and Jarvis's weapons, along with Darby's knife.

The cut on his arm, which he had barely noticed at the time, was hurting like blazes now. He kicked some twigs into the flickering fire so it blazed up brightly, and by the light of the rekindled campfire he tore a strip of cloth off the bottom of his shirt and awkwardly tied it as tightly as he could, one-handed, around his injured arm.

When he looked at the woman again, she was pushing at the corpse. After a moment, Cory realized she was trying to turn the dead man onto his stomach. He wasn't sure why she wanted to do that, but he supposed it wouldn't hurt anything to help her. She didn't cringe away from him this time as he bent and said, "Let me give you a hand, ma'am."

Leaning over the dead man like this, Cory got a first look at his face. The man had been about thirty years old, dark-haired, and probably would have been handsome if his features hadn't been frozen in a grimace of agony. The woman was a couple of years younger. Surely they had been married, Cory told himself. A couple on their way to somewhere, from somewhere, and they had had the bad luck to cross paths with a trio of animals like Enoch, Jarvis, and Darby. When the woman calmed down, Cory would ask her name and where she and her husband had been bound. He didn't want to delay his getting to Vicksburg, since Lucille might be there, but he couldn't abandon this woman. He would have to see to it that she got where she was going, if it was in his power.

Together, Cory and the woman rolled the dead man onto his left side, and then he fell over onto his stomach. Cory distinctly heard gas gurgle inside the corpse, and again he felt sick for a moment. As he swallowed hard, he saw that the man had fallen onto his gun when Jarvis shot him, the horse pistol that Enoch had mentioned. It was indeed old and didn't look like much of a threat.

But the weapon still worked, Cory discovered a second later when the woman gave a strangled cry and snatched it up. She cocked it as she staggered to her feet and pointed it two-handed at Enoch's corpse. She fired, the recoil nearly tearing the gun from her fingers. The bullet took Enoch in the face, smashing his cheek. The woman cocked the gun again and turned toward Jarvis. She fired. It was Darby's turn next, as she drove a slug into his face.

Cory didn't move, figuring the gesture of vengeance wouldn't hurt anything. Then he started to worry as the woman swung around toward him. What if she thought he was one of them, despite all the assurances he had given her that he was not, and took a shot at him, too. He tensed, ready to try to dive away from a bullet.

Instead, the woman tipped the barrel of the gun up, shoved it into her mouth, and pulled the trigger. Cory cried out in shock and horror as the bullet exploded out the back of the woman's head. She folded up on the ground, crumpling like a discarded doll.

Cory stared at her for a long time, his mouth open. Somehow, this death was more shocking than all the deaths he had seen on the battlefield at Shiloh. Finally, he raised a trembling hand and dragged the back of it across his mouth.

He would have to dig a grave, he told himself. It would have to be big enough for the woman and her husband, if that was who he had been. It no longer mattered.

As for the three renegades . . . well, those bastards could lay where they had fallen. Burying was too good for them.

Cory searched for a broken branch to use to scrape out a grave. It was going to be a long night.

A crashing in the brush made him stop and look up, eyes widening. A second later he heard hoofbeats, and before he could move, several riders came out of the trees and reined in sharply at the sight of the campfire and Cory standing there with five corpses scattered around him.

"Well, son," said the Confederate captain who was pointing a revolver at him, "you look like you've been a mite busy."

Chapter Two

BEFORE CORY COULD SAY anything, the captain issued orders to the three men accompanying him, "Somebody drag that body out of the fire. I can't stand the smell of burning flesh."

Cory thought Enoch's smoldering hand smelled pretty bad, too, so he was glad when a couple of the gray-clad troopers dismounted from their horses and pulled the big man's body away from the fire.

"What do you have to say for yourself, mister?" asked the captain.

"I don't know, sir," Cory replied. "What do you want me to say?"

The captain's mouth tightened slightly. "You could start by telling me how all these people wound up dead."

Cory pointed at the woman's husband, or whoever the man had been. "He was shot by that one over there, the one who bled to death from the leg wound. I killed him and the other two men, and the lady shot herself."

"You killed three men? By yourself?" The captain sounded more than a little skeptical.

"I didn't have any choice. If I hadn't, they would have killed me." Cory indicated the bloodstained rag tied around his arm. "I got this when one of them threw a knife at me."

"You'd better start at the beginning."

Cory took a breath and tried to order his thoughts so that he could explain everything clearly. Before he could say anything, however, one of the troopers spoke up. "Cap'n, I know this fella. He's Enoch Barstow. Part of a militia company from North Carolina. Leastways, he was until he deserted a while back." The soldier spat. "Barstow was a sorry son of a bitch, and if them other two was travelin' with him, you can bet they were, too."

"They killed the man, like I told you, and planned to violate the woman," Cory said. "I figure they were planning to kill her, too."

The captain regarded him narrowly. "Were you a friend of theirs?"

Emphatically, Cory shook his head. "No sir. Never saw them before tonight. I was bedded down not far from here when I smelled their smoke. I came looking, thinking maybe they'd share some food with me." He paused, then added, "I hadn't eaten since noon, and that was just a little piece of hardtack."

The nearest trooper made a face. Cory understood. Hardtack was almost universally despised in the Confederate army. For all he knew, the Federals ate the stuff, too, and felt the same way about it.

The captain still looked like he couldn't make up his mind if he believed Cory or not. "What's your name?" he asked.

"Cory Brannon, sir."

"Where are you from, Brannon?"

"Culpeper, Virginia," he answered.

The captain lifted his eyebrows. "You're a long way from home."

"I've been out here for the past couple of years," Cory explained. "Spent some time in Missouri, then worked on a riverboat for a while. The *Missouri Zephyr*."

"Never heard of it," the officer said with a shake of his head. "How come you're not in the army? Or are you a deserter, too?"

"No sir, I'm not," Cory replied, and the indignation in his voice was real. "I just never joined up. But that didn't stop me from fighting at Forts Henry and Donelson and Shiloh."

"You were at Shiloh?" the captain asked sharply.

"Yes sir. I was part of the charges at the Hornet's Nest."

One of the troopers let out a low whistle. "That was some mighty bad fightin'."

Cory nodded. He still sometimes had nightmares about that day. "Yes," he said quietly. "It was."

The captain holstered his gun. "Well, I don't know whether to believe you or not, but I don't suppose I have any reason not to. You've come right out with your answers to everything I've asked you. I'm still not sure how you managed to kill three hard cases like these men, though."

"Like I said, Captain, I didn't have any choice."

"And the woman shot herself?"

Cory felt a fresh wave of nausea at the memory of the suicide. "Yes sir," he choked out. "I figure she and that fella were married, and she couldn't bring herself to live without him."

"Foolishness," the captain said, yet his voice held some sympathy. "Life is always worth living."

Cory wanted to believe that, but he wasn't so sure. When he thought about what he might do if he were forced to watch Lucille gunned down before his eyes, he just couldn't say. If the men responsible for her death were already dead themselves, he might not be able to see any reason to go on living, either.

"We gonna bury these folks, Cap'n?" one of the men asked.

"Of course."

"Even Barstow and them other two?"

The captain considered, then nodded. "Bury all of them. But not in the same grave. I know it'll take longer that way, but it just wouldn't be proper to do otherwise."

Cory agreed with that. He said, "I'll be glad to help."

"All right, Brannon. Dawes, hand this young man a shovel."

For the next hour, Cory and the troopers dug a pair of graves. Unceremoniously, they rolled Enoch, Jarvis, and Darby into the larger of the two holes, then more carefully placed the other two bodies in the second grave.

The captain commented, "I wish we could wrap them in something, but we don't have any blankets to spare."

Neither did Cory. Dry-eyed, he helped shovel the dirt back into the graves. He had done what he could for the man and the woman. It hadn't been enough, not hardly, but it was all he could do.

When they were finished, the captain ordered the fire extinguished. "We're on patrol," he explained to Cory, "and we've got to get back to it. There are rumors that Grant is sending out spies in preparation for an overland attack on Vicksburg, so we're keeping an eye out for them."

Cory's interest quickened, and he hoped the captain would tarry long enough to answer a question or two. "Excuse me, sir, but how far are we from Vicksburg?" Cory knew he was south of the settlement at Grenada, somewhere near the Big Black River, but that approximation was the best he could do.

"It's about 150 miles southwest of here," the captain replied. "Is that where you're bound?"

"Yes sir."

"On foot?"

"That's right."

"You've still got a long walk ahead of you, then."

"Yes sir. But I walked here from Corinth, so I reckon I can make it the rest of the way."

The captain nodded. "Good luck to you, then, Mr. Brannon."

"One last question, Captain."

"What is it?" the officer asked, impatient now.

"Do you have any news from Vicksburg? The Confederacy still controls the town?"

"Of course. The people who live in Vicksburg don't have any quit in them. That bastard Farragut steamed upriver from New Orleans last month and shelled the city, but he was driven back by our batteries and gunboats."

"Was there much damage in the city?"

"Considerable, from what I've heard." The captain frowned at Cory. "Do you have kin in Vicksburg, Mr. Brannon?"

Cory's reply was closer to the truth this time. "Of a sort. I hope to find a Charles Thompson, my fiancée's uncle. She may be staying with him. He's a captain in the Mississippi Home Guard."

In fact, Cory didn't know that the Charles Thompson in Vicksburg was Lucille's uncle, nor did he know that Lucille herself was in Vicksburg. She had gone to Nashville when her father sent her away from Fort Donelson, but when Cory had arrived there, after the fort had fallen to the Federals, he found the Thompson family gone. Not until later, after the battle at Shiloh, had Nathan Bedford Forrest told Cory about hearing of a captain in the Mississippi Home Guard named Charles Thompson. That news had set Cory on the path to Vicksburg in hopes of being reunited with the woman he loved.

"Don't believe I know the man," the captain said. "But I hope you find what you're looking for in Vicksburg, Mr. Brannon."

"So do I, sir."

"In the meantime, you'd best sleep with one eye open. This was a beautiful country once, but the war has changed it."

Cory nodded in understanding. From what he had seen over the past year, he had learned that war changed just about everything—and seldom for the better.

⚊⚊⚊

EXCEPT FOR the guns and ammunition, the Confederate patrol let him scrounge whatever he wanted from the packs of Enoch and the other two deserters, but that didn't amount to much. Cory didn't want their lice-ridden blankets or any of their clothes. He salvaged a canteen, the knife, and a mouth harp that he couldn't play. He might be able to trade it for something later on, though, he reasoned as he tucked it in his pocket. He also took some hardtack that he found in one of the packs. It was better than nothing.

He made his way through the woods for another mile or so, wanting to put some distance between himself and the site of the killings before he bedded down again. When he finally curled up under a tree, he didn't sleep well, and even though he was weary, he was just as glad when the sun came up the next morning and he was able to set off again on his journey.

The Mississippi terrain was low and rolling and heavily wooded. None of the ridges were tall enough to be called hills as far as Cory was concerned. Having grown up in sight of the Blue Ridge, he knew mountains when he saw them. The landscape was broken up frequently by creeks that flowed into the Big Black River. He also came across quite a few fields that had been cleared of brush and trees but now lay fallow, abandoned by the families that had farmed here.

From time to time as he trekked toward Vicksburg, he ran across a farm that was still being worked, usually by a woman and children, the man of the family having gone off to war. More than once as he approached ramshackle cabins, he saw youngsters scurrying off to hide, then a grim-faced woman would appear with an old musket or a shotgun or sometimes just a pitchfork. He knew they took him for a deserter or a renegade, and it saddened him to see people who had once been friendly and hospitable turned so hostile. Anytime he wasn't able to convince them easily that he meant no harm, he moved on without delay, not wanting to worry anybody unduly.

There were plantations, too, still being worked by slaves. Cory found that he wasn't much more welcome there than he was on the small farms, though occasionally he was offered a meal by the matriarch of some vast estate who was struggling to keep things going while her husband was serving in the army. As Cory looked around, he saw that most of the overseers on the plantations were gone, too; this was now a land of white women and children, and slaves. The slaves could have left, but habit and loyalty kept most of them where they were.

The days passed slowly, and Cory spent them trudging along roads choked with yellowish-brown dust, the sun beating down hotly overhead. He figured that he made between fifteen and twenty miles on a good day, but his route twisted and turned so much that he was sure he wasn't getting that much closer to his destination.

Finally he came to a small settlement where the trail crossed a railroad line. The tracks stretched due east and west, and as Cory stood beside the rails and gazed along them, he wondered if the railroad went to Vicksburg. He looked around for somebody to ask.

There was no depot here, just a flag stop, but a man was sitting in a chair under a shed next to the railroad tracks. The chair was tipped back, and snores filled the air. A long-eared dog lounged nearby. Cory walked toward them and called out, "Excuse me? Sir?"

The dog stirred and growled a little, and the man snorted a couple of times under the brim of a hat he kept pulled down over his face. He let the cane-bottomed chair come forward until all four legs touched the ground. After scrubbing a hand over his broad, sunburned face for a moment, he looked up and asked, "What you want, boy? It better be important. I was sleepin' good."

Cory gestured toward the tracks. "Does this railroad go to Vicksburg?"

"It sure does. This here's the Southern Mississippi Railroad, the finest railroad in the South. I should know, since I'm one of the board of directors."

Cory had taken the man for a farmer because he was wearing threadbare overalls and boots with holes in them and an old, sweat-stained hat. He kept his thoughts to himself, though, as he asked, "Do you know when the next westbound train will be along?"

"Was supposed to be through yesterday." The man shrugged. "Schedules ain't what they once was. The army's got a habit of commandeerin' trains whenever they need to move men or supplies from one place to another."

Cory nodded in understanding. "But the tracks definitely go to Vicksburg?"

"Yes sir. That where you're headed, boy?"

"That's right."

The man leaned his chair back against the wall of the shed again. "Well, you just follow them tracks," he said as he pulled his hat down again to shade his eyes. "They'll get you there."

"Much obliged," Cory said, but the man was already taking a deep breath and settling back down into his nap.

Cory started walking along the tracks. He wished he had thought to ask how many miles it was to Vicksburg. At least he didn't have to worry now about getting lost. If he just followed the tracks, he would get where he was going sooner or later.

CORY WALKED at the bottom of the little embankment on which the railroad tracks were laid. He had tried walking on the roadbed itself for a while, but that had proven too difficult. The soles of his shoes were thin, and the rocks of the bed hurt his feet.

Late in the afternoon, with night coming on, he retreated into the woods once more, finding a fairly comfortable spot about fifty yards away from the tracks. He gnawed on a piece of hardtack for a while, then put away what was left of it. He was almost out of food again. After taking a swig of creek water from the canteen, he leaned his back against a tree trunk and dug the mouth harp out of his pack. Frowning at it in the gathering darkness, he wondered if he might learn to play it. He put it in his mouth and blew tentatively. A noise came out of the instrument, but it didn't sound like music to Cory. He experimented for a few minutes, blowing in the harp in different ways, but none of the sounds he produced were anywhere close to melodious. Stubbornly, he kept playing, and suddenly the notes sounded a lot better. They sounded, in fact, just like the song "Dixie."

Cory lowered the mouth harp, and the music continued. He had known that he hadn't suddenly mastered the instrument. Someone else was close by with another mouth harp, someone who actually knew how to play it. Cory hurriedly got to his feet as a man strolled out of the brush, his hands moving the harp back and forth in his mouth as he finished the song with a flourish.

Then the man lowered his arms and grinned at Cory, saying, "Howdy. Heard somebody killin' a cat over here and figured I'd see what was goin' on."

Cory held up the mouth harp he had "inherited" from the dead renegades. "I, uh, was trying to figure out how to play."

"Well, you got a far piece to go, no offense." The man wiped his hand on his trousers, then stepped forward and offered it to Cory. "Name's Pie. Pie Jones. Ain't my real name, o' course, but that's what ever'body's called me since I was a little feller, on account of how much I like to eat pie."

Cory could have guessed that from the man's roundish figure; Pie Jones looked to be almost as wide as he was tall. He had a brown beard and a thatch of sandy brown hair under a floppy-brimmed hat. His ample belly strained at a pair of canvas trousers and a linsey-woolsey shirt with a leather vest over it. Cory also noticed a hunting knife with a long, heavy blade tucked behind the man's belt, but other than that he seemed to be unarmed.

The two men shook hands and Cory introduced himself.

"Pleased to meet you," Pie responded. "You got a reason for bein' out in these woods, besides sparin' innocent folks from havin' to listen to them unholy sounds you was makin'?"

"I'm heading to Vicksburg," Cory said. His instincts told him that unlike Enoch Barstow and his two companions, Pie Jones didn't represent any sort of threat to him. Still, he was going to be cautious.

"Is that a fact?" said Pie. "So'm I. Figured to enlist in the army there and fight me some Yankees when they come down the river. That what you're goin' to do?"

"I don't know yet," Cory replied honestly. "I'm looking for someone, and it all depends on whether or not I find her."

Pie chuckled. "A gal, huh? Well, good luck. You'll need it. Say, you want to sort of stick together, since we're headin' for the same place? I could teach you how to play that thing." He gestured toward the mouth harp.

Cory shrugged. He didn't fully trust Pie, but he didn't want to act overly suspicious and make the man angry at him. "I guess if we're going the same direction . . ."

"Good." Pie reached behind him and brought around a pack that was slung over his shoulder by a broad strap. "I got some ham in here. Want some?"

Cory's mouth instantly watered. If Pie was offering to share his food, he couldn't have anything evil in mind, Cory told himself. Then he remembered the rabbit haunch he had eaten at the deserters' camp.

The lure of the ham was too much, though. Cory said, "Sure. I'm much obliged."

"Shoot, we're partners now, I reckon," Pie said as he took the meat out of his pack, unwrapped some paper from around it, and peeled off a couple of strips from the slab. "Here you go."

"I've got a little hardtack left if you want some," Cory offered, not wanting to take the food without offering to share what he had in return.

Pie made a face. "Biscuits is better." He reached in the pack again. "Here you go. Try one o' these. My granny made a mess of 'em for me 'fore I left the farm. They're a mite dry but still pretty good."

A hundred times better than hardtack, thought Cory as he bit into the biscuit a moment later. He sat down and ate it with the ham. When he finished he felt better than he had in days.

Pie sat cross-legged under another tree and ate his supper along with Cory as night fell. They didn't build a fire. The night was plenty warm without one, and Cory had learned not to call attention to himself as he journeyed through this area where everyone was on edge, waiting for the seemingly inevitable Yankee invasion.

"Seen any fightin'?" Pie asked when they were finished.

"A little," Cory admitted. "I was at Shiloh. And Henry and Donelson before that."

"Lordy mercy," Pie said. "A feller from back home was at Shiloh. He come back with both legs blowed off. Didn't live long after he got home, the poor devil."

Cory nodded. "It was bad, all right. I saw a lot of men killed."

"Them Yankee bastards get you?"

"Not a scratch. I was lucky."

"Dang right! I'm glad I met up with you, Cory. Maybe some o' your good luck'll rub off on me if we're travelin' together."

"I was lucky at Shiloh," Cory said. "I don't know how long it'll last."

"I'm willin' to take a chance." Pie tapped his mouth harp against the palm of his other hand. "Now, you want to start learnin' how to play this here thing, or are you ready for some shuteye?"

After a decent meal, Cory found that he wasn't as tired as he had been earlier. "Maybe I could try to play it for a little while," he said.

"All right. It's just like ever'thing else in life, the first thing you got to do is learn how to hold your mouth right . . ."

Chapter Three

BY THE TIME CORY curled up in his blanket and went to sleep, he still couldn't produce any sounds on the mouth harp that qualified as music, but the notes coming from it were less harsh and dissonant, he thought. He slept well, and after a breakfast of biscuits and ham, he and Pie started walking along the railroad tracks toward Vicksburg.

As they walked, they told each other about their families. Cory explained how his father, John Brannon, had named his oldest son William Shakespeare Brannon after the immortal Bard of Avon. "I reckon Pa knew by heart just about everything Shakespeare ever wrote," Cory said. "He could sit and quote from the plays for hours."

"My daddy couldn't read," Pie said. "For that matter, neither can I. But he was durned near the singin'est man you'll ever see. He knowed all the old songs and hymns. Pretty good fiddle player, too."

"Did he teach you how to play the mouth harp?"

"Nope, I sorta just picked that up on my own. You got any other brothers and sisters?"

"MacBeth Richard Brannon, Titus Andronicus Brannon, Henry Julius Brannon, and Cordelia Ophelia Brannon."

Pie whistled. "Them names are a mouthful."

"They're all characters from Shakespeare's plays."

"How come him to call you somethin' as simple as Cory?"

Cory hesitated then said, "My full name is Coriolanus Troilus Brannon."

Pie threw his head back and laughed. "Reckon I see how come you go by Cory! How'd your ma feel about your pa givin' all you youngsters such highfalutin' names?"

"She didn't much like it. But then she didn't much like my father, either. He was the restless sort. I reckon I got that from him, because I left home as soon as I got old enough."

"Me, I'd've been happy to stay on the farm all my borned days," said Pie, "if it hadn't been for them damned Yankees. I figure it's my duty to help send 'em packin'."

"They won't go easy."

"No, I suppose not. But we can't just let 'em run roughshod over us, neither."

Cory couldn't argue with that. He had fought the Northern invaders before and probably would again.

Cory told Pie about his days on the *Missouri Zephyr* and how he had dreamed of someday being a riverboat pilot. Somewhat more reluctantly, he spoke of his friend Ike Judson, the pilot who had been killed at the battle of Fort Henry, and the *Zephyr*'s captain, Ezekiel Farrell, the man more responsible than anyone else for Cory turning his life around. Farrell had been killed at Fort Donelson, but not before he had taught Cory a great deal about honor and responsibility.

And Farrell's daughter, Lucille, was the woman Cory loved. When he talked about her, he couldn't help but smile, and Pie chuckled. "You got it bad, all right," the big man said. "I hope you find her when we get to Vicksburg."

Around the middle of the afternoon, they came to a trestle that spanned a broad, sluggish stream. They started across and had covered about half of the distance to the far shore when Pie suddenly stopped and held up a hand. "Hear that?" he asked.

"What?" Cory replied, but then to his ears came the same sound that Pie had heard: a shrill whistle, rapidly rising in pitch, and underlying it was a low rumble. Cory felt the steel rails vibrate under his feet.

"Train comin'," Pie said. "We best hustle on to the other side."

They only had about fifty yards to go. Cory was confident they would reach the other side well before the train arrived at the trestle. Still, there was no point in dawdling. He and Pie started walking again, more quickly this time.

Somewhere behind them, the train whistle sounded again.

They had covered about twenty yards, leaving them still thirty yards from the end of the trestle, when Cory heard the sharp sound of wood cracking. Pie lurched to the side and yelped, "Dang!" His hand caught instinctively at Cory's sleeve.

Cory turned around. "What is it?" he asked anxiously. "What happened?"

"One o' the ties must've been rotten," Pie said as he gestured down toward the trestle. "My foot went right through it." He tried to pull his leg up, clutching Cory's arm for balance as he attempted to extricate his foot. "Uh! Sumbitch is stuck."

"Stuck?" repeated Cory. "You mean you can't get it loose?" Even as the words came out of his mouth, he knew how foolish they were.

Pie grinned, but his eyes looked worried. "Yeah, that's it, all right." He wrenched at his leg again. "The splintered ends o' that railroad tie are catchin' on my boot."

"Well, take your foot out of the boot," Cory said, a note of desperation creeping into his voice as he heard the train's whistle again. It sounded a lot closer now, like it was almost upon them.

Pie grunted again as he tugged at his foot. "It don't want to come out," he announced grimly. "My foot must've swole up some since I had them boots off last. Hell, it's only been a couple of weeks."

"Let me try." Cory knelt next to Pie on the trestle and awkwardly grasped his leg above the top of the boot. He pulled at the same time that Pie did. The foot didn't budge, and neither did the boot. Cory looked down through the hole in the trestle and saw that it was indeed the splintered ends of the tie that were holding the boot in place.

The rumbling of the approaching train was loud now, and the vibration of the rails seemed to shake the entire trestle, although that could have been Cory's imagination. Raising his voice so he could be heard over the noise of the locomotive, he suggested, "Maybe I could cut the boot loose."

Immediately, Pie slid his knife from behind his belt. "Use this pig sticker," he said. "Careful, though. The blade's pretty sharp."

Cory took the knife and began trying to work the tip of the blade between the top of the boot and Pie's leg. He knew he couldn't afford to waste any time, but he didn't want to put a bad gash in his friend's leg, either. The knife wound on Cory's arm had healed fairly cleanly, leaving a ridged scar behind, but Pie might not be so lucky.

Cory glanced at the trees on the side of the stream where they had come from. Thick black smoke was visible above the treetops now, and he knew it was coming from the locomotive's stack. The train would be there in a matter of moments. He got the blade in position and began sawing at the thick leather of Pie's boot.

Tightly, Pie said, "You best forget about this and get movin', Cory. You still got time to get to the other end."

Stubbornly, Cory shook his head. "I'm not going to leave you out here."

"Hell, you just met me! You don't owe me a thing."

The knife had made a little progress through the boot. "I'll get you loose. Just hang on," Cory said.

The train appeared in the trees, slowing slightly as it approached the trestle. Cory saw the cowcatcher on the front of the locomotive rushing toward them.

"Cory, get out o' here!" yelled Pie.

Cory sawed frantically at the boot with one hand while pulling at it with the other. The leather began to part faster, and Cory shouted, "Pull your foot up, Pie!"

Pie leaned over to grip the iron framework on the side of the trestle and pulled with all his strength. The point of the knife gouged into his leg, drawing a shout of pain from him, but the side of the boot ripped even more and the big man's foot came free with a popping sound. The next second, the locomotive's whistle shrilled deafeningly as the engineer spotted the two figures on the trestle. The train rattled out onto the bridge, bearing down on them.

"Jump!" Cory shouted.

He hung on to Pie's knife as the two of them scrambled through an opening in the trestle's framework. The locomotive was practically on top of them as they flung themselves from the bridge and plummeted down the twenty feet to the surface of the river. With a pair of huge splashes, they went into the water.

Cory had no idea if Pie could swim or not. He had been able to draw a breath into his lungs just before he hit the water, so he didn't panic as he plunged deeply under the surface. He had learned to swim in Dobie's Run, the creek near his home back in Virginia. He waited until he had stopped sinking, then started kicking for the surface.

His head popped out of the water, and he dragged in more air. Then he started looking around for Pie. Seeing no sign of his friend, Cory shouted, "Pie! Pie!"

With another big splash, Pie broke the surface. He shook his shaggy head, spat water out of his mouth, and gasped for breath. Cory swam over to him.

"Are you all right?"

"I . . . I reckon," Pie said breathlessly as he continued treading water. "I . . . I ain't much good at this."

"Can you get to shore?"

"I'll sure try."

Together, they swam to the riverbank, Cory giving Pie a hand whenever the big man needed it. At least this stream wasn't as cold as the Tennessee River had been back in February, when the *Missouri Zephyr* had been blown out of the water by Yankee gunboats and Cory and Captain Farrell had been forced to swim for their lives. After a few minutes, Cory and Pie reached the shore and clambered out. Water streamed from their clothes and hair.

Pie glared up at the trestle. "I just lost a perfectly good boot," he said.

"I hung on to your knife," Cory said. He held out the blade.

Pie took it. "Thanks. And thanks for savin' my life. You should've run when you had the chance."

Cory shook his head. "I couldn't do that."

"Why in blazes not?"

"I guess I've seen too many friends die already."

Pie looked at him for a second, then stuck his hand out. Cory shook it, and neither of them needed to say anything else.

"Well," Pie commented after a moment, "it's goin' to be a long ol' walk to Vicksburg with only one boot."

—————

As IT turned out, it was neither that long nor that painful. They had followed the railroad tracks for another half-mile when a road crossed the steel rails and then turned to parallel them. They followed the road, which made walking easier, and a few minutes later the creaking of wheels sounded behind them.

Cory and Pie stopped and turned to watch a wagon rolling toward them. Handling the reins of the mule team was a black man in late middle age. His face was heavily lined and his hair was white under a broad-brimmed black hat, but his shoulders were still wide and strong. A white girl about ten years old perched beside him on the seat. She wore a frilly dress and carried a parasol to shield herself from the sun. She used it to point at Cory and Pie as the wagon came closer, and they heard her say, "Look, Henry. Why don't we stop and give them a ride?"

"Can't hardly trust nobody on the road these days, Miss Maggie," the driver replied. He flipped the reins, clearly determined to keep going, and Cory and Pie stepped back off the road to give the wagon plenty of room. The vehicle rattled past.

Cory supposed he didn't blame the black man for not wanting to stop. He and Pie probably looked pretty disreputable. Their clothes were still damp, and Pie was missing a boot.

Pie grinned at Cory and said, "Got me an idea." He plucked his mouth harp from his pocket and brought it to his lips. The instrument had survived the dunking in the river, and Pie had shaken it dry as best he could. Now he began to play, launching into a fast, delightful tune that Cory didn't recognize.

"Stop!" the little girl cried out as she heard the music. "Oh, please stop, Henry!"

The driver reined in, bringing the wagon to a halt about ten yards along the road. Now that it had gone past them, Cory could see that the back of it was filled with burlap bags, no doubt some sort of crop being taken to market in Vicksburg.

Pie continued playing the mouth harp, tapping his sock-clad foot in the road as he did so. Smiling happily, the little girl twisted around on the seat so she could watch him. She started clapping her hands in time to the music.

Cory wondered if he ought to dance a jig right about now. That was probably what his father would have done under these circumstances. Cory decided against it, knowing that his dancing talents were negligible.

Pie finished the tune with a masterful flourish and bowed deeply from the waist as the little girl laughed and applauded. "That was wonderful!" she called to them. "Do you know any more songs?"

"Hundreds, little missy," Pie replied.

The girl turned to her companion. "Oh, please let them come with us, Henry. The ride into town is so long and boring."

"Your father'd have my hide if'n he knew we picked up a couple of tramps, Miss Maggie—"

"They're not tramps. You're not tramps, are you, sirs?"

"No, ma'am," said Pie. "Just a couple o' country boys on our way to the city."

The driver leaned down and picked up something from the floorboard at his feet, then turned and lithely hopped down from the wagon. Cory saw that he now had a shotgun tucked under his arm. He came to the back of the wagon and said quietly,

"Miss Maggie wants me to invite you fellas to ride with us to Vicksburg. You got any sort o' devilment in mind?"

"Not a bit," Pie said.

"And we'd surely appreciate the ride," Cory put in. "You can see for yourself, my friend lost a boot a ways back."

Henry grunted, unmoved by Pie's loss of footgear. "Climb in the back," he said. "But you'd best behave yourselves."

"We will. Don't you worry 'bout that," Pie promised.

As they climbed into the wagon and settled down on the full burlap bags, Maggie said, "You'll play some more songs, won't you?"

"Only if you sing along," Pie told her.

She clapped her hands again. "I know lots of songs! What's your name?"

"They call me Pie. Pie Jones."

"Pie," she repeated in delight. "That's a funny name."

"And I'm Cory."

"Hello, Cory." As the driver stepped back up to the seat, Maggie said to him, "I'm going to ride in the back with Mr. Pie and Mr. Cory."

"Gal, you better just—" Henry stopped and sighed. Clearly, he was accustomed to the girl's headstrong ways. "All right. You go sing with the gentlemen. Your father always said you got a voice like a songbird, and I got to agree with him."

Maggie climbed agilely over the back of the seat as Henry got the wagon moving again. She sat herself down on a bag next to Pie and asked, "Do you know 'Camptown Races'?"

"I sure do," he said, starting to play the familiar tune. The young girl sang along with him.

Cory was sitting closer to the wagon seat. He said to the driver, "One of my brothers is named Henry."

Henry grunted, "That so? You don't sound like you come from these parts. Where you from, massa?"

"You don't have to call me that," Cory said. "I'm nobody's master."

Henry turned his head enough to look back at Cory for a moment, then he shrugged and nodded.

"I'm from Virginia," Cory went on.

"Long way from home."

"That's what people keep telling me."

"Why you goin' to Vicksburg?"

Cory turned around and leaned over the back of the seat so that he and Henry could talk more easily. "I'm looking for some people. A man named Charles Thompson, and his niece, Lucille Farrell."

Henry shook his head. "Don't reckon I know 'em."

"The little girl . . . does her father own a plantation near here?"

"Wouldn't hardly call it a plantation, but it's a good-sized farm. Me and a couple of other boys take care of it, and of Miss Maggie and her mother."

Something about Henry's voice struck Cory as odd. "What about the girl's father?" he asked quietly. "Did he go off to the war?"

Henry stared straight ahead down the road. "He went off . . . and he ain't comin' back." His words were so quiet that Cory could barely hear them. He knew the little girl would not have heard over the music and her own singing.

Cory leaned forward even more. "He's—"

"Shiloh," Henry said tautly. He didn't have to say anything else for Cory to understand what he meant.

"Nobody told her?"

"That's the way her mother wants it. That's what we do."

Cory looked off at the countryside rolling past the wagon and listened to the girl's clear voice as she sang happily, accompanied by Pie's mouth harp. A part of him felt like Maggie should have been told that her father was dead, but at the same time, he could understand why the girl's mother had kept the knowledge from her. Maggie would grow up soon enough and know everything that this war had taken from her.

By late afternoon, the wagon was nearing Vicksburg. Maggie had fallen asleep on one of the sacks next to Pie, and the big man was dozing, too. At Henry's invitation, Cory stepped over the seat and sat beside the slave.

The terrain had grown more rugged, and the road veered to the northwest away from the railroad to twist through a range of hills cut by steep, brush-choked ravines. As the road climbed to a pass and then reached it, Cory got his first land-side look at the city of Vicksburg, spread out on a series of hills along the Mississippi River. In the distance to the north, Cory could see the horseshoe bend that the great river made, turning sharply back to the south before turning north again. The city itself was dominated by a massive building with majestic white columns surrounding it on all four sides.

"That big buildin' is the Warren County Courthouse," Henry said. "It's so big and fancy I hear it puts some state capital buildin's to shame."

"It's impressive, all right," Cory agreed. And so was the rest of Vicksburg, he thought. He went on, "Do you know anything about the Yankees shelling the town?"

Henry glanced over his shoulder and saw that the little girl was asleep. "We don't talk about the war much where Miss Maggie can hear it. But since she's dozin' . . . Couple months ago, some Yankee admiral came sailin' up the river and sent a message to the officers at the garrison tellin' them they'd better surrender. They sent a message back tellin' him they didn't know how to surrender and didn't figure to learn. So he turned his ships around and went back down the river."

That didn't jibe with what the Confederate cavalry officer had told Cory after the encounter with the renegades. "I thought the Yankees attacked the city."

"I'm gettin' to that," Henry said. "Last month, the ol' admiral came back. What he didn't know was that a heap of cannons been moved onto the bluffs overlookin' the river. He got a warm welcome when he started firin' into the town."

"Then the Yankees *did* shell Vicksburg?"

"Yep. They couldn't knock out those cannons, though."

Cory was less concerned about military matters than he was about the damage that might have been done to the city and its inhabitants, possibly Lucille. "What about the people who live there? Were very many of them hurt?"

"Some, I reckon," Henry said with a shrug. "I heard about how some houses and businesses got blown up by those mortar shells. But not many folks were killed because when the Yankees were shellin', people would go down in their basements or into caves in the hills. The shells couldn't get them there, especially in the caves."

Cory nodded. Though he didn't care for the idea of Lucille's cowering in some underground lair while shells burst above, that was infinitely better than the possibility of her being killed in one of the attacks. *If* she was even in Vicksburg, he reminded himself. He couldn't be sure of that.

"You know a lot about what's been going on in town," he commented to Henry.

"For a country nigger, you mean?" Henry laughed, but there wasn't any real humor in the sound. "Miss Sarah—that's Miss Maggie's mama—she asks me for the war news every time I come back from town. So I ask questions, and I listen good."

"She must not think it's too dangerous, or she wouldn't let her little girl come with you into Vicksburg like this."

Henry shook his head. "We stop at a mill on the edge of town. We never get too close to the river. For a while, everybody figured the Yankees were goin' to attack by land, too, but there hasn't been any sign of that, so it's safe enough to travel around on the main roads."

"I've heard rumors about an invasion, too," Cory said, recalling what the Confederate captain had told him.

Henry flapped the reins and said, "I reckon they'll come soon enough. I never heard of a Yankee who knew how to let well enough alone, have you?"

Cory looked at him with a frown. He had never thought much about slavery one way or the other, since his family had never held slaves nor had much to do with those who did. "You don't want the Yankees to come down here and set you free?"

For a long moment, Henry didn't say anything, and Cory worried that he might have offended the man. Then Henry said, "There are some things that need changin', that's for sure. Just 'cause Miss Maggie's folks always treated us right doesn't mean it's that way all over. Seems to me there ought to be a way to change things without fightin' a war over it, though." He looked over at Cory. "And as for bein' free . . . I could leave Miss Sarah any time I want. So could the other boys. Ain't nobody to stop us. But we're not goin' anywhere."

"I'm sure she appreciates your help."

"She's a strong woman, I reckon, but she couldn't get along by herself, just her and Miss Maggie. Nothin' is goin' to happen to hurt them two, not anymore. Not while there's breath in this body." Henry spoke low and fervently, and then he reined in sharply. In a more normal tone, he went on, "This is the mill. Far as we're goin'."

The mill was a large building. Cory looked around and saw that they were on the outskirts of the city. From here on, there were a lot more buildings. "Where would I find someone who's an officer in the Mississippi Home Guard?" he asked.

"Go on down to the river. There'll be plenty of soldiers around. I'd ask one of them, if I was you."

Cory hopped down from the seat. In the back of the wagon, Pie sat up and looked around, a little bleary-eyed. "Are we there yet?" he asked.

"We're here," Cory told him. "This is Vicksburg."

Pie's eyes got wider as he took in the city sprawled on the hills. "Dang. It's even bigger'n I thought it'd be."

Maggie sat up and rubbed her eyes. "Oh!" she exclaimed in disappointment. "We're here. We didn't get to sing enough, Mr. Pie."

"Maybe some other time we'll sing some more, sweetie," Pie told her.

"You'll come to see us on the farm?" the little girl asked eagerly. "I'm sure Mama would like to hear you play the mouth harp. She loves music."

"Well, maybe someday, if we ever get back over that way."

"No, you have to promise," Maggie insisted.

Pie shrugged his broad shoulders. "All right. I promise we'll come see you."

Henry stepped down from the wagon seat and said solemnly, "She'll hold you to that, you know."

"Well, that's fine, 'cause I mean it." Pie climbed out of the back of the wagon and then reached up to lift Maggie and set the little girl on the ground. "There you go, honey. Me an' Cory got to be movin' on now."

"Good-bye, Mr. Pie," she said. "Good-bye, Mr. Cory."

"Good-bye, Maggie," Cory told her. He turned to Henry and put out his hand. "Thank you."

Henry hesitated, then took Cory's hand. "You come on out to the farm any time you want. It's just off the Jackson road, about twelve miles east. You'll be welcome."

"We'll do that," Cory promised.

Pie caught Maggie up in his arms and gave her a hug, his whiskers making her laugh merrily, then he fell in step alongside Cory as they walked toward the main part of the city. "So this is Vicksburg," the big man said as they walked.

"Yes," said Cory, and he hoped that he would find what he was looking for here.

Chapter Four

WILLIAM SHAKESPEARE BRANNON HAD seldom felt better in his life, he reflected as he leaned back against the trunk of a tree on the bank of the creek called Dobie's Run. He had a cane fishing pole in his hand, but his eyes were closed and he didn't really care if he caught anything or not. A gentle breeze, a little warm for late September, washed over the rolling hills of Virginia's Piedmont region and brought with it the smells of vegetation and rich dark earth that Will recalled so fondly. He was home.

"Mac," Will said without opening his eyes, "there's not really a war going on, is there?"

Will's brother Mac was sitting on the bank and leaning against another tree a few feet away. He grunted and said, "I wish there wasn't."

So did Will. But every time he moved, he felt painful reminders of what he had been through during the past eighteen months. His leg was stiff and sore sometimes, especially when the weather was damp, and occasionally he felt a twinge deep in his side, piercing enough so that he wondered if the wound there had healed completely. The aches and pains had come courtesy of the Yankees, whom Will had battled twice at Manassas, up and down the Shenandoah Valley with Stonewall Jackson, around Richmond during the Confederacy's desperate defense of its capital, and finally at a little stream in Maryland called Antietam Creek. Two weeks ago, unlike Dobie's Run, the Antietam had run red with blood during that awful day when huge armies from the North and the South had clashed there.

"I don't much want to go back," Will mused.

"They shoot deserters," Mac pointed out lazily.

"Well, there is that to consider—" Will felt a tug on his line. He sat up and opened his eyes. "Got one."

55

He gave a little jerk on the pole to set the hook, then began pulling in the line. Mac sat up and watched as Will drew the fish out of the creek. As it flopped and fought, throwing droplets of water in the air, its scales sparkled brilliantly in the sun. It was a good-sized trout, almost a foot long, and strong.

Will came to his feet and lifted the fish at the end of the line. He looked at it for a moment then grasped it carefully and worked the hook free from its mouth. When the hook was loose, Will tossed the fish back into the stream. It landed with a splash and shot away, disappearing under the surface.

"Would've made good eating once Ma fried it up," drawled Mac.

"Yeah," Will said. "I reckon so." He stretched, feeling a slight pull in his side again as he did so. "Time we were getting back to the house."

Mac pulled his line out of the water. "I guess you're right. Titus is supposed to come to supper this evening."

"That means he'll have his wife with him."

"Maybe," said Mac. "If he can budge Polly off Mountain Laurel."

Mac stood up and tilted the cane pole over his shoulder as he fell in beside Will. The two eldest Brannon brothers walked through the fields back toward the farmhouse where they had grown up. The resemblance between them was slight but definite. Will was a little taller and heavier and had black hair instead of Mac's sandy brown. His features were harsher and more angular. Mac had a gentleness about him, especially around the eyes. Riding with Gen. Jeb Stuart's cavalry and several battles had not been able to take that away. Will, on the other hand, had been more prone to violence, even during the years he had upheld law and order in Culpeper County by serving as its sheriff. It was the ease with which his hand sought out a gun that had led to the death of Joe Fogarty and the feud that had caused Will to enlist in the army to protect his family from the vengeance of the rest of the Fogartys.

It had also caused his banishment from the family farm by his mother, Abigail. That had hurt worse than anything else.

But now he was back, and Abigail seemed to have accepted him once again. After the battle near Sharpsburg, Maryland, along the bank of Antietam Creek, the Confederate forces had withdrawn into Virginia. That withdrawal had ended near Culpeper, where the army had gone into bivouac. Will suspected that neither side wanted to fight again any time soon after the carnage in Maryland. The troops from both North and South wanted to rest for a while and lick their wounds. The respite might even last all the way through the coming winter. Will hoped so. If several months passed without any more battles, the armies might get out of the habit of fighting. Then maybe the leaders of the Union and the Confederacy could work out some way to end this terrible war before anyone else was killed.

In the meantime, with their home so close, Will and Mac had been able to get passes from their commanders, and they had come back to the Brannon farm for a visit. Will knew he would never forget the terrible uncertainty he had felt as his mother stepped onto the porch and looked at him for a long moment before reaching out to embrace him. If she had turned him away then, it would have hurt more than any Yankee bullet ever could.

She had drawn him into her arms and back into the family, though, and during the week since then Will had been happier than he would have thought possible.

The only disturbing thing was the business of his brother Titus marrying Polly Ebersole. That had taken Will completely by surprise, and he still wasn't convinced it was a good thing.

The farmhouse came into sight, and Will's keen eyes spotted the carriage parked in front of it, between the house and the barn. He recognized the Ebersole carriage, having seen it often enough in Culpeper. Duncan Ebersole, the owner of the plantation called Mountain Laurel, was the richest man in the county, and he liked to be seen riding in the fancy carriage drawn by a matched pair of black horses. Will hoped that Ebersole hadn't come along with Titus and Polly. He had never liked the man.

"Has Titus talked to you about his marriage?" Will asked Mac as they came closer to the house.

"Not much. He says he's happy, but . . ."

"Yeah, I know what you mean. I know he's been mooning over that girl for years, but I never figured that he really had a chance to marry her."

Mac laughed, but there wasn't much humor in the sound. "Strange things happen when there's a war going on."

Will just grunted in agreement.

One of the family dogs, a blue heeler known as Skeeter, came loping toward them, barking and wagging his stump of a tail. The commotion drew their brother Henry out onto the porch, where he grinned and lifted a hand in greeting. The youngest of the Brannon boys, the stocky, dark-haired Henry was barely out of his teens. He called, "Catch anything?"

Will spread his empty hands. Mac said as they came up to the porch, "Will hooked a nice one, but he threw it back."

Henry looked shocked. He asked, "Why'd you do that, Will?"

Will frowned uncomfortably, because he wasn't completely sure why he had tossed the fish back into the creek. "I decided to let him fatten up some more," he finally said. "I'll catch him again next time."

Henry's grin grew wider. "Not if I catch him first."

"Help yourself, little brother." Will inclined his head toward the house and asked quietly, "Did Polly come with Titus?"

Henry grew more solemn. He came down the steps to join his oldest brothers. "She did," he said, "but I don't think she's too happy about it."

"Titus shouldn't have married her," Will said.

"She's a mighty pretty girl."

"And her father hates us."

Henry shrugged. "Mr. Ebersole's got Titus in charge of defending Mountain Laurel if the Yankees come. I tell you, for a while this year it looked like they were going to swarm over the whole county. I reckon we got off lucky. Might've been a lot worse if you boys in the army hadn't pushed them back north."

"Maybe they won't come again," said Mac.

Will hoped that was the case, but he doubted it. He had seen enough of the Yankees by now to figure that they wouldn't give up easily.

The sound of hoofbeats made the three of them turn and look down the lane to the main road. In the late afternoon light, they saw a man riding toward them on a dappled gray horse. He was broad-shouldered and brawny and was dressed in a sober black suit and black hat.

"Reverend Spanner," Henry said in surprised recognition. "What's the preacher doing here?"

A woman's voice said from the doorway of the farmhouse, "I invited him." Abigail Brannon stepped out onto the porch. She put a hand to her grayish-brown hair, patting it to make certain it was in place, then smiled toward the newcomer.

Will and Mac glanced at each other, each of them trying not to appear shocked. If they hadn't known better, they would have thought that their mother was acting like a woman interested in a man.

Not Abigail. That just wasn't possible, thought Will. Ever since the death of his father, Abigail had dedicated herself to her children and the Lord. There wasn't room for anything else in her life.

"This fella is the preacher who took Reverend Crosley's place at the church?" Will asked quietly.

Henry nodded. "Yep. And he can spout the hellfire-and-brimstone better'n Reverend Crosley ever could."

The rider drew his mount to a halt and swung down from the saddle. He was in late middle age. His full mustache and the hair under the broad-brimmed hat were white, in sharp contrast to the tanned, leathery skin of his face. He carried himself like a younger man, however, and his voice was deep and resonant as he said, "Sister Abigail, how are you?"

"I'm fine, Reverend. Welcome."

The preacher turned to Will and stuck out his hand. "You must be Will," he said. "I'm Benjamin Spanner. Pleased to meet you, son. I've heard a lot about you."

Will glanced at his mother as he shook hands with the minister. "All about what a terrible heathen I am, I expect," he said.

"Will!" Abigail scolded.

Spanner threw back his head and laughed heartily. "There might have been a few times when I was asked to intercede with the Lord on your behalf. But I've heard, too, about how you've been fighting the Yankees. You're a captain, aren't you?"

Will nodded and said, "In the Thirty-third Virginia, part of the Stonewall Brigade."

"The gallant Stonewall Jackson. You boys are famous."

Will shrugged. "Just trying to get the Yankees to leave us alone."

Spanner shook hands with Mac and Henry, then turned toward the porch again and asked, "Am I in time for supper, Abigail?"

"You certainly are, Reverend."

Spanner shook his head. "I'll remind you again, dear lady, to call me Benjamin."

"Of course. Benjamin."

The name sounded odd coming from his mother's lips, Will thought. And it looked mighty odd the way she took hold of the preacher's arm and squeezed it for a second as Spanner stepped up onto the porch. "Come sit down in the parlor," she said, "while Cordelia finishes getting the food on the table."

When the two of them had gone on into the house, Will looked at Henry and whispered, "What in blazes was *that* about?"

Henry grinned. "Can't you tell? Ma's sweet on the reverend."

Will shook his head. "No. That's just not possible."

"You'd better get used to it," Mac said. "I saw it start before I joined up with the cavalry. She's smitten, all right."

Will would have sooner believed that the sun could rise in the west the next morning, but he couldn't dispute the evidence of his own eyes. He just shook his head.

"Better put those cane poles in the barn and come on inside," Henry said. "Ma won't like it if we aren't hospitable to the preacher."

Will and Mac did as their little brother suggested, then went into the house and turned through the arched entrance into the parlor. Abigail and Reverend Spanner were sitting on the divan, a respectable distance between them. Titus and his wife, Polly, were in the parlor, too, and Will sensed that an awkward silence had developed.

Will tried to break it by smiling and saying, "Well, Titus, I hadn't seen this lovely bride of yours since we've been home. Hello, Polly."

Polly Ebersole Brannon returned the smile and took Will's hand when he held it out to her. "Hello, Will," she said. "How are you?"

"Just fine," he said. "And yourself?"

"Wonderful, of course." She turned the smile toward Titus. "Married life is treating me very well."

"I reckon I could say the same for Titus. That gloomy face of his looks about as happy as I've seen it in a long time."

Titus didn't look particularly happy at the moment, but Will didn't figure it would hurt to stretch the truth a little. Titus stood up from the chair where he had been sitting and came across the room to shake Will's hand. He was in his midtwenties, with long, dark brown hair, and he had cultivated a close-cropped beard since Will had left home. "Henry said you were down to the run fishing," Titus said. "Catch anything?"

Will shook his head, not wanting to explain again about the trout he had thrown back.

"You boys sit down," Abigail said, "and we'll have a nice visit."

Will and Mac did as their mother requested, but Henry said, "I'm going out to the kitchen to see how Cordelia's getting along with supper." He hurried from the parlor before Abigail could stop him.

She laughed. "That boy and his appetite," she said.

"I reckon we all have appetites," Reverend Spanner said. "That's what makes us creatures of the world and why we have to work to ascend to something higher."

"Yes, that's right," Abigail agreed. Will thought he saw a faint flush on his mother's cheeks. Maybe it was there because of the preacher's comment about worldly appetites, he mused, but then he firmly pushed that line of thinking out of his head.

He turned to Polly instead and asked, "How's your father doing? Is he still in charge of the militia around here?"

Polly shook her head. "There's not any real militia left in the county. The men are all off fighting."

Titus's jaw clenched a little tighter. Will saw the reaction but tried not to let on that he had.

"Everything on Mountain Laurel is all right," Polly continued. "It's been something of a struggle, of course. The army has required so much of what we produce."

Will nodded. The army was like a hungry giant, gobbling up supplies from the countryside and the people who lived there. A lot of officers felt it was their right to commandeer whatever they needed or wanted. Will had done his best not to be that way. He never wanted the civilians in the South to be as afraid of their own army as they were of the Yankees.

"I heard that Yancy Lattimer was wounded," Polly went on, sounding more concerned now. "Is that true?"

Will nodded solemnly. "He was badly hurt during the battle in Maryland." He debated briefly whether to be blunt about Yancy's injuries, then decided that Polly had a right to hear about it. She had known Yancy since childhood. "He lost a leg."

One of Polly's hands went to her mouth in horror. "Oh, no!"

Will ignored his mother's disapproving look and nodded. "The last I heard, his boy Roman was taking him back home. Yancy was lucky. There wasn't any blood poisoning or gangrene. He ought to recover . . . but I reckon he'll never be the same."

"Terrible," murmured Reverend Spanner. "Just terrible."

"Yes sir," agreed Will. "It surely is."

Yancy Lattimer had been more than a fellow officer to Will. He had been a good friend, a comrade in arms, and Will was grateful to him for the way Yancy had helped him through his first days in the army. Yancy was an aristocrat, the son of a wealthy planter who had grown up at Tanglewood, one of Culpeper County's finest plantations. He was also a graduate of West Point who had served for three years as an officer in the army before resigning his commission and coming home to Virginia when the war broke out. Yancy had had no reason to befriend someone like Will—but he had, and Will missed his friendship now.

"I remember dancing with Yancy at many of the balls we had at Mountain Laurel," said Polly. "He was so dashing, so handsome. I don't suppose he'll ever be able to dance again."

Will figured there were things Yancy would miss more than dancing, but he didn't say anything. To someone like Polly, being unable to enjoy a party was probably the worst thing she could imagine.

Henry came back into the parlor. "Cordelia says to tell you that supper's on the table and you'd better come get it before she throws it to the hogs."

His sister's voice sounded sharply from the dining room. "Henry Brannon!" Cordelia exclaimed. "I never said any such thing!"

Reverend Spanner chuckled as he stood up and extended his arm to Abigail. "Shall we?" he asked.

She hesitated then came to her feet and linked her arm with his. "I'm sorry about all the squabbling among the children."

"Nonsense. I enjoy being around youngsters. I never had any children of my own, you know."

"You and your late wife were never blessed with children?"

"My wife's not late," Spanner said with a grin. "Never had one of those, either."

"I see," Abigail said primly.

Will tried not to roll his eyes as he followed them into the dining room.

One of the best things about being home—other than not being shot at—was being able to eat his mother's and sister's cooking again. After living on hardtack, pone, salt jowl, and jerky for months on end, a home-cooked meal was a luxury beyond imagining. Even though fresh provisions were in short supply in the county, Abigail and Cordelia usually managed to scrape together enough floor to make a mess of biscuits, and there were still hams hanging in the smokehouse and a couple of hens that laid fairly regularly, along with a dependable milk cow. The garden had produced well during the summer, and there were still fresh beans and corn and greens. The Brannons, despite their modest means, were living as well or better now than most of the people in Culpeper County.

Cordelia stood near the head of the table, lovely in a blue dress patterned with little yellow flowers. She was the youngest of the Brannons, only eighteen, and also the only one to inherit their father's fiery red hair. Cordelia's curls fell in thick waves around her shoulders.

"I don't know what's wrong with Henry," she said with a quick glare at her brother. "I never said anything—"

"That's all right, dear, we know," Abigail said. "We're well aware of your brother's penchant for mischief."

"Aw, I was just joshin'," Henry said.

Abigail ignored him. "Before everyone sits down . . . Benjamin, would you say grace?"

"It would be my privilege and pleasure to do so, ma'am," Spanner replied.

They all moved to their places around the long table, then bowed their heads. As they did so, Will glanced around surreptitiously. All the Brannons were home except for Cory—wandering Cory—and Will was gratified that they had made it through the war so far. Many families had not been so lucky. They had lost husbands, fathers, sons, and brothers. Men had gone off to the war and never returned, and some of those who did come back would be haunted or even crippled forever by what had happened to them. All across the South, the losses were multiplying.

And in the North, Will suddenly found himself wondering, were there families who stood around their dinner tables like this and gave thanks that so far the war had not snatched away any of them permanently? Were there supper tables with empty places that would be forever empty?

Of course that was true, Will thought as Reverend Spanner began praying. Yankee soldiers died just like their Confederate cousins. And to those left behind, the deaths hurt just as much. Will knew that the Union had provoked the war by issuing a call for troops to carry out an invasion of the Confederacy, as well as the refusal to turn over Fort Sumter after South Carolina had seceded. It didn't matter as much now who had started the war, though. Will had seen enough fighting, enough death, to know that both sides bled the same color. A dying Yankee cried out in pain the same as a fallen Reb, and tears of loss knew no North or South.

He should have been paying attention to what the preacher was saying, Will knew, but he had never been much of a praying man. He looked again through hooded eyes at his family and hoped that no more tragedy would strike them.

"Amen," Reverend Spanner said, and Will repeated the benediction with the others, even though it rang hollow in his heart.

Chapter Five

TITUS SLAPPED THE REINS angrily against the rumps of the horses, sending the carriage rolling faster along the road. There was plenty of light from a full moon to guide him. The speedy pace made the ride rougher, and as Polly bounced a little on the padded seat, she said, "Slow down, Titus. There's no need to rush."

"Figured you'd be in a hurry to get home," snapped Titus, "seein' as you had such a bad time this evening."

"I was polite to your family. I even smiled at them."

"And you didn't say a dozen words the whole night."

Polly sighed. "It's just like you to exaggerate everything, Titus. I was as friendly as I can possibly be, and you know it."

"Maybe," he said. "Maybe that's right. You were as friendly as you can possibly be to my family."

She turned her head away from him, and he could sense the anger in her, could almost feel it radiating from her stiff body like the rays of the sun on a hot day. The only difference was that sunshine was warm, and what he felt coming from his wife was as cold as ice.

How could things change so fast? he asked himself. In a matter of a couple of months, he had gone from being the happiest man in the world to wondering if he would ever know any joy again. He had been aware when he married Polly that her father didn't like him, of course. It would have taken a blind man to miss the fact that Duncan Ebersole could barely tolerate him. But Titus hadn't cared about that. All he wanted was to be married to Polly.

And at first everything had been just fine. Better than fine. The passionate bond he had experienced every time he kissed Polly had not prepared him for the true pleasures of married life. He had been with women before, but never one who was as

69

eager and inventive as Polly. He supposed that was because she'd been a virgin and had stored up a whole lot of randiness. A few times, she had even embarrassed *him* a little. Nice Southern girls shouldn't have been able to even guess about such things, let alone do them so well.

Then, abruptly, that had all stopped. Polly had grown chilly toward him, and every day it got worse. Titus had no idea what caused the change, and nary a clue how to fix it. He had tried being as nice and romantic as he knew how, he had tried being more aggressive, he had appealed to her in every possible way he could think of. Polly just insisted that nothing was wrong, that she loved him as much as ever, but there was a barrier between them as high and sturdy as any brick wall.

Thank God he'd had his work to keep him busy. His father-in-law was relying on him to lead the defense of Mountain Laurel if that ever became necessary, but slowly, Ebersole was coming to rely even more on his new son-in-law. Several of the plantation's overseers had gone off to join the army, so Titus had been taking on some of their duties. He didn't like dealing with the slaves—the Brannon family had never owned any or needed any—but he wanted to make himself valuable to Ebersole. If he could get the planter to come around to liking him, maybe Polly's attitude would change, too.

Several minutes had passed since their last exchange, so Titus broached the silence by saying, "I reckon Will and Mac will have to go back to the army pretty soon."

"I don't see why," Polly said dully. "Nobody's fighting now."

"It won't stay that way," Titus predicted. "I hear that ape Lincoln was pretty mad at McClellan for not chasin' after our boys after what happened in Maryland. McClellan's got to do something so that Lincoln won't think he made a mistake by leavin' him in charge of the Yankee army."

Polly glanced over at him, interested in spite of herself and her anger. "Do you think so?"

"You can bet on it."

"Do you think the Yankees will come this way again?" There was an edge of fear in Polly's voice. Virginia had gotten off lightly during the last Federal push into the state. It might not be the same next time. It would be just like the Yankees to lay waste to every place they came across.

"If they do, they'll be sorry," Titus said boldly. "It was a mistake for Lee to go gallivanting off up into Maryland. Our boys weren't ready for that. But if we're fighting on Virginia soil it'll be different. Nobody's goin' to beat us on our home ground."

"I hope you're right."

Titus felt himself relaxing slightly. Talking to Polly like this helped. Their common hatred for the Northerners allowed them to put aside their problems with each other, at least for the moment.

A few minutes later, they reached the tree-lined lane that led from the main road to Mountain Laurel. Titus had no trouble following it in the bright moonlight. As the carriage drew nearer the huge plantation house, he spotted a light glowing from one of the downstairs windows. He had expected the place to be dark. Ebersole was not a man who kept late hours.

A young black man was sitting and dozing with his back against one of the columns that supported the porte-cochère over the house's front entrance. As the carriage rattled up, the slave leaped hurriedly to his feet and ran forward to catch hold of the harness on one of the horses. "I take care of 'em fo' you, Massa Titus," he called.

"Thanks, 'Lonzo," Titus replied as he stepped down from the carriage. He realized he was the only one on the plantation who would even think of expressing appreciation to a slave for doing a job that was expected, but old habits died hard. Abigail Brannon had taught all of her children to be polite, even the more wayward ones like Titus.

He turned and reached up to help Polly down from the seat. As he did so, his hands spanned her slender waist, and when her feet hit the ground she was standing quite close to him, close enough so that he felt the warmth of her breath on his cheek. He kept his hands on her waist and slowly slid them around to the small of her back. Sensing a yielding within her, he pressed gently, and she came even closer to him. Her face was only inches from his. It would have been so easy to bring his mouth down on hers, to taste once again the sweetness of her lips . . .

The front door banged open, and a harsh voice demanded, "What the hell're ye doin' out there? Who's that? Polly, is that ye an' that husband o' yers?"

Polly gasped and flinched away from Titus at the first sound of her father's voice. She turned toward the doorway and said, "Yes, it's just us, Father."

"Well, dinna stand out there all night. Come on in th' house." Duncan Ebersole's words were spoken with a thick tongue, and Titus knew his father-in-law had been drinking again. The effects of whiskey were something with which Titus was intimately familiar, since until a couple of weeks before his wedding to Polly, he had been pretty much of a drunk himself.

"We're coming, Father," Polly said. She caught hold of Titus's arm and tugged at him as she hissed, "Come on!"

Ebersole beckoned with a hand at them as he turned and stumbled back into the house. Titus hesitated. "Your pa's drunk," he said quietly.

"He is not!" Polly pulled harder on his arm. "Please, Titus. Come in with me."

"I thought I might walk down to the stables and check on the horses," Titus said. He was just looking for an excuse to avoid Ebersole. If his father-in-law wanted an argument tonight, that was just too bad. Titus was in no mood to give him one.

"Titus, you have to come in with me," said Polly, and this time her voice quavered. Titus realized with a shock that she no longer sounded angry. She was frightened instead.

"All right," he said. "I'll go with you. Just rest easy, Polly."

Her fingers dug almost painfully into his arm through the sleeve of his coat. "You won't leave me?"

"No. I won't leave you."

She sighed in relief, and her voice had some of its usual crispness as she said, "Let's go then."

Light spilled through the open doorway. Titus and Polly went into the foyer, their footsteps ringing on the brilliantly polished hardwood floor and echoing from the tall, vaulted ceiling. Ebersole called from their right, "Come into the parlor, you two."

They turned and went into the lavishly furnished room where Ebersole was waiting for them. He stood next to a window where the heavy drapes had been pulled back. This was the lighted window Titus had noticed as the carriage approached Mountain Laurel.

Ebersole had his back to them as he stood there and swirled brandy in a crystal snifter. He swayed slightly, and Titus thought that it had taken more than brandy to get Ebersole that drunk. He wondered what Ebersole wanted.

Abruptly, the planter lifted the snifter and downed the rest of the brandy. He swung around and glared at them. Ebersole was a medium-sized man who carried himself as if he were larger. He was balding, but the reddish-gray hair he had left was worn long. He sported a neatly trimmed beard as well. Tonight, he wore an open-throated white silk shirt over tight brown whipcord trousers. When he spoke, especially when he had been drinking as was the case now, his voice carried the distinct burr of his Scottish ancestry.

"So, th' two o' ye ha' been over to th' Brannon farm, have ye? Did ye have a good visit?"

"Of course, Father," Polly replied.

"Everyone there all right?"

Titus nodded. "I suppose so. Will and Mac are still home on leave."

"Wha' about that pretty little redheaded sister o' yers, Brannon? How's she doin'?"

Something about the way Ebersole spoke of Cordelia made Titus bristle. "She's fine," he snapped. "Why do you ask?"

"Jus' bein' frien'ly—" Ebersole began, but Polly took a step toward him and interrupted.

"Father, you're up too late," she said. "You know you need your sleep. You ought to go on to bed."

Ebersole drew himself up and glared at her. "And would ye be tuckin' me in now? Who's the parent here, an' who's the wee bairn?"

"I haven't been a wee bairn for a long time," Polly muttered. She held out a hand toward her father and went on, "Please—"

Ebersole turned sharply away from her and strode across the room toward the fireplace. A large portrait hung over the mantel. "D'ye hear that, darlin'?" he demanded of the painting. "Our daughter's givin' th' orders around here now."

Polly was pale as her gaze followed her father. Titus wasn't sure what was going on here. He looked back and forth between Polly and the painting, struck as he always was by the uncanny resemblance between his wife and the woman in the portrait— Polly's mother and Ebersole's late wife. Titus had seen the portrait every day since he had moved to Mountain Laurel, and on a few occasions before that. In the painting, Polly's mother was sitting in a chair in front of the window where Ebersole had been standing earlier, and the view behind her showed the lane with its twin rows of mountain laurel trees receding into the distance. She wore a gown of muted rose, and her long blonde curls fell loosely around her shoulders. She was probably the second most beautiful woman Titus had ever seen. Only her daughter was more lovely.

"I'm not trying to give orders, Father," Polly said tightly. "But you've been drinking, and you ought to go on to bed. If you don't, you're going to be sick in the morning."

Ebersole was going to be sick anyway, thought Titus. He knew a hangover in the making when he saw one.

Polly went on, "Let me call one of the servants to help you—"

"No!" Ebersole was still holding the brandy snifter. He flung it into the cold fireplace without warning, shattering it with a crash. "I dinna want any damned niggers fussin' over me! I can put meself to bed when I'm good an' ready!"

Polly glanced at Titus, and in her eyes was a mute appeal.

Titus took a deep breath and let it out in a weary sigh. There was no way this encounter could end well, he told himself, and yet he could not refuse Polly anything she wanted. Regardless of the growing friction between them, he wanted her to be happy with him.

He stepped forward and said, "Mr. Ebersole . . . Duncan . . . maybe you'd better do like Polly says." He reached out and touched Ebersole's arm.

Ebersole's fist came up like a shot and crashed into Titus's jaw. The unexpected impact was blinding, and for a second Titus was senseless as he flew backward, fell over an end table beside one of the divans, and tumbled to the floor with the wreckage of the fragile piece of furniture scattered around him. Awareness came flooding back in on him as he lay there, and anger accompanied it. How dare Ebersole strike him like that!

Once before, on the night of the magnificent ball at which he had kissed Polly for the first time, Titus had been physically assaulted here at Mountain Laurel. That time, it had been Ebersole's overseers who had handed him a thrashing, and Titus had been unable to fight back. He had known, though, that Ebersole had ordered the beating.

But this time, Ebersole had struck his own blow, and there were no burly overseers here to stay between him and his victim. Titus wasn't going to meekly accept the pain and humiliation tonight. Instead, roaring a curse, he came up off the floor and started toward the plantation owner. Ebersole stood waiting for him, feet widespread so that his drunkenness made him sway only slightly.

With a cry of "No!" Polly threw herself between her husband and her father. "Stop it, both of you!"

"Get out of the way, Polly," Titus grated. "He's had this comin' for a long time."

Grinning savagely, Ebersole lifted both hands and motioned for Titus to keep coming. "Have at me, ye damned skalleyhooter! I been achin' to gi' ye a beatin' ever since ye forced yer way into me home."

"He didn't force his way in," Polly said, her head snapping toward her father. "He's my husband, and I love him."

"Love!" snorted Ebersole. "Ye dinna kin what love is."

"I know what it isn't," she hissed. She turned to Titus and put a hand on his chest, gently pushing him back. "Go on to our room," she said. "I'll take care of Father."

"He's crazy!" Titus flared. "I'm not going to leave you with him."

"I'll be all right," she said in a low, determined voice. "Please, Titus, do as I ask. Just go to our room, and I'll be there in a little while."

Titus looked at Ebersole, who stood there blinking his bleary eyes belligerently. He still wanted to put his fist right in the middle of the planter's face, but he supposed Polly was right. Brawling with his father-in-law wasn't going to make things any better at Mountain Laurel. Besides, he reminded himself, Ebersole was drunk. He might be sorry about all this in the morning. Titus didn't expect that—Ebersole wasn't the sort to ever feel sorry about anything he did; he could always find a reason to justify his behavior no matter what—but Titus supposed it was at least possible. Finally he nodded and said to Polly, "If you're sure that's what you want . . ."

"It is," she said without hesitation. "Please, Titus, just go. I can handle him." The fear she had shown earlier was gone now, replaced by a bleak resignation.

"All right." He glared at Ebersole for a second longer, then turned and left the parlor.

The bedroom he shared with Polly was on the second floor of the big house. By the time Titus reached it, he was still seething with anger. He practically tore his clothes off and yanked on a nightshirt, then crawled into the massive four-poster bed and blew out the candle that one of the house slaves had left burning on a table beside the bed. There was no point in trying to stay awake for Polly, he thought. She wouldn't want anything to do with him when she came to bed.

Titus figured he was too angry to fall asleep easily. He surprised himself by dozing off almost immediately. He had no idea how much time had passed when he was awakened by the mattress shifting underneath him. He heard Polly's breathing as she crawled under the covers.

Then, to his even greater surprise, he felt the warmth of her breath on the back of his neck as she moved against him, molding her body against his. Her hand caressed his hip.

Titus lifted his head. "Polly . . . ?"

"Shhh," she said. "Don't talk. Just turn over and hold me."

Titus rolled over and pulled her into his arms. She clung to him with a sort of desperation. Her face rested against his shoulder, and he felt his nightshirt grow damp from the tears on her cheeks. He tightened his embrace around her and asked, "What's wrong? Your father—"

"Don't talk," Polly said again. "Please."

"But are you all right?"

She gave a hollow little laugh. "All right? Of course I'm all right. Please, Titus . . ."

"I'm shuttin' up," he said. He stroked her back and her hair. Her legs twined around his. She was wearing a thin cotton gown, and the heat of her body so close to his was searing.

Titus couldn't stop the reaction that came over him. He expected her to turn away from him in revulsion, as she so often did these days, but instead she pressed closer to him and then urged him to move so that he was above her.

Wordlessly, they came together. Titus sensed there was something unsettling about this, but he was too caught up in the passion of the moment to even think about stopping. Whatever had gone wrong between them, maybe tonight would help repair the breach, he told himself.

All he could do was hope.

—⟩⟨—

MAC STOOD with his arms folded on the top rail of the fence and watched his horse cantering around the field. In the moonlight, the silver gray stallion was difficult to see, but Mac's keen eyes were able to pick out the horse, its powerful muscles working smoothly under its sleek hide as it ran.

Beside Mac, Will scratched a sulfur match into life and lit his pipe. "That stallion of yours looks anxious to get back to work," he commented as he shook out the tiny flame.

Mac nodded. "He got used to the war."

"What about you?" asked Will. "You ever get used to it, Mac?"

Mac looked down at the ground and shook his head. "God, no. I hope I never do."

"That makes it harder on you," Will pointed out.

"Maybe so." Mac looked at his older brother. "But have *you* gotten used to it?"

For a long moment, Will didn't answer. Then he said, "Sometimes I think I have. I've been in enough battles, come close enough to dying, so that the thought of it doesn't bother me that much anymore. But then there are some nights . . ."

"Bad dreams?" Mac asked after letting a moment of silence slip by.

"Not always dreams. Sometimes I'm awake. But I see things in my head." Will puffed solemnly on the pipe then went on. "You know, sometimes I can't remember any of their faces, not a damned one of them, and other times I can see every one as plain as day."

"Who?" Mac asked, though he thought he might already know the answer.

"All the men I've killed," Will said flatly.

Mac nodded. That reply was what he expected. "I know what you mean. The same thing happens to me."

"Anyway, you'd better take your horse out for a gallop or two," Will said, and Mac knew his brother was deliberately changing the subject. "Otherwise he's liable to turn wild again."

"I doubt that. He was ready to be tamed as soon as he saw I was smart enough to catch him."

Will chuckled. "I'm not so sure who caught who. Sometimes I think you belong to that stallion, instead of the other way around."

"Maybe you're right. He sure takes good care of me." Mac hesitated, then went on, "You may think I'm crazy, but sometimes it seems like he knows what's going to happen before it happens. He's jumped out of the way several times when a Yankee was about to shoot me in the back. He saved my life."

"Sounds to me like you've just been mighty lucky."

"I'm not sure luck has anything to do with it." Mac started to go on then stopped. Will really *would* think he had lost his mind if he started talking about how sometimes he thought of the stallion as some sort of ghost horse or magical spirit or . . . or something that Mac couldn't even come close to explaining. He was just going to have to keep all those feelings to himself. Instead he said, "Polly was mighty pretty tonight, wasn't she?"

Will grunted. "Polly Ebersole was always pretty. That don't make her the right girl for Titus."

"Her name's Polly Brannon now."

"She'll always be an Ebersole," Will said with a shrug. "I wonder if Titus is happy. He didn't look much like it tonight."

"Henry tells me that he was all right at first," said Mac. "Titus had been drinking a lot, and then that marriage business sort of came up unexpectedly. Henry says after the wedding, he'd never seen Titus any happier."

"A fella gets married, he's generally in a pretty good mood for a spell," Will said dryly.

"Yeah, I reckon so. I just wish it had lasted longer for Titus."

"He should have brought Polly back here to the farm to live."

"I suppose Ebersole wouldn't hear of it."

The tobacco in Will's pipe burned down. He tapped the dottle out and stepped on the glowing coals. "Titus made his own bed. I just reckon I'm glad he's still around here to help look after the farm."

Mac nodded and looked again at the ceaselessly pacing stallion who was eager to once again smell the smoke of battle. "That's right," Mac said. "Two soldiers in the family are enough."

Chapter Six

F OR A CITY THAT had been under attack not long before, Vicksburg seemed like a bustling, vital place. The sidewalks were crowded with people, and horses and wagons and buggies filled the streets. The county courthouse was the most dominating feature on the landscape, but many of the other structures were almost equally imposing. As he and Pie walked along the streets, Cory saw banks and office buildings and theaters and an orchestra hall. The railroad depot was a gabled building of red sandstone only two blocks from the river's edge. The area along the riverfront was filled with warehouses that had once handled all the goods from the river traffic. Given the fact that Federal forces controlled both the upper and lower Mississippi, Cory expected that the warehouses would be empty now, but he saw that wasn't the case. In fact, quite a bit of cargo seemed to be going in and out of the big buildings. Wagons from the docks along the river carried goods to the warehouses, and other wagons carried them away, heading out to north, east, and south. Cory frowned as he saw that. With the riverboats unable to travel freely up and down the Mississippi, where were those supplies coming from?

As the two men reached one of the bluffs overlooking the river, Cory turned and gazed back at Vicksburg. The city looked more familiar to him from this angle. He had seen it before, from the deck of the *Missouri Zephyr* as the riverboat plied the waters of the great river. He had even gone ashore here a time or two with Ike Judson and Ned Rowley, the other pilot, but only to have a meal and a beer in a waterfront tavern. He had never explored the city itself until now.

Looking along the bluff, Cory saw the redoubts where cannon had been installed. Several of them were massive Columbiads. Their huge barrels were angled down toward the river in perfect position for firing on any Yankee vessels that ventured too close. At the moment, Cory didn't see any boats on the river. Its broad, slow-moving expanse was empty.

Even though there was no threat right now, all the guns were manned. Their crews sat around talking and playing cards, while an officer at each of the gun emplacements continually scanned the river with field glasses, watching for any sign of a new Northern assault.

Pie said with a grin, "You reckon I could get me a job shootin' one o' them cannons?"

"I don't know," Cory replied. "Is that what you want to do?"

"I never fired nothin' bigger'n a squirrel rifle. I reckon it'd be pretty excitin' to touch off one o' them big sumbitches."

"Well, then, let's go see where you sign up, and I'll ask about Colonel Thompson."

The nearest artillery battery was set just below the top of the bluff. The two men went down a set of broad steps that had been hewn into the sandstone itself and approached a lieutenant who was watching the river.

"Beg your pardon, sir," Cory said. "My friend here would like to enlist, and I have a question."

The lieutenant lowered his glasses and turned toward them. Cory saw that he was about his own age, perhaps even a little younger. He sported a goatee to try to make himself look older, but it didn't really succeed.

"I don't have time for civilians," the officer snapped. "Whatever you want, make it quick."

"I'm looking for an officer in the Mississippi Home Guard," Cory said. "He's a colonel, I think, and his name is Thompson, Charles Thompson."

"You're in the wrong place," the lieutenant said impatiently. "The Mississippi Home Guard mans the defenses on the inland side of the city."

Cory's heart sank. He hadn't noticed any defenses as he and Pie were coming into Vicksburg on the wagon, but he supposed there could have been some. Now he was on the wrong side of the city, and he would have to walk all the way through Vicksburg before he would even have a chance to find the man he was looking for.

He ventured one more question. "Do you happen to know Colonel Thompson, Lieutenant?"

"Never heard of him." The lieutenant was looking at Pie now. "You want to enlist, do you?"

"Yes sir. I want to shoot one o' them cannons."

The lieutenant smirked. "You don't look to me like you have the makings of a gunner, but someone as big as you ought to be able to manhandle shells quite easily. We can always use another loader." He turned and pointed to a tent on the nearby bluff. "See the company clerk. He'll sign you up."

Pie hesitated. "Well, I don't know . . . I sort of had my heart set on shootin' a cannon."

"Suit yourself." The young officer turned back toward the river and lifted his field glasses, clearly no longer interested in talking to either of them.

He snapped around again, though, when a woman's voice called from behind Cory and Pie, "Hello, Lieutenant O'Reilly."

Cory's breath seemed to freeze inside his body, and his throat was suddenly blocked by an impassable boulder. The sound of his pulse beating in his head rose to a thundering roar as loud as if all those Columbiads had been fired at once. He tried to make himself turn around, but his muscles refused to obey his commands.

The lieutenant smiled past Cory and Pie and said, "Good afternoon to you, Miss Farrell. You've come to lift the spirits of our troops again, I see."

"That's right. I've brought some fresh-baked tarts."

Slowly, Cory began to turn. He was only halfway around when the young woman who had come up behind him gasped, took an involuntary step back, and cried out in disbelief, "Cory!" The straw basket she was carrying slipped from her fingers to fall to the ground, and the tarts wrapped in linen inside the basket slipped out and scattered haphazardly.

"Miss Farrell!" exclaimed O'Reilly. "Are you all right? Are you afraid of this man?"

"Afraid?" Lucille Farrell said in a half-whisper. "The only thing I was afraid of was that I would never see him again."

"I'm here," Cory said quietly to her. "I'm really here, Lucille." He held out his hands toward her.

She let out a strangled sigh and reached to take his hands, and then she fell into his arms. They caressed each other desperately.

"Well, it appears that they know each other," the lieutenant said. Cory heard him only vaguely. He was too occupied with the way in which, having Lucille in his arms again, all his senses seemed to burst.

She was so warm, and she smelled so good. As his lips found hers, the sweet taste intoxicated him faster than any of the moonshine whiskey cooked up by the Fogartys back home ever could have. He wanted to hold her and kiss her forever.

But he wanted to look at her, too, to let his eyes drink in the sight of her, the sight he had ached for during the long, lonely months they had been separated. He stepped back, resting his hands on her shoulders, and gazed at her in awe and wonderment.

She was as beautiful as ever. Slightly below medium height, with a richly curved body, long honey-colored hair, and brown eyes so deep and warm a man could lose himself in them. She looked up at him with her chin angled at a slightly defiant tilt, as usual. She wore a gray dress and was bareheaded on this warm summer day.

As he stared at her, Cory was so overcome with emotion that he found himself unable to speak. His mouth opened, but no words came out, no matter how hard he tried. He wanted to tell her how much he loved her and how much he had missed her and how glad he was to see her again, but none of that would emerge. The power of what he was feeling was so strong that it kept everything else locked up tight within him. Finally, with an effort, he was able to whisper her name.

It was enough. She whispered his name in reply, and they embraced again.

Pie scratched at his beard and said to O'Reilly, "If all you've got right now is loadin' jobs, Lieutenant, I reckon I'll wait about enlistin'."

"You don't want to fight the Yankees, is that it?" O'Reilly said scornfully. His attention wasn't really on Pie, however. He kept looking at Cory and Lucille with a frown on his face.

Pie's eyes narrowed. "I want to fight Yankees just as much as the next man, and prob'ly more'n some. But I'll do it my own way."

"I could conscript you, you know. The Confederacy needs all the able-bodied fighting men it can get. Our losses have been heavy."

"You could try," Pie said with a shrug. "Ain't it better, though, to have fellas fightin' alongside you that want to be there?"

The lieutenant turned away in disgust. "Get out of here," he snapped. "You and your friend, too. This is a military installation, and it's no place for civilians."

Cory heard that and could not ignore the slur. He released Lucille enough to slip his arm around her shoulders and say, "Come on. We're not wanted here."

O'Reilly said over his shoulder, "My comments did not apply to Miss Farrell, of course. She is always welcome."

Lucille looked uneasily at Cory. "I *did* bring tarts for the men who are posted here."

Cory understood. The lieutenant had said Lucille came to boost the spirits of the soldiers at the batteries, and Cory had no doubt that she did. A visit from a lovely young woman, especially one bearing freshly baked pastries, would go a long way toward relieving the boredom of being on constant watch for the enemy. He said to Lucille, "Go ahead," then looked around quickly for a place they could rendezvous later. He pointed toward a small tavern wedged between two warehouses a block away. It was the first place that caught his eye. "We'll be waiting over there for you."

"All right," she agreed. She came up on her toes and kissed him again. "You'll have to tell me everything that's happened since I saw you last."

"Of course," he said, but he immediately realized that he really didn't mean it. Not fully, anyway. Too many terrible things had occurred. He wondered suddenly if she even knew that her father was dead.

That could wait. For now, he gathered up the tarts and the basket she had dropped, handed them to her, and then said to Pie, "Come on. We're going over to that tavern for a little while."

"That's all right by me," declared Pie. "It's been too long since I had a chance to wet my whistle."

They went back up the broad sandstone steps, and Cory paused at the top to look back at the gun emplacement. Lucille was still there, talking to the lieutenant. She took one of the tarts from the basket and gave it to him, then moved on to bestow her gifts on the other members of the artillery detachment.

Cory could hardly believe he had found her again. Now that he had, he swore to himself that he would never let her go.

———

THE SHADE inside the tavern felt good after being in the hot sun all day. The place wasn't busy. Cory picked a table near the door, where he would be able to see Lucille as she approached, and he sat down while Pie went to the bar to get them something to drink. He came back with a bucket of beer and a couple of mugs. As he placed them on the table and sat down opposite Cory, he said, "So that's the gal, huh?"

Cory nodded. "That's the gal," he agreed. "Miss Lucille Farrell."

"She's mighty nice-lookin'. Seemed sweet, too." Pie dipped the mugs in the bucket and then set one of them in front of

Cory. Cory hesitated, then picked it up and drank some of the foaming beer from it.

"I'm sorry you weren't able to enlist and get the job you wanted," he commented.

Pie shrugged, the massive shoulders going up and down. "Aw, it don't matter. I was thinkin' I might join that Mississippi Home Guard you been talkin' about. That pipsqueak lieutenant said they been mannin' the defenses outside o' town. That sounds pretty good to me. I'm a fair shot with a rifle."

Cory remembered how the Northerners had carried out a two-pronged attack on Fort Donelson, shelling the fort from gunboats on the Cumberland River and at the same time striking at it overland from the west with troops. A similar fate might await Vicksburg. The Yankee gunboats were already making a nuisance of themselves. North of the city was the Yazoo Swamp, a vast, marshy expanse that would make it difficult if not impossible to launch an invasion from that direction. The way into the city was open to the east, however, along the railroad. That was the way Cory and Pie had come, and Cory hadn't seen anything that would prevent an army from following the same route.

"I expect if you join the Home Guard, you'll see some action," Cory said.

Pie downed a healthy swallow of the beer and then licked foam off his lips. "That's what I'm lookin' for," he said with a grin.

Cory was still looking out the open door of the tavern, watching for Lucille. He didn't want her to have to come into the establishment to search for him. A waterfront dive like this was no place for a lady. Since his gaze was turned toward the river, he was in position to see something coming toward the city in a steep arc through the air, hard on the heels of a strange thumping noise. A second later he heard a high-pitched whine.

"Mortar!" shouted the bartender. The man went diving to the floor, as did the other customers in the tavern, with the exception of Cory and Pie. They sat at the table, frozen by surprise.

Less than a block away, the explosive shell struck a ware-house, and the force of the blast was strong enough to shake the ground and send Cory and Pie tumbling out of their chairs. Cory lay stunned for a second, then pushed himself up on his hands and knees and said, "What the hell!"

"Get under cover, you damned fool!" shouted one of the tavern's patrons. As Cory looked around in confusion, he saw that all the customers except for Pie and him had scrambled under-neath tables. The furniture wouldn't offer much protection, but any shelter was better than none in the middle of a bombardment.

And that was exactly what was happening to Vicksburg, Cory realized a moment later as another shell burst nearby with shat-tering force. He remembered the way the officers at the artillery batteries along the bluffs had been watching the river, and he wasn't sure how the Yankee gunboats could have gotten close enough to shell the city without an alarm being sounded first. At the moment, that didn't really matter, he told himself. He pushed himself to his feet. Lucille was still out there some-where, among the gun emplacements along the Mississippi.

"Cory!" Pie shouted as his friend dashed for the doorway of the tavern. "Dang it—" Hurriedly standing up, Pie lumbered after him.

As he emerged from the tavern, Cory looked around wildly, searching for any sign of Lucille. The cannons along the river thundered into action, answering with their roar the deep-throated thumps of the mortars on the Yankee gunboats. More explosions sounded behind him as Cory ran toward the bluffs.

He took the steps leading down to the closest battery in a couple of bounds. The Confederate artillerymen were working feverishly. One man had a long pole with a water-soaked wad of cotton attached to the end of it. He ran the pole down the length of the cannon barrel to extinguish any sparks left from the previ-ous shot, thus preventing an accidental explosion. Two men car-ried a shell from a nearby pile while a fourth soldier put the firing charge in place. The shell was rammed home, the fuse was set, and the gunner took hold of the lanyard attached to the friction trigger. O'Reilly stood nearby, his field glasses to his eyes, calling out adjustments in aim. One of the soldiers turned a wheel attached to the cannon's carriage, lowering its barrel a bit. The lieutenant shouted, "Fire!"

The gunner pulled the lanyard. The sound of the cannon firing was so loud it was like two heavy fists against Cory's ears. He staggered slightly, then recovered his balance and rushed up to the lieutenant. His own voice sounded strangely muffled in his ears as he shouted, "Where is Miss Farrell? Have you seen her?"

O'Reilly ignored him, concentrating instead on the river.

Cory reached out and grabbed the officer's shoulder, swinging him around roughly. "Miss Farrell!" he said, and he was able to hear himself more clearly this time. "Where is she?"

O'Reilly looked both harried and angry. He brought up his arm and knocked Cory's hand off his shoulder. "Let go of me, damn you! Can't you see we're under attack?"

"I have to find Miss Farrell!"

O'Reilly waved along the bluff toward the north. "She was going that way," he said. He put his hand on the butt of the pistol on his hip. "Now get out of here, or I'll shoot you myself."

Cory stared at the young officer for a second, then broke into a run along the bluff. He was aware that Pie was huffing along behind him, but he didn't look around.

The other cannons were firing sporadically. Their shots were aimed toward the river, almost two hundred feet below. From the corner of his eye, Cory saw water fly into the air, the high-flung droplets sparkling in the late afternoon sunlight, as Confederate shells splashed into the Mississippi. He saw smoke as well, forming a haze in the air above a line of trees along the riverbank. The Yankees must have used the trees to cover their approach to Vicksburg. They could have stopped their engines before coming too close and then silently poled the boats into position to launch the barrage. That would explain how they had taken everyone by surprise.

Now, having struck at the city, the Yankees would be on their way, firing up their boilers and running before the Confederate guns could do too much damage to them. It had been a good plan, and the part of Cory's brain that had learned more about military tactics over the past year could almost admire the Northerners' audacity.

But if those bastards had hurt Lucille—!

He didn't see her at the first three batteries he came to, but as he approached the fourth one, he saw the westering sun glint on her long hair as she knelt beside a fallen soldier. She had pulled up her gown and was ripping a piece off the already ragged bottom edge of her petticoat to serve as a makeshift bandage. As Cory hurried up to her, she wrapped the strip of fabric around the soldier's bloody arm and tied it tightly.

"There," she said to the trooper, whose face was pale and strained. "You'll be all right."

Cory caught hold of her shoulder. "Lucille! Are you hurt?"

She stood up and turned to face him. There was blood on her hands, but he told himself it had come from the wounded soldier. "Cory!" she exclaimed.

He caught hold of her and restrained the impulse to shake her. "Are you all right?" he asked. He couldn't bear to think of losing her again after finally finding her.

"I'm fine," she told him. When he continued staring at her and his hands trembled on her upper arms, she said more emphatically, "I'm not hurt, Cory. I'm all right."

"Thank God." He was so shaken that was all he could manage to say, so he repeated it and embraced her.

The guns were falling silent now, and the quiet sounded odd after the deafening cacophony that had filled the air only moments earlier. After holding Lucille for a couple of minutes, Cory stepped back and said, "I was afraid you'd been . . . that the explosions . . ."

She shook her head. "Most of the shells fell in the city. The gunboats have a difficult time dropping their shells on our batteries, especially when they're as close as they were today. I don't think anyone was expecting them to attack in broad daylight."

Cory certainly hadn't been expecting it. His thoughts had been full of his reunion with Lucille and little else.

He looked around for the basket she had been carrying earlier but didn't see it anywhere. "What happened to your basket?" he asked, even thought the question sounded foolish to him.

"I dropped it somewhere when the shelling started," she said. "I'm afraid I don't remember where. I wanted to pitch in and help if I could, so I started bandaging wounds."

Pie said, "Is this what you lost, ma'am?"

The couple turned and saw the big man holding the straw basket with its bright ribbons. It looked peculiar as he held it gingerly with fingers as long and thick as sausages. "I saw it layin' over yonder," he went on, "and figured it might be yours."

Lucille reached out and took the basket from him. "Thank you, Mister . . . ?"

"I was so overcome by seeing you earlier that I forgot to introduce the two of you," Cory said. "Lucille, this is my friend Pie Jones. Pie, this is Miss Lucille Farrell."

Pie tugged on the brim of his hat. "Mighty pleased to meet you, Miss Lucille." He glanced at the confusion around them. "Reckon it could've been under better circumstances, though."

"Much better," agreed Lucille. "I'm pleased to meet you, Mr. Jones, and thank you again for recovering my basket."

"Shoot, call me Pie. That's all I been answerin' to since I was knee-high to a grasshopper." A broad grin spread across Pie's bearded face.

"All right, then, Pie, but I'm Lucille."

The big man nodded. Cory took Lucille's arm and turned her toward the city. "We'd better go," he said. "Just in case the Yankees come back."

"The people are in more danger than these gunners," Lucille said grimly. "The Yankees think they can batter us into submission, but they're wrong. Vicksburg won't ever surrender."

Cory didn't know about that. He didn't like to consider the possibility of the Northern invaders ever winning anything. But right now, unpatriotic though it might be, he didn't give a hang about the war. All he cared about was Lucille. He just wanted to sit somewhere quiet with her and hold her hand and look at her and tell himself how lucky he was to be with her once again.

"You're both coming with me," Lucille said as they climbed the steps to the street. "I know Uncle Charles and Aunt Mildred will want to meet you."

"Then your uncle is the Charles Thompson who's a colonel in the Mississippi Home Guard?" asked Cory.

"That's right. How did you know about that?"

"A friend told me," Cory said. He didn't explain that the friend was Bedford Forrest or that the information had come to Cory in the aftermath of the savage battle at Shiloh. "I knew your uncle had left Nashville, and I hoped the one here at Vicksburg was the right man—and that you were still with him."

"I had nowhere else to go," Lucille said. "Not after we received the news about—" Her voice caught for a moment before she could go on. "About my father."

So she knew that her father was dead. Though he experienced a twinge of guilt at his reaction, Cory felt relieved that he wouldn't have to be the one to tell her. He had not been looking forward to breaking the news of her father's death.

He wasn't going to completely escape, however. Lucille went on, "Were you with him . . . at the end?"

Cory took a deep breath. "I was."

"I want you to tell me all about it." Her hand tightened on his arm as they walked along the street. "But not now. Later."

They were near the southernmost artillery battery when someone came hurrying up behind them. Lieutenant O'Reilly called, "Miss Farrell!"

The three stopped and turned to face the officer. O'Reilly took off his hat and asked, "Were you injured in the attack, Miss Farrell?"

"No, I'm all right, Lieutenant," she told him. "But thank you for your concern for my welfare."

"Of course I was concerned," O'Reilly said. "I know how much your visits mean to the men."

"I do what little I can to help our noble cause."

"It's a great deal indeed," said O'Reilly. He glanced at Cory and Pie, and his tone was cooler as he said, "I see your friends found you."

Lucille squeezed Cory's arm. "Yes, and thank you for helping them, Lieutenant."

Cory said, "He didn't—" but stopped as Lucille's hand tightened even more on his arm.

O'Reilly smiled. "I'm always glad to come to the assistance of a lovely lady such as yourself."

Lucille returned the smile while Cory did his best not to glare. She said, "Why don't you come to dinner at my uncle's house tomorrow night, Lieutenant?"

"The pleasure would be all mine, Miss Farrell."

"At six o'clock, then."

"Six," repeated O'Reilly.

The three civilians turned to walk on down the street, and Cory said under his breath, "I don't like Lieutenant O'Reilly."

"Don't be silly," Lucille told him. "The lieutenant is a fine officer and dedicated to the cause of the Confederacy."

"Maybe," Cory said shortly.

But he had seen the way O'Reilly looked at Lucille, and he had a feeling the lieutenant was dedicated to other things besides the cause of the Confederacy.

Chapter Seven

A S THE CITIZENS OF Vicksburg began clearing the damage
from the latest Yankee shelling, Lucille led Cory and
Pie across the city to a modest but neatly kept frame dwelling
in a neighborhood not far from the courthouse. The house had
been whitewashed recently, and so had the picket fence surrounding the small front yard.

"We were lucky to be able to rent this place when we got
here," Lucille said as she opened the gate. "The gentleman who
owns it is in the army, and his wife and children went to stay with
relatives in Jackson."

"It looks very nice," Cory said.

"Yes, it is. The trip here from Nashville was hard. We got out
of there one jump ahead of the Yankees, and while we were traveling we usually had to sleep underneath the wagon. It was wonderful to get here and have a real bed again."

By the time Cory had arrived in Nashville to search for
Lucille, following the fall of Forts Henry and Donelson, a Federal army under Gen. Don Carlos Buell had occupied the city.
The Confederate army in Nashville had withdrawn rather than
defend the city, a decision Cory still thought had been wrong.
From Nashville, Buell's men had moved west, while an army
under Gen. Ulysses S. Grant had come from the west. The
Southern army, which had regrouped after the loss of the two
river forts, struck quickly at Grant, hoping to cripple that part of
the Northern army before it could join forces with Buell. That
had led to the battle of Shiloh, a bloody two-day affair that had
first seen the Confederates winning before fortune had ultimately turned against them and led to a Union victory.

Cory knew he would never forget the things he had seen and
done during the savage battle near the little church whose name
meant "place of peace." But for now anyway, he was able to

push them to the back of his mind and concentrate on the wonderful sensations of being with Lucille again.

"I slept on the ground every night during my journey here," he said, "so I know what you mean."

Lucille led them up a flagstone walk to a small front porch with a couple of wicker chairs on it. She opened the door and called, "Aunt Mildred? We have company."

A small, birdlike woman with graying red hair came hurrying along a hallway toward the foyer of the house. She was wearing an apron over a dark brown dress, and as she approached she untied it and slipped it off, holding it behind her back as she came into the entryway. "Company?" she said. "Why, Lucille, you should have given me some warning—" She stopped short, her eyes widening as she saw the blood on her niece's hands. "Lucille!"

"It's all right, Aunt Mildred," Lucille said quickly. "I'm not hurt. I helped bandage some soldiers' wounds after the shelling awhile ago."

"That was awful," Mildred Thompson said. "I was so worried about you when I heard the explosions. I knew you'd gone down to the batteries with those tarts I baked."

"I was fine. It was frightening, but none of the Yankee shells came that close to where I was." Lucille set the basket aside on a small table, then took Cory's arm. "Aunt Mildred, this is Cory Brannon," she announced. "I've told you all about him."

"Of course." Mildred smiled and took Cory's hand. "We've heard a great deal indeed about you, young man. It's a pleasure to finally meet you. I know my brother Ezekiel thought very highly of you."

"And I thought highly of him, too, ma'am," Cory said solemnly. "Captain Farrell was one of the best men I ever met."

"He certainly was." Mildred turned to look at Pie. "My, you're certainly a big one, aren't you?"

"Yes'm," Pie replied with a grin as he tugged off his hat.

"Aunt Mildred, this is Cory's friend, Pie Jones."

The older woman took Pie's hand as well. "What sort of a name is Pie?" she asked bluntly.

He continued grinning and patted his belly. "Fittin'."

Mildred laughed. "Do you like peach cobbler, Mr. Jones?"

"One of my favorites, ma'am."

"Well, then, we'll have some after supper. You *are* staying for supper, aren't you?"

"Of course they are," Lucille said before either Cory or Pie could frame a response. "They'll be staying with us while they're in Vicksburg. Won't you?"

Cory hesitated. The house was rather small, but with the weather as warm as it was, he and Pie could easily sleep on the porch. And he didn't want to be any farther from Lucille than he had to be. He said, "If it's all right with your aunt and uncle . . ."

"Certainly it's all right," Mildred said. "Charles isn't here right now, but I'm sure when he gets home he'll welcome you boys with open arms. Now, why don't you make yourselves comfortable while Lucille and I see to supper."

"We're much obliged, ma'am," Pie told her.

Mildred turned toward the kitchen, and Lucille came up on her toes to give Cory a quick kiss on the cheek. "Go into the parlor and sit down," she told him. "I'll be back in a bit."

Reluctantly, Cory let her go. She followed her aunt toward the rear of the house as Cory and Pie stepped through an arched entrance from the foyer into a smartly furnished parlor.

Carefully, Pie lowered his bulk into an armchair near a cold fireplace. The chair had lace doilies on the arms and back. He fingered one of them and said, "I never seen the like."

Cory remembered such homey touches from his own childhood. In fact, as he sat down on a claw-footed divan and rested his hands on his knees, he looked around the parlor and thought about how much it reminded him of his home. The Brannon farmhouse hadn't been as fancy as this place, of course, but his mother had always kept it spick-and-span and had done what she could to create an air of gentility. There was even a framed embroidered sampler of the Lord's Prayer hanging on the wall of this room. Back home it had been the Twenty-third Psalm.

They had been sitting there for about half an hour, talking quietly and enjoying the faint sounds of Lucille and her aunt bustling around the kitchen, when footsteps sounded on the porch and a moment later the front door swung open. A tall man in a uniform consisting of a dark gray jacket and lighter gray trousers came into the foyer. He took off his hat, revealing a thatch of salt-and-pepper hair, as he called in a deep, resonant voice, "Mildred, I'm home." He started through the foyer, only to pause as he noticed the two strangers sitting in his parlor. His free hand moved toward the flap of the holster on his hip.

Cory stood up quickly, holding out his hands so that the officer would see he was unarmed and meant no harm. "It's all right, Colonel Thompson," he said. "We're friends."

Mildred hurried out from the kitchen and said, "Charles, what are you doing? You weren't about to pull a gun on our guests, were you?"

The man relaxed a little. "I wasn't expecting anyone else to be here," he said. He stepped into the parlor and held out his hand to Cory. "I'm Col. Charles Thompson, as you seem to know already."

"Cory Brannon, sir," Cory introduced himself as he shook the colonel's hand.

Thompson's eyebrows rose. "Lucille's friend? The one who was on the *Zephyr* with Zeke?"

"That's right, sir." Cory nodded toward Pie, who had stood up from the armchair. "And this is my friend Pie Jones."

Thompson shook hands with Pie. "Pleased to meet you, Mr. Jones."

"Call me Pie, Colonel. I been thinkin' about joinin' up with your outfit to fight Yankees."

Thompson nodded in approval as he looked over Pie's powerful form. "We'd be glad to have you. The Home Guard will need every man it can get to defend the city from the Yankees."

"Cory and Pie are going to be staying with us for a while," Mildred told her husband.

"Excellent." Thompson waved the two men back into their seats. "Sit down, gentlemen, sit down. Make yourselves at home."

Mildred went back to the kitchen while Thompson hung his hat and pistol belt on a hook and then sat down in the parlor with Cory and Pie. In a quiet voice, he asked, "Have you seen Lucille?"

"Yes sir," Cory said with a glowing smile.

"She was quite worried about you, you know, after we received the news of Zeke's death. She was afraid you might have been killed in the fighting as well."

"Luck was with me," Cory said with a shrug. "I came through Donelson all right, and then Shiloh after that."

"Shiloh? My God. I've heard about what happened there, of course. I'd say you're fortunate just to be alive."

"Yes sir," Cory agreed.

Thompson lowered his voice even more. "Lucille is going to want to know all the details of what happened to her father, if you haven't given them to her already."

"No sir."

"I hope you feel kindly enough toward her to be judicious in what you tell her."

"I'll make it as easy as I can on her," Cory promised. "I don't want to see her hurt any more than you do, Colonel."

Thompson nodded. "I know that. I'm aware of her fondness for you. I'm glad you've survived and that you've been reunited. That will certainly lighten her heart." He looked over at Pie. "What about you, Mr. Jones? Have you seen any action?"

"Nope," replied Pie. "That's why I'm lookin' to join up somewheres. I talked to a feller in the regular army about shootin' some o' them cannons over by the river, but he just wanted me to haul shells around."

"Who would that be?"

Cory said, "His name was O'Reilly."

Thompson snorted. "Jack O'Reilly can be insufferable. He is, however, a decent artillery officer. But I'm just as glad I don't serve with him directly."

Pie leaned forward and clasped his hands together. "You reckon you got a place for me in the Home Guard, Colonel?"

"We can find a place, Mr. Jones," Thompson assured him. "Or perhaps I should start calling you Private Jones, so that you can become accustomed to it."

Pie grinned. "Private Jones," he repeated. "Sounds good to me."

Lucille came into the room. She was wearing an apron now, and Cory thought its wholesome appearance made her even more beautiful. She bent over and kissed her uncle on the cheek, then announced, "Supper is ready."

Thompson got to his feet. "Come along, gentlemen. I can't promise you an elaborate meal, but I can assure you that it will be delicious."

Lucille hung back to let her uncle and Pie go first, then she fell in beside Cory and took his hand in hers. He felt his heart swell at her touch, and her shy smile made him want to pull her into his arms and kiss her again.

Time enough for that later, Cory told himself. Now that they were together again, they had all the time in the world.

As THEY ate, Cory learned more about their hosts. Charles Thompson had been an officer in the army and had served with distinction during the Mexican War before retiring to a career in business in his hometown of Nashville. He had married Mildred Farrell while establishing himself in banking and real estate. The only child they were destined to have had died in infancy, but the marriage had survived this tragedy and Charles and Mildred had grown even closer because of it. They had come to be especially fond of their niece Lucille, who had visited them often as she was growing up. Cory got the feeling that Mildred thought a riverboat wasn't a fit place to be raising a young lady, but no one could argue with the way Lucille had turned out. Cory certainly wasn't going to.

"When Fort Donelson fell and General Johnston decided to withdraw our troops from Nashville, I knew we could remain there no longer," Thompson said. "It was time I took an active part in defending our homeland. I'd had letters from an old friend of mine who served in Mexico with me, and I knew he was an officer here in the Mississippi Home Guard. We came here. and he arranged a commission for me."

"I hated to leave our home in Nashville," Mildred put in. "But we knew there was no choice. We couldn't live under a Yankee army of occupation." She looked at Cory. "You said you went there to look for Lucille. What has happened to the city? Have the Yankees destroyed it?"

Cory shook his head. "It's not too bad. There was no real fighting when the Federal troops got there, so there wasn't much damage. Of course, now there are Yankee soldiers all over the place, and it's been hard on the people because they can't get enough supplies. The Yankees commandeer anything they want."

"Supplies," Thompson repeated grimly. "That's going to be a problem here, too, before much longer."

Cory leaned forward. "I was surprised, sir, to see so much activity around the docks and the warehouses. You still have goods coming in from somewhere."

"From Texas and Arkansas," said Thompson. "Ships can bring cotton and grain and cattle down the Red River to the Mississippi and then steam north this far. From Vicksburg those goods go out by rail to the rest of the South. But with the Yankees pushing west and south through Arkansas, they may eventually be able to cut that supply line. That's why we've been looking at other options."

Cory was intrigued by that statement, but Thompson didn't seem to want to elaborate on it at the moment, and Cory was not going to be rude enough to press the matter. He and Pie were guests in the colonel's house, after all.

After supper was finished—including bowls of warm peach cobbler that brought a huge smile to Pie's face—Cory, Pie, and Thompson went out to the porch to enjoy the evening. Cory and Thompson sat in the wicker chairs while Pie lowered himself onto the porch steps. Thompson and Pie filled pipes and lit them. Cory watched fireflies darting around the front yard.

"You've seen the Yankees firsthand, lad," Thompson said after a few minutes. "Tell me, are we going to be able to stop them?"

"I'm no military strategist, Colonel," Cory said with a shake of his head. "I'm not even a real soldier. I just happened to be in some places where I had to do some fighting."

"You survived Shiloh," Thompson said. "That makes you a soldier as far as I'm concerned. I'd like your opinion."

Cory thought about the question for a moment. He wanted to say something positive and encouraging, but when he finally opened his mouth, the truth was what came out. "There are just so *many* of them."

Thompson nodded. "And for an army fighting in a land that's not their own, they're very well supplied. If we lose this war, that may well be our undoing."

Cory frowned. This was the first time he had heard anyone admit even the possibility that the Confederacy might not prevail. "You don't think we'll win, sir?"

"I didn't say that. I believe our cause is just, and we're fighting to protect our homeland, rather than being the invaders. That gives us a natural advantage. But any soldier knows that, in war, there are victors and there are losers."

Pie spat into the yard. "Beggin' your pardon, Colonel," he said, "but I ain't intendin' to see us lose to a bunch o' no-account Yankees who got no business bein' down here in Dixie."

Thompson reached over and clapped a hand on Pie's shoulder. "Well said, Private Jones. It's just that attitude which gives me hope the Confederacy will emerge triumphant in the end. The Yankees may outnumber us, but by God, they can't outscrap us!"

Cory hoped the colonel was right. He was no longer that sure himself.

A short time later, the ladies came out of the house, having finished the after-dinner chores. Cory and Thompson stood up and gave their seats to Lucille and Mildred. They joined Pie on the porch steps.

"Could you . . . could you tell us a little about my brother's passing, Cory?" Mildred asked.

Cory looked at Lucille, and in the light that came from inside the house, he saw her nod. He hesitated a moment longer, brushing a mosquito away from his face. "All right. You know about what happened at Fort Henry. Lucille was there for most of it."

"Yes, but Father sent me away before the worst of the battle," said Lucille. "All I know is that the *Zephyr* was destroyed with all hands on board except for you and Father."

Cory nodded. "After you left for Nashville, Captain Farrell and I volunteered to help defend the fort."

He didn't mention how Farrell had descended into drunkenness for a short period of time because of the grief and guilt he felt at the loss of his boat and his crew. Captain Farrell and Ike Judson had been good friends and long-time companions on the river, and the captain had been almost as close to Ned Rowley. The crew of the *Zephyr* had been like a second family to Farrell. Cory had an inkling of how he had felt, because the rivermen had started to become a second family to him, too, before that rainy February day had ended it all.

"We were carrying a message for one of the officers when the Yankees attacked," Cory began. "We helped push them back, but the captain . . . the captain was fatally wounded in the fighting."

With a catch in her voice, Lucille asked, "Did he . . . did he say anything before he died?"

"He told me how much he loved you," Cory replied softly. "And he made me promise to find you and take care of you. I'm glad I'm finally going to be able to keep that promise."

Thompson squeezed Cory's shoulder. Mildred was crying quietly, almost silently. With an obvious effort, Lucille asked, "Did he . . . suffer much?"

"No," Cory said without hesitation. "It was very fast."

She nodded and whispered, "Thank you."

Cory sat there and stared into the gathering shadows, remembering other things: the lanky Confederate soldier from Texas who had befriended him and talked about someday having a ranch on a river called the Brazos before dying in battle at Fort Donelson; the daring Colonel Forrest, who had led his cavalrymen in an audacious escape rather than surrender to the Yankees; the time Cory had spent as a prisoner of the Yankees following the surrender of the fort, until he had been suddenly and unexpectedly paroled along with hundreds of the other captives; the desolation he had felt upon arriving in Nashville and discovering that Lucille was gone; the horrors of Shiloh, always the horrors to which his mind returned unbidden . . .

Pie slipped his mouth harp from his pocket and began to play. The tune was "Dixie" but the way Pie played it, the song had a slow and mournful air at sharp odds with its usual jauntiness. The music was poignantly beautiful, and Cory knew he would never be able to hear it again without thinking of this moment together on the porch as the soft black night fell over Vicksburg.

Chapter Eight

OVER THE NEXT FEW weeks, Cory almost came to feel as if Vicksburg had always been his home. He spent his days walking the streets of the city with Lucille or visiting the defenses manned by the Home Guard. The guardsmen were engaged in digging rifle pits, erecting earthworks, and clearing magnolia trees and cane brush off the heavily wooded hills so that when the Yankee assault finally came, the Federal troops would have to charge across open ground. Cory pitched in to help, as did Pie Jones. Pie was officially sworn in as a member of the Guard, but Cory continued his practice of serving as a civilian volunteer. He had given his word to Captain Farrell that he would protect Lucille, and if the time came when they had to flee from the city, he wanted to be able to leave without being a deserter.

Cory saw Colonel Thompson's prediction about the flow of supplies into Vicksburg slowing down begin to come true. Fewer ships were steaming up the Mississippi from its junction with the Red River near Simmesport, Louisiana. Cory didn't know if the slowdown was caused by military activity in Arkansas or the natural drain on resources that seemed to be affecting the entire Confederacy. He knew that Thompson was growing more worried, however, and wondered what was going on with those "other options" the colonel had mentioned that first night.

It wasn't long before he found out. After supper one evening, Thompson invited Cory and Pie to sit out on the front porch with him again. This had not become a habit, because the men were usually too tired after their day's work to do anything except go to sleep. Tonight, though, Thompson led Cory and Pie onto the porch and began filling his pipe from a tobacco pouch. Pie did likewise. After he had puffed his pipe into life, Thompson exhaled a cloud of smoke and said, "I'm looking for volunteers for a new mission, gentlemen. I thought you might like to have first crack at it."

"If it means fightin' Yankees, I'm all for it," Pie answered without hesitation. "So far, the only fightin' I've done has been with a shovel."

Thompson smiled thinly. "The work of shoring up the city's defenses is vitally important, Private Jones . . . but you're right, it's not very exciting. However, the job I propose to carry out now probably does not directly involve battle with the Union forces, either. But it might not be without its own particular dangers."

"What is it you intend to do, Colonel?" Cory asked bluntly.

"After discussing the matter with General Smith and General Pemberton, the conclusion has been reached that something has to be done to ensure the continued flow of supplies into Vicksburg."

Cory knew that Gens. Martin Luther Smith and John C. Pemberton were the commanders of the regular Confederate forces in and around Vicksburg. If this mysterious mission that Charles Thompson was proposing had been approved by those two officers, then Cory knew it had to be vital to the Confederacy itself.

Thompson drew on his pipe again then asked, "Have you heard of the Vicksburg, Shreveport, and Texas Railroad?"

"That's the new line being built on the other side of the river, isn't it?" Cory asked. He had heard talk about the railroad but didn't know any details.

"It's been completed as far as the settlement of Monroe, on the Washita River." Thompson added dryly, "I'm afraid Shreveport is a bit out of reach at the moment."

"So you've got a railroad that goes west a ways," said Pie. "What good does that do you?"

"From Monroe it's only about 120 miles to the Texas border. That would be within reach of a wagon train."

Cory felt his pulse suddenly quicken. "You're thinking about taking a wagon train to Texas, loading it up with supplies, and bringing them back overland to Monroe?"

Thompson pointed the stem of his pipe at Cory and said, "That is exactly what we're thinking of, lad."

"It could work," Cory said, feeling his excitement growing. His restless nature, the facet of his personality that had led him to leave home in the first place, needed no urging for him to realize that this might be his long-awaited chance to see the nearly mythical land known as Texas. He was certain that Thompson was going to ask him and Pie to come along on the trip.

But then, abruptly, his spirits sank. Such a journey would take weeks, and he couldn't leave Lucille here in Vicksburg for that long. He had his promise to her father to consider.

"What about the Home Guard?" asked Pie. "I thought we was supposed to be protectin' the city."

"Keeping Vicksburg's inhabitants from starving to death *is* protecting it," Thompson pointed out. "Right now, the Yankees seem to have abandoned the idea of shelling the city into submission, but no one really believes they won't be back, probably before winter. With luck, we could bring in at least two trainloads of supplies by then. Our group will be a mixture of volunteers from the Home Guard and regular troops on detached duty. General Smith and General Pemberton have placed me in charge of the operation, and I'd like for you two fellows to be my first recruits."

"I've heard there's wild injuns in Texas," Pie said.

"I honestly don't know about that. But we *will* have to worry about renegades and cutthroats once word gets out about what we're doing. Those supplies could be worth a fortune. Not to mention the possibility of encountering Yankee soldiers trying to reach the Red River."

"I'm sold," Pie nodded emphatically. "When are we leavin'?"

"As soon as possible." Thompson turned to Cory. "What about you, lad? Will you join us?"

Cory wanted to say yes. The adventure that Colonel Thompson was proposing called out to him with a siren song almost impossible to resist. But he couldn't forget his promise . . .

"I'd like to, sir," he said with a voice choked with emotion, "but Lucille—"

"What about Lucille?" asked a new voice, and the young woman in question stepped through the open front door and onto the porch. "What are you being so secretive about, Uncle Charles, and what does it have to do with me?"

Thompson smiled and nodded toward Cory. "You'd best ask your young friend here."

She looked at him sternly. "Well, Cory, what about it? What's going on here?"

Cory struggled to find the words. "Your uncle asked me to . . . to come with him on a mission for the Confederacy. A vital mission, I suppose you could call it."

Thompson put in, "Yes, and we'd like to keep our plans confidential for as long as possible, so as not to complicate matters. But I think telling you about it is an acceptable risk, my dear."

Lucille looked at Cory and waited.

"We're going to Texas," he heard himself saying. The restlessness within him would not be denied.

"Texas?" she repeated, surprised.

"That's right." Cory rushed on before he could let himself think too much about what he was saying. "We can go to Monroe, Louisiana, on the railroad, then take a wagon train to Texas from there and load it up with supplies. It may be the only chance Vicksburg has."

"Oh. It sounds like a good idea."

Cory couldn't tell if she was upset by the prospect of him leaving or not. He had known Lucille only for a year or so, and during much of that year they had been separated. So he still had trouble at times knowing what she was thinking and feeling, despite the closeness he felt for her.

"I'd say it's vital to the survival of the Confederacy," Thompson said. "If Vicksburg falls, the Yankees will have succeeded in splitting us asunder. That's been their military strategy all along. And it would give them complete control over the Mississippi River, too. As Vicksburg goes, so goes the war."

"Then if you can help, you have to go," Lucille said to Cory. "How long will you be gone?"

Cory looked at the colonel, who shrugged. "I don't know," Cory said. "Several weeks, I suppose, if all goes well."

"All right." Lucille stepped closer to Cory and put her hand on his arm. She brushed a kiss across his mouth. "Good luck."

Pie said, "I'm goin' along, too, you know."

Lucille laughed and turned toward him, coming up on her toes to kiss his bearded cheek. "And good luck to you, too, Pie," she said.

"So it's decided, then," Colonel Thompson said. "You lads are coming with me."

"It looks like we are," said Cory. He glanced again at Lucille. She was still smiling, but there wasn't enough light on the porch for him to get a good look at her eyes.

He wasn't sure he wanted to know what he would see there, anyway.

ONCE THE operation was underway, things moved quickly. Thompson arranged for the use of a train with the directors of the Vicksburg, Shreveport, and Texas Railroad. The owners of the new rail line were more than happy to cooperate. Not only would they be paid for the use of their train and tracks, but ensuring the continued flow of supplies into Vicksburg could only be good for their business in the long run.

Cory, Pie, and Thompson were given cavalry mounts and crossed the Mississippi on a ferry. The train was being put together at the depot of the VS&T, but while that was being done, the three men would ride ahead on horseback to Monroe to make arrangements for the wagons they would need. Some army wagons could be shipped on the train, but they would require more than that for the trip to Texas.

Lucille and Mildred accompanied the three of them on the ferry to say good-bye at the depot. Cory felt as if he were being pulled in two as he looked at Lucille standing on the station platform, as beautiful as ever in a dark blue dress and bonnet. He put his arms around her and looked deeply into her eyes, saying, "I'm sorry to be leaving you again so soon, Lucille, when I promised I would stay with you and take care of you."

"I'll be fine, Cory," she assured him. "What you're doing is important to me, too, you know." She sighed. "But I *will* miss you." She kissed him.

Nearby on the platform, Charles and Mildred Thompson were saying their good-byes, too, leaving Pie to wander over to where the horses were hitched. He was carrying an army rifle under one arm, and Cory and Thompson were armed with a pistol each. Neither the colonel nor Pie were in uniform, since they didn't want to attract attention to themselves.

Lucille had her face pressed against Cory's chest and he was stroking her hair when Thompson coughed discreetly and announced, "We had better get started."

Cory forced himself to let go of Lucille and step back. She mustered up a smile and said, "Good luck, Cory. Hurry home."

"I will," he promised. Not trusting himself to actually go if he lingered any longer, he turned and walked quickly to the horses.

Pie was already mounted, and Thompson was swinging up into the saddle. The colonel wore high-topped black boots, brown trousers, a brown jacket over an open-throated white shirt, and a broad-brimmed black hat. He looked more like a successful planter than a soldier and former banker. Pie was wearing the clothes he had worn when Cory first met him, although they had been washed and the holes patched by Mildred, and the big man had a new pair of boots as well.

Cory wore a new hat, shirt, trousers, and boots, all of them bought for him by Lucille—over his objections. His old garb had been good enough for him, he protested, but she wouldn't be persuaded not to make the gesture. The Colt holstered on his hip, though, was the one Forrest had given him.

His horse was a brown gelding. He gathered up the reins, put his foot in the stirrup, grasped the saddle, and swung up onto its back. Finally, he dared to turn his head and look at the station platform where Lucille and Mildred stood side by side. Both women smiled and waved. The three men returned the waves, then heeled their horses into motion.

"It never gets any easier," Thompson said quietly as they rode along the tracks away from the depot.

"What do you mean, sir?" asked Cory.

"Leaving behind those we love. It never gets any easier."

"No, I don't suppose it does." Cory hesitated, then went on, "I swore to myself I would never leave Lucille again."

"You'll be back with her soon," Thompson said confidently. "What we're doing now is for the greater good."

"Besides," Pie put in with a grin, "ol' Cory here has got itchy feet. Ain't that right, Cory?"

For a second, Cory felt a flash of anger, but then he realized there was no point in denying what Pie had stated. He managed a rueful chuckle and said, "I've always wanted to see what's on the other side of the hill, that's true."

"You won't find many hills here in Louisiana," said Thompson. "You'll have to settle for seeing what's on the other side of the bayou."

COLONEL THOMPSON was right about at least one thing: Louisiana was flat. There were a few ridges along the river, but they were narrow and within a few miles had sloped down to a level stretch that seemed endless. The land was covered with a rich, dark soil composed mostly of silt carried down from the north over the centuries by the river, which had changed its course numberless times in the past. There were also occasional areas of thick, sticky clay. The road to Monroe ran through several plantations. The three riders passed cotton patches, orchards, and fields of waving grain. The uncultivated areas were covered with thick grass and stands of small pine trees. The terrain was similar enough to what Cory had seen in Mississippi that it didn't seem foreign to him. He wondered if Texas would be different.

From Vicksburg to Monroe was about eighty miles. The three men planned to cover the distance in four days, though that estimate might have to be adjusted depending on how well the horses held up. The first train on the VS&T was scheduled to arrive in Monroe in a week, so that would give Cory and his companions two or three days to round up some wagons.

This was the most riding Cory had done in a long time, and by the end of the first day in the saddle, his muscles were aching. They stopped that evening at a tavern where rooms could be rented. Cory suppressed a groan as he dismounted. Pie was moving a little gingerly, too, he noticed. Only Colonel Thompson seemed unbothered by the long hours on horseback, and Cory couldn't figure that out. The colonel hadn't been riding lately, either.

Thompson smiled as he saw the way the two younger men were hobbling. "Sorry to say, you'll probably feel worse tomorrow," he said. "But by the third day, I expect you'll notice at least a slight improvement."

"How do you do it, Colonel?" Pie asked with a pained grimace. "You look like you ain't hurtin' at all."

"I took the precaution of putting extra padding in my breeches," Thompson replied. He slapped himself on the rump. "Never felt a thing."

"You could have warned us," Cory grumbled.

"A lesson learned through experience is a lesson never forgotten."

Cory clenched his jaw and didn't say anything. Thompson was a colonel, after all, and Lucille's uncle.

A supper of fried ham, pone, and coffee that was mostly chicory and grain made all three of them feel better. He sat on a bench with his back against a log wall and stretched out his right leg on the bench. That eased his muscles even more. He sipped what was left of the brew in his cup and listened to the war talk going on among the tavern's handful of customers.

The word from back east was that the Yankee army under Gen. George McClellan had driven up the Virginia Peninsula almost all the way to Richmond before a series of vicious battles over a week's time had pushed them back, nearly into the sea. Gen. Robert E. Lee, who had recently been placed in command of the Confederate forces, had orchestrated those audacious maneuvers.

There were times, here in the west, when they seemed far removed from the rest of the war, Cory reflected. And yet he knew that what was going on along the Mississippi might turn out to be just as important to the final outcome of the conflict.

The tavern keeper was a thick-bodied, balding man who stayed behind the bar. A tall young woman had served the meals, and Pie had practically licked his lips as she bent over and gave him a view down the low neckline of her dress. Red hair was piled up high on her head. Cory thought she was pretty enough, but nowhere near as beautiful as Lucille, of course. When they were finished eating, she came back to pick up their plates, and Pie said, "You sure are a honey. What's your name?"

She didn't answer but started to turn away instead, carrying the empty plates. Pie put out a hand and caught hold of her wrist.

"I asked you your name, ma'am," he said, still polite but sounding a bit impatient now.

"Pie . . . ," Colonel Thompson said in a warning tone.

Cory leaned closer to his friend. "You'd better let go of her, Pie," he said quietly. "That man behind the bar may be her father, and he's watching you."

Pie released her wrist. "I'm sorry, ma'am. I reckon I wasn't thinkin'." He took off his hat and held it over his heart. "I was plumb overcome by your beauty, I reckon."

She looked down at him, and Cory was surprised to see a faint smile tug at the corners of her mouth. "Rachel," she said quietly. "My name is Rachel. But Grat's not my father. He's my husband."

Pie looked completely embarrassed now. "I'm mighty sorry."

"It's all right," Rachel told him. She went back to the bar, carrying the plates.

Pie ran his fingers through the tangled thatch of his hair. "Dang it," he muttered. "Didn't mean to make a fool o' myself. I purely do love redheaded women, though."

"You should see my sister, Cordelia," Cory said. "Although on second thought, maybe you shouldn't."

Thompson got to his feet. "Let's turn in, gentlemen. We have a great deal of riding to do tomorrow."

Cory tried not to moan as he stood up.

They had rented two rooms, one for the colonel, one that Cory and Pie would share. The rooms were dirt-floored lean-tos built onto the rear of the log tavern building. The single bunk in each room was made of thin straw ticking. Staying here would be better than sleeping outside, but not by much, Cory thought as he looked around the place by the light of the stubby candle the tavern keeper had given them. The man hadn't cracked a smile since they had been there, Cory noted, and he didn't seem happy to have them as customers. But the tavern wasn't doing much business, so Cory supposed any coins were better than none.

They took off their boots and hats, and Cory removed his gun belt. Otherwise, they were fully dressed as they stretched out on the bunk. Pie blew out the candle and set it on the floor. The lean-to had one window that was covered with an oilcloth shade. It didn't let in much air, and the room was like an oven. Mosquitoes buzzed around Cory's ears. He resigned himself to spending a long, miserable, mostly sleepless night.

To his surprise, he dozed off quickly, and he had no idea how long he had been asleep when something abruptly woke him. In the faint moonlight that came through the cracks around the window shade, he saw Pie sitting up beside him on the bunk. Cory heard a whisper of steel on leather and knew that his companion had just drawn his knife. "Who's there?" Pie asked in a harsh whisper.

Instantly, Cory had visions of Grat, the dour tavern keeper, trying to murder them and rob their corpses. He tensed his muscles, preparing to throw himself off the bunk if gunfire erupted.

But instead of Grat's voice, he heard a woman's voice whisper, "Shh! It's me, Rachel."

"Ma'am?" Pie exclaimed.

Cory relaxed slightly. So Rachel's job here at the tavern involved more than just serving food and drink, he thought. He felt a twinge of revulsion. He didn't understand how any man could send his wife in to do such a thing.

Pie swung his legs off the bunk and stood up. "Ma'am, what're you doin' here?" he asked. Cory saw movement in the room and knew that Rachel had come closer to them.

"It's not what you think," she said, and now Cory could hear how her voice trembled with strain.

"I wasn't thinkin' nothin'," Pie told her sincerely. Now Cory felt ashamed that he had immediately jumped to a conclusion while Pie had been willing to give the young woman the benefit of the doubt.

"I need to know—" Rachel began, then her voice choked off. She was terrified, Cory realized. She regained control of herself and went on, "I need to know where you're going."

"We're, uh, bound for Monroe," Pie said hesitantly. Clearly, he was unsure how much Colonel Thompson would want him to reveal about their plans.

"Thank God," she breathed. "Can you take me with you?"

"Take you with us?" Pie repeated. "Why?"

"Because I've got to get away from Grat. *I've got to!*" She covered her face with her hands and began to sob.

Suddenly, Cory felt a sense of unease. What if this was a trick to find out where they were bound and what they intended to do when they got there? Cory couldn't think of any reason why Grat would want to know that badly enough to play such a trick with his wife, but the colonel had warned them how valuable a trainload of supplies from Texas would be. That could be motive enough in itself.

"I'm not sure we can help you—" he started to say, but Pie whirled toward him.

"Hush up!" the big man snapped. He turned back to Rachel. "'Course we can help you, ma'am. But I ain't sure how kindly the law would look on it if we was to give you a hand in runnin' away from your husband."

Rachel wiped her nose with the back of her hand and said, "He's not really my husband. He just tells people he is. He really keeps me here like a . . . a prisoner."

"Dang it, that ain't right. It just ain't." Pie looked at Cory. "Get your boots on and go wake up the colonel. We're gettin' out of here, and we're takin' Miss Rachel with us."

"Pie, we can't do that." Cory knew he had to make his friend listen to reason. If they ran off with Rachel, Grat might come after them or even set the law on them. Helping this woman could jeopardize the mission that had brought them to Louisiana in the first place. He couldn't come right out and say that in front of Rachel, but somehow he had to make Pie understand. "We have business to take care of—"

Pie's hand closed over Cory's arm. He leaned closer and whispered, "What would you do if it was Miss Lucille who was askin' for help?"

Cory swallowed. "Damn it, Pie, that's not fair."

"You'd help her and you know it."

Cory took a deep breath, let it out in a long sigh, and then muttered, "All right." He bent over and reached for his boots. "But we'd better be as quiet as possible. I'll go wake the colonel."

"Miss Rachel an' me'll get the horses."

"I . . . I can't thank the two of you enough," Rachel said.

"No need to thank us," Pie assured her. He sat down on the edge of the bunk and began pulling on his boots.

Cory buckled on the belt holding his holstered Colt and then settled his hat on his head. He went to the door that led to the main room of the tavern and eased it open. The place was dark, all the customers long since gone home for the night. He wondered where Grat slept.

He took a step into the main room and turned toward the colonel's door, hoping they wouldn't all get killed tonight before their mission had even gotten started good.

Chapter Nine

CORY MOVED OVER TO the door of Colonel Thompson's room and opened it as quietly as possible. He stepped inside, thankful the rooms had dirt floors. There were no floorboards to creak under his weight. In the dim light, his eyes made out the shape of the colonel's bunk and the colonel lying on it, facing away from him. Cory took a step toward the bunk. He hoped Thompson wouldn't make any sort of outcry when he was awakened.

Cory didn't have to worry about that. Thompson was already awake. He rolled over and lifted his pistol, earing back the hammer with a metallic click. "Stop right there, you brigand," Thompson ordered in steely tones. "I'll blow a hole right through you if you come a step closer."

Cory froze in his tracks. The colonel had jumped to the same conclusion he had earlier, that the interloper was a robber and possible murderer. He hissed, "Colonel, it's me, Cory."

"Cory?" Thompson sat up and lowered the pistol. "What in blazes—"

"Please be quiet, sir," Cory whispered as he came closer to the bunk. "We have to leave."

"Leave? But it's the middle of the night. Why—"

"It's that Miss Rachel, sir," Cory said, wishing he didn't have to explain all this. "She asked us to help her get away from Grat, and Pie promised her we would."

"Blast it! We can't afford to get involved in someone's marriage problems."

"That's what I told Pie," Cory said, "but he wasn't of a mind to listen."

"No, I suppose not. I saw how he was looking at that woman." Thompson swung his legs off the bunk and placed the pistol on the mattress beside him while he pulled on his boots. "Is there any way out of this?"

"No sir, not that I can see. Not without causing more trouble for Miss Rachel."

Thompson sighed and stood up. "Very well. We'll have to get the horses—"

"Pie's already gone to do that. Miss Rachel is with him."

"I don't feel right about this, helping a woman run away from her husband."

"She says Grat's not her husband. He just makes her stay here."

Thompson grunted. "That's possible, I suppose. In that case, I don't mind as much. I hate that this is going to interfere with our mission, though."

"Maybe it won't," Cory said, but he didn't really believe that.

Thompson put on his jacket and hat, and they left the lean-to through the window, rather than going out through the tavern's main room. Grat had insisted that they pay for their lodging in advance, so there was no legal reason they couldn't leave whenever they wanted to. Maybe the tavern keeper would think they had just pulled out early, before anyone else was up. Maybe Grat would believe it was just a coincidence that Rachel disappeared on the same night.

Sure, thought Cory. And maybe the Yankees would see that they were in the wrong and go on back home, too.

Pie and Rachel led the horses out of the small pen behind the tavern. Cory and Thompson took the reins of their mounts, and Pie gestured toward the woods that came up almost to the pen. "I figured we'd lead the horses off thataway, through the woods. Best not to mount up until we've put some distance 'tween us and this place."

"I agree," the colonel said. He nodded to Rachel and tugged on the brim of his hat. "Ma'am."

"I can't tell you how much I appreciate this, Colonel," she said. "I think I'd rather die than stay here another day with that . . . that man."

"No one has to die," Thompson said. "Come along, all of you, quietly."

They led the horses through the woods, moving slowly because the shadows were so thick under the trees. The soft loam cushioned their steps so that they didn't make much noise. Rachel seemed to know where she was going. The men allowed her to take the lead.

After about a quarter of an hour, they came to a narrow game trail. "This will take us back to the main road," Rachel said quietly. They were far enough away from the tavern now that they no longer had to whisper. "I think we can ride now."

"You'll ride with me," Pie said.

"Actually, the lady should ride with Cory," Thompson put in. "He's the lightest of us, and if one of the horses is going to have to carry double, it should be his."

"Dang it—" Pie said.

"No, the colonel's right," Rachel told him as she placed a hand on his arm. "We have to get away, and I'm sure Cory doesn't mind."

Cory wasn't that fond of the idea, but he said, "Uh, no, of course not. You can ride with me, ma'am."

She moved over next to his horse as he mounted. When he was settled in the saddle, he took his left foot out of the stirrup and reached down to give her a hand. She pulled her dress up, put her foot in the stirrup, and grasped his hand with both of hers. She swung up behind him, sitting on the gelding's back just behind the saddle. Her arms went around his waist.

The colonel took the lead now, following the game trail back toward the road. Cory and Rachel came next, and Pie brought up the rear. As they rode along, Cory was acutely aware of how Rachel's body was pressed against his back.

It was a matter of necessity, he told himself, and it didn't really mean anything. Pie was the one who was smitten with the redheaded woman, not him. The woman *he* loved was back in Vicksburg.

But Rachel was warm and soft in all the right places, and as Cory blew his breath out between clenched teeth, he thought about how glad he was going to be when this ride was over.

—⧫—

EVEN THOUGH it seemed they had successfully slipped away from the tavern, Cory halfway expected at any moment to see Grat pop up in pursuit of them, roaring and shooting. Their trip through the night remained quiet and uneventful, however. After an hour they reached the main road and turned west toward Monroe.

They rode for another hour before Thompson reined in and motioned for the others to follow suit. "Perhaps we should get off the road and find a place to stop for a few hours. It would mean sleeping on the ground, ma'am. Would you be averse to that?"

For the past half-hour, Rachel had been trying to doze off, Cory knew. Her head had lolled forward and come to rest against his shoulder several times. So he wasn't surprised when she said, "Not at all."

"Good. My companions and I embarked on this journey prepared to camp out if need be, so I think we can come up with enough blankets to form an extra bedroll." Thompson heeled his horse into a walk and turned off the road. "Let's find a suitable place."

They rode through a stand of pines until they came to a clearing. When Cory looked up through the opening in the trees, he saw that the sky had a faint grayish tinge to it. False dawn, he thought. The real thing would be along in a couple of hours.

What with worrying about the trouble they were possibly in, he hadn't thought that much about his sore rump during the ride. Of course, his muscles still ached, and he became more aware of his discomfort as he dismounted. But it wasn't too bad, he told himself.

"We're well out of sight of the road," the colonel said, "but I think we should post a guard anyway, just in case of pursuit."

"I'll stand watch," Pie volunteered. "I ain't sleepy."

Cory couldn't make that claim. He had to stifle several huge yawns as he unsaddled the gelding. A couple hours more sleep sounded pretty appealing to him.

"All right," Thompson agreed. "But wake us at any sign of trouble."

"Sure thing," Pie promised. When he had taken care of his horse, he sat down on a deadfall with his rifle cradled in his arms. Cory noticed that Rachel took the blankets the colonel gave her and made her bed not far from where Pie was sitting.

He found a relatively comfortable spot for himself and rolled in his blankets. Weariness claimed him almost immediately. He slept soundly and didn't awaken until true dawn was graying the sky.

Cory heard quiet voices as he awoke. He didn't move, but just lay there instead with his eyes closed, listening as Pie and Rachel talked. He knew he was eavesdropping, but he didn't care. Pie was his friend, and Cory was going to look out for him as much as he could. And he still didn't fully trust Rachel.

"—been off the farm until I come to Vicksburg," Pie was saying. "You ever been there?"

"No, I haven't," Rachel said. "I was born down close to Baton Rouge and lived there until . . . until I came up here with Grat."

"He really ain't your husband?"

"No, he's not," she said emphatically. "I'd never marry a man like him. He . . . he has a brutal streak a mile wide."

"He beats you?" Pie asked hollowly.

Rachel's reply was faint, but Cory was able to make it out. "Yes."

"That sumbitch. I'd like to get my hands 'round his neck. I'd pure-dee choke the life right out'n him, only that'd be too good for him."

"I wouldn't want you to do that, Pie," Rachel said. "That would just get you in trouble, and I'm not worth it."

"Now, don't go talkin' 'bout yourself like that, Miss Rachel!"

"You don't know . . . you don't know all the things I've done, all the things he made me do . . ."

"I don't care," Pie said grimly. "I'm sorry 'bout you bein' hurt by him, but that don't change who you are."

"Doesn't it?"

"No, ma'am. Nary a bit."

Rachel laughed softly, humorlessly. "At first, when you grabbed my wrist, I thought you were just like any other man, Pie. But then you apologized. No man has ever told me he was sorry before. I knew then you were different. I knew you and your friends might actually help me."

"Yes, ma'am. We'll do whatever we can."

"Where are you going?"

Cory waited tensely to hear what Pie would say. It was inevitable that their plans would become known once they got to Monroe and began assembling the wagon train they would take to Texas. But until then, Thompson wanted the details of their mission kept secret as much as possible.

"Like I said back yonder at the tavern, we're bound for Monroe," Pie replied after a moment. "After that, I don't rightly know."

"I don't know if that's far enough away," Rachel said. "Grat might find me there."

"You reckon he'll come lookin' for you?"

"I honestly don't know. He hates to lose money—"

She stopped short, and Cory wondered why. So did Pie, because the big man asked, "What's money got to do with it?"

"He . . . he thinks that having me around brings more business into the tavern."

"Well, I can sure understand that. If I lived around these parts, I'd sure go there just to gaze on you, ma'am."

Pie might have accepted Rachel's answer, but Cory wasn't sure he did. Her hesitation had hinted that there might be more to the situation than she was willing to admit. Maybe she was like an indentured servant had been back in the colonial days. Maybe Grat had paid someone—her father?—for her to come with him to the tavern.

Cory didn't know, and he supposed it didn't really matter. But he was curious, and he told himself that he would keep an eye on Rachel.

Now, though, it was time that they were moving again. He stuck his arms out of his bedroll and stretched, yawning to let Pie and Rachel know that he was awake. A few yards away, Thompson was stirring, too.

Pie stood up and said, "Mornin', fellers. Ever'thin's quiet 'round here."

Cory climbed out of his bedroll. He saw that Rachel was still sitting on the deadfall and knew she had been there beside Pie while they were talking. He gathered up his blankets and rolled them neatly. Nearby, Thompson did the same. The colonel asked, "Have you heard anything from the direction of the road?"

Pie shook his head. "Nary a thing."

"Grat's a heavy sleeper," said Rachel, "and he's not an early riser, either. I'm the one who gets up to start the fire and cook breakfast. So he probably doesn't even know I'm gone yet."

"We can only hope that is the case," Thompson said.

They broke camp quickly, without building a fire. As they rode through the gray dawn, they made a rough breakfast on hardtack and jerky from their saddlebags. Cory thought about how a hot meal and a cup of coffee would have tasted and tried not to be too disappointed. He could do without a little if it meant helping an innocent person—and he was becoming convinced that Rachel was indeed innocent.

She was behind him on the horse again this morning, and again he tried to ignore the necessary intimacy. If by midday there was no sign of pursuit from the tavern, he was going to suggest that she ride with one of the others for a while. It was a legitimate request, he told himself. Carrying double all the time would wear out his horse. It would be better to alternate the extra burden, though it was difficult to think of someone as pretty as Rachel in that manner.

Around the middle of the morning, they reached a bayou that was too wide to be forded. However, someone had built a ferry where the road crossed the stream. It was crude, little more than a raft attached to a pair of thick ropes tied between trees on each bank, but it would do to get them across. As they rode up, the hoofbeats of the horses alerted the ferryman that someone was there. He came out of a shanty built beside the road. He was an old man, toothless and barefoot, and a straw hat with a ragged brim shaded his face as he looked up at the travelers. "Need to get across the bayou, do you?" he asked.

"That's right," Thompson replied. "How much?"

"Well . . ."

Cory heard the wheedling tone in the ferryman's voice and was prepared for him to quote an outrageous price.

"Three hosses, three dollars. I don't charge for people."

That was high, but not too bad, Cory thought. The colonel paid without hesitation, taking three silver dollars from a pouch he carried in a pocket inside his coat. "There you are," he said. "Now, if you please, we'd like to get started."

"Day's already too hot to move right fast," the old man said. He ambled over to the raft. "Come on."

They dismounted and led their horses to the bank of the stream. It wasn't easy getting the animals to step out onto the raft. As it shifted under their weight, the horses moved around nervously, blew their breath out through their nostrils, and rolled their eyes. Cory and Pie each held tightly to the reins as they murmured quietly to the horses in an attempt to calm them. Cory wished his brother Mac was here. No one was better at communicating with animals than Mac. He seemed to be able to talk their language.

The raft was small and crowded. The ferryman said to Thompson, "You'll have to help me pull on the ropes."

"Very well." The colonel gripped the rope on one side, while the old man took the other. Together, they began hauling the raft across the placid surface of the slow-moving bayou.

As the ferryman pulled on the rope, he kept shooting curious glances at Rachel, and finally, when the raft was about halfway across, he said, "You're that gal from Grat's tavern, ain't you? Back down the road a spell?"

She shook her head. "I don't know what you're talking about. I don't know anybody named Grat."

"Sure you do. I remember you plain now." The man cackled. "Seen you in there plenty o' times. I got an eye for a pretty gal, 'specially one with hair like that."

"Shut up and keep pullin'," snapped Pie. "You been paid to ferry us across, old man, so why don't you do it?"

"Don't go gettin' uppity with me, boy," the ferryman growled back at him. "'Sides, I was talkin' to the gal, not to you."

Cory saw one of Pie's big hands clench into a fist, so he said in a low, warning tone, "Not now, Pie." They didn't need trouble out here in the middle of the bayou.

"I never saw you before," Rachel said firmly to the old man and turned away from him.

He shook his head. "You can say what you want, but I know what I know."

There was a tense silence on the raft during the next few minutes as it completed the crossing. When the logs bumped against the western bank of the bayou, Pie stepped off quickly and led his pair of horses with him. Cory followed, leading the gelding, and then Thompson and Rachel stepped off, the colonel holding Rachel's arm to steady her.

"Colonel, listen here," Pie said urgently. "If Grat comes lookin' for her, that old man'll tell him he ferried us across. I say we best kill him."

The ferryman's eyes widened in fear as he heard Pie's words. He started pulling the other way on the rope he held, but the ferry barely moved away from the bank.

"We're not going to kill anyone—unless we have to," Thompson said. He looked at the ferryman. "You there!"

The old man was almost quaking now. "Y-yeah?"

"You haven't seen us, have you?"

The ferryman blinked in confusion. "What?"

The colonel drew his pistol but didn't point it at the ferryman. He repeated patiently, "I said, you haven't seen us, today or any other day. We never crossed this bayou on your ferry."

The old man wiped the back of a hand across his mouth. "That . . . that's right," he said. "I never seen you. I 'specially ain't never seen no redheaded gal!"

"That's exactly the response I hoped to hear." Thompson reached inside his coat with his free hand and took out another coin. He tossed it toward the ferryman, who forget about being afraid long enough to pluck it deftly out of the air.

The colonel continued, "Consider that a bonus. But if we find out that you've gone back on your word, we'll return sooner or later. I give you my word on that. And the next time, I won't restrain my large friend here from doing whatever he pleases."

Pie's bearded face stretched into a savage grin as he glowered at the ferryman.

"Let's go," Thompson said. "I don't believe we have anything to worry about."

Cory decided this was as good a time as any for his suggestion about Rachel switching horses. "Colonel," he said, "do you think it would be all right if Miss Rachel rode with Pie for a while? I don't want my horse to get too worn out."

"I think that would be fine," Thompson said.

Pie and Rachel were both smiling already. Pie mounted up, then helped Rachel climb on behind him. With a feeling of relief, Cory swung up into his own saddle. He was glad they were trying to help Rachel, but he was just as glad she was riding with Pie now and not with him.

And from the looks of the grin on his face, Pie didn't mind a bit.

THE NEXT three days passed with far less trouble than Cory had feared when they left the tavern in the middle of the night with Rachel. Grat had to know by now that she was gone, but either he had decided not to pursue her or he hadn't been able to figure out where she might have gone and with whom. The second night they camped out again, but the third night they spent in an inn at a small crossroads settlement. And late in the afternoon of the next day, they reached Monroe.

The town was small and dominated by the new railroad depot, with a few other businesses on either side of a short main street and a scattering of houses on a couple of cross streets. One of the businesses was a wagon yard, and that was where Colonel Thompson headed as soon as they had ridden into the settlement. Cory, Pie, and Rachel followed him.

During the days they had been on the road, nothing had been said to Rachel about the reason they were going to Monroe, but now that they had arrived, Cory didn't see how they were going to keep it from her. The colonel must have felt the same way, because as they reined up in front of the wagon yard's barn, he turned to Cory and Pie and said, "If you want to tell Miss Rachel why we're here, go ahead, lads. The time for secrecy is of necessity at an end."

Pie glanced at Cory and said, "The colonel means we can tell the truth, right?"

Cory nodded.

"Look," Rachel said from her seat on horseback behind Pie, "you don't owe me any explanations, any of you. You've done more for me already than I ever dreamed anyone would do. I can take care of myself from here on." She started to dismount, but Pie reached around and stopped her.

"Where you gonna go?" he asked her. "Gonna find another tavern here in Monroe to work in? If that's what you wanted, you could've stayed where you was."

"What else can I do?" she asked, a note of desperation creeping into her voice.

"You can go with us to Texas," Pie answered without hesitation. Cory and the colonel both looked at him in surprise. Thompson had said it was all right to reveal their mission, but he hadn't mentioned anything about inviting Rachel to accompany them.

She looked shocked, too. "Texas?" she repeated. "You're going to Texas?"

"Yep," Pie said. "Goin' to take a wagon train there."

"Why?"

"Well . . . I reckon the idea is sort of to save the whole danged Confederacy."

Chapter Ten

RACHEL LOOKED AT CORY and Thompson and asked, "Does he mean it?"

"Perhaps my young friend overstates the case a bit," said the colonel, "but our mission *is* very important to the cause of the Confederacy. What we are attempting to do is nothing less than ensure the future of Vicksburg as a Southern stronghold."

"We're going to Texas to buy supplies," Cory added, knowing that Thompson's high-flung talk might be a little less than clear. "We'll bring them back here by wagon train, then carry them to Vicksburg on the railroad."

Rachel looked at the spanking new depot of the Vicksburg, Shreveport, and Texas line. It was a large, whitewashed building at the other end of the street. "But . . . there's no train here," she said.

"There will be," Thompson assured her. "It's due to arrive three days from now."

"You can't get from here to Texas and back in three days, especially not with a bunch of wagons."

"Of course not, but that was never the plan. The train will commence its regular run between Monroe and Vicksburg. There are plantations here in the area that will be able to furnish a certain amount of goods. By the time we return, the train crews will be familiar with the route and there should be no problems transporting the supplies from Texas."

Rachel thought about it and then nodded. "I suppose you're right. I heard a lot of talk about the war, there in the tavern, but I never gave it much thought. I was too busy trying to get by from day to day myself."

Cory suspected that was true of a lot of people. It had certainly been the case with him while he was working as a wharf rat in New Madrid. The nation had been splitting in two, and he truly hadn't given a damn. He had been much more worried about starving to death or freezing.

"So how about it?" Pie asked her. "Are you comin' with us to Texas or not?"

"Private Jones," the colonel said, and now his voice had an edge to it, "I think we should discuss this later. Right now I have to see how many wagons are available, and how soon we can obtain others if we need them. In the meantime, why don't you and Cory take the young lady to that boarding house down the street and see about getting her a room?"

"I . . . I can't pay for a room," Rachel said miserably.

"That will not be a problem," Thompson said. "I'll be glad to take care of the expense for now."

"All right," Pie grumbled. "But I don't see why we can't just take her with us."

"Come on, Pie," Cory said. He didn't want his friend getting into any more trouble than was necessary.

The boarding house was a two-story wooden building. They left the horses tied in front of it and went inside, finding a middle-aged woman in a parlor that was furnished with shabby but clean furniture. She looked a little askance at Pie, then turned her attention to Cory and Rachel. "Can I help you?" she asked.

"We were looking for a room for the young lady," Cory said.

The woman frowned. "I run a respectable house here, you should know that."

"Yes, ma'am," Cory said quickly. "We could tell as much, that's why we stopped here. My friend and I won't be staying." Pie glanced at him but didn't say anything.

"Well, then, in that case . . . I suppose I could find a room for you, dear," the woman said to Rachel. "What's your name?"

"Rachel. Miss Rachel Hannah."

The woman smiled. "I'm acquainted with some Hannahs down near Baton Rouge. Fine family, just fine. Would you happen to be related to them?"

"Yes, ma'am. I was raised at Cottonwood Point."

The woman clasped her hands together and said, "My, my! That magnificent plantation! I visited there many years ago. Why, you must be one of Rutherford's girls! I remember Rutherford Hannah had the reddest hair of any man I've ever seen."

"Yes, ma'am," Rachel agreed. "He was my father."

"Was?"

"He passed away two years ago," Rachel said.

"Well, now, I'm mighty sorry to hear that," the woman said, pursing her lips. She stepped closer to Rachel and took her arm. "You just come over here and sit down and tell me all about what's been happening down yonder. How in the world did a girl from Cottonwood Point wind up all the way up here in Monroe?"

Cory was wondering that himself. He and Pie had learned more in the past few minutes about Rachel's background than they had during the three days they had ridden together, but what Rachel had told the woman didn't make much sense. If she was the daughter of a wealthy plantation owner, how had she become an involuntary servant to a backwoods tavern keeper?

As Rachel sat down next to the woman on a sofa, Pie said, "Reckon you'll be all right here, Miss Rachel. We'll head on back down to the wagon yard."

Rachel nodded. "Thank you," she said. "Thank you both for everything you've done."

"'Tweren't nothin'," Pie mumbled as he looked down at his boots and twisted his hat in his hands. "You think about what I asked you, hear?"

"I will," Rachel promised.

Cory took hold of Pie's arm and steered the big man out of the boarding house. They didn't bother mounting up again; instead, they just led their horses back along the street toward the wagon yard.

"What in blazes were you thinking?" Cory asked in a low-pitched voice. "We can't take a woman with us to Texas. It's going to be too dangerous."

"More dangerous than stayin' here and waitin' for that sumbitch Grat to find her?" Pie shook his head. "We don't know what we're goin' to run into over there. Might not be no trouble at all."

"Maybe not, but you still shouldn't have asked her without talking to the colonel about it first."

Pie snorted. "He'd've just told me not to do it."

"Maybe for good reason."

"Maybe so," Pie said with a shrug, "but you wouldn't have such a burr under your saddle if it was Miss Lucille we was talkin' about."

"Blast it, Pie, that wasn't fair back at the tavern, and it's not fair now. Lucille and I . . . well, I expect we'll be married one of these days."

"Just like me and Miss Rachel," Pie said. "I knowed it as soon as I seen her. There ain't no other woman in the world for me."

Cory sighed in exasperation. "You remind me of my brother Titus. He used to moon over a girl named Polly, but he never had a chance in hell of marrying her."

"Are you sayin' me an' Miss Rachel ain't goin' to get hitched?" Pie demanded.

"Oh, hell, I don't know. Why don't you ask her that, too?"

Pie looked thoughtful. "Maybe I will," he said. "Maybe I'll just do that. Much obliged for the suggestion."

Cory sighed again, glad that they had gotten back to the wagon yard.

They found Thompson in earnest conversation with a balding man who had bushy brown whiskers. "There's a sawmill just down the river a piece, and a wheelwright here in town. I already got half a dozen frames started. We'll get them extra wagons built for you in no time, Colonel."

"The Confederacy will thank you, Mr. Dawson, and see that you're well paid besides." Thompson looked over and saw Cory and Pie. "Did you get the young lady settled?"

"Yes sir," Cory replied. "That's all taken care of."

"Good. I have excellent news to report here as well. Mr. Dawson, the proprietor of this establishment, has half a dozen wagons on hand, and he's agreed to build us half a dozen more as quickly as possible." Thompson turned back to the owner of the wagon yard. "Do you think we could have them in a week's time, Mr. Dawson?"

The man rubbed his whiskery chin and frowned in thought. "That's pushin' mighty hard . . . but we'll give it a try. I'll need some money in advance for lumber and supplies . . ."

"Of course. Shall we step inside and settle the financial details?"

Thompson and Dawson went into the barn, leaving Cory and Pie outside to look around the town. The Washita River, sluggish between tree-lined banks, flowed from north to south just east of the settlement. Monroe reminded Cory slightly of Culpeper, his hometown back in Virginia, though Culpeper was larger and busier.

Pie nodded toward a nearby building with a crudely lettered sign that read Black Horse Tavern. "What say we go get a drink?" he suggested, licking his lips.

"You go ahead. I'll wait for the colonel."

"You sure?"

"Yeah. That way when he's through, I can tell him where you are. We'll come by over there and get you."

Pie nodded again. "All right," he said, then he shambled over to the tavern and disappeared inside.

Cory sat down on a bench next to the barn and leaned back against the wall, cocking his right ankle on his left knee. He tipped his hat down over his eyes as if he were about to doze off, but he wasn't sleepy.

He was thinking about Rachel and what she had told the woman at the boarding house about being from a plantation near Baton Rouge. There had to be some truth to the story. Rachel was the one who had volunteered the name of the place—Cottonwood Point. Was she really the daughter of the owner? There must have been a resemblance, because the woman at the boarding house hadn't seemed to have any trouble accepting Rachel's story.

It was none of his business, Cory told himself, and besides, the point would soon be moot. He was sure the colonel wouldn't allow Rachel to go with them to Texas. She would have to stay here in Monroe.

The colonel came out of the barn a few minutes later, trailed by Dawson, who was saying, "I'll get my boys to work right away, Colonel."

"Very good. It's been a pleasure doing business with you, Mr. Dawson."

The wagon yard owner grinned. "Pleasure's all mine. I'm bein' well paid to do something that'll help us run those damn Yankees back up north where they belong."

Thompson smiled tightly and nodded. "We can certainly hope so." He turned to look at Cory. "Where is Private Jones?"

Cory pointed. "He wanted to get a drink."

"Go fetch him and then come down to the depot. I'll be there having a talk with the stationmaster."

Cory nodded in acknowledgment and started toward the tavern. Before he got here, he heard raucous music coming from inside. That was Pie playing the mouth harp; Cory had no trouble recognizing the sound.

He pushed back the already partially open door and stepped inside. The interior of the tavern was dim, lit only by a lamp with a smoke-grimed chimney. Pie stood beside a crude bar formed by placing wide planks across some whiskey barrels. A couple of men had linked arms and were dancing a drunken jig in time to the music. Several other men stood around grinning at the spectacle.

Cory's eyes almost passed over the figure of a man slumped on a chair in a shadowy corner. The man had the chair tipped back so that its front legs were off the puncheon floor. His foot rocked the chair back and forth slightly. He had a piece of straw clenched between his teeth and was rolling it from one side of his mouth to the other. Above that mouth, a hooked nose arched out prominently, and higher still, dark, hooded eyes burned with a peculiar intensity as they took in the scene.

Despite the heat and humidity, Cory's heart suddenly felt like a chunk of ice in his chest.

Cory would never forget the face of the man sitting in the corner. He had last seen that cruel visage in Cairo, Illinois, as the man spoke to some Union army officers on the platform of the train station. Months before that, Cory had gotten a good look at it in the garish light of torches wielded by a mob intent on burning the *Missouri Zephyr* as it sat at anchor in New Madrid. The man was Jason Gill, an ardent abolitionist and *agent provocateur* for the Northerners.

What was he doing sitting in a tavern in Monroe, Louisiana?

Those thoughts flashed through Cory's head in less than the blink of an eye. He lowered his head slightly so the brim of his hat would shield most of his face. He didn't know if Gill had noticed him or not, and even if the man had, the Yankee might not have recognized him. Gill hadn't spotted Cory in Cairo, and Cory figured he had changed quite a bit since that night in New Madrid eight or nine months earlier. He wasn't dressed in rags now, nor was he gaunt and haggard from months of near starvation and exposure to the elements. Moving confidently, he walked to the bar but avoided glancing in Gill's direction.

Pie finished his song and lowered the mouth harp to catch his breath. One of the half-soused men who had been dancing urged, "Play us another, big fella."

Cory put a hand on Pie's arm. "We need to get going," he said.

"So soon? Hell, I was just gettin' warmed up."

"Yeah, sonny," put in the other dancer. "You can't take this gent away from us. He's goin' to play us 'nother song!"

Cory didn't want to call any more attention to himself than he had to, not with Jason Gill sitting there in the corner. "You can come back later," he said to Pie. "Mr. Thompson's waiting for us." Cory deliberately avoided referring to Thompson as "Colonel" and hoped that Pie had noticed and would follow his lead. Now that he knew Gill was in Monroe, they might have to reconsider the need for secrecy.

"Well, if them's the colonel's orders . . . ," Pie boomed, and Cory winced. Still, he didn't let himself look toward Gill. He just tugged on Pie's arm.

"Le' go of him, damn you!" one of the dancers shouted, and with no more warning than that, he swung a fist at Cory's head.

The blow wasn't very fast, and the man who threw it was off balance because he was drunk. Cory had no trouble ducking away from the roundhouse punch.

Pie rumbled a curse and threw a punch of his own, his massive shoulders bunching as he drove a hamlike fist into the face of the man who had just swung at Cory. The man flew backward and fell over a chair, crashing to the floor of the tavern. "Swing at my friend, will you?" Pie yelled.

The other man who had been dancing happily only moments earlier grabbed a bucket of beer off the bar and whipped it at Pie's head. Cory called a warning, but Pie moved too slowly. The bucket shattered on his head, staggering him and drenching him with beer. Pie caught his balance by slapping a hand down on the bar, then shook his shaggy head like a bull and charged toward his attacker, sweeping him up in a bear hug.

"He's got Arvey!" yelled another man. "Get 'im 'fore he busts his ribs!"

Several men leaped toward Pie.

Cory bit back a curse as he suddenly found himself in the middle of a roaring, cursing, flat-out brawl. One of the tavern's patrons tackled him, and he had no choice but to fight back. As he was slammed against the bar, he drove his clenched fists into the ears of the man holding him. The man howled in pain and loosened his grip enough for Cory to tear free. He shoved the man away to get room enough for a punch, then buried a fist in the man's belly. The man's breath gusted out into Cory's face, sour with the fumes of raw whiskey. Cory batted him aside with a backhanded blow.

Someone else jumped him from behind. Cory almost went to his knees, but he desperately caught himself on a table and remained upright. If he fell, he might have the life trampled out of him, he knew. He slashed backward with an elbow, then turned and hooked a punch to the jaw of the man who had grabbed him.

A few feet away, Pie was more than holding his own. He was like a bear beset by small, yapping dogs, and he effortlessly swatted away the men around him. After a moment, the men who were still conscious started backing away from Cory and Pie, and the fracas came to an uneasy conclusion. Cory was just glad there hadn't been any gunplay. The colonel was going to be upset enough about what had happened.

From behind the bar, the tavern keeper ordered angrily, "You fellas get the hell out of here and don't come back! You're just lucky nothin' got busted up but a bucket, or I'd have the law on you!"

"We're goin', we're goin'," muttered Pie. He had dropped his mouth harp. He bent down and picked it up, inspected it to make sure it hadn't been hurt, then stowed it away in his pocket. He and Cory edged toward the door.

Cory cast a glance at the chair in the corner. It was empty. Jason Gill had slipped out of the tavern during the fight.

Had Gill recognized him? Cory had no way of knowing, but he was sure of one thing.

No good ever followed Jason Gill.

———

THOMPSON WAS waiting impatiently at the depot with the station-master, a man he introduced as Luther Bradley. "These are my assistants, Private Jones and Mr. Brannon," the colonel went on, frowning at Cory and Pie. "I'm not sure what they've been doing. Slopping hogs, perhaps, to judge by their appearance."

Cory didn't think they looked anywhere near that bad. They were just a little rumpled up from the fight in the tavern.

"We, ah, ran into a little trouble," Cory said.

"Nothin' we couldn't handle," Pie added proudly. "Just got into a scrape with some fellas up yonder at the tavern."

"The Black Horse?" Luther Bradley asked. "That's the worst place in this part of Louisiana. No one goes there except ruffians and highwaymen."

"Well, we didn't know that," Cory said. He took off his hat and pushed the crown back into place where it had been dented slightly during the brawl.

"You're both all right?" asked Thompson.

"Shoot, yeah," Pie answered. "It'd take more'n those ol' boys to ruffle our feathers, wouldn't it, Cory?"

"I suppose so." Cory wanted to tell Thompson about seeing Jason Gill in the tavern, but he preferred to wait until he could speak to the colonel privately.

Thompson nodded, already forgetting about the fight. "Mr. Bradley tells me that a telegraph line is about to be completed between here and Vicksburg. That will certainly make things easier once the supply line is established."

"I guess the first train is still on schedule?" Cory asked.

Bradley answered, "As far as I know. I've got my orders from the directors of the line to cooperate with you gentlemen any way I can, so just tell me what you need me to do."

"I've already spoken to Mr. Dawson at the wagon yard," said the colonel. "I suppose the next item on our agenda will be finding some place to stay while we're here in Monroe."

"There's a boarding house run by Miz Fay, or you can stay here at the depot. There are some quarters for railroad employees, and I suppose we can make an exception for you fellas. You're close enough to working for the railroad."

Thompson nodded his thanks. "That will enable us to keep a close eye on the operation. We're much obliged to you, Mr. Bradley."

"No sir, it's the rest of us who are obliged to you for trying to keep the supply lines open."

"What do you know about Texas? What are the best places to obtain supplies?"

Bradley suggested, "Why don't we go on in my office? I've got a map of East Texas. I'm not sure it's 100 percent accurate, since I've never been over there myself, but I reckon it's close enough to get a general idea."

Cory put out a hand to stop Thompson as the colonel started to turn toward the office with the stationmaster. "Colonel, I need to talk to you for a minute," he said. "In private."

Thompson frowned again. "Mr. Bradley *is* privy to our plans, Cory. I don't think we need to keep secrets from him."

"Maybe not," Cory said quietly, "but I'd really rather speak to you alone."

"Very well," Thompson said with an exasperated sigh. "Come along the platform with me."

They walked toward the other end of the platform, leaving a clearly puzzled Pie and Bradley behind them. The boards of the platform showed little use. Everything about the station was new, but within a few days, trains would be coming and going, and with them would come people. The sleepy little hamlet of Monroe was about to get a whole lot more important.

"What is it?" Thompson asked when they reached the far end of the platform, out of easy earshot of the other two.

"Before the trouble broke out in the tavern, I saw a man there named Jason Gill."

"Gill?" Thompson repeated, his face darkening with anger and surprise. "The abolitionist?"

"That's him," Cory said.

"You must be mistaken. What would a Northern agent such as Gill be doing in the middle of Louisiana?"

"A lot of Yankees are where they're not supposed to be," Cory said. "And I didn't make a mistake, sir. I've seen Gill several times, close up. It was him, all right."

"Did he see you?"

"I don't think so, but I can't be sure."

"Would he recognize you?" asked Thompson.

"I can't be sure of that, either."

Thompson rubbed his chin as he frowned in thought. "Well, this certainly puts a new face on things. I suppose it's too much to hope for that our friend kept his mouth closed for a change."

"I don't know how much he said before I got there," Cory replied honestly. "He was playing the mouth harp when I came in. But he could have been bragging about our mission earlier."

"If Gill gets wind of what we're doing, he'll try to spike our plans. Mark my word. I've heard that the man's tenacious, that he's a veritable bulldog once he gets on the scent."

"He's a troublemaker," Cory said flatly. "If he's down here pretending to be a Southerner, he's up to some sort of mischief. You can count on that."

"Do you think he might try to stop the wagon train?"

"Gill will do anything to get what he wants. He came close to getting a mob to burn the *Missouri Zephyr*."

Memory made Thompson's eyes light up. "Yes, I recall now. Lucille said something about that. She said that you warned them of Gill's plans and probably saved the boat."

"I wouldn't go that far," Cory said. "Captain Farrell faced the mob down with a cannon. That's what really saved the boat."

"Nonetheless, you know more about Gill and how he operates than any of the rest of us. What do you think we should do?"

"Watch our backs," Cory said grimly. "Because if Gill gets wind of what we're doing here, he'll try to put a knife in them, sure as hell."

Chapter Eleven

ALTHOUGH CORY WAS EXTREMELY watchful over the next three days, he saw no more signs of Jason Gill. The abolitionist must have left Monroe, he decided. As small as the settlement was, if Gill had still been there, Cory was sure he would have seen him somewhere. At least, that was what he hoped. He supposed Gill could be holed up somewhere in town, surreptitiously keeping an eye on them.

Colonel Thompson spent part of each day at the wagon yard, keeping track of Dawson's progress on the new wagons. Dawson had a couple of elderly white workers and several slaves toiling long hours to complete the vehicles. There was also the matter of finding oxen or mules to pull the wagons. Accompanied by Cory and Pie, Thompson made several trips to the plantations in the area, searching for livestock he could buy. Once they learned for what purpose the animals were to be used, some of the plantation owners donated the stock to the Southern cause. Cory, Pie, and the colonel drove the animals back to Monroe and kept them in a pen behind the wagon yard.

They didn't go out of their way to spread the news of what they were doing in Monroe, but word got around anyway. It was unavoidable, especially once the colonel began looking for men to work as drivers. It was there he encountered more of a problem than any of them had expected. Most of the able-bodied men in the area had already volunteered either for the regular army or the militia, and they were off fighting the Yankees. Those who were left were either too old, too young, crippled, or unsuitable in some other way. There were the layabouts who frequented the Black Horse Tavern, of course, but Thompson didn't trust them after what Luther Bradley had told him about them. Neither did Cory. He had seen for himself what sort they were.

Thompson was pacing worriedly up and down the depot platform on the day the first train was scheduled to arrive. He had been able to find only five men to hire as drivers. Cory, Pie, and he could each handle a wagon, but that still left four wagons without drivers. "Perhaps we could use some slaves," he muttered, more to himself than to his two companions.

A thumping sound made Cory glance over his shoulder. He saw a man coming along the platform toward them, a determined look on his face. The man's right leg was gone below the knee and had been replaced by a stout wooden peg. He was in his late thirties, with sandy hair and a broad, tanned face. The muscles of his arms and shoulders bulged against his threadbare shirt. Other than the missing leg, he seemed to be in the peak of condition.

"Colonel Thompson?" he inquired as he limped up to the three men waiting on the platform.

"I'm Thompson. What can I do for you, sir?"

"I hear you're looking for drivers to take a wagon train to Texas." The man thrust out his hand. "I'm Allen Carter. I want to go with you."

The colonel shook hands with Carter, but he looked down pointedly at the wooden peg as he did so. "I appreciate the offer, Mr. Carter," Thompson began, "but under the circumstances—"

"Don't let this damned stump fool you," snapped Carter. "I can handle a team just fine. I've driven oxen and mules before. There's nothing wrong with my hands and arms and shoulders, and they're all I need to haul on reins and crack a bullwhip."

"Yes, I suppose that's true," Thompson said. "Still, the journey will be long and rather hard—"

Again Carter interrupted. "The Yankees blew my leg off at Manassas. Can't be anything between here and Texas any worse than that." A strained note entered his voice. "Just give me a chance, Colonel, and I know you won't be disappointed."

Cory could see the pride on Carter's face and knew how much it must have cost this man to have to beg for what he wanted. He was hoping the colonel would say yes, and after a moment, Thompson nodded.

"All right, we'll give it a try. You don't happen to know anyone else who might be willing to take on the job, do you?"

"As a matter of fact, I do." Carter looked around the platform, then said in annoyance, "Where in blazes did that boy get off to? I thought he was right behind me." He lifted his voice. "Fred? Fred, where'd you go?"

A young man came around the corner of the station building and looked curiously toward them. "Did you call me, Pa?"

Carter gestured to him. "Get over here!" To Thompson, he added, "This is my boy Fred." He lowered his voice and added, "He's not quite right in the head, but he'll work hard and do what you tell him to."

Fred Carter was smiling vacantly as he came up to the others. He was about Cory's age, with a shock of raggedly cut hair a shade darker than his father's. He greeted the men around his father with a simple hello.

"Fred, this is Colonel Thompson," Carter told him.

"Colonel?" Fred repeated. He stood up straighter and saluted. Then he looked at his father, grinned, and asked, "Did I do that right, Pa? I tried to do it just like you taught me."

"You did fine, Fred."

Thompson held out his hand. "I'm pleased to meet you, Fred. These are my friends, Cory and Pie."

Fred shook hands all around, then poked Pie in the chest with a finger and laughed. "I like your name," he said. "I like Pie."

"So do I," said Pie, grinning back at him. "That's how come they call me that."

"I like grits, too, but I'm glad nobody calls me Grits."

Thompson took Carter a few paces aside and asked quietly, "Are you positive this is a good idea, Mr. Carter?"

"He'll be fine, I promise," Carter said. His broad, powerful shoulders suddenly slumped wearily, and he scrubbed a hand over his face for a second before continuing, "His ma passed on a few months ago. There's just him and me. And I can't leave him here by himself. If I go to Texas with you, Fred's got to go, too."

"You're sure he can handle a team?"

Without hesitation, Carter nodded. "I taught him. He'll do the job for you, Colonel."

Thompson took a deep breath then sighed. "Very well. I understand your dilemma, Mr. Carter. Perhaps going with us will be a good solution for you and your son."

"And it'll give me a chance to do something to get back at those Yankees," Carter added. Cory saw his hands clench into fists and then slowly unclench.

The distant sound of a locomotive's whistle made them all turn and look toward the east along the tracks. Luther Bradley came hurrying out of the depot and pulled a watch from the pocket of his frock coat. He flipped it open and checked the time. "Right on schedule!" he said excitedly.

Cory felt his own pulse speed up a little. Within a matter of weeks, the trains that came here to Monroe would be rolling back to Vicksburg carrying the supplies from Texas that were so vital to the Confederacy. If the South was going to have any chance to withstand the Northern onslaught, the plan hatched by the colonel had to work.

Cory saw smoke rising above the trees and knew it came from the locomotive. A few moments later, the tall, diamond-shaped stack appeared. The cowcatcher thrust out proudly on the front of the massive engine. With a squeal of brakes and a clatter of drivers, the train began to slow. Steam hissed, and clouds of the stuff, mixed with smoke, billowed out as the engine passed the platform, momentarily blinding the men who stood there. Cory tried not to cough.

The train came to a halt with the first of the passenger cars next to the platform. A clean-shaven, nattily uniformed Confederate officer was already waiting at the door of the car. He made the long step down to the platform as soon as the train was completely stopped, without waiting for a porter to bring a set of portable stairs. Colonel Thompson and Pie came to attention and saluted the officer.

"General Smith, sir," Thompson said. "Welcome to Monroe. I didn't expect to see you here."

Cory recognized the man as Martin Luther Smith. The general had been in command of the Confederate defense of New Orleans. When that effort failed and Admiral Farragut captured the Crescent City for the Union, Smith had withdrawn upriver to Vicksburg, where he was now in charge of the city's defenses. He returned the salutes. "At ease, Colonel. I wanted to see for myself how our plan is working out."

"Quite well so far, sir," replied Thompson. "I have arranged for wagons, teams, and drivers. Within a few days, the wagon train will be ready to depart."

That was stretching things just a mite, thought Cory. With the addition of Allen and Fred Carter, they were still lacking two drivers. Maybe General Smith could send someone from Vicksburg to take those final two spots.

"I'm glad to hear it," the general said. "Now, I have something of another surprise for you, Colonel." He turned toward the car and extended a hand. "Ladies?"

Cory caught his breath as Mildred Thompson appeared in the doorway of the railroad car. The porter had put the steps in place, and Thompson sprang forward to assist his wife as she started down them to the platform. "Mildred!" he exclaimed. "What are you doing here?"

A smile curved her lips. "One would think that a loving husband would tell his loving wife that he was glad to see her, rather than sounding so surprised."

"Of course I'm glad to see you, my dear," Thompson said. As she reached the platform, they embraced. When he lifted his head and smiled, he added, "But I *am* a bit surprised. We didn't discuss your coming here to Monroe."

"We decided to accompany General Smith on the spur of the moment."

We? Cory thought as he saw movement again in the doorway of the railroad car. His heart began to slug heavily in his chest.

Lucille stepped out of the car and started down the steps. Unlike the colonel, Cory seemed rooted to the spot where he stood. Lucille looked typically lovely in a bottle-green traveling outfit and a matching hat with a small plume. When she reached the platform, she smiled at him and said, "Cory, aren't you glad to see me?"

Those seven words broke the spell that had frozen him in place. He practically leaped forward and pulled her into his arms. She laughed and returned the embrace. When his lips found hers the kiss they shared was both sweet and passionate.

"Dang it all," Pie said. "My gal ain't here, or I'd get in on this, too."

Cory and Lucille finally broke the kiss, and he stared into her eyes with the realization of just how much he had missed her since leaving Vicksburg. Most of the time, he had been too busy to brood about being separated from her, but it was always there, like a hole inside him that only she could fill.

Luther Bradley, the stationmaster, stepped up to General Smith and introduced himself. "It's an honor to meet you, General," he said. "Why don't you and the ladies come with me to my house? I'm sure Mrs. Bradley could be persuaded to make some lemonade."

"That sounds fine, Mr. Bradley. It is rather warm out here, and the smell of smoke is quite strong. Would you perhaps have a carriage for the ladies?"

"There's a spring wagon that belongs to the railroad." Bradley tugged off his cap and bowed to Lucille and Mildred. "If you ladies would kindly follow me . . ."

Cory didn't want to let Lucille out of his sight, so he said, "I'll drive the wagon." No one objected.

Thompson spoke briefly to Allen Carter. "You and the boy meet us at Mr. Dawson's wagon yard in the morning."

Carter nodded. "We'll be there."

They all left the station. Cory helped Lucille and Mildred onto the seat of the spring wagon, then climbed up beside them and took the reins. The pair of draft horses that were hitched to the wagon began moving stolidly as Cory flapped the reins and called out to them. Thompson, Smith, Bradley, and Pie all walked along beside the wagon, keeping up with it easily.

The stationmaster lived in a nearby whitewashed frame house that was one of the nicer dwellings in Monroe. Mrs. Bradley, who wasn't expecting company, was a bit flustered to see such a large group suddenly on her doorstep, but she recovered quickly, invited everyone in, and at her husband's suggestion went into the kitchen to make lemonade. "Luther, why don't you help me?" she asked coolly, and Bradley looked a little nervous as he followed her out of the parlor. Cory suspected the stationmaster was about to get a tongue-lashing for issuing the impulsive invitation.

The Thompsons sat together on a brocaded divan, leaving the others to sit in armchairs arranged in a half-circle around the room. General Smith leaned forward in his chair, clasped his hands together, and said, "So tell me, Charles, how is the plan proceeding?"

"Quite well, actually," replied Thompson. "We arrived here with no trouble and immediately set to work making arrangements for the trip to Texas. As I said at the station, we should be ready to depart within a few days."

"How many wagons?"

"A dozen. And they're good-sized wagons, too. I think we'll be able to carry enough supplies to fill several freight cars."

The general frowned. "At first glance that's impressive, but it won't last very long."

"Eventually I plan to have several wagon trains operating at the same time, so there will be a near constant flow of goods from eastern Texas," Thompson said. "I am told that there are good roads between here and Shreveport and Marshall, which, according to Mr. Bradley, is one of the largest cities in Texas."

Looking somewhat abashed, Bradley slipped into the room from the kitchen in time to hear the colonel's comment. The stationmaster nodded in agreement. "Yes sir, General, that's right. There are plantations all over East Texas, and Marshall is the center point for them."

"Not only that," Thompson put in, "there are many excellent ports on the Texas coast that the Yankees have not been able to close. I hope to import goods from overseas through these, then have them brought overland to Marshall."

"If Vicksburg can hold out until we get the railroad built to Shreveport, that'll make it even easier," added Bradley.

"How long will that require?" asked Smith.

Bradley had to shrug and spread his hands. "That's really hard to say. It's difficult getting steel for rails now, not to mention reliable men to lay the tracks. But the VS&T will be working at it as best we can. You can rely on that."

The general nodded. "I do rely on that, Mr. Bradley. The entire Confederacy is, to an extent, relying on what you gentlemen are able to accomplish. I must admit, though, it sounds as if you have the situation well in hand."

Mrs. Bradley returned from the kitchen with a pitcher of lemonade and glasses on a silver tray. She served the cool beverage and then asked Smith, "Will you be staying with us long, General?"

Smith sipped the lemonade, licked his lips in satisfaction, and replied, "I won't be staying at all, I'm afraid, ma'am. I'll be returning to Vicksburg this evening on the train. I can't be away from the city for very long at a time."

"What about you and Miss Farrell, Mrs. Thompson? Surely you intend to have a longer visit than one afternoon." Mrs. Bradley might have been surprised by her visitors, but like any Southern lady, her hospitality rose unhesitatingly to the occasion.

"Well, I hadn't really thought about it . . . ," Mildred began.

Cory looked at Lucille. He hated to think that in a few hours, she might be on the train back to Vicksburg. Now that they were together again, he didn't want her to leave. She must have been able to read that emotion in his eyes, because she said, "I'd like to stay for a few days, if it's all right with everyone. Unless, of course, it would interfere with your work."

It might, thought Cory, but right now he didn't care. He just wanted to be able to spend more time with her. He said, "We can get the wagon train ready in plenty of time, can't we, Colonel?"

"Of course," Thompson replied. He took his wife's hand. "You're welcome to stay if you want, darling, as long as it won't be putting Mrs. Bradley out."

"Not at all," the stationmaster's wife assured them. "We have a couple of spare rooms."

"It's settled, then," said Lucille. She smiled at Cory, and all he could do was return the smile. He was almost dizzy with happiness. Right now, at this moment, the war seemed far, far away.

And though he knew better, he wished it would just stay there.

———

GENERAL SMITH ate supper with the others at the Bradley house, then returned to Vicksburg on the train, which could make the run from Monroe in about three hours. The general promised to send two army teamsters back to the settlement on the next train, which took care of the problem of finding enough drivers for the wagon train. He offered to send enough men to drive all the wagons, but Colonel Thompson turned him down. "I want some of our drivers to be local men," the colonel explained. "They'll be more familiar with the territory between here and Texas."

Over the next couple of days, Cory managed to spend quite a bit of time with Lucille, since the operation was proceeding so smoothly. The two of them went to the boarding house with Pie, and Cory introduced Lucille to Rachel. The two young women hit it off immediately, and within an hour it seemed as if they had known each other for years. That made Pie beam, and when he caught a moment alone with Cory on the porch, he grinned and said, "One o' these days maybe we can have us a double weddin'. You can get hitched to Miss Lucille, and I'll marry up with Miss Rachel."

"Have you actually *said* anything to Rachel about how you feel about her?" Cory asked.

Pie kicked at the porch planks with the toe of his boot. "Well . . . I don't reckon I have."

"Why not?"

Pie glanced around guiltily and then said, "Don't you go tellin' nobody, but that gal scares the dogwater out o' me."

"Rachel? She's a nice girl." The idea of the massive Pie being afraid of anything, let alone Rachel, seemed ludicrous to Cory.

"Yeah, but I never been around one so nice an' so pretty. When you first met up with Miss Lucille, weren't you never scared of her?"

Cory frowned. Now that he thought about it, she had been rather intimidating at first. He had never seen a woman so beautiful, or one who affected him so strongly. "I guess I know what you mean," he said. "But you have to tell her sooner or later."

"What if she says she don't want nothin' to do with a big ol' backwoods boy like me?"

"Well, it's better to find out one way or the other, isn't it?"

Pie rubbed his nose with the back of his hand. "I don't know. Might be nice to dream a while longer first."

Cory clapped a hand on his friend's brawny shoulder. "Do what you think is best," he said. "Just don't wait too long."

"I won't," Pie promised, but Cory wasn't sure the big man meant it.

The wagons were taking shape at the wagon yard, and when they were finally finished and lined up along the road beside Dawson's place, they were quite a sight.

"As long as we can get the hardware and the lumber, we'll keep buildin' while you're gone to Texas," Dawson promised.

"Ought to have quite a few more wagons finished by the time you get back."

Thompson nodded. "Splendid. And if you could arrange for more livestock . . ."

"I'll do what I can, Colonel."

The next morning, the wagon train was assembled in the town square. Cory had spent a nearly sleepless night, knowing that he would have to say good-bye again to Lucille, so his shoulders ached and his eyes felt gritty as he got ready to climb onto the seat of the wagon assigned to him. One of the local men who had been to Texas several times was going to drive the lead wagon, followed by Thompson, Pie, Allen Carter, Carter's son Fred, Cory, the other men who had been hired locally, and finally the two soldiers sent to Monroe by General Smith.

Quite a crowd was on hand to see the travelers off. If there had ever been any secrecy shrouding this mission, it was long gone. Cory saw several of the men from the Black Horse in the crowd, but he didn't spot Jason Gill. He and the others would have to worry about the wagon train being attacked by renegades, but Colonel Thompson insisted the possibility of such a thing, while real, was unlikely. The group would be well armed and able to fight off most attacks.

Lucille and Rachel were there to say good-bye to Cory and Pie. Cory would have expected the two young women to dress up a bit more for the occasion, but they were both wearing plain, functional dresses and sun bonnets. Cory drew Lucille into his arms and kissed her for a long moment, savoring the warm sweetness of her lips because he knew he might not taste it again for several weeks. Up toward the front of the line, Thompson was bidding farewell to Mildred, and Pie was awkwardly shaking hands with Rachel.

Cory hugged Lucille tightly and buried his face for a moment in her thick, honey-blonde hair. "I wish I never had to let you go," he whispered.

"You don't have to," she said.

Cory lifted his head as Colonel Thompson stepped up onto the box of the second wagon and called out, "Wagons ho, men!"

"Lucille," Cory said brokenly, "I . . . I have to go."

"But not alone."

"What?" he asked, confused and then suddenly apprehensive.

"You and Pie don't have to go alone," Lucille said, "because Rachel and I are going to Texas with you."

Chapter Twelve

GEORGE B. McCLELLAN, THE commander of the Union force known as the Army of the Potomac, was no more immune to political considerations than any other high-level military officer. A lifelong Democrat, the general known fondly to his men as Little Mac was on the opposite side of the political fence from his Republican commander in chief, Abraham Lincoln. Ever since he had put McClellan in charge of the army, Lincoln had been under considerable pressure to replace him. The failure of the Union's Peninsular campaign had been laid, rightly or wrongly, at the feet of McClellan. He was too cautious, people said, too slow to strike at the Rebels.

Following the stalemate in the blood-drenched fields along Antietam Creek—which was hailed as a victory in the North only because Robert E. Lee's army had withdrawn from the field of battle—the feeling was that McClellan should have pursued the Southerners across the Potomac into Virginia. McClellan had failed to do so, citing the fatigue of his men and his horses after the massive battle they had just fought. That was a reasonable excuse, but feeling the pressure from his Cabinet and other advisers, Lincoln was in no mood for excuses. McClellan had to do something quickly, and he had to show some results this time.

Accomplishing something quickly, however, seemed to be a task the general was incapable of performing. Nearly six weeks after the battle, in October 1862, he did manage to move more than a hundred thousand troops across the Potomac and into Virginia. They advanced slowly down the Orange and Alexandria Railroad to the vicinity of Warrenton, less than thirty miles north of Culpeper, where a large part of the Confederate army had gone into bivouac. But instead of continuing to move his men southward, McClellan's natural caution once again took over, and there at Warrenton the Army of the Potomac sat.

Meanwhile, General Lee had split his army, leaving the First Corps, under James Longstreet, in Culpeper while sending the Second Corps, commanded by Thomas J. "Stonewall" Jackson, back across the Blue Ridge Mountains to the town of Winchester in the Shenandoah Valley. Longstreet's corps, the smaller of the two, was bolstered somewhat by the presence of the cavalry of Jeb Stuart. Still, they were decidedly outnumbered by the Federals, and as the crisp coolness of autumn settled over the Virginia landscape, it brought with it an inescapable air of tense anticipation.

MAC BROUGHT the stallion to a halt at the edge of the woods. The thick stretch of trees offered plenty of concealment, but Mac would have been seen immediately if he had tried to cross the open fields beyond. He lifted a telescope and peered at the sprawling Yankee camp less than half a mile away.

The tents that housed the Federal troops extended almost as far as the eye could see, even aided by a spyglass. The Army of the Potomac not only had plenty of manpower, but as Mac swept the telescope from one side of the encampment to the other, he saw scores of cannon, vast numbers of horses and mules, and a multitude of wagons that were no doubt loaded with supplies. The Yankees had everything they needed to wage war . . . except the willpower on the part of their commander.

Mac lowered the spyglass and tucked it in his saddlebag. He backed the stallion several yards deeper in the woods before he turned the animal. The path he followed twisted and turned torturously through the thick growth, and it took him fifteen minutes to work his way back to where he had left the rest of the patrol.

As Mac rode up, the young officer in charge lifted a hand in greeting. A full beard did little to make the man appear older.

Despite his youthful appearance, he wore the uniform of a brigadier general. Fitzhugh Lee, nephew of Robert E. Lee, was one of the youngest and most able commanders under Jeb Stuart. He was also Mac Brannon's commanding officer, and as far as Mac was concerned, Fitz Lee had no business being this close to the Yankees on a routine patrol. That was Lee's nature, though—impulsive sometimes to the point of recklessness. He couldn't stand to be away from the action for very long.

"Well, Mac, are the Yankees still there?" asked Lee with a grin as Mac reined in.

"You saw the smoke from their fires, General," Mac replied.

"Indeed I did. What are they up to these days? Still sitting on their rear ends?"

Mac nodded. "Yes sir."

"They didn't look like they were preparing to move?"

"Not at all," Mac said without hesitation. "Their rifles were stacked, their cooking fires were going strong, and I don't think a horse in camp had a saddle on it. None of the wagon teams were hitched up, either."

Lee chuckled. "Hard to believe your namesake would be content to just sit and wait, but I suppose we should be grateful for small favors."

Mac tried not to bristle as he said, "I was named for the character MacBeth, not McClellan. Sir."

"Of course I know that. I meant no offense, though I can certainly see why you would take it that way." Lee stroked his beard and grinned. "MacBeth was an able military commander, if I remember the play correctly."

"Until his ambition got the better of him," said Mac.

"Ah, yes, the fatal flaw. Well, McClellan's flaw seems to be sloth." Lee turned his horse and waved for the other eight men of the patrol to follow him.

Mac brought the stallion alongside Lee's horse and rode beside the general, knowing that Lee wouldn't mind. The two men were as close to being friends as a general and a newly promoted lieutenant could be. They had fought side by side in several battles since Mac had joined the horsemen the previous spring.

"We'd best head on back to Culpeper and report what we've seen," Lee continued. "Although I have to admit that the idea of a quick raid on the Union camp is rather appealing. Did they have sentries out?"

"A few," Mac said.

"We could ride in there, hit them before they knew who we were or what we were doing, and then gallop off before anyone could stop us."

"Yes sir, we sure could," Mac said. He hoped Lee would talk himself out of the foolhardy idea before they all got killed. Mac knew that a cavalryman's success depended in large part on speed and audacity, and he was sure they could take the Yankees by surprise, just as Lee said. But a ten-man patrol attacking an army the size of the one camped near Warrenton was about as ludicrous as a flea trying to topple an ox. Just about as futile, too, Mac judged.

"But Beauty's orders were to not engage the enemy unless fired upon," Lee said, "so we'd better follow them. He'd be upset if we didn't."

"Yes sir," Mac agreed. Beauty, as Lee referred to his friend and commander, Gen. James Ewell Brown Stuart, would certainly be put out if Lee's patrol went and got themselves killed. Mac wouldn't be too happy about it himself.

The cavalrymen emerged from the woods and hit the Warrenton Turnpike. They made better time now as they trotted their mounts south toward Culpeper and R. E. Lee's headquarters.

In the two weeks since he had returned to active duty following his visit to the farm, Mac had made several such patrols to check on the Yankees, but that was all he had done. Since the Confederate army's First Corps was bivouacked near Culpeper, it wasn't difficult for Mac to continue visiting his home. He ate supper at the farm at least twice a week.

Will, on the other hand, had left with the Second Corps to travel back across the Blue Ridge to the Shenandoah Valley. The farewells he had made to his family had been difficult. Mac knew how much it had pained Will to leave now that he had been accepted back into the family.

A little more than a year had passed since all the trouble with the Fogartys had begun. It seemed even longer to Mac. So much had happened, so much had changed. He thought about that as he rode along the turnpike beside Lee, and he couldn't help but wonder how much more change the future would bring.

Nothing ever stayed the same when there was a war going on; that was for certain.

—◦◦◦—

WEARING UNION blue, Nathan Hatcher sat beside the campfire and watched the dancing tips of the flames. All around him he heard men talking and laughing, but he didn't take part in the joking. It was easier not to draw attention to himself when he kept quiet. Any time he opened his mouth and spoke, his drawl betrayed his Southern heritage. A Virginian, born and raised, he sat in the midst of a hundred thousand Yankees, all because he had made the choice that he couldn't support the Confederacy.

It hadn't been a choice, not really, Nathan reflected. His conscience had dictated that he oppose slavery and that he should stand up for his beliefs. He could have stayed in Culpeper and continued working as Judge Darden's clerk in the old man's law office. The fact that he hadn't enlisted in the Confederate army caused some resentment toward him on the part of the townspeople, but he could have lived with that. He might have even been able to live with the disappointment in him that Cordelia Brannon had felt.

But once he had told Cordelia the truth on her brother Titus's wedding day, everything had become crystal clear for him. He had to leave Culpeper County, had to leave the Confederacy and all it stood for. He had gone north and had nearly been shot for a Rebel spy when he was caught behind Union lines. Only the intervention of a sympathetic Federal officer had saved him. Captain Pryor had known what it was like to be a Southerner fighting for the Union, because he was from Texas. The captain had helped Nathan enlist in the army so that he could fight for the side he believed in.

Perhaps that hadn't been much of a favor after all, Nathan had thought more than once since then. Like tens of thousands of other soldiers, he had wound up at Antietam Creek on that fateful September day. An artillery shell had burst near him and knocked him unconscious for a time, and when he came to, he had been surrounded by death. Corpses in blue and gray and butternut were sprawled everywhere he looked. Half-crazed with fear and shock, he had picked up a gun and threatened the only person he saw moving on the battlefield, a Confederate captain.

That Rebel officer had turned around, and Nathan had found himself staring into the face of Will Brannon, Cordelia's oldest brother. Will's features were so haggard and grimed with powder smoke and dirt and blood that Nathan hadn't recognized him at first.

Will hadn't recognized *him* at all. Instead he had just turned away in disgust, leaving Nathan there amidst the carnage. Finally, Nathan had stumbled away, looking for the remnants of his company.

He still had nightmares about that battle, even though he had taken part in it only marginally. Afterward, he had thought seriously about deserting, but he hadn't been able to bring himself to do that. He still believed in the Union, believed that the country had to remain united. So he had stayed, hoping that the next time he was faced with the challenge of battle, he would acquit himself more honorably.

Now the Army of the Potomac was back in Virginia again. Before the war, Nathan had been to nearby Warrenton several times on legal business for the judge. If he'd had a horse now, he could be home, in Culpeper, in less than an hour.

As he stared into the fire and twilight fell, he wondered what Cordelia was doing at that moment. The Brannon family was probably just sitting down to supper, he decided.

"Hey, Reb."

Nathan looked up to see a young, dark-haired officer with flowing mustaches standing over him. He came quickly to his feet and saluted. "Yes sir!" he said, then added, "But I prefer not to be called by that name, sir."

"Ah pree-fer not tuh be called by thet name, suh," the officer drawled with a mocking grin. "Well, then, what do you want us to call you, Reb?"

With an effort, Nathan controlled the anger he felt welling up inside him. Lieutenant Baxter was a jackass, plain and simple. Vain, cruel, and arrogant, he had been a thorn in Nathan's side ever since Nathan had become part of First Corps. In fact, it had been Baxter who had come close to giving the order to have Nathan shot as a spy—before Captain Pryor had stepped in.

"Private Hatcher, sir," Nathan said, keeping his voice emotionless.

"All right, Private Hatcher, I need a volunteer for a mission, and you're it."

"Yes sir."

Baxter smirked at him. "Don't you want to know what it is?"

"I'm a soldier, sir. I follow orders."

"How admirable. You're part of Corporal Barcroft's foraging detail. Get your rifle and report to him immediately at the wagon yard."

"Yes sir." Nathan saluted again and started to turn away.

"Hatcher." The lieutenant's cold voice stopped him.

"Sir?"

"I've told Barcroft to keep an eye on you. I still don't trust you."

There was nothing Nathan could say to that. He simply stood with his back ramrod stiff, his chin up, and his eyes straight ahead until Baxter went away. Then Nathan picked up his rifle and walked toward the area where the supply wagons were parked. He thought it was rather late in the day for a foraging detail, but no one had asked his opinion of the matter, of course.

He was worried, though, about being under Barcroft's command. The corporal was a large, harsh man, nearly twice Nathan's size, and he hated Southerners with a passion that was probably unequalled in the Union army, or so Nathan thought. Barcroft never failed to make insulting, obscene remarks about all Southerners, and Virginians in particular, every time Nathan was within earshot. Nathan was sure he was doing it on purpose.

The rest of the detail was already gathered at the wagon yard. Barcroft and four other men were waiting for him. As Nathan walked up, Barcroft sneered and said, "Finally climbed out of your hog wallow, eh, Reb?"

"Private Hatcher reporting as ordered, Corporal." It would be best, Nathan told himself, to keep this as detached and professional as possible. He didn't have to like Barcroft or the other men in order to work with them.

"You're late," snapped Barcroft. "'Course, I don't expect anything else from a stupid Rebel."

"I came over here as soon as Lieutenant Baxter told me to," Nathan replied.

"Shut your damned mouth and fall in. I didn't ask for any explanation."

Nathan gave a mental shrug and moved over to join the detail. Arguing with Barcroft wasn't going to do him any good and would probably just make matters worse.

You're here to help save the Union, Nathan reminded himself. That was what was important.

The six men left the camp, Barcroft telling the sentries that they were going on a foraging detail. They walked toward the village of Warrenton, less than a quarter of a mile away. Shadows were gathering, and Nathan thought it wouldn't be long until full night had fallen.

When they came to the first house on the outskirts of the settlement, Corporal Barcroft said, "This'll do."

"What are we looking for, Corporal?" Nathan asked. The house was small, with only a tiny garden patch behind it. There was no barn, so there wouldn't be any horses or cows or pigs for the troopers to commandeer. Nathan couldn't think of anything these people could have that the Federal army would want.

"You just let me worry about that, Reb," snapped Barcroft. "You're just here to make sure these people do what we tell them to do."

Nathan felt a twinge of uneasiness inside him. He didn't mind so much fighting Confederate soldiers; that was, after all, what happened in war. But he didn't like the idea that they might have to fight Southern civilians, too.

A lamp was burning in the house. Nathan could see its warm yellow glow through some gauzy curtains over a window in the front room. Barcroft stalked up to the porch and stepped heavily onto it. Holding his rifle in his left hand, he balled his right into a fist and pounded on the door facing.

"Open up in there!" he called. "By order of the Army of the Potomac!"

Nathan saw a shadow moving on the other side of the curtain, but other than that there was no response for a moment. Then the door opened a couple of inches.

"What do you want?" asked a frightened old man.

"Open up," Barcroft said again. "We're here to requisition supplies in the name of the United States Army, by the authority of Gen. George B. McClellan."

"I . . . I don't have anything," the house's elderly occupant quavered. "There's no food . . . Ma and me are about to starve ourselves . . ."

Without warning, Barcroft drove the heel of a booted foot against the door, slamming it open and knocking the old man backward. The old man cried out in pain and surprise. Nathan stiffened in shock.

Barcroft stepped through the now open doorway and shouted, "Refuse to cooperate, will you? I'll teach you a lesson, you old Rebel bastard!" He lifted his rifle in both hands, poised to drive the bayonet fastened to the end of the barrel into the old man's frail body.

"No!" Nathan cried out without thinking. "Leave him alone!" He threw himself forward, dashing toward the house. Inside, a woman began to scream. Probably the old man's wife, horrified at what Barcroft was about to do to her husband.

Something heavy landed on Nathan's back from behind, and he suddenly felt himself falling. He tried to catch his balance and right himself, but it was no use. He toppled forward, the weight on his back and his own momentum sending him down. He slammed painfully against the porch steps, and the impact knocked the breath out of him. All he could do for a couple of seconds was lie there and gasp for air.

He looked up in time to see Barcroft kick the old man in the side, hard. Something snapped with a noise like a slender branch breaking. The old man screamed thinly.

The old woman started to flail at Barcroft. He backhanded her away from him. "Shut up!" he yelled. He kicked the old man again. "Shut up that mewling, you damned traitor! You're lucky I don't burn this house down around you."

Nathan tried to push himself up off the steps, but a foot planted itself between his shoulder blades and pushed him down again. His face struck one of the risers. He felt blood well from his nose.

Barcroft turned away from the old couple and growled, "Get him on his feet." A pair of troopers lifted Nathan, one on each side of him. He stood unsteadily between them and would have fallen if not for their brutal grips on his arms.

Barcroft swaggered down the steps and stood in front of Nathan. "The lieutenant said you'd show your true colors as soon as we threatened some of these no-account Rebs. He was right, wasn't he, Hatcher?" Barcroft's hand cracked across Nathan's face in a vicious slap. "Wasn't he?"

Nathan's lips were bleeding now, too. The lower half of his face was awash with crimson. He said thickly, "Le . . . leave 'em alone . . . no need to . . . hurt anybody."

"Except you, you traitor. You've really been a Reb all along."

Nathan wanted to cry out that Barcroft was wrong, that he was a true supporter of the Union, but he was too dizzy and hurt too much. Barcroft probably wouldn't listen to him anyway, he realized. He knew now that this foraging detail had been a sham. They hadn't been after supplies. It was nothing more than a trap designed to force him to oppose what Barcroft had been doing. And since Barcroft was in charge of the detail, that made Nathan guilty of disobeying orders. Right from the start, what was happening tonight was just a clever ruse on the part of Lieutenant Baxter so that he could have his vengeance on Nathan.

Not even Captain Pryor would be able to intervene successfully once it was known that Nathan had interfered with a superior in the performance of his duties. Nathan would be court-martialed and hanged, maybe shot. At the very least, he faced time in a military stockade, unless the tribunal decided to just throw him out of the army. And Baxter would see to it that he didn't get off that easily, Nathan told himself.

Barcroft handed his rifle to one of the other men and began rolling up the sleeves of his uniform tunic. "Keep an eye on those old bastards," he said. "I'm going to teach this Reb a lesson he'll never forget."

Two of the troopers watched the old couple, who weren't in any shape to cause any trouble, while the other two hung on to Nathan's arms. Barcroft stepped closer to Nathan and swung his right arm, burying his fist in Nathan's midsection. The brutal blow was like an artillery shell exploding in Nathan's guts. The pain was so bad he couldn't even scream. All he could do was make a gurgling sound.

"You'll thank me for this, Reb," Barcroft said as he set himself to throw another punch. "The lieutenant could've had you hauled in front of a firing squad. He gave you to me instead."

Again, Barcroft hit Nathan in the stomach. Then again and again, short, compact swings that still packed plenty of strength behind them. After a few minutes of the beating, Nathan felt consciousness slipping away from him. He didn't even try to hang on to it. He let it go willingly, surrendering himself to the black tide that washed over him.

Chapter Thirteen

ITUS ROLLED OVER AND felt the empty space in the bed beside him. He blinked his eyes open and murmured, "Polly?" There was no answer.

Sitting up, Titus ran his fingers through his tangled hair and looked around the bedroom. It was early; only the faint gray light of dawn came through the gaps around the curtains over the windows. It was enough illumination for him to tell that Polly wasn't here. The sheets on her side of the bed were cool. It had been a while since she had gotten up.

Titus swung his legs out of bed and stood up. He stumbled across the room and opened the door, looked out into the hallway. The corridor was deserted except for a slave about twelve years old who slept curled up on the floor beside the door to Duncan Ebersole's room. It was the boy's job to tend to Ebersole during the night if the planter needed anything.

Titus was about to call out to the slave and wake him so that he could ask the boy if he'd seen Polly, when the door to Ebersole's room opened quietly. Polly herself stepped out into the corridor, a pale figure in a flowing white robe. She eased the door closed and then stepped carefully around the sleeping slave so as not to awaken him. Only when she had started down the corridor toward the room she shared with her husband did she look up and see Titus standing there in the half-open doorway watching her. She stopped short, and her hand went to her mouth in surprise. Then she came toward him again, motioning for him to go back into the bedroom.

He frowned in confusion, but he stepped back and let her come into the room. She closed the door behind her and then turned to face him.

"What are you doing awake so early?" she asked.

"Woke up and you were gone," he said. "I thought something might be wrong."

Polly shook her head. "No, nothing's wrong. Nothing at all."

"What were you doing down there in your father's room?"

"I was in the hall . . . going to the privy . . ." Even in the dim room, he could see the blush that spread across her face. ". . . when I heard him cry out. I thought something was wrong, so I knocked. He didn't answer."

"How come the boy didn't wake up and see what was wrong?" asked Titus.

"That worthless boy could sleep through the last trump," Polly said crisply. "I intend to speak to Father about him. At any rate, I went inside and found him having a nightmare. He was shouting and thrashing around, so I thought it best to wake him. He didn't want to wake up, though, and I was about to fetch you to help me when he finally did."

"Wakin' up a fella who's havin' a nightmare isn't always the smart thing to do," Titus pointed out. "My brother Henry like to knocked my head off one time when I shook him because he was talkin' so loud in his sleep."

"Well, Father was fine once he was good and awake," Polly said. "He calmed down once he realized it was just a nightmare."

"What was he dreamin' about?"

Polly shook her head. "He wouldn't say. I just imagine it was something to do with the Yankees, though." She sighed. "They're a nightmare for all of us, awake or asleep."

Titus couldn't argue with that. Instead he said, "Well, it's too late to go back to sleep now. I'm up, so I might as well stay up." He put his hands on Polly's arms and rubbed up and down as he inclined his head toward the bed. "You want to . . . ?"

She shook her head curtly and said, "No, I'm still tired. I'm going to try to sleep." She turned away from him.

Titus stood there for a moment, frowning, then shrugged his shoulders. "I'll get dressed and get out of here, so I won't bother you."

"Fine." Polly slid beneath the covers and pulled them up over her. Her back was still turned to him.

Titus just shook his head and reached for his trousers. There was nothing else he could do.

⸺

AFTER MAKING sure that the morning's work on Mountain Laurel was being tended to by the overseers and the slaves, Titus saddled his horse and rode over to the Brannon farm. When he was growing up, he had thought the farm was the biggest place in the world, containing as it did all sorts of fields and woods and even a creek. As an adult, he had known that there were much larger pieces of property in the county, of course. But now, after living for several months on the Ebersole plantation, he could plainly see how small and insignificant his family's home really was.

Henry was in one of the fields, hoeing weeds out of the crop of fall wheat he and Titus had planted there. When he saw Titus coming, he stopped what he was doing and waved, then leaned on the hoe to wait. Titus reined in at the edge of the field and swung down from his saddle. "Howdy, little brother," he called as he walked between the rows of wheat.

"Come to lend a hand?" asked Henry. "We can sure use you. The woodbox needs to be filled for winter, and Cordelia can't hardly do it. I was about to decide that she'd have to do this hoeing while I split the wood."

Titus hesitated. "Well . . . actually I was thinkin' about ridin' on into town to have a drink, and I thought you might like to go with me."

Henry glanced up at the sun. "Shoot, it's not even mid-morning yet! Anyway, I thought you'd given that up since you got married to Polly."

"Pretty much have." Titus couldn't explain it, but he had been edgy all morning. It was more than just frustration because

Polly had turned away from him. He was sure of that. Something else was wrong, and he thought that a little whiskey might soothe his nerves. Now, under the prod of Henry's disapproving stare that reminded Titus so much of their mother, he almost let his temper get away from him. He took a deep breath and with an effort forced a grin. "Ah, hell, you're right. What was I thinkin'? You go ahead with the hoein'. I'll ride up to the house and get that wood split."

"All right," Henry said with a nod. "Thanks, Titus."

"No thanks necessary. I'm still a member of this family, ain't I?"

Henry didn't say anything, and after a minute Titus turned and went back to his horse.

As angry as he was at his little brother, Titus knew Henry was right: drinking wasn't going to solve his problems, no matter how much he wanted that to be true. Right now, no matter how hard he thought about it, Titus just didn't see a solution.

Abigail and Cordelia were glad to see him. He went around to the back of the house where the woodpile was and started splitting the pieces of wood so that they could be burned in the fireplace. It was a chore Titus had done many times before, so he had no trouble with it. Despite the crisp autumn air, swinging the heavy ax was hard work, so after a while he took off his jacket. His mind began to wander, lulled by the routine of lifting the ax and then bringing it down to bite deeply into the wood.

He had tried every way he knew how to win over Duncan Ebersole. The man simply didn't like him. Of course, Ebersole's natural arrogance made him look down on just about everybody else in Culpeper County. But he seemed to harbor a special dislike for Titus, and the only reason for that animosity, as far as Titus could see, was Polly. Ebersole had made no secret of the fact he thought Titus wasn't good enough to even court his daughter, let alone marry her. Then Polly had stood up to him and forced him to accept the marriage. Under those circumstances, Titus wasn't surprised that Ebersole bitterly resented him. He had hoped, though, that his father-in-law would gradually come around and see that he wasn't such a bad sort after all. So far there had been no sign of that, other than a few moments of obvious, forced insincerity. And the hostility went both ways, Titus had to admit to himself. He didn't like Ebersole any more than Ebersole liked him. He had been willing to make an effort to get along, though.

Titus wondered if the man's nightmare early that morning had indeed been about the Yankees. The thought of Ebersole thrashing and sweating and crying out in fear was a far cry from the attitude of icy superiority with which the plantation owner habitually carried himself. Titus found himself grinning and thinking that he would have liked to have seen that. Ebersole would hate it if his son-in-law saw him in such a vulnerable state.

Thinking about that gave Titus a little extra energy, and he finished off the wood-splitting quickly. He closed the now full woodbox and went to the back door.

"Box is full, Ma," he called into the house.

"Thank you, Titus," Abigail said as she came to the door. "It's nearly time for lunch. You'll stay, won't you?"

Titus hesitated. Polly had been asleep when he left Mountain Laurel—or at least pretending to be asleep—so he hadn't told her when he would be back. Nor had he said anything to anyone else about when to expect him to return from the Brannon farm. For that matter, he hadn't even mentioned where he was going.

But why should he worry about that? he asked himself. Nobody on the plantation cared whether he was there or not except Polly, and as cool as she'd been to him this morning, she probably wouldn't mind if he was gone for a while longer.

"Sure," he said with a nod. "I'll be glad to stay. Thanks, Ma."

The meal was just pone and greens. Food was getting scarce, even on the farms that had produced crops this year. It was going to be a hell of a lean winter, Titus told himself. Because of the war, some folks were going to starve.

But the Yankees didn't care. The Yankees didn't care about anything. Whenever Titus thought too much about what those damned Northerners had done to his homeland, he burned inside with rage and regretted that he hadn't joined the army along with Will and Mac. If it hadn't been for Polly, he would have, he told himself. The rest of the family wouldn't like it, but he wasn't that much help to them these days, anyway. Might as well be off fighting the Yankees, so as to bring the war to a close that much sooner. That was the only way to really help anybody in the South, including his family.

Titus kept those thoughts to himself as he shared in the meager fare offered to him and enjoyed a few minutes of companionship with his mother and sister and brother. "What do you hear from Cory?" he asked as he was chewing a bite of pone.

"He's in Vicksburg, on the Mississippi River," Cordelia replied. "He said he was staying with a family there and working on the railroad, of all things."

Titus chuckled and shook his head. "That Cory. He does get into a heap of things."

"At least he gets to travel around," said Henry. "He's not stuck here on the same ol' farm his whole life." He glanced at his mother.

Abigail caught the look and returned a stern frown. "There'll be time enough for gallivanting around when you're older, Henry Brannon, if that's what you're bound and determined to do. But some people think it's best to put down roots and stay in one place. That's the only way things will grow."

"Anyway, one fiddle-footed Brannon is enough," Titus said.

"What about Will and Mac?" Henry challenged.

"That's entirely different," she said. "They're off defending our home. They're not traveling around because they enjoy it."

"Well, I wouldn't mind seein' some new places," said Henry, "even if it meant fightin' some Yankees along the way."

"You just get that thought out of your head, little brother," Titus said sharply. "You're not goin' anywhere."

After lunch, Titus mounted his horse and rode back toward Mountain Laurel. He felt a mixture of emotions: dislike for Ebersole, wariness where Polly was concerned, disappointment that things hadn't worked out better between the two of them. But his fate was inextricably linked with hers now, so all he could do was try to make the best of it.

As he turned into the lane that led to the house, he saw a buggy he didn't immediately recognize parked in front. It was painted black and had fancy silver ornamentation on it. A slave in high-topped black boots, white trousers, a red jacket, and a black top hat sat on the driver's box, staring straight ahead. Titus had never seen such a fancy getup. A moment later, as he drew closer, a couple of figures came out of the house and strolled toward the buggy. One of them was Ebersole, dressed in a suit and tie instead of the more casual garb he usually sported around the plantation. The other man was a stranger, portly and well dressed in brown tweed and a dark brown beaver hat. He shook hands with Ebersole and then climbed into the buggy. The driver cracked a whip and sent the matched team of grays down the lane. The buggy rolled past Titus, who reined his horse to the side of the path to let it go by.

Ebersole was waiting for him when he rode up to the front of the house a moment later. "Where the devil ha' ye been?" he demanded. His face was flushed with anger, but it also held a gray tinge, as if something had greatly disturbed him.

Titus didn't answer until he had swung down from the saddle and handed over the reins to a slave who hurried out to take the horse. Then he turned to Ebersole, whose features had grown even more red with impatience, and said, "I went over to the farm to lend a hand."

"The farm, is it? Yer family's farm?"

"That's right. I still have a responsibility over there." Titus told himself to stay calm and not allow Ebersole's brusqueness to irritate him.

"What about yer responsibilities to me an' my daughter?"

"I checked with the overseers before I left," Titus said. "Everything seemed to be all right."

"All right, is it? No, everything is *not* all right! D'ye kin who that was who just left?"

Titus shook his head. "Never saw him before."

"His name is Bradford Challis. He owns th' largest bank in Richmond."

A frown creased Titus's forehead. Why would a Richmond banker come all the way up here to Culpeper County, especially when the Yankee army was only a couple of dozen miles away?

"D'ye know why Challis was here?"

"I was just wondering about that," admitted Titus.

"Because I owe him money, o' course!" Ebersole clenched his fists. "A man can own a fine plantation an' still be cash poor sometimes and need a loan. But ye wouldn't know about that, since ye've never been anything *but* poor."

Despite his best efforts, Titus's temper flared. "My family—" he began.

"Yer family's like all the other families in this county," Ebersole cut in. "White trash, nothin' but white trash."

It was Titus's turn to ball his hands into fists. "Damn it, you can't talk like that!" he exclaimed.

Ebersole went on as if he hadn't heard Titus's angry response. "But that is a nice piece o' land they farm. Nice enough that Challis was willin' to accept it as collateral for the money I owe him."

For a second the meaning of Ebersole's words didn't penetrate Titus's brain. When they did, his jaw dropped, and he stared at his father-in-law with anger and amazement. "What did you say?" he asked.

"I put up the Brannon farm to secure the debt I owe to Challis's bank," Ebersole said matter-of-factly.

"But . . . but you can't do that!" Titus sputtered. "You don't have any right to that property. That's Brannon land! My father homesteaded it years ago, when he first came to the Piedmont."

"Aye, but you're married to my daughter now. What's hers is yours, and what's yours is hers. I knew ye'd want to do yer part to help out."

Titus was stunned as he tried to wrap his mind around the outrageous things Ebersole was saying. "You have no legal right to do that," he finally said. "Even if you think my assets are part of your holdings now, I only own a small part of the farm. Really, as long as my mother's alive, I don't own any of it."

A humorless grin stretched across Ebersole's face. "Aye, but this is a time of war, and a bank can't afford to fail when it's proppin' up the Confederate treasury. If Challis wants to, he can just declare an emergency and take the land, and no judge is goin' to say he can't."

"This is crazy!" Titus roared. "You can't just . . . just ignore the law!"

"The man with the money ignores wha'ever he wants to ignore," Ebersole said smugly.

Titus took off his hat and raked his fingers through his hair. He knew that Ebersole might be right. Even though what Ebersole was proposing was highhanded and obviously illegal, with the war going on anything was possible. Eventually, when everything was sorted out, a court would probably rule against him, but by then it would be too late. The Brannons might have already been forced off their land.

"You son of a bitch," he said, his voice trembling.

The smirk fell off of Ebersole's face. "Ye canna talk to me like that," he snapped.

"I'll talk to you any way I want to, you damn thief!" Titus was far too angry to control his temper now. He didn't care that he had been trying to mollify Ebersole ever since he had married Polly. He didn't care what Polly would say or think if she heard him cursing her father. All that mattered to him was the rage that blazed inside him.

Ebersole's hand flashed up and cracked across Titus's face in a hard slap. "Get off my land!" he shouted.

Titus was staggered by the blow, but he quickly caught his balance. He was about to swing a punch of his own when the unexpected blast of a nearby gunshot made him flinch and look around for the source of the sound. Had the Yankees snuck up on the plantation and launched an attack?

There were no more shots, and no Yankees to be seen. Instead, Polly stood in the doorway of the big house with a heavy pistol in her hands, gray smoke curling from the barrel. The weight of the weapon required her to use both hands to support it, and her arms trembled from the strain. She wasn't pointing the gun at Titus and Ebersole, but she could have swung it in their direction fairly easily.

"Stop it!" she screamed at them. "Stop it, both of you!"

"Put that gun down!" Ebersole roared. "Ye'll hurt yerself!"

"Stop fighting, or I swear I'll shoot both of you," she said, her voice quieter now but no less upset.

"Polly, this is crazy," Titus began. "You don't know what your father's done—"

"I don't care. I'm sick to death of both of you. Always picking at each other, making life miserable for everyone around here. I ought to let you fight! I ought to let you beat each other to death like a couple of stupid animals!"

Ebersole tried again. "Polly, I'm orderin' ye to put that gun down—"

"Shut up! You don't have any right to give me orders."

Ebersole drew himself up and glared at her. "I'm yer father, an' dinna ye ever forget it!"

Polly's answering laugh was hollow. She said, "You haven't acted like my father for a long time, and you know it."

"Watch yer mouth, girl." The flush had faded suddenly from Ebersole's face. He was pale now, as if he had seen something that frightened him.

"I'm not listening to you anymore," she went on as if she hadn't heard him. She was breathing rapidly and heavily, almost panting. "I'm not listening . . ."

Suddenly, her arms could no longer support the heavy pistol, and the barrel drooped toward the ground. Her knees gave out, causing her to pitch forward. Ebersole sprang toward her, catching her with one arm while he used the other hand to wrench the gun out of her now unresisting fingers.

"Polly!" Titus cried. He started toward her, too, but Ebersole was closer, and he had his arm solidly around Polly before Titus could do more than take a couple of steps.

Ebersole swung toward him with a look of triumph. The gun that was now in his hand came up. "Stand back!" he ordered. "Take another step an' I'll blow a hole in ye!"

Titus stopped, knowing that Ebersole meant the threat. Taut and quivering with the strain of wanting to go to his wife, he said, "Polly?"

She let out a moan as she sagged limply against her father. Her eyes rolled up in her head as she fell. Now, supported by Ebersole, she shook her head slowly as her near faint wore off.

"I told ye to get off my land," Ebersole went on, brandishing the pistol. "I'll give ye ten minutes. And ye might as well know now, my daughter will be divorcin' ye. She never should've married a scut like you in the first place."

"You can't do that," Titus said hollowly.

"The hell I can't. What law there is in this county answers to me."

"If my brother was still sheriff—"

"Ah, but yer brother's long gone, ain't he? He ran away the first chance he got."

The insult directed at Will made Titus even more furious, but for the moment he put that aside and looked at his wife instead. "Polly," he said imploringly. "You've got to tell your father he can't do this."

Slowly her head lifted. Some of her blonde curls had fallen in front of her face. She pushed them aside and looked at Titus out of dull, defeated eyes. "You'd better just go," she said. "There's nothing either of us can do to change things. I see that now."

Ebersole's vicious grin widened. "Ye see? She wants ye gone."

Stubbornly, Titus shook his head. "No, Polly. It doesn't have to be like this—"

"You wouldn't know what it has to be like," she cut in. "You'd never know. Never . . ."

Ebersole eared back the hammer of the revolver. "Go," he hissed. "And dinna come back."

"You'll want me here when the Yankees come," blustered Titus.

"I'll deal with th' Yankees. Get off my land, 'fore I shoot ye where ye stand."

"You and that banker of yours will never get your hands on our farm."

A malicious light glittered in Ebersole's eyes. "A trade, then," he said. "I'll send word to Challis that I've changed my mind. I'll find some other collateral for that loan. Yer family's farm will be safe, at least from the bank. But only as long as ye never set foot on Mountain Laurel again."

"But . . . but my wife's here!"

"Not yer wife for much longer, boy. Not for much longer."

"Polly . . . ?" Titus whispered in despair.

She raised a limp hand. "Go. Just go."

"Come with me. We'll go back to the farm and make a life for ourselves there. He can't stop you."

Polly just shook her head and then buried her face against her father's chest.

"See? She does'na want ye anymore. Now, are ye leavin', or do I kill ye?"

For a long moment, Titus didn't say anything. Then, in a voice full of pain, he told Ebersole, "I'm going." He turned toward his horse.

"I'll have one o' the niggers bring yer things to that precious farm o' yers," Ebersole said. "So ye'll have no reason to ever come back here."

Titus didn't say anything. He swung up into the saddle and tugged on the reins, turning the horse away from the house. A part of him wanted to look back at Polly, but he couldn't bring himself to do it. It was bad enough that she had betrayed him like this. If he never saw her again, it would be all right with him. He kicked his heels against the horse's flanks and sent it galloping down the long, tree-lined lane that led away from Mountain Laurel. Away from everything he had held dear.

But no longer.

Chapter Fourteen

A RGUING WITH A WOMAN, Cory Brannon had learned to his dismay, was like trying to teach a pig to sing. It was an utter waste of time.

"Now," Lucille said from where she sat beside him on the wagon seat, "aren't you glad Rachel and I didn't listen to any of your nonsense last summer?"

She had asked that question at least once on every trip to Texas, Cory thought as he flapped the reins against the backs of the mules pulling the big wagon. Women never tired of being told by the men in their lives that they were right, whether they actually were or not.

The thing of it was, Cory really was glad Lucille and Rachel had talked their way into coming along on that first trip. Having to leave her behind had always bothered him, and although he hated to put her in a situation that might be dangerous, he had to admit that so far the wagon train journeys had been safe as houses. Under those circumstances, anything that meant he got to spend more time with Lucille was all right with Cory.

"I'm glad," he said sincerely.

"I knew you would be. I told Rachel we'd just have to tell you and Pie what you really wanted."

This was the third trip to Texas, and so far the supply line that Colonel Thompson had set up with the assistance of Cory and Pie was functioning perfectly. Goods came into the town of Marshall from all over East Texas, more than enough to fill the dozen wagons. The efforts of Mr. Dawson, owner of the wagon yard in Monroe, Louisiana, to build more wagons had been slowed by a shortage of axles and wheels, but soon he would have enough ready to make up another train. Once those wagons were ready, one train could be leaving from Monroe about the same time as the first one was leaving Marshall. That would double the amount of supplies that could be carried back to Vicksburg on the railroad.

Work on the Vicksburg, Shreveport, and Texas line was proceeding even more slowly, and Cory had already given up on the idea that the railroad might reach Shreveport before the end of the war. But the roads were good between Monroe and Marshal, and the wagon train could make the trip in under three weeks.

Now, in October 1862, the wagons were nearing Marshall again. Cory looked around, never tiring of the Texas scenery. The woods were thicker here, the pine trees somehow greener than they were in other places. Taller, too. He had heard some of the townspeople in Marshall make the claim that everything was just naturally bigger in Texas. They seemed to believe it, too.

One thing was sure enough bigger, thought Cory, and that was the mosquito that was sucking blood out of the back of his left hand. He held the reins with his left and used his right to swat the varmint. Its demise left a red smear on the back of his hand. Lucille made a face at the sight.

"It's autumn," she said. "When are the mosquitoes going to go away?"

"Not any time soon, I reckon," said Cory. "At least not until the weather cools off a lot."

So far that hadn't happened. Autumn or not, a muggy heat still lay over East Texas and Louisiana.

The nights would be chilly this time of year back home in Virginia, Cory mused. The thought made him a little homesick, but not too much. He had Lucille beside him, and he had come to realize that wherever she was, that was home, too, as far as he was concerned.

The wagons rolled down the main street of Marshall. Charles Thompson drove the lead wagon, since he knew the route as well by now as any of the local men. Fred Carter was next in line, followed by his father, then Pie and Cory and the other wagons. Cory had to admit that Fred had done a good job of handling his team, just as Carter had promised he would. And the young man was very friendly and good-natured, making Cory that much happier the colonel had taken a chance on Carter and his son.

The citizens of Marshall recognized the wagons and their drivers. Several of them called out greetings. Colonel Thompson returned the welcome with a wave, then brought his wagon to a stop in front of a large warehouse. The other drivers followed suit.

A man came and bustled up to Thompson as the colonel stepped down from the wagon box. Ed Loomis owned the warehouse and was the local cotton broker. The two men shook hands, and Loomis said heartily, "Hello, Colonel. Mighty nice to see you again."

"It's good to be back, Ed," Thompson replied. "I hope you have enough supplies to load us up and get us back on the road."

"We sure do," said Loomis. He added in a conspiratorial tone, "And that, ah, special shipment we talked about is finally here, too. I locked it up in the shed out back."

Thompson stiffened. "Indeed?" He turned to Cory and Pie as they walked up, "Mr. Brannon, Mr. Jones, come with me, please."

Cory glanced at Lucille and gave a tiny shrug. She frowned slightly, then turned to Rachel, who had been standing with Pie and holding the big man's hand.

"Come on, Rachel," she said. "Let's go on over to the Saddler House and let the men take care of their business."

"All right," the redhead agreed, and the two women started down the block toward a nearby restaurant.

Thompson turned to Allen Carter and instructed, "Have the men start loading the goods from the warehouse, would you, Mr. Carter?"

"Sure, Colonel," the one-legged man replied. Not only had his wooden leg not interfered with his ability to drive a wagon, the natural leadership qualities that might have made him an officer in the army had led Thompson to rely on him more and more. He effectively functioned as the colonel's second-in-command on these wagon train journeys.

Thompson, Loomis, Cory, and Pie walked around to the back of the warehouse. Thompson unlocked a big padlock on the door of the shed attached to the rear of the building, and the four men stepped inside. The long wooden crates stacked inside the shed reminded Cory of coffins. Loomis picked up a crowbar and pried the top off of one.

The warehouse owner peeled back layers of canvas and oilcloth, and the light that came through the open door suddenly reflected off brightly polished rifle barrels. Loomis picked up one of the weapons and displayed it proudly. "Enfield rifles, gentlemen. Straight from England. We have four crates full of them, plus another two crates of Kerr revolvers and two crates of ammunition. A British ship landed them in Galveston a month ago." He held the rifle out to Thompson.

The colonel took it and examined it with obvious satisfaction. "This is splendid, Mr. Loomis. General Smith has had word from Chief of Ordnance Gorgas that more such shipments are on their way to us. With weapons such as these, we'll give the Yankees a warm welcome should they try to take Vicksburg."

Thompson handed the rifle to Cory. He was no expert on such things, but he thought it looked like a fine weapon. "I reckon my brother Titus would like to get his hands on one of these," he said. "Although you might have a hard time convincing him to give up that old Sharps of his."

The colonel said, "We'll load the crates in the morning. I want each of our drivers armed with one of these rifles. The crates will be split up, no more than one per wagon."

Cory understood the reasoning for that. If anything happened to one of the wagons, Thompson wanted to lose as few of the guns as possible.

"I want two men standing watch over this shed at all times tonight," Thompson went on. "We'll leave for Monroe first thing in the morning, but until then I want these guns protected."

"We'll watch over 'em good, Colonel," said Pie. "Won't we, Cory?"

Actually, Cory had been hoping that the colonel would recruit the guards from among the Texans so that he could have dinner with Lucille and then spend a whole night in a real bed for a change, but he knew Pie was right. The safety of the weapons was paramount.

"Sure," he said with a nod. "We won't let anything happen to them, Colonel."

Thompson nodded in return. "I'll see about some volunteers among the men for the other shifts."

Pie said, "Let's see how heavy these boxes are, Cory." He took hold of one end of a crate and Cory took the other, and with grunts of effort, they lifted the heavy container. The crate still reminded Cory of a coffin, and the thought suddenly hit him that he and Pie looked like pallbearers.

For some reason, a shiver ran down his backbone.

———

LOOMIS ASSURED Colonel Thompson that he had kept the existence of the British rifles and pistols as quiet as possible, but there were probably quite a few people in Marshall who either knew or had guessed what was in the heavy crates stored in the shed. A shipment of weapons like this could be very valuable. Cory was armed with his pistol, and Pie had an army rifle tucked under his arm as they stood guard over the shed that night.

Cory leaned against the wall and thought about Lucille, who no doubt was sitting in the Saddler House at this very moment and enjoying a good supper. Later, she would climb the stairs to one of the rooms in the hotel and sleep in a real bed between clean sheets. Cory bit back the groan that came up his throat. The thought of a hot meal was enticing enough. The vision in his mind of Lucille in a filmy white nightdress sliding into bed was almost more than he could stand.

So far he hadn't asked Lucille to marry him. Setting up the supply line to Vicksburg had seemed too important, and besides, he was already spending a great deal of time with her.

But as much as he enjoyed holding Lucille and kissing her, the time was coming for them to take the next step. Cory hoped that she wanted that as much as he did, and that she would say yes when he proposed. When they got back to Vicksburg from this trip, he told himself, that would be the time.

As if Pie were privy to his thoughts, the big man asked idly, "When are you and Miss Lucille goin' to get hitched, Cory? The way you talked about her while you was lookin' for her, I figured you'd ask her to marry you right off."

"I planned to," Cory admitted. "But then we got involved in this whole wagon train business, and it seemed like there was just too much going on. I've been thinking about it, though, and I believe the time is coming. What about you and Rachel? I know the two of you have been courting."

"Well, yeah, I reckon so," replied Pie, sounding a little embarrassed. "I never dreamed a beautiful gal like her would ever be interested in a big ol' galoot like me, but she said yes when I asked her to go walkin' with me, and she lets me come to Miss Fay's boardin' house to court her whilst we're in Monroe. I reckon she really does like me."

From what Cory had seen of the way Rachel acted around Pie, he knew his friend was right. He grinned and asked, "Have you ever kissed her, or do you just hold hands?"

Pie bristled. "That ain't any o' your business, Cory Brannon. Miss Rachel's a doggone lady. I don't ask you what you and Miss Lucille get up to while you're courtin', do I?"

"Sorry, Pie," Cory said with a chuckle. "I didn't mean any offense. I withdraw the question."

"Durned well better."

Cory reached into his pocket and took out the mouth harp he had scavenged months earlier. "You know, I never did learn how to play this thing. I'm not sure why I'm still carrying it around."

Pie took his own harp from a pocket of his overalls. "You ain't never goin' to learn how to play if you don't practice," he said. "Listen here." He brought the harp to his mouth and coaxed a long, mournful chord out of it. "Now, try that."

"How?" Cory asked helplessly.

Patiently, Pie explained, and after a few minutes, Cory began to get the hang of it. What few musical skills he had developed had gotten rusty during the months of not playing, but as he kept trying, his confidence grew and the sounds coming from the mouth harp began to sound better.

"There you go," said Pie. "Before you know it, you'll be standin' under Miss Lucille's window playin' for her."

Cory hadn't thought about that. He shook his head. "I'm not ready for that."

"A fella is usually ready for more than he thinks he is. All he's got to do is try."

That was good advice, thought Cory. He brought the harp to his mouth again and began to play, and to his surprise, the notes actually sounded pretty good this time.

CORY GOT a few hours' sleep at the hotel then was up early the next morning to help with the loading of the guns. The weapons were spread out among the wagons as Colonel Thompson had ordered the day before, and Cory had one of the crates of revolvers in his wagon. All the other goods from the warehouse were already loaded, so it was not long after sunup when the wagon train was ready to roll. Thompson bade farewell to Ed Loomis, then climbed onto his wagon and stood on the seat to wave for the others to follow him. One by one, the big, unwieldy vehicles lurched into motion as the teams of mules and oxen strained against their harnesses.

Lucille sat beside Cory on the wagon seat. She seemed to be worried about something, he realized after an hour or so. There was a frown on her face, and her answers to his comments were short, almost curt. Not liking the idea of spending more than a week on the road with Lucille angry with him, he said, "What's wrong? Did I do something?"

"What?" Lucille asked distractedly, then she gave a little shake of her head. "Oh, no, Cory, you didn't do anything wrong."

"You seem upset. I just thought—"

She laid a hand on his hand. "Not at all. I'm not upset. I'm just worried about Rachel."

"Rachel?" Cory repeated in surprise. "What's wrong with Rachel?"

"That's just what I've been asking myself. You'd think she would be happy that Pie is in love with her—"

"Wait a minute," Cory broke in. "Pie is in love with her? Has he told her that?"

"Well, not in so many words," admitted Lucille, "but can't you see it? Rachel and I certainly can."

Cory shrugged. Clearly, he was not the only one who had noticed what was going on between Pie and Rachel. "I suppose I knew about it. Pie hasn't said much, though. He keeps all that to himself." He paused then went on, "You say Rachel's unhappy with the way he feels about her?"

"She seems to be. She's afraid he's going to ask her to marry him or something crazy like that. Those are her words, not mine."

"Then you don't, ah, think marriage is crazy?"

"Of course not! What gave you that idea?"

"Nothing," Cory said quickly. "I didn't say I thought marriage was crazy, or that you thought it was crazy, or that—"

"Cory, you're babbling," Lucille said firmly. "The question is, what are we going to do about Pie and Rachel?"

"Do? Why do we have to do anything?"

"They're our friends! We can't let them be unhappy."

The way Cory saw it, he wasn't responsible for making anybody else happy, only himself and Lucille. All this talk about marriage made him wonder if he shouldn't wait until they got back to Vicksburg to propose. Maybe *this* was the right time after all.

"Lucille, I—"

Again he was interrupted, this time by a sudden crackle of gunfire from up ahead. The wagon train was well out of Marshall by now, and thick piney woods stretched as far as the eye could see on both sides of the road. That was where the shots were coming from. Muzzle flashes were visible in the deep shadows under the canopy of branches, and bullets whined through the air. Cory jerked his team of mules to a stop and grabbed Lucille, practically flinging her over the back of the seat into the wagonbed. "Stay down!" he shouted at her as he snatched up the Enfield rifle from the floorboard at his feet. The thick, heavy planks of the wagon's sideboards would stop most bullets, so he hoped Lucille would do as he told her.

Colonel Thompson had warned them on every trip that they might be attacked. The wagon train full of supplies was a tempting target for the bands of renegades and deserters that roamed the woods of East Texas and Louisiana. If word of the weapons shipment had gotten out, it would be even more enticing. But every driver had been in combat before except for Fred Carter, and they weren't going to give up without a fight. Cory heard shots ringing out from the other wagons as he dropped into a crouch on the wagon box and brought the rifle to his shoulder, cocking it as he did so.

He saw a muzzle flash in the trees and heard the bullet rip through the canvas over the wagonbed, only a few feet away from him. He pressed the trigger and felt the Enfield kick hard against his shoulder. While the powder smoke that geysered from the barrel was still floating around his head, he began reloading with a paper cartridge he took from the pouch attached to his belt.

More bullets thudded into the wagon, and Cory prayed the sideboards were too sturdy for them to penetrate. He cast a glance through the opening in the front of the canvas cover and saw that Lucille was huddled on the floor of the wagon, watching him with fear in her eyes. It was fear for him, not for herself, he realized as she met his gaze and said, "Cory—"

A bullet snatched his hat off his head. He grated, "Damn it!" and fired again. With so many trees all around them, it was impossible to tell if his shots were hitting anything or not.

A Rebel yell came from the woods, and men began to charge out of the trees. It was bad enough they had to fight the Yankees, Cory thought as he dropped the empty rifle and jerked his Colt from its holster. They shouldn't have to battle their own countrymen.

But these raiders weren't real Confederates, he told himself. They were outlaws, only interested in what they could steal and who they could kill.

He rolled over the back of the seat as bullets chewed at the wood. Landing on his knees in the wagonbed, he swiveled around and leaned over the seat to fire the Colt at the renegades charging out of the pines.

They were bearded men dressed in the ragged remnants of Confederate uniforms. Deserters, like the ones Cory had been forced to kill back during the summer. Now, as he emptied the Colt toward them, he saw a couple of men stagger back and fall under his bullets.

The charge broke under the fire from the wagons. Some of the renegades turned and ran. Clearly, they hadn't expected the men with the wagons to put up such a fight. The ones who weren't willing to give up the attack were shot down before they could reach the wagons.

"Get the wagons moving!" Thompson bellowed from the lead vehicle. "Let's get out of here!"

Cory jammed his empty pistol back in the holster and scrambled over the seat to grab the reins. He took the whip from its holder and lashed the mules mercilessly, shouting at them as he tried to get them moving. The balky animals broke into a grudging trot.

"Cory, behind us!" Lucille screamed behind him.

His head jerked around in time to see one of the deserters running up behind the wagon. He was brandishing a Bowie knife in one hand, and he used the other to grab the tailgate as he leaped onto the back of the wagon and tried to clamber inside. Lucille was between Cory and the renegade, and Cory's gun was empty. He was about to drop the reins and take on the deserter hand to hand when Lucille lifted the pistol from the floorboards beside her. Cory barely had time to recognize it as one of the Kerr revolvers from the crate before Lucille aimed the gun at the renegade with both hands and pressed the trigger.

The man's eyes widened in shock at the sharp crack of the pistol and the impact of the bullet in his chest. He was flung backward, landing on his back in the road with his arms and legs splayed out. Cory had just a glimpse of him lying that way before the wagon behind him ran over the man.

"Oh, my God, oh, my God," Lucille was saying over and over.

Cory kept the wagon moving but reached back with one hand to grip her shoulder tightly. "You're all right, Lucille," he told her. "You did just fine. That was smart thinking, loading that pistol like that."

She turned a shocked face toward him. "I . . . I killed him," she said.

"And he had it coming," Cory said.

Lucille began to cry, but she nodded. "There . . . there was nothing else I could do."

Cory squeezed her shoulder. Words didn't help much at a time like this, he thought, remembering how he had felt when he'd thought he had killed Lydell Strunk back in New Orleans. The fact that Strunk had later turned up alive had no bearing on the feelings Cory had experienced when he was convinced he had brought a human life to an unnatural end.

He prayed that Lucille would never grow as accustomed to killing as he had.

Thompson kept the train moving at a faster than normal pace for a couple of miles before calling a halt. When all the wagons were stopped, he climbed down hurriedly and ran along the train, checking on each of the drivers. Cory and Pie were doing the same thing. Cory felt a wave of relief wash over him when he saw that the big man seemed to be unhurt.

"Is Rachel all right?" he asked.

Pie nodded. "What about Miss Lucille?"

"She's fine," Cory said, even though he knew Lucille was still upset about having to shoot the renegade.

Allen Carter had a ragged, bloody tear in his shirt where a bullet had grazed his side. He was white-faced and clearly in pain as he half-fell from the wagon box to the ground, but as Cory, Pie, and the colonel bustled up, he said, "I'm all right. Go see about Fred."

Fred had already jumped down from his wagon, and he hurried forward to his father's side. "Pa!" he exclaimed. "You're hurt!"

"What about you, boy?" Carter asked. "Were you hit?"

Fred shook his head. "No. I don't know what happened. Was that shooting? It was so loud."

Carter put an arm around his son's shoulders and embraced him tightly. "Yes, it was loud," he agreed, a small catch in his voice. "But it's over now."

Two of the other drivers were wounded, one of them seriously. Seeing the way blood drenched the man's midsection, Cory was amazed that he had been able to get his wagon moving and keep the team under control while hurt that badly. Wounds like that were usually fatal.

"Good work, Ted," the colonel said to the man as they came up to the wagon. "Here, we'll help you—"

It was too late for that. Clutching his belly where the bullet had torn through him, the man swayed to the side and then toppled off the seat before any of the others could catch him. Thompson sprang forward and knelt at the man's side to check for a pulse, then shook his head dispiritedly. "He's gone," Thompson announced as he stood up and took off his hat.

Cory and Pie removed their hats, too, as did the other members of the group who had come up behind them. After a moment of silence to honor the fallen man, Cory cleared his throat and said rather awkwardly, "We'll need somebody to drive this wagon—"

"I'll do it," Rachel said.

Pie swung around toward her. "You can't—" he began.

"Yes, I can," declared Rachel. "I've driven wagons before that were almost this big, back home on the plantation."

"You're sure?" Thompson queried.

Without hesitation—and without looking at Pie—Rachel nodded and said, "I can do it, Colonel. You have my word on that."

"Very well, Miss Hannah. It appears you'll get a chance to be a teamster."

Pie tried again. "Dadgum it—"

"We'd best get this man buried and then get started again," the colonel said. "I don't think those reprobates will try to attack us again after the reception we gave them, but I'd like to put some more distance between them and us anyway."

Cory was in full agreement with that, and he had reached a decision on another matter, too. Now that danger had reared its head, as he had feared from the first that it might, Lucille would never again make one of these trips. And if she didn't like it, that was just too bad, because as her husband he would forbid her to come along next time.

Because he wasn't going to leave Vicksburg again until Lucille Farrell was his wife.

Chapter Fifteen

MAC RAN THE CURRY comb over the sleek, silver gray hide of the stallion. The horse turned his head from time to time and nipped at him, but the bites always missed. It was a game, but Mac had learned to keep an eye on the stallion anyway. From time to time, if he grew too careless, the horse would actually bite him. It was as if the stallion were trying to point out to him the value of staying alert. Mac was more likely to stay alive that way.

"Good evening, Lieutenant," a voice said from behind.

Mac lowered the comb and turned his head. He thought he recognized the voice, and as he looked at the officer standing there in the gathering dusk, he saw that he was right. Maj. Jason Trahearne had spoken, but as usual, the major was more interested in the stallion than he was in Mac. Trahearne's eyes greedily watched the horse.

"Good evening, Major," Mac responded properly with a crisp salute.

Trahearne casually returned the gesture. He was about the same age as Mac but shorter and stockier. The major was the son of a wealthy plantation owner and had entered the army as an officer. So far, his career had been undistinguished, though Mac supposed he was courageous enough. Trahearne had led his men into battle and hadn't shirked his duty. He just hadn't managed to accomplish much.

The major tugged at one of his long, bushy sidewhiskers that came down almost to his chin. "I was thinking I might go as high as five hundred dollars for that nag of yours," he said.

Mac's eyes widened a little in surprise. There had been plenty of years when the Brannon family farm hadn't made more than five hundred dollars in profits. Now here was Trahearne, offering to pay him that much for one horse.

Unfortunately, this was the one horse in all the world Mac would not sell for any price.

He shook his head. "Sorry, Major. This stallion's still not for sale."

Trahearne glowered at him in the dusk. "You're a fool, Brannon," he snapped.

Mac couldn't resist goading the man. "A fool with a mighty fine horse, I reckon."

For months now, almost since the day Mac had joined the cavalry, Jason Trahearne had made a nuisance of himself with his efforts to buy the stallion from him. Trahearne was clearly accustomed to getting whatever he wanted, and during their first encounter he had relied on the fact that he was an officer and Mac only a lowly private to settle the matter. Mac was going to sell him the horse, and that was that.

Only Mac had refused, and Trahearne's blustery threat to commandeer the horse had collapsed when Fitzhugh Lee overheard the argument. Lee had smoothly interceded on Mac's behalf, letting Trahearne know that he wouldn't stand for such tactics. Since then, Trahearne had resented Lee as well as Mac, but seeing as how Lee had been made a brigadier general in the meantime, there was nothing he could do.

Now that Mac was a fellow officer, threats stood even less chance of working, but there was nothing to prevent Trahearne from continuing to offer to buy the stallion. It was tiresome and annoying, but Mac supposed he would just have to tolerate it.

Trahearne's face darkened with anger at Mac's comment. "You think you're as good as the rest of us because of that horse," he accused. "I ought to have a word with General Stuart about your insubordination, Lieutenant. We'll see what he thinks about your brash behavior."

Considering the fact that Jeb Stuart was capable of some pretty brash behavior himself, Mac didn't take that threat too seriously. He said, "I'm off duty, Major, so if you don't have any military matters to discuss . . ."

Trahearne turned on his heel and stalked away. Mac could not help but grin as he watched the major leave. He had few pleasures these days. Petty though it might be, frustrating Jason Trahearne was one of them.

A short time later, the music began, as it did every night after supper while the cavalry was camped. General Stuart loved the strains of a good song almost as much as he relished riding into battle, so he had gathered a sizable number of subordinates who could either sing, play a musical instrument, or both. As the merry fiddling got underway, Mac drifted toward the general's tent.

Corporal Hagen, a giant of a man with a bushy black beard, was dancing a jig as he often did, while most of the men clapped in time with the music. Enlisted men as well as officers were welcome at these nightly get-togethers, so there was always a large crowd. Mac stood at the edge of the audience and watched with a grin as Hagen cavorted. The big man had ridden with him on several scouting missions in the past, and Mac considered him a friend.

Stuart sat on a three-legged stool near the fire, clapping with the rest of the men. He was hatless and smiling. He had taken advantage of the respite in the fighting to have his wife and children brought to the camp, and he had spent the past few days visiting with his family, which he often did whenever battle was not imminent. Jeb Stuart took war seriously enough, but he wasn't going to let it interfere too much with his enjoyment of life. Watching him now, Mac had no trouble understanding why Stuart's men were so fiercely devoted to him. The general was like a knight in an old storybook, a genuine hero.

After a while, Mac grew tired and started back toward his tent. His route led him close to the rope corrals where the horses were kept, and he suddenly heard a familiar sound cutting through the cold night air. It came from a horse and was full of anger and defiance. Immediately, several other horses joined in the commotion.

That first shrill trumpeting, though, had come from the big silver gray stallion. Mac was sure of that. He bit back a curse and broke into a run, angling past several tents toward the corrals.

From the corner of his eye, he saw a shadowy figure leap out from behind one of the tents. Instinct tried to twist him in that direction to meet a possible threat, but he didn't react quite quickly enough. Something crashed into the side of his head and sent him staggering sideways. He tripped on a tent rope and went down hard.

Blinding pain ripped through Mac's head as he struggled to push himself up from the ground. His attacker had hit him with a gun butt or a club of some sort, and he was afraid that his skull had been fractured. He forced himself to ignore the agony as he came up onto his hands and knees. Vaguely, he heard a grunt of effort and knew that another blow was probably coming his way.

He threw himself to the side, hoping that he wasn't rolling right into the attack. Instead he crashed into a pair of legs. His assailant toppled over, falling on top of Mac. He shoved the man off, feeling the rough fabric of a uniform tunic against his hands as he did so. His attacker was a soldier, which came as no surprise since he was in the middle of a camp full of thousands of Confederate troops.

The struggle had been carried out in grim silence so far. With scores of troopers in earshot, Mac knew he could shout for help and men would come running. But he was filled now with an anger that fed off his pain, and as he rolled over again his arm shot out at the dimly glimpsed figure on the ground beside him. The impact that shivered up his arm as the punch landed made his head hurt even more, but it was satisfying at the same time. Mac's fist crashed into the man's face again, bouncing his head off the ground.

With a groan, the man went limp. Mac stumbled to his feet. He guessed his head wasn't broken open after all, because he could see more clearly now and the pain in his skull was beginning to subside slightly. He started to run toward the corral again, his movements awkward and jerky at first but smoothing out quickly.

"Stop those horses!" someone shouted. "They're stampeding!"

The rope corrals were fairly sturdy for what they were, but they wouldn't stand up for long under the battering that a herd of spooked horses would give them. If the herd broke free and went rampaging through the camp, they could cause considerable damage. Some of the men might even be trampled to death. Injuries would occur, that was certain.

Mac came in sight of the corrals. The horses were a shapeless, shifting mass, but suddenly a silver gray form shimmered in the moonlight as it loomed over the other animals. The stallion had reared up on his hind legs, and his forelegs were lashing out at a man who was trying to get a halter on him. The man cried out in pain as one of the stallion's hooves struck him on the shoulder and sent him spinning off his feet.

Falling down in the middle of that frightened mass of horses was a death sentence. Mac skidded to a stop as he heard the man shriek. The scream was cut off in the middle. Mac felt a cold finger go down his back at the knowledge of what that sudden silence meant.

There was nothing he could do now for the man in the pen. Instead, he took a deep breath, put a couple of fingers in his mouth, and let out a shrill whistle. The sound cut through the confusion, and the stallion's head swung toward Mac. The big horse began bulling his way through the herd, biting and slashing with his teeth at any of the horses that didn't get out of his way quickly enough. Mac ducked under the ropes as the stallion came up to them. In a flash, he had grasped the stallion's mane and pulled himself up onto the horse's back. He began riding bareback in a circle around the corral, calling out to the nervous horses as he did so. Any time the herd surged toward the ropes, the stallion was there to drive them back.

In a matter of moments, the horses began to calm down. More troopers ran up carrying halters and ropes, but Mac motioned for them to stay back. He rode around the corral, talking to the horses in a soothing voice, until the danger of the stampede seemed to be over. With the help of the stallion, Mac had averted a possible disaster.

General Stuart came striding up to the corral, followed by Fitz Lee, Corporal Hagen, and a large group of officers and enlisted men. "Is that you on that horse, Brannon?" Stuart called.

Mac slipped down off the stallion and bent to duck under the ropes again. "Yes sir," he replied.

"Well, you've certainly raised quite a commotion, Lieutenant. Would you care to explain what this is all about?"

"Beggin' your pardon, General," said one of the men who had arrived at the corral shortly after Mac. "The lieutenant here didn't cause the trouble. He stopped it. If he hadn't got up on that horse of his, the whole bunch of 'em would've probably busted out and raised holy hell."

"I see. Then what *did* cause the trouble?"

"Someone was trying to steal my horse," Mac said. His thoughts came together all at once, and what he had said made sense. Someone had slipped into the corral and tried to put a halter on the stallion, and the big silver gray horse had reacted as he would have to any stranger trying such a thing. He had protested strenuously, and his outrage had stirred up the rest of the herd to the point of panic. The would-be thief had met his fate under the hooves of the maddened horses. Mac pointed into the corral and went on, "I reckon you'll find him in there—what's left of him."

"You mean someone was trampled?" Stuart asked.

"Yes sir. I saw him fall, and he didn't have any chance to get out."

Grim-faced, Stuart ordered, "Someone take a look."

"I'll go," Hagen volunteered. He slipped into the corral and gradually herded the horses back toward the far side of the enclosure. When Hagen came to a dark shape sprawled on the ground, he called, "Here he is, Gen'ral."

"Somebody fetch a torch,"ordered Fitz Lee.

Mac more than halfway expected the light of the torch to reveal the mangled corpse of Maj. Jason Trahearne. Instead, when the flickering glow washed over the face of the dead man, Mac only vaguely recognized him and was unable to put a name with the face. All he knew was that he had seen the man around the encampment several times. The dead man wore a captain's uniform that was stained with blood and dirt from the fatal trampling. His face was largely untouched, however, except for the huge dent in his forehead that had no doubt taken his life.

"Captain Curwood," Stuart said. He knew the dead man even if Mac didn't. Stuart looked sharply at Mac. "Are you sure you want to accuse this man of trying to steal your horse, Lieutenant?"

Mac was as convinced of that as ever. Now that he had had a moment to think about it, he recalled where he had seen the dead Captain Curwood before: sitting in front of Trahearne's tent playing cards. If Curwood was one of Trahearne's cronies, Trahearne could have talked him into helping in the attempt to steal the stallion. But Curwood was the one who had risked—and lost—his life.

Mac could tell that wasn't what the general wanted to hear. In the absence of actual proof, Stuart wouldn't want one of his officers accused of being a horse thief. Mac said slowly, "That was just a guess on my part, sir, and maybe I jumped to a conclusion. I really didn't see what happened."

"In any regard, this is a tragedy," Stuart said. "Captain Curwood was a fine officer."

"Yes sir," Mac agreed, even though he hadn't known Curwood all that well.

Stuart sighed. "Fitz, we'd better see about a burial detail."

"Of course, sir," Lee said. "I'll take care of it."

"If you don't need me, sir . . . ," Mac ventured.

Lee nodded. "You can go on about your business, Lieutenant."

"Thank you, sir."

Mac's business at the moment was the man who had jumped him while he was running toward the corrals. He walked quickly toward the spot where the brief fight had occurred, but when he got there no one was around. His attacker must have regained consciousness and skulked away.

He was convinced that it had been Jason Trahearne. He rubbed his right fist in his left palm. That was the fist he had used to strike his assailant in the face, and he remembered now how he had felt bushy sidewhiskers on the man's cheeks. It had been Trahearne, he was sure of it. Trahearne had sent Curwood into the corral after the stallion, letting the other officer handle the dangerous task while Trahearne himself merely watched to make sure the theft wasn't interrupted. It was Trahearne who had leaped from the shadows to strike Mac down.

"Mac?"

He turned quickly and saw Fitz Lee standing there. The general went on, "I know who Curwood's friends were, Mac. Beauty doesn't want to think badly of any of his men, but you and I both have a pretty good idea of what happened tonight, don't we?"

"Could be, sir," Mac replied curtly.

"After this, you'd better keep your eyes wide open. If it was up to me, I'd cashier Trahearne right out of the army, but it's not. He won't forget what happened to Curwood."

Mac rubbed his sore knuckles again. Trahearne probably didn't give a damn about what had happened to Curwood.

But he would likely never forgive Mac for punching him in the face.

⸻

NOT SURPRISINGLY, Maj. Jason Trahearne's face was bruised and somewhat swollen the next morning. When Mac saw him,

Trahearne gave him a cold-eyed stare full of hate. "Ran into a tree branch last night in the dark," Mac overheard the major explaining to another officer.

"You must have been in a hell of a hurry," the man commented dryly. That made Trahearne's eyes flick toward Mac again, and Mac knew he was seeing living proof of that old saying about how looks could kill . . .

If Curwood had been able to get the stallion out of the corral, Trahearne must have planned to spirit the horse away from the camp and send it back to his father's plantation. There was no way Trahearne could have ridden the animal without having it recognized as being stolen. This affair had gone beyond a simple desire on Trahearne's part to possess the stallion, Mac knew. The only thing that mattered to Trahearne now was that Mac not have the horse. Trahearne was motivated by sheer spite.

Fortunately—depending on how you looked at it—it quickly became obvious that Trahearne, along with all the other members of Robert E. Lee's command, soon were going to have other matters to occupy their time. Around midday, the general officers were summoned to Lee's tent, and Mac went along as Fitz Lee's aide-de-camp.

Robert E. Lee sat on a chair underneath a tree, his legs crossed. James Longstreet, distinguished with his high forehead and long beard, sat to Lee's right, while Jeb Stuart sat at the commander's left hand. The other officers and aides gathered around.

"Gentlemen," Lee began, "we have received word that President Lincoln, having grown tired of the slowness and caution of General McClellan's movements, has replaced him as the commander of the Army of the Potomac."

Lee paused. Mac could tell that several of the officers were almost bursting with questions, but they remained silent, willing to let their white-bearded commander proceed at his own pace.

"General Ambrose Burnside is now in command of the Federal army," Lee continued after a moment. "We have reason to know him well."

That was certainly true, Mac reflected. General Burnside had been in command of the Union left flank during the battle of Sharpsburg. It was his men who had made charge after bloody charge in an attempt to capture a small stone bridge that spanned Antietam Creek. Late in the day, they had finally succeeded, but the arrival of Confederate reinforcements led by Gen. A. P. Hill had driven the Yankees back across the bitterly disputed stream. Burnside had expended all his reserves in capturing the bridge, so he'd had nothing left with which to defend against the Southern counterattack.

This time when Lee paused, Longstreet asked, "What do you think Burnside will do, General?"

With a frown of concentration, Lee replied, "He will have to do *something*, if for no other reason than to demonstrate to President Lincoln the contrast between himself and General McClellan. Our scouts report that he is concentrating his forces in the vicinity of Warrenton, as if he plans to move soon."

Mac knew the town of Warrenton quite well. It had served as the headquarters of the Confederate army for a time, and it was at Warrenton that he had joined the cavalry. Since then, however, the Union troops had occupied the settlement, which was no more than thirty miles north of Culpeper on the Orange and Alexandria Railroad. If Burnside wanted to, he could move on Culpeper in a hurry.

"Perhaps it would be wise to bring General Jackson and his men back from Winchester," suggested Longstreet.

That would be all right with Mac. It would mean he could see Will again, and there was no better group of fighting infantry in the world than the famous Stonewall Brigade.

Lee pondered the idea for a moment then shook his head. "From Warrenton, General Burnside can move in any of three directions," he said. "He can cross the Blue Ridge and strike at Winchester, come straight down the railroad to Gordonsville and Culpeper, or shift east to Fredericksburg. That seems unlikely to me, but we must be prepared for all eventualities."

"Wait to see which way the rabbit's going to jump, you mean," observed Stuart.

Lee smiled faintly. "Exactly, General."

The meeting broke up shortly after that. For the time being, the plan was for the scouts to keep a close eye on the Yankee encampment at Warrenton. At the first sign of impending movement, the Confederate forces would shift to block the Federals and hope that Burnside, who had a reputation for being stolid, unimaginative, and almost as cautious as McClellan, was not attempting a feint.

That evening, Mac saddled the stallion and rode out to the farm. Abigail, Cordelia, and Henry were glad to see him, as always. After saying hello to all of them, he led the stallion into the barn to put it in a stall for the evening.

A figure sauntered out of the shadows inside the barn. Mac caught a whiff of the sharp tang of raw whiskey as the figure resolved itself into his brother Titus. "Howdy, Mac," Titus said.

"Hello, Titus," Mac said as he began loosening the cinch on the cavalry saddle. "What are you doing here? I thought this time of day you'd be over at Mountain Laurel, sitting down to supper with Polly and her father."

An ugly laugh came from Titus. "Don't reckon that'll be happening again any time soon. I ain't welcome on the plantation these days."

"Not welcome?" repeated Mac. "But you're Polly's husband."

"That don't seem to mean as much as it once did."

Titus's voice was even more laden with bitterness than it was with whiskey. Clearly, he and Polly had had a terrible falling-out. Nothing else could have driven him to leave her. After making marriage to her his goal for so many years, the sweetness of the union obviously had turned to ashes in his mouth.

Mac put a hand on his brother's shoulder. "I'm sorry to hear that, Titus—" he began.

Titus shrugged off the hand and turned away, saying, "It don't matter."

"Of course it does."

Titus ignored that. He said, "I'll put your horse up . . . unless you don't trust me to."

Mac hesitated a heartbeat. Titus sounded so downtrodden, Mac didn't want to do anything that might make him feel even worse. "Thanks," he said. "I'll leave the stallion with you then." He patted the horse on its silver gray shoulder, so that he would know Mac wanted him to cooperate. The stallion tolerated Titus the same as he did Henry and Cordelia.

"Tell Ma not to wait supper on me," Titus called after him as Mac started out of the barn.

Mac stopped. "You're not coming inside?"

"Not right now. I'm not very hungry. Maybe later."

What he meant was that he wanted to stay out here in the barn with his jug of corn squeezings, Mac understood. Titus had straightened up for a while, but this rift with Polly had pushed him right back into his old ways.

Mac sighed, knowing there was nothing he could do to help right now. With over a hundred thousand enemy troops right up the road, he had more with which to concern himself than one wayward brother.

But that wouldn't stop him from worrying about his family, including Titus. Nothing could do that.

Chapter Sixteen

Ｔitus wiped the back of his hand across his mouth. His heart was thudding heavily, almost painfully, in his chest as he rode up the lane toward the plantation house. A cold November wind blew through the bare branches of the mountain laurels that gave the estate its name. The sky was thickly overcast, and the gloom suited Titus's mood just fine.

But Polly could bring the sunshine back into his life with just one word, if only she would.

Titus hunched his shoulders and pulled his hat down a little tighter on his head. He didn't owe Polly Ebersole—Polly Ebersole *Brannon*, he reminded himself—one damned thing, and yet he was here anyway to give her a last chance to redeem herself. He had waited, watching the house from a distance, nipping occasionally from the flask he carried inside his coat to keep him warm, until he had seen Ebersole drive away in the fancy black coach. Titus had known his father-in-law would be leaving because he had sent him a letter claiming to be from the secretary of that banker in Richmond, Bradford Challis. The letter had asked Ebersole to meet Challis today in Culpeper on a matter of urgent business. Titus thought it was a pretty smooth trick, even if he did say so himself.

He reined his horse to a stop under the canopy built on the front of the house. As he swung down from the saddle, he looked around nervously, halfway expecting one of the overseers to come up and challenge his right to be here. The only person he saw, though, was an elderly maid who opened the front door and peered out curiously. "I thought I heard somebody out here on a hoss," the slave said. "What you want, Massa Titus?"

Titus whipped the horse's reins around a post, then strode toward the door before he lost all the courage he had gotten from the flask. The maid had no choice but to step back hurriedly out of his way as he said, "I'm here to see my wife."

"Miss Polly, she indisposed—"

"The hell with that," snapped Titus. "I'm going to see her. Is she in her room?"

"Don't you be goin' up them stairs, Massa Titus—"

"Stay here," he commanded.

He went up the stairs two at a time, and when he reached the second-floor landing, he stalked along the corridor toward the room he had shared with Polly while he lived here. His courage and determination ebbed away a little more with every step, but he forced himself to ball his hand into a fist as he reached his destination. He pounded on the closed door and called loudly, "Polly! It's me, Titus! I have to talk to you!"

No response came from inside. His fist thudded against the door again. "Polly!"

The click of another door opening startled him. His breath hissed between his teeth as he turned toward the sound. Polly was framed in the opening of this door as she said, "Titus? What are you doing here?"

She clutched the edge of the door with one hand as if she really were sick. There were dark circles under her eyes, and her blonde hair was in disarray. She wore a silken dressing gown and held it tightly closed with her other hand.

"Polly?" Titus said in confusion. "I thought that was your father's room."

"We've changed rooms," she said curtly. She asked again, "What are you doing here?"

"I came to see you, of course," Titus said as he moved toward her. She drew back slightly, as if getting ready to slam the door in his face, and he stopped short and held up both hands placatingly. "I just want to talk to you."

"My father told you never to come back here."

"Your father told me a lot of things," Titus said. "That don't mean I have to listen to him." He ventured a step closer. "Polly . . . I came back for you."

"Wha . . . what?"

"Come with me now," Titus said urgently. "While your father's gone. Just throw a few things in a carpetbag and come with me to the farm. We'll make us a home there. I'll build a cabin for us down by the creek. It won't be much at first, but once the war's over—"

Polly's hollow laugh stopped him. "Do you really think the war will ever be over?"

"Sure it will," said Titus, trying to sound more convinced than he really was. "It can't be too much longer before those stupid Yankees see that we won't let 'em run our lives. They'll give up and go home."

Polly shook her head. "I wish I could believe that."

"It's true. But . . . but the war doesn't really have anything to do with us. You and me can be happy together, Polly, if we can just get away from this place."

"This is my home." She laughed again. "Home, sweet home."

"A woman's supposed to leave her folks and cleave unto her husband. That's what it says in the Good Book." Titus was desperate enough to try any argument, even religion. He just wished he remembered more of the things he'd heard Reverend Crosley preaching about over the years.

"It says to honor thy father and thy mother, too." Polly giggled, and Titus suddenly wondered if she had been drinking. That would explain the dark circles under her eyes. "I have to honor my father, Titus."

"No, you don't," he argued. "What you've got to do is come with me, so we can be like a regular husband and wife again—"

"No!" She practically screamed the word at him. "Things can never be right again! Can't you see that?"

"Sure they can, if we try." Titus felt the last of his hope slipping away. He cast about in desperation for something, anything, to say that might convince Polly he was right, but there was nothing. He had made his case, and that was all he could do. "Please," he whispered. "Please try."

She looked at him for a long moment out of dark, haunted eyes, opened her mouth to say something, then closed it. She stepped back, and the door began to swing shut.

"Polly!" Titus cried. For one wild instant, he thought about shouldering the door open, scooping her up in his arms, and carrying her away from here by force. If he did that, though, Ebersole would probably just come to the farm with all his overseers and any other men he could round up, and they would come with shotguns and dogs, and people would get hurt. Maybe Polly, maybe someone else in his family. He couldn't risk it, he realized, not even for Polly.

His beloved Polly.

The door clicked shut.

Titus stared at it, feeling the last of whatever was human in him flicker out like the last glow of a candle. When he couldn't stand it anymore, he turned and walked heavily along the hall and then down the stairs. Several more elderly slaves were waiting at the bottom of the winding staircase, no doubt summoned by the maid.

"Miss Polly, she be all right?" the woman asked.

"I didn't lay a finger on her," grated Titus. "She's fine."

"She won't go with you?"

Titus shook his head and pushed past the slaves. As he went out of the house, he heard the maid mutter, "Oh, Lawd, that poor girl . . ."

He suppressed a snort of contempt. He wasn't going to waste any sympathy on Polly. *He* was the one with the broken heart, not her.

He untied his horse, mounted, and rode back down the lane. As he reached the end of it, he saw the carriage rolling toward him along the road. Ebersole hadn't had time to get to Culpeper and back after discovering that the so-called meeting with Challis was a ruse. He must have forgotten something.

Titus could have wheeled his horse around and galloped away, but he was in no mood to run from Ebersole like a whipped dog. Instead he reined in and sat there in the cold wind, waiting patiently and not even feeling the chill. He slipped his hand inside his coat and curled his fingers around the butt of the pistol that he had brought with him. If Ebersole wanted trouble, then Titus had nothing to lose by giving it to him.

The driver brought the carriage to a stop beside Titus's horse, and Ebersole glared up at him from the window of the vehicle. "What are ye doin' here, Brannon?" he demanded. "I told ye I'd have ye shot if ye set foot on this plantation again!"

"You're welcome to try," Titus said flatly.

Ebersole must have sensed the danger in the air, because he frowned and said, "I dinna want more trouble with ye, lad. Why have ye come?"

"To say good-bye to Polly," Titus heard himself saying. As a matter of fact, that was exactly what he *hadn't* done. He had been too frustrated and disappointed and upset to remember his plans. If she refused his plea to leave Mountain Laurel, then he'd intended to tell her what he had decided to do. When the moment came, however, those intentions had been completely forgotten.

"Good-bye?" repeated Ebersole. "Where are ye goin'?"

"Depends on where the army sends me, I reckon," Titus said. "I'm joinin' up."

Ebersole sat back. "Are ye now? 'Tis bloody well about time ye did yer part for the Southern cause. What did Polly say?"

"I didn't tell her."

Ebersole looked slightly confused by that, but he put it aside and said, "Well, then, despite our differences, lad, let me wish you luck."

Titus knew Ebersole was hardly sincere. It would be perfectly all right with his father-in-law if the Yankees killed him. In fact, in the old man's eyes, that would be the best solution.

But it wasn't going to happen. A humorless grin stretched tightly over Titus's face as he said, "Much obliged, Ebersole. You're goin' to help me fight the Yanks, you know that?"

Now Ebersole was getting really confused. "How do ye mean?"

"Every time I line my sights on one of those Federal bastards and put a bullet through his head . . . I'm goin' to be imagining that he's *you.*"

With that, Titus wheeled his horse and kicked it into a gallop. As he rode away from Mountain Laurel, he could still see the flabbergasted rage on Ebersole's face in that final moment as Titus's words sank in on him. Titus laughed. Ebersole's expression was small consolation for what he had finally lost today, once and for all, but it was better than nothing.

Now all Titus had to do was tell the rest of his family about his decision.

———

"ABSOLUTELY NOT," said Abigail Brannon. "I forbid it."

"You don't have any say in this, Ma," Titus said defiantly. "It's my decision to make, and I've made it."

The air in the parlor of the Brannon farmhouse was thick with tension. Titus stood on one side of the room, Abigail and Cordelia and Henry on the other. Titus hunched his shoulders a little and glanced down at the floor as the other three glared at him. "I'm goin'," he muttered.

"You'll leave us to take care of the farm by ourselves," Henry said. "But you don't care, do you?" He laughed harshly. "Not that you're much good these days, anyway, not since you've gone back to drinkin'."

Titus's gaze jerked up. "I won't be talked to that way by my little brother."

"I'll talk to you any way I please," Henry shot back. "I'm tired of carryin' your weight, Titus."

"You never—"

"Yes, he did, Titus," Cordelia said softly, her voice quivering with emotion. "We've all had to take up the slack that you left these past months. I don't like saying it, and I don't want you to go off to the war, but it's true."

Abigail folded her arms across her chest. "I've sent two sons off to war. Three if you count Cory. That's enough for this family. Titus, I want you to go upstairs and forget all about this foolish notion. You should fall down on your knees and ask the Lord to guide you into the proper path." She turned her head and spoke to Henry. "And I want you to go out to the barn and find your brother's jug. Get rid of it."

Henry started toward the door, but Titus moved quickly to head him off. He put a hand in the middle of Henry's chest and shoved him back. "You all think I'm just a worthless drunk!" he raged. He reached inside his coat and jerked out the flask. "Well, maybe that's all I am, but I'm not gonna let you boss me around anymore!"

Her face turning pale, Abigail stepped forward and held out her hand. "Give that to me."

"No ma'am." Titus laughed and moved back beyond her reach. He pulled the cork from the neck of the flask with his teeth, then spat it into his other hand. Upending the container, he took a long pull from it. Satisfied, he glared at his mother. "There. I ain't goin' to hide no more. I'll do my drinkin' right out in the open, thank you very much."

Henry's hands were clenched into fists. "Blast it, Titus, stop it! What's got into you?"

"I'm tired of everybody else makin' up my mind for me. I been listenin' to you preach at me for years, Ma. Do this, don't do that. Praise the Lord! And Will an' Mac were just as bad, always tryin' to keep me on the straight an' narrow. You're turnin' into just as much of a self-righteous bastard as they are, Henry."

"Titus!" Abigail was aghast.

"Now you're gonna fuss at me 'cause of my language, Ma?" He laughed. "The hell with all of you! I'm goin' to fight Yankees, and you can't stop me! None of you!" He turned and lurched toward the door.

"Titus!" Henry sprang forward, grabbing his brother's shoulder.

Titus spun around. He was royally drunk, but that had never affected his reflexes. His fist came up and cracked into Henry's jaw, knocking the younger man backward. Henry's feet tangled in a throw rug as he tried to catch his balance, and he tumbled to the floor, landing heavily.

Cordelia cried out and hurried to Henry's side. Abigail didn't move. She seemed rooted to the floor of the parlor. Her eyes glittered with anger as she said, "The Devil has stolen you away from us, boy. Satan has blinded you to what's right."

"The only devil I know is Duncan Ebersole, and him and that bitch daughter of his have opened my eyes," Titus said, his lip curling in contempt. "I wasn't good enough for them, and I ain't never been good enough for the rest of the high an' mighty Brannons! That's why I'm leavin'."

"Then go!" Cordelia cried raggedly from where she knelt beside Henry. "Just go and stop tearing all of us apart!"

Titus stared at her for a moment, blinking blearily. Then he turned on his heel and stalked out of the parlor. A second later, the front door of the farmhouse slammed behind him.

He took another drink from the flask as he walked unsteadily toward the barn and tried not to think about Cordelia's sobs. As cold and hard as he had become inside, he still wished that he hadn't had to make his sister cry.

But there hadn't been any tears from his mother. No sir, Abigail Brannon wasn't going to cry over losing something as worthless as he had become.

Titus rode out a few minutes later, his Sharps rifle across the saddle in front of him and the flask tucked safely in his pocket.

———

THE CAMPFIRES spread nearly from horizon to horizon. Titus had seen the army camp before, but not at night. It was more impressive this way.

His breath fogged in front of his face as he swung down from the saddle and led his horse toward the sentries who stood guard at the edge of the encampment. "Hold it, mister," one of the soldiers called to him. "State your name and your business."

"I'm Titus Brannon, and I've come to enlist." Titus hoped that his voice wasn't too thick with drink. If the troopers took him for a sot, they might send him away and tell him to come back when he was sober. Titus didn't want to wait. He might lose his nerve if he did.

To his surprise, the sentries lowered their rifles, and the one who had challenged him said, "All right, you'd best talk to the cap'n, I reckon." He turned and pointed. "It's that big tent right yonder."

"Much obliged," Titus said with a curt nod of his head. "What outfit is this, anyway?" Mac was in the cavalry, and Titus didn't want any part of that. The Stonewall Brigade, including Will's company, was still on the other side of the Blue Ridge in the Shenandoah Valley, so he didn't have to worry about inadvertently volunteering for that group.

"This is General Cobb's brigade," replied the trooper. "Georgia boys, born and bred."

"Well, I'm a Virginian," Titus said, "but if you'll have me, I'd be proud to join up."

The soldier jerked a thumb over his shoulder. "Go talk to the cap'n like I said, Virginny. It'll be him who says yay or nay."

"Can I leave my horse here?"

"Sure thing."

Titus tied the reins to a post that had been driven into the ground for that purpose, then walked over to the tent the sentry had pointed out. He carried his rifle with him, cradled in the crook of his left arm.

A corporal was sitting on a stool in front of the captain's tent. "What do you want?" he asked as Titus walked up.

"Fella over yonder told me to talk to the captain about enlistin' in the army."

The corporal leaned over to the opening in the front of the tent and called, "Cap'n, got a civilian out here who wants to join up."

"Send him in, Burris," a voice replied from inside the canvas structure.

The corporal held the entrance flap to one side. Titus ducked through the opening and found himself in a good-sized tent. A folding table had been set up, along with several chairs. A lantern sat on the table, throwing its light over several maps that had been unrolled and their edges weighted down by various items of equipment, including a pistol and a bayonet. A balding man with a sand-colored beard glanced up at Titus. "I'm Captain Stevens," he said. "What can I do for you?"

"I've come to enlist," Titus said for what seemed like the tenth or twelfth time. It took these Georgians awhile to get things through their head, he supposed.

"You're from Virginia?"

"That's right," replied Titus, then he added, "sir," figuring that it couldn't hurt.

"This brigade is from Georgia."

"We're all fightin' the Yankees, aren't we?"

A faint smile appeared on the captain's face. "Yes, of course. What's your name?"

"Titus Brannon."

Captain Stevens didn't appear to recognize the name. Titus had been afraid he would run into an officer who knew Will or Mac. He didn't want anybody running to them to tell them that their brother had joined the army. It was none of their business.

"That's a pretty good looking rifle you have," Stevens said, nodding toward the Sharps. "Can you use it?"

"You won't find a better shot in the whole state of Virginia. Or in Georgia, for that matter." Titus had never seen the sense in being modest about his skill.

"Oh, ho, is that so?" Stevens replied with a grin. "Proud of yourself, aren't you, Brannon?"

Titus shrugged. "Just statin' the facts, Cap'n."

Stevens got to his feet. "Come on. I want a demonstration of this uncanny ability of yours."

Suddenly, Titus felt uneasy. He had figured the army would just sign him up without any rigmarole. He hadn't counted on having to pass some sort of test before being allowed to fight Yankees. Wasn't the army supposed to be short on manpower, especially after all the casualties at Sharpsburg?

He wasn't one to pass up a challenge, though. Never had been. So he said, "What is it you want me to shoot?"

Stevens led the way out of the tent. "Come along to the edge of camp," he said. "We don't want to start a panic by shooting off a gun in the middle of the army. Corporal Burris, get a candle and come with us."

The corporal obeyed, fetching a stub of a candle from inside the tent and hurrying along behind Titus and Stevens. When they reached the pickets, Stevens said, "Rest easy, boys. We're just going to have a little shooting exhibition."

Titus heard mockery in the captain's voice, and it made him burn with anger inside. "I'm ready whenever you are, Cap'n."

"Burris, light that candle and take it out, say, a hundred yards from the edge of camp," Stevens ordered. "Find some place to set it down."

"Yes sir."

Titus loaded the Sharps while the corporal scurried off into the darkness. The tiny flame dwindled until it was barely visible. It grew a little brighter when Burris placed the candle on a low tree branch that was bare of leaves now in late November.

Burris came trotting back and asked, "How's that, Cap'n?"

"Just fine, Corporal. Thanks." Stevens turned to Titus. "Can you see that candle flame, Brannon?"

"I can see it," Titus said.

"Can you put it out from here? Or at least hit the candle?"

"I can put it out," Titus said. He licked his thumb, rubbed it over the sights of the rifle, and lifted the weapon to his shoulder.

One of the soldiers who had gathered around said in a loud voice, "Hell, nobody can make a shot like that!"

Titus wasn't sure the fellow was wrong. He was aiming at a tiny target in bad light. He squinted over the barrel of the rifle as he settled the stock against his shoulder. His arms, accustomed to the weight of the Sharps, held it steady. He wished he hadn't drunk quite so much whiskey earlier in the day. Usually liquor didn't muddle his head or affect his eyesight too much, but a shot such as this required the utmost concentration. He took a deep breath and held it as he gently stroked the rifle's trigger.

The blast of the shot, which would have been loud under the best of circumstances, seemed unnaturally so. The buttplate kicked heavily against Titus's shoulder. The evening breeze caught the cloud of smoke that billowed from the muzzle of the rifle and blew it in Titus's face. His eyes stung and watered from the acrid tang of burned powder. For a second he couldn't see . . .

A low whistle of admiration sounded from beside him. "Good Lord," Captain Stevens said. "I honestly didn't think it could be done. Not at that range."

Titus lowered the Sharps and grinned as he looked at the spot where the candle flame had been glowing just a moment earlier. Now there was only darkness there.

"The wick must've gone out," said Burris.

"Bring the candle back with you," Stevens ordered.

Titus turned to the officer and asked, "Are you ready to sign me up, even though I ain't from Georgia?"

"Anybody who can shoot like that, I want him in my company regardless of where he's from."

Burris came trotting back. He gave the candle to Stevens, who held it up and studied it in the light of a nearby campfire. "Clipped the wick off clean as you please," he said. He tossed the candle to Titus, who caught it awkwardly in one hand while the other held the Sharps. "Here's a keepsake for you, Brannon. A reminder of your first day in the Confederate army."

Chapter Seventeen

MAC HEARD THE GALLOPING hoofbeats before he saw the rider approaching out of the dusk. As the horseman came closer, however, it was impossible to miss him because of his imposing size. Mac leaned forward in the saddle as Corporal Hagen rode up to him and reined in. The sides of Hagen's horse were covered with lather from the hard run. Its breath plumed around its nostrils in the cold air. The corporal's mount was large and sturdy—the horse had to be to carry Hagen's great bulk—but clearly Hagen had put it to the test.

"You must have important news, Corporal," Mac said. Along with several other men, he had waited here near Warrenton while Hagen scouted closer to the town and the Federal encampment there.

Hagen nodded. "Important as can be, Lieutenant," he said. "The Yankees are on the move. Looks like at least a full division headin' southeast toward the Rappahannock, and from the looks of what's goin' on in the camp, I figure the rest of 'em plan to pull out sometime mighty soon."

Mac had expected as much. For the past few days, Confederate scouts had reported what appeared to be preparations for movement in the Union camp. That information had led Robert E. Lee to order that an even closer watch be kept on the Northerners.

"Good work, Corporal," Mac said to Hagen, then wheeled the stallion around. "I'll go on ahead," he told the rest of the patrol. "You men follow as quickly as you can."

Nods of agreement came from the other soldiers. They all knew that none of their horses could keep up with Mac's stallion when he let the big horse have its head. And it was important that this news be carried back to Lee's headquarters as quickly as possible.

Mac heeled the stallion into a run that soon left the rest of the patrol far behind in the gathering shadows. As he rode, he pondered what Hagen had told him. It was difficult to know exactly what the Union movement toward the Rappahannock might mean: the Yankees could be bound for Fredericksburg, which would be an important prize if they intended to march on Richmond once more, or they could be splitting their forces in an attempt to string out the Southern line of defense. The whole thing could even be a trick of some sort, though according to several staff officers, Burnside had never shown any inclination for fancy maneuvers in the past.

The one good thing that Mac could see about the whole situation was that if the Yankees were heading southeast, it was less likely they would attack Culpeper County. The Brannon farm was safe, if only marginally so.

When he reached the Confederate encampment a short time later, Mac went directly to Robert E. Lee's tent. The white-bearded commander was alone when Mac was ushered into the tent by a sentry. Lee looked up from a table covered with several maps, returned Mac's salute, and asked, "What news, Lieutenant Brannon?"

"One of the Federal divisions has moved out and is proceeding southeastward toward the Rappahannock, sir," Mac reported. "According to Corporal Hagen, the other two divisions are also preparing to break camp."

Lee nodded, not seeming surprised. "According to General Stuart, Corporal Hagen has sharp eyes. So do you, Lieutenant. Did you observe this movement, as well?"

"No sir, but I do not doubt Corporal Hagen's report."

"Nor do I," declared Lee. "You're dismissed, Lieutenant, but if you should happen to see General Longstreet or General Stuart or General Lee, please tell them that I should like to see them immediately."

"Yes sir," Mac said, saluting again. He ducked through the tent's entrance flap and stepped back into the chilly night.

He had hoped they could make it through the rest of the winter without any more fighting, but it appeared that was not to be. He couldn't imagine that General Lee would allow Burnside and the rest of the Yankee army to move unopposed across the Virginia countryside. Richmond had already survived one Federal assault that had carried the Yankees almost to the city itself before they had been driven back down the Peninsula. That effort would be wasted if the Yankees were to march into the capital from the other direction without a fight.

It wasn't his job to decide tactics, Mac reminded himself. Instead, even though General Lee had couched it in the form of a polite request, Mac went looking for Stuart, Longstreet, and Fitz Lee so that he could deliver the news to them as well.

THE NEXT day, just as Hagen predicted, the second and third Grand Divisions of the Union army left the encampment at Warrenton and marched southeast toward the Rappahannock. Confederate scouts watched them along the way and brought back reports that they were headed straight for Fredericksburg at a fast march. Indeed, in less than a week all three of the Union divisions reached the villages of Falmouth, on the northern bank of the Rappahannock, just upstream and across the river from the city of Fredericksburg, and Stafford Heights, directly across from Fredericksburg itself.

There were no bridges spanning the Rappahannock at these points because they had been destroyed by the Confederates just in case the Yankees might ever want to use them. That day had come, and the Northern forces were faced with either attempting to ford the river or staying on their own side. Gen. E. V. Sumner, commander of the Right Grand Division, the first one to reach the scene, wanted to make the ford, but orders quickly came from Burnside forbidding him to do so. If the river rose, rendering the fords impassable, Sumner and his men would be cut off, trapped on the Confederate side of the Rappahannock. Burnside had already sent for pontoon boats so that they could be used to build bridges across the river. In the meantime, the Yankees waited.

And waited.

———

THE MEN marching along the muddy road had to be footsore and weary, but no complaints came from their lips. Instead, they strode along in grim-faced silence, never lessening their pace unless they were ordered to do so by the officers who rode on horseback alongside them.

Will Brannon was one of those officers, and as he looked over the line of marching men in their ragged, threadbare clothes and bare feet, he felt a surge of pride. Stonewall Jackson's foot cavalry. They had come to be known as that during the summer campaign when they marched at dizzying speeds from engagement to engagement in the Shenandoah Valley and befuddled three Federal armies. They were indeed foot cavalry, the Stonewall Brigade, and Will was proud to be a part of it. No group of fighting men surpassed their courage and dedication to their cause. Some might come close, a few might even equal the Stonewall Brigade, but none would ever be better.

Now they were on their way to another fight, and after a couple of months of inactivity around Winchester, they were more than ready for action.

The order to halt and fall out for a brief rest came back along the column of marching men. "That's far enough, Darcy," Will called to Sgt. Darcy Bennett, his right-hand man in command of this company of the Thirty-third Virginia. Most companies were now led by lieutenants, but when Will had enlisted, right after the beginning of the war, there had been plenty of captains to go around.

A lot of those captains were dead now, Will reflected grimly as he swung down from the saddle of the rangy dun that had carried him through most of the war's campaigns. He looped the horse's reins over one of the bare branches of a bush and stretched, easing muscles sore from long hours on horseback. His side twinged, and so did his thigh, reminders of his wounds.

Jackson's men had come through Brandy Station, north of Culpeper on the Orange and Alexandria Railroad, then crossed the Rapidan River and passed north of the town of Chancellorsville on their way to Fredericksburg. Another few miles would see them at their destination. Will was a little puzzled that they had stopped to rest so close to where they were going. It seemed to him that it would have been better to push on and get there.

As soon as he had made sure his men were all right, he walked forward and soon understood why the column had halted. A summit meeting of sorts was going on next to the road. Will saw General Jackson in his long gray coat and campaign cap talking to Robert E. Lee and James Longstreet. The other two commanders must have ridden out from Fredericksburg. All three men were in earnest conversation. Several other officers stood close by, obviously keenly interested in what was being said but not wanting to intrude on the high-level discussion.

Will walked up, thumbing his hat to the back of his head, and nodded to William Caskie, an artillery captain he knew only slightly. Caskie quietly greeted him.

"What do you hear?" asked Will. "Are the Yankees waiting for us?"

"They're waiting, all right," Caskie replied. "From what I've overheard, they're just sitting across the river, not doing anything. No one seems to know why, unless they're waiting for reinforcements."

From everything Will had heard, the Union army was already considerably larger than the forces under Lee, Jackson, and Longstreet. If they were waiting for more men before attempting to cross the Rappahannock, then Burnside was running McClellan a close second when it came to moving slowly and carefully.

The conversation between the three generals broke up, and they went back to their horses. When Jackson had mounted up, he waved his arm forward and called, "Move out!" Gradually, the long column of men lurched into motion again.

A short time later, as the troops approached Fredericksburg from the west, Will was able to see the long dip to the south that the river made. The town was lined up neatly on the south bank, and about a mile behind it was a long ridge that paralleled the Rappahannock. Across the river was another such ridge. Will's keen eyes spotted movement on the ridge across the river, and when he took out his field glasses, he saw the Union batteries lined up along the front of the bluff. From there the Yankees had a commanding field of fire over the river.

But so did the Confederates who had placed their riflemen along the ridge on this side of the river. It was something of a standoff, Will thought. Whoever tried to cross the river first would be heading into a thicket of trouble.

Burnside had more than enough men to assault the Southern positions, however. As Will swept his glasses over the rest of the Union position, he estimated that their camp was at least twice as large as that of the Confederates, meaning that the Rebels were outnumbered by at least two to one.

The arrival of Jackson's corps would alter the odds a little, but the Yankees would still hold a clear numerical superiority. It was a good thing he and the rest of the Southern boys were better fighters, Will told himself as he put the field glasses away.

He heard a rider coming up behind him but didn't look around until a familiar voice said, "Like what you see?"

Will turned and grinned at his brother on the big silver gray stallion. "Not much," Will replied. "How are you, Mac?"

"All right," his brother replied.

"What are you doing here?" It had been weeks since the two had seen each other, and Will was glad to be reunited with him.

"General Stuart sent out the cavalry to escort you boys from the valley into camp." Mac gestured toward the riders who were forming into lines that flanked the long column of Jackson's men. "A gesture of respect from the mounted cavalry to the foot cavalry, I guess you could say."

Will kept his dun moving steadily as Mac rode beside him. "What do you hear about Burnside's plans?"

"I'm not sure he has any," Mac said with a dry laugh. "We figured he's been waiting for somebody to come along and build him a bridge over the river, but his pontoon boats showed up a couple of days ago and so far he still hasn't budged."

"They haven't started?"

Mac shook his head. "Not yet."

After a moment, Will predicted, "He'll get around to it. He didn't move three divisions to Fredericksburg just to have them sit there the rest of the winter."

"Are you sure about that?" asked Mac.

Will had to admit that he wasn't. Still, his instincts told him that Burnside had to move. He had to, or else risk being painted with the same brush that had tarred McClellan.

Jackson's men marched into the camp, skirting a rugged hill known as Marye's Heights. They passed above and behind the town of Fredericksburg and began pitching their tents in the flat land below the town, at the far right end of the defensive line. If they stayed in this position and if the Yankees attacked as everyone expected, the Stonewall Brigade would form the Confederate right.

"Who has the middle?" Will asked as Mac dismounted to help his brother set up a tent.

"Longstreet has the middle and the left," Mac said. "Hood, Pickett, and McLaws will take up most of the middle if there's any fighting, and Anderson will have the left."

Will grinned. "You must hear a lot, being Fitz Lee's aide."

"Enough to know what's going on," Mac admitted.

Will clapped him on the shoulder. "You're already a lieutenant. At the rate you're going, you'll be a general before this war is over, Mac."

"I hope not," Mac said fervently. "I hope it never lasts that long."

—⊶⊷—

THE UNIFORM jacket Titus was given had belonged to another soldier. He never asked what had happened to the previous owner, but judging from the small, roughly patched holes in the front and back of the tunic and the faded brown stains around them, it hadn't been anything good. Titus tried not to think about the fact that he was wearing a dead man's clothes.

The Georgians in Captain Stevens's company had accepted him grudgingly. That he could outshoot all of them was both resented and welcomed. None of them liked to admit that a Virginian might be better than a Georgian at anything, but having Titus fighting beside them might mean that a few more of them would come through the war alive.

Still, he had no close friends in the company, so it wasn't unusual for him to spend most of his time alone. On this bleak December day he sat with his back against the low stone wall at the bottom of Marye's Heights, smoking his pipe. The air was foggy, and whenever Titus blew out a cloud of gray pipe smoke, it vanished almost immediately into the mist. Even though he was on guard duty, there was no point in looking toward the Rappahannock River a couple of hundred yards away. He couldn't see more than a fourth of that distance.

A patchy layer of snow covered much of the ground along the river. The air was quite cold, and Titus pulled on the thin blanket he had wrapped about him, drawing it tighter around his shoulders. Twenty yards to his left, the soldier on duty at that position let out a loud snore. Titus glanced over and saw that the man's head had fallen forward on his chest as he slept. If any of the officers caught him sleeping, he would be in a great deal of trouble. Titus thought about calling over softly to him in an attempt to wake him up, then decided against it. He didn't owe him anything.

His hand slipped inside his tunic and his numb fingers fumbled with the small brown bottle there. He took it out, worked the cork loose, and took a quick nip. The whiskey warmed him slightly, but not much.

On a day like this, he thought, the best place to be was in a warm bed with an even warmer woman. Like Polly.

It was too damned bad that was never going to happen again.

Titus sipped from the bottle. He hadn't heard a word from Polly since he'd joined the army. That came as no surprise. She had made it clear on the day of their final, fateful argument that she was choosing her father over him. He was certain she no longer cared what happened to him, if indeed she ever really had. So even though she could have gotten a letter to him, he wasn't expecting one.

But no one else had written, either, and that hurt most of all. Nobody had so much as jotted him a few lines. Titus supposed they were still angry with him for deserting the farm and enlisting. They would never understand that he just couldn't stay there any longer. He could not bear to know that he was so close to Polly but could no longer have her.

So he hadn't minded when the army had packed up and left Culpeper to come to Fredericksburg. This was where the Yankees were now, and he had joined up to kill Yankees, after all.

Boots crunched on the snow nearby. A figure loomed up out of the fog, seeming almost supernaturally large as it towered over Titus. He started up from where he was sitting against the wall, already forming an excuse for not keeping an eye on the river and the Yankees on the other side of it. The man standing over him wore an officer's greatcoat and hat.

"Sorry, sir—" Titus began.

"Don't worry, Titus. I'm not here to see how good a soldier you are. I reckon I know the answer already."

Titus's hands tightened on the Sharps rifle. It was his personal rifle, the one he had brought with him from the farm. He figured he could kill Yankees with it better than anything else.

"Will?" he said in surprise.

"Yep," his eldest brother said. "Don't take on so. You can't be any more surprised to see me than I am to see you. You're supposed to be home, helping take care of the farm, not to mention that wife of yours."

Titus's lips pulled back in a grimace. "Then don't mention her," he snapped. "It'll be all right with me if you never say anything about her again."

"Finally chose her old man over you, did she?" asked Will, unknowingly echoing Titus's thoughts of a few minutes earlier.

"Shut up about Polly," said Titus, forgetting for the moment that he was talking to an officer. They weren't soldiers to each other right now; they were brothers. "How'd you know I was over here?"

"I heard somebody talking about a rifleman in Cobb's Brigade who's been picking off Yankee gunners at those batteries on Stafford Heights. They said his name was Brannon, and I figured it was too much of a coincidence to be anybody else." Will gestured toward the river and the ridge on the other side where the Union batteries were set up, even though nothing was visible in that direction at the moment except fog. "That's got to be a mile or more. A Sharps can carry that distance, but not many other rifles. And nobody's better with a Sharps than you. I thought I'd better come take a look at this famous marksman."

Titus propped a hip against the stone wall and shrugged. "I've taken some potshots at those Yankee bastards and been lucky a few times."

"You've got a natural talent. You never made a lucky shot in your life."

"Maybe not," Titus admitted.

Will moved a step closer to him. "What are you doing here, Titus? How could you run off and leave Ma and Henry and Cordelia like that?"

"Like what?" Titus barked back at him. "You mean like you and Mac did?"

Will lifted a hand and rubbed his face wearily. "You know why I left," he said. "I had to. And I didn't much like it when Mac joined the cavalry. You know that, too. Damn it, Titus, it's like the whole family is falling apart."

Titus shrugged. "War does that. Henry can take care of things at home, though. The family'll be all right."

"Until Henry runs off and joins the army, too."

Titus straightened away from the wall. "If he does that, he'll have a whippin' coming to him, and I'm just the fella to give it to him."

Will uttered a harsh laugh and said, "You don't understand, do you? One by one we've gone off to the war, assuming that the ones left behind would take care of things at home. What happens when there's nobody left to go and fight?"

"The womenfolk will be all right, I tell you." Titus gestured angrily toward the northwest. "They're way up yonder in Culpeper County, and the Yankees are *here*, Will. This is where the next fight's goin' to be."

"You're probably right about that. But there's no guarantee that the fighting won't wind up back home."

"There ain't no guarantees in anything," said Titus. "I remember a preacher sayin' 'Until death do you part,' but it didn't work out that way."

For a long moment, Will didn't say anything. Titus supposed he didn't have any argument. Finally, Will spoke quietly. "I could order you to go back home."

"The hell you could. I'm part of Cobb's Brigade, not the Thirty-third Virginia. You're not my commanding officer."

"I could order you as your older brother."

"I'm not goin' anywhere," Titus said flatly. "If you're so worried about the farm, why in blazes don't *you* go back there?" When Will didn't answer, Titus laughed. "Same reason I don't. You haven't killed enough Yankees yet, have you?"

"They're still here, aren't they?" Will said grimly.

"That's right. They're still here."

Will took a deep breath. "I'm disappointed in you, Titus, but I reckon I shouldn't have expected anything else. You never have cared much about what happens to anybody else."

The scornful words hit Titus painfully. He wanted to yell at Will that that wasn't true, but he knew it wouldn't do any good. Instead, through thinned lips that were growing numb from the cold, he said, "You think whatever you want, big brother. You just think whatever you want about me."

Will stared at him for a moment longer, than started to turn away. He paused to say, "You neglect your duty again, soldier, and you'll be in a lot of trouble."

"Yes sir, Captain, sir," Titus replied with a sneer.

This time Will turned sharply and stalked off into the fog. Under the circumstances, Titus was glad to see him go. One more bridge burned, he told himself. Until now he had gone out of his way to avoid meeting up with Will or Mac, but maybe that had been a mistake. Maybe it would have been better to have a showdown with his brothers and get it over with.

Suddenly, he heard voices out of the fog and realized they were coming from the direction of the river. As he turned toward the Rappahannock, Titus forgot about his personal problems. The voices from the river could mean only one thing:

The Yankees were coming.

Chapter Eighteen

TITUS LOOKED AT THE sentry who had been asleep earlier. The man was on his feet now, leaning forward over the stone wall. Titus figured the soldier had been roused by the argument between Will and him and was now trying to look as if he had been alert all the time.

"They're making a lot of noise over there," Titus called to him, and he jerked his head in a nod.

"I hear 'em, too," he called back. "Who do you reckon it is?"

Titus bit back the sarcastic reply that sprang to his lips. He might be fighting alongside that soldier in a few minutes; no point in antagonizing the man, he told himself. "Must be Yankees," he said. "There ain't none of us in that direction. This wall is the front line."

"What'll we do?" The other sentry sounded worried, as well he might considering how many Federal troops were on the other side of the river.

Titus came to a decision. "Go back and tell the corporal of the guard that the Yankees are up to something," he said.

"What about you?"

"I'll go take a look and see if I can find out what it is."

The other sentry stared at Titus in disbelief, then waved a hand toward the thick fog. "You're goin' out in that, knowin' there might be a hundred thousand Yankees waitin' for you?"

"There's not that many on this side of the river," Titus said confidently. "Couldn't be. They haven't had time to ferry that many across. Now go on like I told you."

Titus didn't stop to think that he was giving orders now, as if he were an officer, too. Finding out what the Yankees were doing just seemed like a job that was tailor-made for him. Impatiently, he waved the other sentry into motion, then swung his legs over the wall and started slipping forward cautiously.

In the sky above him, the thick clouds and fog were suddenly pierced by a shaft of sunlight. The glare of it seemed almost blindingly bright after the gloom that had held Fredericksburg in its grip all morning. Titus winced and narrowed his eyes. The break in the overcast lasted only a couple of seconds, and then the fog closed in again, seemingly as impenetrable as ever.

That might have been just a fluke, thought Titus, or it was possible the sun was beginning to burn away the clouds and fog. If that happened—and if there were indeed Federal troops on this side of the river—he might be letting himself in for trouble. He was counting on the fog to hide him, just as the Yankees were probably counting on it to conceal whatever they were doing.

As Titus came closer to the river he began to hear other noises: the creaking of ropes as they hauled something heavy, the slap of water against what sounded like the sides of boats, orders called out in low voices. He trotted past a couple of warehouses that now stood empty. Fredericksburg was at the head of the navigable waters of the Rappahannock and had once been the center of a bustling river trade. In more peaceful times, three-masted schooners would have been docked at the city's wharves and the warehouses along the waterfront would have been full of goods. The war had changed all that.

The clouds shifted and broke apart again as Titus reached the edge of one of the docks. Again sunlight slanted down through the opening. Instinctively, Titus sought cover, crouching down behind a pair of rotting crates stacked atop each other. He gripped the Sharps tightly as he peered around the corner of the crates.

Sunlight played over the surface of the river, rolling back the fog. At this point, the Rappahannock varied between 400 and 440 feet wide. Titus had no trouble making out the pontoon boats that were being hauled into position along the opposite shore by the Yankees. Union soldiers clambered over the pontoons, laying down wide, thick timbers to form the beginnings of a bridge.

Burnside had finally gotten up off his backside, Titus thought. The Yankees were moving at last. This probably wasn't the only bridge they were building this morning, and if they were able to span the Rappahannock, the troops could cross much more quickly than if they had to be ferried over. That speed was necessary if an attack on the Confederate defenses was to have any chance of succeeding.

"Thought you'd sneak up on us, eh, boys?" Titus muttered to himself as he watched the Yankee engineers go about their work. A humorless grin stretched across his face as he lifted the Sharps to his shoulder. "We'll just see about that."

He drew back the hammer of the heavy rifle and aimed toward the pontoon boats. A few minutes earlier, he had wanted the fog to remain in place so it would hide him from the Union soldiers, but now he hoped the sunlight wouldn't go away. The illumination made aiming the Sharps a lot easier. He drew a bead on a man who was carrying one end of a thick timber that would be laid down to help form the bridge.

Titus inhaled, held the breath, adjusted his aim slightly, and squeezed the trigger. The Sharps boomed, sounding a bit muffled by the overcast but still loud. The butt kicked hard against his shoulder, but he was used to the recoil. He was used to the smoke that came from the barrel of the weapon, too, and knew how to squint past it to see the results of his shot.

The Yankee jerked violently, dropped his end of the timber, and spun halfway around before tumbling off the pontoon boat and splashing into the river. Titus heard angry, frightened shouts from the man's companions.

He ignored them. He was already reloading. With practiced ease, he closed the Sharps's breech and raised the rifle again.

The bridge extended about thirty feet into the river. Some of the blue-clad soldiers were scrambling over the bridge planks toward the riverbank; others hunkered down where they were. A few glared defiantly at the opposite bank of the river. An officer bellowed orders, trying to get the men back to work.

Titus shot him in the head. The man's skull seemed to explode, sending his hat spinning high into the air. He toppled off the pontoon.

Still grinning, Titus reached into his cartridge box for another round. As he reloaded, he heard another shot ring out from a rifle on this side of the river. A glance at the Yankees told him that one of them was staggering, hand clasped to a bullet-shattered shoulder. Another Rebel sniper joined in the work, Titus thought.

Maybe they ought to have a contest to see how many of those damned Yankees they could kill. That would liven things up a mite, Titus told himself.

FOR THE next half-hour, the sound of shots filled the air along the river as sixteen hundred sharpshooters from William Barksdale's Mississippi brigade moved forward to harass the Union bridge-building effort. For a while, the Yankees stayed at it stubbornly, but as more and more of them were knocked off the pontoons by sniper fire, they gradually abandoned their task. The clouds continued to roll back, and the fog evaporated in the strong sunshine. As Titus looked up and down the river, he could see that he had been right in his guess: the Yankees had tried to span the Rappahannock in half a dozen different spots. Each try had failed, thanks to the deadly fire of Titus and the Mississippians.

Titus wondered where Will was. His big brother wouldn't be so high and mighty now if he could see how Titus was doing. He had killed or badly wounded at least a dozen of the blue-clad soldiers.

The firing died away as the last of the Yankees fled, leaving the pontoon boats where they were. Lacking human targets, Titus began drawing a bead on one of the pontoons. It wouldn't float so good if he could manage to hole it below the waterline, he thought. He squeezed off the shot and saw water kick into the air where the heavy lead pellet struck, but he had to wait for a couple of minutes before he could be certain that the pontoon was gradually sinking in the river. He grinned triumphantly.

The big guns in one of the Federal artillery batteries atop Stafford Heights suddenly roared. Titus's eyes widened in surprise. He heard a menacing whine and flattened himself, pressing his face against the rough planks of the dock and covering his head as best he could with his arms after dropping the Sharps beside him.

The whine grew ear-splittingly loud, then the warehouse exploded that was across the waterfront street from the dock where Titus lay. The blast shook the dock underneath him and the sound slammed against his ears, making him cry out in pain and shock. Debris from the explosion pelted around him. A piece of board came spinning through the air and struck him in the back. Titus yelled again.

More explosions rocked the waterfront as Titus rolled over and staggered to his feet. He scooped up the rifle and started to run. He was out in the open with no protection from the Yankee bombardment. Another shell burst not far to his right, and the impact nearly tumbled him off his feet. Somehow he managed to keep running away from the river.

The Yankees had enough cannon on the ridge to flatten every building along the river if they wanted to, Titus told himself. The smart thing to do would be to pull back to the stone wall where he was supposed to be. But if all the Rebel sharpshooters ran away, the Yankees would be able to build their bridges unhindered. Titus didn't think it would be a good idea to let that happen.

He hurried along an alley between two of the warehouses. The bombardment continued as blasts sounded from both his left and his right. Luck had been with him so far; he had avoided a direct hit. If one of those bursting shells struck him, there wouldn't be enough of him left to scrape up, Titus thought grimly.

There were houses behind the warehouses along the water-front. Titus ran into the front yard of one of them as he saw a man standing on the porch beckoning urgently to him. Many of the residents of Fredericksburg had fled the town when the Yankees showed up on the other side of the river, but here was one stubborn townsman who had stayed behind. He called, "Come on in here, soldier! You'll be safe inside."

Titus knew that wasn't true. If the Union bombardment could flatten those big stone warehouses, it could make kindling out of a frame house like this one. But Titus ran up to the house anyway, since he didn't really have anywhere else to go.

The man, stocky with curly brown hair, held the door open. Titus hurried past him into a foyer. At that instant, a shell landed in the street directly in front of the house. The blast threw Titus forward and nearly knocked him off his feet. He caught his balance and turned around, only to see the man who had waved him up here lying face down across the doorsill in a rapidly spreading pool of blood. With a shocked cry, Titus dropped to one knee and grasped the man's shoulder to roll him over. To his horror, he saw that the man's throat was gone, ripped out probably by a flying piece of canister from the bursting artillery shell. The man's eyes stared sightlessly up at the ceiling of his foyer.

Titus grated a curse. This man had died because he had come to his door to offer sanctuary. Of course, any second another shell could land on the house itself and reduce it to rubble, he told himself. Still, he couldn't help but feel a twinge of guilt.

He pulled the man inside the foyer and slammed the door shut. He looked around, saw that a parlor opened up to the right. It was well furnished, with plenty of homely touches that told Titus a woman lived here as well. He called, "Anybody home?"

There was no answer. The dead man probably had sent his wife to stay with relatives or some such, but he had stayed behind for some reason. That decision had cost him his life.

Quickly, Titus searched the house. It was indeed empty. A window on the second floor offered him a good view of the riverfront and the devastation that the Yankees were raining down upon it. Clouds of powder smoke lay thick over the Rappahannock, having drifted down from the Union batteries on the heights. More smoke came from warehouses and other buildings along the waterfront that had caught on fire from the explosions. Some of the structures had been blasted into nothingness, leaving only gaping craters behind. Others still stood, but without their roofs and huge sections of their walls.

Faced with a bombardment such as this, all a man could do was hunker down, wait it out, and hope for the best, Titus told himself. He pulled a chair up to the window and sat down after using the butt of his rifle to knock out the remaining pieces of glass that hung in the pane. The window had been broken by the nearby explosion, and if there was another blast close by, Titus didn't want any of those razor-sharp shards flying at him.

He placed the Sharps across his lap and took out his bottle. There wasn't much whiskey left in it. He swallowed what there was, replaced the cork, and put the bottle back inside his pocket. As the warmth of the liquor spread through him, he was glad the bottle hadn't gotten broken earlier. The whiskey offered at least a little solace.

Through providence or blind luck, no more shells exploded near the house where Titus sat and watched the bombardment. The shelling continued for another ninety minutes. Finally, the cannon fell silent, and an eerie calm drifted down over the waterfront. A gentle wind gradually brushed away the smoke, revealing the hellish destruction that remained of the waterfront. The river cleared of smoke as well. As the gray haze cleared, Titus abruptly leaned forward when he saw movement resume on the far side of the Rappahannock.

The Yankee engineers were working their way back out onto the pontoon boats, carrying timbers for the bridges they were once more trying to build.

"Those damn fools," Titus said aloud. He cocked the Sharps and rested the barrel on the window sill to steady it. The range was a little longer now, since he had retreated to this house, but with the added elevation of being on the second floor and the nice shooting platform the broken-out window provided, he knew he could make the shot. He centered his sights on one of the tiny figures moving out onto the pontoons.

The Sharps roared.

Across the river, the Union soldier went flying backward as if a giant had just punched him in the chest. He fell lifelessly into the water.

Titus started to reload, and he smiled as he heard the crack of more shots coming from the southern side of the river. Some of the sharpshooters surely had been killed in the bombardment.

But not all of them, Titus thought. No sir, not all of them.

SEVERAL MILES to the southeast, near the spot where Massaponax Creek ran into the Rappahannock, Gen. Thomas J. Jackson had set up his headquarters. The ridges that paralleled the river farther north and west tapered down to nothing at this point, so there was only an open plain about two miles wide between the Confederate forces and the river. The Southern pickets were alert for any sign of an attack, and an air of urgency gripped the camp as the Union artillery opened up on the Fredericksburg waterfront. This could be a prelude to a general assault, Jackson's officers thought.

Instead, word swiftly came by courier from General Longstreet that the Yankees were merely attempting to dislodge the Rebel sharpshooters who were hindering the building of their pontoon bridges. When Will Brannon heard that, he had mixed emotions. He was glad the Yankees weren't attacking, but he knew his brother Titus was up there where the bombardment was concentrated.

Will was standing near one of the campfires, absorbing what warmth he could because the cold always made his old wounds ache more, when he saw Mac approaching on the stallion. Mac lifted a hand in greeting, then swung down from the saddle and joined Will by the fire, leading the horse by its reins.

"Did you find Titus?" he asked. "Was it him we'd heard about?"

Will nodded. "It was him, all right," he said heavily.

"Damn it!" The exclamation was unusual coming from Mac, providing a good indication of how upset he was. "He ran off and left Ma and Henry and Cordelia alone there on the farm?"

"Left his wife, too," said Will. "There was some sort of big trouble between him and Polly and Ebersole. I reckon that was what really made him decide to enlist."

"He could've just gone home. He didn't have to abandon the farm."

"We did," Will said curtly.

"That's—" Mac stopped, grimaced, and then went on, "I was about to say that was different, but maybe it wasn't. We did what we felt we had to do, and I reckon Titus did, too."

"Doesn't mean we have to like it or agree with it."

"No, it doesn't." Mac shook his head wearily. "Where did you find him?"

Will waved a hand vaguely toward the town, where the Federal bombardment was still going on. "Up there."

Mac's eyes widened. "You mean he's in the middle of that shelling?"

"He was close by there when I left him. I don't know where he is now."

Mac took off his cap and raked his fingers through his brown hair. "Maybe one of us should go look for him," he suggested.

Will looked sharply at him and asked, "What are your orders?"

"Well . . . General Stuart's holding the cavalry in reserve right now and sending out patrols on scouting missions."

"So you're liable to have work to do before the day's over."

Mac shrugged. "Maybe. Fitz told me I could visit you but not wander off too far."

"Same here," Will grunted. "Our orders are to maintain our position and see what the Yankees do. Titus is just going to have to take his chances. It was his decision to enlist."

Will knew it sounded hardhearted to talk about their brother like that, but that was the way it had to be. He and Mac were soldiers, and their duty had to come first.

"Sure," Mac said after a moment. "Titus takes his chances, just like the rest of us." His voice was hollow, though, and he didn't sound at all convinced of what he was saying.

Another volley roared out from the Union batteries, then the big guns fell silent. Both Brannon brothers turned toward the river at the sudden quiet.

"You reckon they're through?" asked Mac.

"I don't know. Maybe they've stopped so they can see if they got all the sharpshooters cleaned out." Titus had surely been one of those, Will thought. Had he been able to find a safe place to wait out that awful shelling?

A moment later, they both heard the faint, distant crack of rifle fire, and a grin broke out on Mac's face. "Some of our boys are still there," he said.

Will nodded. What Mac said was true enough . . . but there was no way of knowing if one of the survivors was Titus.

———

THIS DIDN'T hardly seem like war, Titus thought as he reloaded the Sharps. It was more like shooting squirrels out of a tree. All he had to do was draw a bead, squeeze off a shot, watch a dead Yankee tumble into the river, reload, and do it all again.

The Union engineers weren't so stubborn this time, however. After only a few minutes, they abandoned their efforts to span the river and pulled back. Titus was glad for the respite. It would give the barrel of his rifle a chance to cool down.

He wished he had a little more whiskey.

A short time later, the Yankees started moving around again. This time they didn't come creeping out onto the pontoons. Instead, regular boats put out from the far shore and were rowed quickly toward Fredericksburg. Titus squinted toward the river, trying to make out what the Yankees were doing. The boats, more than a dozen in all, were crammed full of soldiers and bristled with rifles. The bombardment hadn't managed to drive out the Confederate sharpshooters, so now they were sending over troops to take on the task. That would mean house-to-house, maybe even hand-to-hand fighting.

Titus chuckled in anticipation. He was ready for them. He lifted the Sharps. *Might as well give 'em a little welcome before they get all the way across,* he thought.

All along the riverfront, the sharpshooters began concentrating their fire on the Union boats. The Yankees were packed into the craft so tightly that when they were hit they didn't topple overboard but just sagged against their comrades. Some of the men at the oars were killed, but each time the dead man was pulled out of the way and someone took his place. The river crossing had to be hell every foot of the way, but still the Yankees came on.

Titus bit back a curse. More boats were being launched on the other side of the river. The sharpshooters wouldn't be able to stop all of them. Some of the bluecoats were going to reach Fredericksburg.

Titus stood up and clattered down the stairs to the first floor. "Sorry, mister," he muttered as he stepped over the body of the dead homeowner and went out the front door. He didn't know, would never know, the man's name. Just one more anonymous casualty of war, Titus thought.

He ran toward the docks, dodging shell craters as he did so. When he reached the wharves, the leading boats were only about fifty yards away. Titus threw the Sharps to his shoulder and fired. He was close enough now that he was able to see the crimson stain suddenly blossom on the front of a Yankee's uniform. Some of the men in the boat returned his fire, and he ducked back around the corner of a warehouse as bullets thudded into what was left of a half-collapsed brick wall.

After reloading the Sharps, he ventured a look and saw that the boats were almost to the wharves. He fired again, a shot that was answered by a hail of lead. There were too many. He and the other sharpshooters who were left could kill half of the Northerners, and they would still be outnumbered four or five to one. This attack, though costing a high toll in Union lives, was going to accomplish what the shelling had not been able to do.

Titus slid another cartridge into the breech and slapped it closed, then spun around as he heard hoofbeats thundering toward him. Someone shouted, "Titus!" His finger eased on the trigger as he recognized the cavalryman riding along the rubble-strewn alley between a couple of devastated warehouses.

"Mac!" Titus called. "Over here!"

Titus had no idea what Mac was doing here, but at the moment he didn't care. Mac extended a hand as he rode up and reined the big stallion to a twisting halt. Titus grabbed his brother's wrist. He heard the Yankees yelling close by and knew they were probably piling onto the riverbank. A second later, as Mac was hauling him up onto the back of the stallion, a bullet whipped past Titus's ear.

Titus barely had time to slide his free arm around Mac's waist as he settled himself behind the saddle. Then Mac wheeled the stallion and heeled it into a gallop. More slugs whistled around them as they raced along the alley.

A part of Titus wanted to turn around, to face the Yankees head-on and show them how a Southerner could fight. Show them how a Southerner could die, more likely, he thought. For now the odds were just too high.

The prospect of death didn't scare Titus. He would have almost welcomed it, because that would mean he would no longer feel the incredible pain of losing Polly. But if he was dead, he couldn't kill any more Yankees, and he wasn't through with that yet. Not by a long shot.

"Thanks, Mac!" he shouted in his brother's ear as they both bent low over the stallion's back, giving the Yankees a smaller target.

Mac didn't say anything. He just sent the stallion soaring in a perfect jump over a pile of rubble that blocked the alley. They turned a corner, and then they were gone.

Chapter Nineteen

AFTER SITTING ACROSS THE river from Fredericksburg for several weeks without budging, once Gen. Ambrose Burnside decided to move, he was not going to allow anything to stop him. He had called on the commanders of the three Grand Divisions to provide volunteers for the highly hazardous task of rooting out the Confederate sharpshooters, and although many of them died in the process, that was what the Union soldiers did. By midafternoon, after several hours of furious house-to-house fighting, the Federals were in control of the riverfront area on both sides of the Rappahannock.

With the danger from the Rebel snipers disposed of, the engineers were able to return to their bridge building. Their work continued the rest of the day and stretched on into the night, but eventually the six pontoon bridges were completed.

Come morning, the Union army could begin to cross the river.

———

TITUS HUNKERED on his heels beside the campfire and sipped from a cup of what was supposed to be coffee but was mostly burnt grain. It would have tasted a lot better with a healthy dollop of spirits in it, he thought, but at least it was better than nothing. The coffee was warm, like the campfire, and the night was cold.

Mac had gone back to rejoin Stuart's cavalry after dropping Titus near the stone wall at the base of Marye's Hill. From the way Mac talked, Titus had a feeling that his brother had disobeyed orders by riding into Fredericksburg to look for him. Mac had gone first to Cobb's division, where some of the soldiers had told him that Titus had slipped into the town to harass

273

the Yankees. Luck had led him to Titus near the newly landed Union troops.

Titus hoped Mac wouldn't get in trouble for what he had done. At the same time, he was glad Mac had been there to pull him out of that tight spot. If he had stayed at the riverfront to put up a fight, he would have surely been either killed or captured.

Captain Stevens came over to the campfire. Titus stood up and saluted, but Stevens quickly returned the salute and waved him back down. "I hear you had quite an adventure today, Private Brannon," he said as he sat down on a camp stool.

"I picked off a few more Yankees," admitted Titus.

"Perhaps as many as a score of them, judging from the stories going around the camp."

Titus shrugged. "I didn't keep count," he said honestly. "Thought about it, but there just didn't seem to be time."

"That's a lot of men."

"A lot of Yankees, beggin' your pardon, Cap'n."

Now that he thought about it, Titus realized that he *had* killed twenty or more Union soldiers today. Twenty men who had awakened that morning with hopes and dreams of their own, families and memories, living and breathing and just being human, all snuffed out now. Snuffed out one by one because Titus Brannon had moved the index finger of his right hand an eighth of an inch. That was all it took to pull the trigger of the Sharps.

Looking at it like that, he should have felt bad about it, Titus supposed, or at least felt *something*. But he just drank the rest of the so-called coffee and dashed the dregs into the fire. They were only Yankees, after all.

"I've spoken with General Cobb about your actions today, Brannon," the captain went on. "He agrees with me that your efforts should be recognized in some way. So as of now, you're Corporal Brannon."

Titus grunted. If they'd wanted to thank him for shooting Yankees, he would have appreciated a bottle of whiskey a lot more than a promotion. But he merely nodded and said, "Thank you, sir. I'll try to live up to it."

"You'll have your chance," Stevens said dryly. "You'll be one of the men charged with holding that stone wall when the Yankees attack tomorrow or the next day."

That news didn't surprise or dismay Titus. The wall was a good position, plenty thick enough to stop bullets and a solid place to rest his rifle while he was aiming at the enemy. He nodded and said again, "Thank you, sir."

After a moment, Stevens said, "You know, I think you're going to make a hell of a soldier, Brannon. Nothing gets to you, does it?"

Titus thought about Polly, then tamped the pain down deep inside him and said, "No sir. Not much."

———

THERE WAS fog again the next morning, but that did not stop the Federal forces from beginning their advance across the newly built pontoon bridges. Often, when stealth was called for, dirt was laid down on the planks of such bridges to muffle the sound of thousands of feet tramping across them. In this case, the Rebels knew quite well that the bridges were in place and being used, so there was no need for secrecy. Through the fog, the Southerners could hear the tramp-tramp-tramp of marching men all morning long.

The crossing continued even after the fog was burned away by the pale winter sun, just as on the previous day. Brigade after brigade of Union troops entered Fredericksburg, occupying the mostly empty city that had been half-destroyed by the bombardment of the day before. The Confederate artillery on the heights behind the town was just out of effective range, so the Yankees didn't have to worry much on that score. And since the snipers and skirmishers had been driven out the day before, they faced no real danger. There were a few isolated shots as the day passed, but for the most part nothing happened except that Burnside finally succeeded in shifting 130,000 men from one side of the river to the other.

Night fell again, and the Yankees made camp wherever they could in the devastated city. Nathan Hatcher found himself alone, as usual, huddled beside a small fire he had made using pieces of shattered wood from the wall of a destroyed house. He looked at the rubble surrounding him and wished it had never had to come to this. War was terrible.

But not as terrible as slavery, not as terrible as fracturing the delicate union of the nation, he told himself stubbornly. That could not be tolerated.

Since his beating at the hands of Corporal Barcroft and the other troopers on the foraging detail, Nathan had been careful not to let himself get drawn into such a trap again. He stayed by himself as much as possible, and the other soldiers were more than willing not to associate with him. Given his background as a Virginian, they were never going to trust him, he thought. And although they shared a common goal—preserving the Union—he found that he disliked the Yankees as much as they disliked him.

There were other campfires only a few yards away, but no one came over from any of them to join Nathan. He boiled water to make a cup of extremely weak coffee, ate his meager rations by himself. When he was finished, he reached inside his jacket and took out a small book to read for a few minutes by the fading light of the fire. It was a Bible, and reading the verses made him think of the Baptist church back in Culpeper, and that made him think of Cordelia Brannon.

Cordelia! He missed her so badly, missed the talks they had had and the sound of her laughter, missed as well the way she had felt in his arms and the warm, sweet taste of her mouth when she kissed him. There could have been something real, something solid and powerful between them, if the war hadn't interfered.

Right now he would have settled for the briefest touch of her hand . . .

"Ow!" he exclaimed as someone kicked his leg.

"On your feet, Reb," Lieutenant Baxter said harshly. "You've got sentry duty tonight."

Nathan scrambled up, snatching his rifle from the ground beside him as he did so. "Yes sir," he acknowledged.

"You'd better keep your eyes open, Hatcher. You know how those damned inbred Johnny Rebs like to skulk around."

"Yes sir," Nathan forced himself to say.

Baxter started to turn away then stopped and said, "You know, I think we'll be going into battle tomorrow. Think you'll be able to kill those Reb cousins of yours—or are you going to turn tail and run?"

Baxter wanted him to desert. Nathan knew that. Baxter would have liked nothing better than to catch him trying to run away. The lieutenant had probably expected that to happen after the incident with Barcroft. But Nathan had been determined not to give Baxter any excuse to cause him more trouble.

"I'll do my duty, sir," he said.

Baxter grunted. "See that you do." He stalked off into the night.

Nathan trudged away from what was left of his fire, heading for the picket lines where he would report to the sergeant of the guard. He had heard all the talk today about how tomorrow they were going to roust the Rebels and drive them back away from the Rappahannock. Tonight might well be his last night on earth.

He wished he could see Cordelia again, just one more time.

———

THE FOG was back again the next morning, bringing with it the usual dank chill. Mac paused to rub his hands together for warmth, then continued with the task of saddling the stallion. The rest of Stuart's cavalry was getting ready to mount up.

From where he was, near the mouth of Massaponax Creek, Mac could look northwestward along the Rappahannock. Hamilton's Crossing, with a small hill behind it, was closest to him.

That was where the bulk of Jackson's forces were concentrated. Mac hadn't seen or spoken to Will this morning, but he supposed his older brother was over there somewhere, waiting for the Union attack like the rest of them.

Beyond Hamilton's Crossing was the town of Fredericksburg itself, its once neat streets now littered with rubble from the shelling and serving as a haven for the Yankee soldiers who had crossed the river the day before. Behind the town ran the long ridge, bristling with Confederate cannon and rifles and bayonets, and at the limits of Mac's vision rose Marye's Hill. That was the area where Mac had left Titus a couple of days earlier. Titus was probably still there, huddled behind that low stone wall with the rest of his company.

Fitz Lee cantered his horse over as Mac swung up onto the stallion's back. "Ready for some action today?" asked Lee. He sounded almost eager for battle.

"Yes sir," Mac replied. "You're convinced the Yankees will attack?"

"Burnside didn't go to so much trouble to get them on this side of the river without meaning to bring the fight to us," Lee said with a decisive nod. "They'll come, never you fear."

Mac wasn't worried that the Yankees would *not* attack, but he didn't plan on pointing that out to Fitz Lee. The young brigadier lived for battle, like Stuart and so many of the other cavalrymen. Mac was sure that Lee felt fear just like anyone else; he was human, after all. But Lee was able to put that fear aside and give himself over to the excitement of the moment, glorying in the thrill of combat. Mac didn't know but what that was a better way to be. Worrying certainly didn't accomplish anything. He needed to capture some of that devil-may-care sort of flair for himself. Maybe after this battle was over, he would see about getting himself a colorful bandanna to wear . . .

The fog began to lift. Mac took out his watch and glanced at it. The time was just after nine o'clock in the morning of December 13, 1862.

—⊶⊷—

IF NOT for the fact that men would soon be killing one another, the fields between the Rappahannock River and the Confederate lines at Hamilton's Crossing would be a beautiful sight this morning, Will thought as he sat on horseback and looked out over the ground. The fog had burned away, leaving the sun to shine down brilliantly on the thin layer of snow. The sunlight struck reflections from the snow and from the bayonets of the rank upon rank of Union troops who were lined up several hundred yards away, ready to move toward the Confederate line.

Will had come forward to get an idea of what the situation might be. His company, under the watchful eye of Sgt. Darcy Bennett, was still in the rear along with the rest of the Stonewall Brigade. Will didn't like it, but for now he and his men would be held in reserve. Given the fact that they were so badly outnumbered by the Federal forces, however, Will was confident they would be needed before the day was over.

Movement to his left caught his eye, and he turned his head to see Jackson riding toward him. Jackson, who normally wore a rumpled old greatcoat and a battered campaign cap, was turned out this morning in an obviously new uniform. The gray trousers and tunic were crisply pressed and spotless; the gray hat on Jackson's head fairly shone from the brushing it had been given. He reined in next to Will and said with a faint smile, "You see me garbed in new raiment this morning, Captain Brannon."

"Yes sir," Will said. "I, ah, noticed."

"The uniform was a gift from General Stuart, and I thought to please him by wearing it. I dispensed with the scarlet sash and the ostrich plume on the hat, however."

Will looked down at his horse for a second in the hope that Jackson wouldn't see the wide grin that played over his face. While such finery as the general described would look all right on the dashing Jeb Stuart, Will couldn't imagine Stonewall Jackson wearing such foofaraws.

The general gestured toward the distant Yankees. "Yonder are the Philistines, Captain, and it falls to us to smite them."

"Yes sir." Will thought the general sounded even more like a preacher today than usual. "I reckon we'll smite 'em just fine."

"We certainly will. I am inspecting our positions, so I suppose I should continue. God's will be done. Good morning to you, Captain."

"Good morning, sir." Will saluted. Jackson returned the salute and rode off, still alone with no adjutant or circle of staff officers around him. Will supposed Jackson thought he could best judge the readiness of his men alone.

They were as ready as they were going to be, Will told himself. If they'd had a few more days, they could have dug some trenches and thrown up some earthworks, but it didn't really matter. The Confederate defenders had the best position. The Yankees would have to come at them in the open.

That was exactly what was beginning to happen, Will saw. Several Yankee officers rode out in front of the assembled ranks and began reading from documents they held up in front of them. Reading the orders for the day, Will told himself. Those orders would send the Northerners marching straight into the teeth of the enemy.

Will waited where he was until he saw the Federals start forward, marching precisely and in neat rows. Their musicians began to play. Moving up alongside the Union infantry came the field artillery. From the heights on the other side of the river, the boom of cannon could be heard, and smoke began to rise. With a whistle and a roar, the first Yankee shell slammed into the field well in front of the Union advance. The Federal gunners were trying to clear the way for the troops. A few moments later, the Yankee field artillery opened up as well, but they were joined by the Confederate batteries. Shells began to rain down on the Yankees. A long, ragged volley of rifle fire ripped out from the Confederate lines. The Yankees, caught out in the open, began to fall.

The carnage was well underway. Will turned his horse and rode back toward his men, knowing that their turn to take part in the killing would come soon enough.

—⟨⟩—

A HARSH laugh came from Titus's mouth as he knelt behind the stone wall. The barrel of the Sharps rested on top of the wall and was pointed toward the long ranks of blue-uniformed men who marched out of Fredericksburg and started in perfect formation across the open ground between the town and the ridge.

"Look at 'em," Titus said. "Look at those stupid Yankee bastards. They're comin' right at us."

To his right, another trooper in butternut licked his lips nervously. "Yeah."

"Don't worry," Titus assured him. "They'll never get this far. We'll cut them down before they can reach us."

"You think so?"

Titus patted the stock of the Sharps. "I know so."

Captain Stevens rode up behind his company. Titus glanced over his shoulder and saw that the captain had drawn his saber. "Hold your fire until they're closer, boys!" called Stevens. "I know you could start picking them off now, but we want them good and close."

Titus eared back the hammer of the Sharps and settled his cheek against the smooth wood of the stock. The rattling strains of martial music came faintly to his ears. The Yankees could play their drums and fifes, he thought, and they could sure march pretty, but those things weren't going to do them a damned bit of good today.

Suddenly, firing broke out in the distance. Titus heard the crackle of musket and rifle fire that was punctuated by the booming of artillery. The sounds of battle came from the southeast along the Rappahannock. The Federal forces must have tried to attack there first, Titus told himself. Down there was where Will and Mac were, Will with Jackson's brigade, Mac with Stuart's cavalry. Titus hoped they were getting in on the fight. As the minutes passed and Captain Stevens continued to order the men to hold their fire, Titus began to grow jealous. His finger on the trigger of the Sharps wanted to get to work.

With a huge roar, the cannons on the heights behind the stone wall opened up. At almost the same instant, the leading edge of the marching ranks of Union troops reached a drainage ditch that cut across the field. Titus could see the ditch from where he was, but evidently the Yankees had had no idea it was there. Several men in the front ranks tumbled into the ditch, unable to stop in time to avoid it. That threw the march into confusion that turned into utter chaos a second later as the shells began to burst among them.

"Let 'em have it!" shouted Captain Stevens.

At last! Titus thought exultantly. He aimed the barrel of his rifle toward the drainage ditch, and as one of the Yankees scrambled up out of it, Titus drew a bead on him and stroked the trigger. The Sharps roared and kicked against his shoulder, and less than half a heartbeat later, the Yankee's head exploded in a spray of crimson and gray and white.

Titus reloaded as powder smoke began to drift along the wall, looking like tendrils of the fog that had hung over the landscape earlier. It smelled a lot worse than fog. Its acrid tang bit at Titus's nose. He was used to the smell and ignored it as he got ready to fire again.

The Confederate gunners continued to pound the field in front of the heights. The exploding shells gouged out huge holes in the earth and blew the Yankee soldiers into pieces of something that no longer resembled humanity. Titus saw men flying through the air, their blue uniforms aflame, and land in smoldering heaps. It was a terrible slaughter, and Titus contributed to it by picking off several of the Yankees as they rushed around looking for any sort of shelter, none of which was to be found.

Each time Titus squeezed the trigger of the Sharps and saw one of the enemy tumble to the ground, he felt a hot rush of excitement go through him. This was what he had been born to do, he realized. He killed and killed again and then killed some more. He was loading and firing so fast that the barrel of the Sharps began to glow a cherry red. When he saw that, he grimaced in disgust. He wasn't ready to stop shooting.

If he didn't, however, the barrel would melt and then he wouldn't be able to shoot Yankees at all. He pulled the weapon back and withdrew, falling back to the other side of the sunken road behind the stone wall. Another man took his place.

Captain Stevens was still riding back and forth, excitement shining on his face. "Brannon!" he called. "Are you hurt?"

"No sir," Titus replied. "Just giving my rifle a rest." He held up the Sharps so that Stevens could see the barrel. The captain nodded in understanding, then suddenly jerked forward in his saddle. He was facing toward Titus, so Titus was able to see Stevens's eyes widen in shock and pain. The captain opened his mouth to speak, but if he said anything, Titus couldn't hear it. He saw the blood that welled from the corners of the man's mouth, though. A second later, Stevens toppled out of the saddle and fell to the ground in a limp sprawl that told Titus he was dead. Titus saw the stain on the captain's coat where a bullet had bored into his body.

So some of the Yankees were putting up a fight after all, Titus thought. They should have just turned tail and run. He wrapped his fingers around the barrel of the Sharps, checking to see if it had cooled off enough for him to resume firing. He decided that it had, so he headed back to the stone wall, not even looking down as he strode past the sprawled body of his captain.

Chapter Twenty

NATHAN SWALLOWED HARD, WISHING he could get some saliva in his mouth. It remained as dry as cotton, however. His fingers clenched harder on his rifle each time the big guns on the heights roared out another volley.

He stood not far from the river, waiting nervously as he had waited all morning with his company. They had not been among the first men ordered forward but had been held in reserve instead. The cannonade had started around midmorning, followed within moments by the sounds of rifle fire, but from where they were on the outskirts of Fredericksburg, Nathan and his fellow troopers could not see exactly what was happening. The air above the open ground between the town and the ridge where the Confederates were waiting was too clogged with smoke to permit a good view. Nathan knew, however, that the Rebel shells were falling on the field, and those terrible explosions had to be taking a toll.

He wasn't the only one aware of that. He heard someone mutter, "They must be cutting those poor bastards to pieces." A glance confirmed that the words had come from Corporal Barcroft. Nathan blinked in surprise as he saw Barcroft lick his lips worriedly. He hadn't thought that Barcroft had any fear of the enemy in him, only hatred.

Barcroft looked around and spotted Nathan watching him. Instantly, the big corporal's attitude changed. He stiffened, and his head lifted defiantly. "What the hell are you lookin' at, Reb?" he demanded.

"Nothing," murmured Nathan.

The cannon on Stafford Heights thundered again as they flung their shells toward the battlefield. Barcroft laughed harshly. "Hear that?" he rasped at Nathan. "Our gunners are blowin' those damned Rebs to pieces."

It might well be the other way around, Nathan considered, as Barcroft had just said when he thought no one was listening. The Union batteries commanded the river and the town of Fredericksburg, but the Confederate cannon were better positioned to hammer at the battlefield itself.

Nathan didn't say that. He looked down at his feet in silence instead, and after a few moments when he glanced at Barcroft again, the corporal had looked away. Nathan breathed a little easier. With what he might be facing today, he didn't want to get in a fight with Barcroft, too.

The guns continued to roar, and Nathan continued to wait. Wait for his turn to die.

UNLIKE SOME of the other horses, the big silver gray stallion stood quietly and calmly instead of dancing around out of eagerness to get into the action. Mac could have almost gone to sleep in the saddle if it had not been for the nearly constant roar of artillery and the sharp whipcracks of rifle fire.

Stuart's cavalry was arranged in a long line behind two groups of four cannon each that were raking the left end of the Union advance. Mac was near the center of the line next to Fitz Lee, who was watching the battle avidly. Most of the action in this area was concentrated to their left, where the Yankees had tried to advance to Hamilton's Crossing, the spot where two roads and the Richmond, Fredericksburg, and Potomac Railroad all intersected. A thick triangle of woods filled the area between one of the highways and the railroad, and those woods were full of Confederate sharpshooters and artillery. Mac could barely see the trees now because of the smoke that wreathed them.

He could see the results, though. The Yankees had abandoned their slow, orderly march when their ranks had been ripped apart by rifle fire and artillery. Most of the soldiers who had not been cut down immediately charged forward, yelling and shooting. Only a few tried to turn and run, and Mac had to give the ones who didn't flee credit for their courage. Not for their common sense, perhaps, but no one could doubt their bravery, no matter what color uniform they wore.

With cannon in front of them in the trees and to their exposed left, the Yankees were hit hard, but still they came on. Mac leaned forward in the saddle as he watched, wondering if they were going to make it to the trees. That would mean hand-to-hand fighting in the woods.

Fitz Lee growled, "Damn it! Is there no place for cavalry in this battle?"

At the moment, there wasn't, thought Mac. The Union and Confederate armies were two behemoths confronting each other squarely across the open ground between them. The cavalry couldn't dash out onto the field of battle when the air there was filled with bullets and balls and exploding shells. All they could do was stand and wait, ready to act if needed.

LIEUTENANT BAXTER forced his horse through the press of men from his company. The troopers had to move or be trampled. "Get ready!" Baxter called. "Get ready to move up!"

Nathan got out of the way of the officer. Baxter might hesitate before riding down some of his men, such as Corporal Barcroft, but he wouldn't hesitate to send his mount plowing over the soldier he considered a turncoat Virginian and a dirty Reb. As the lieutenant rode by, Nathan saw how pale he was under the stiff brim of his campaign cap. Baxter's dark, waxed mustache stood out in sharp relief against his face.

Baxter was afraid, too, thought Nathan. Any man with a shred of sanity would be terrified going into this battle. Everyone knew that the Union forces greatly outnumbered the Confederates, and yet somehow it was the Rebels who held the upper hand.

The fateful orders came from the rear, and Baxter drew his saber and waved it toward the Confederate lines. "Forward, men!" he bellowed. "Quick time, now! Stay in your ranks!"

Nathan felt numb, but he forced his muscles to move. This would be the first action he had seen since that day near Antietam Creek, and he had missed most of that battle while he was unconscious from the concussion of the bursting shell. Still, he had seen enough of war that day to forever dispel any notions he might have had about it being somehow glorious and noble. A cause might be noble, and the results of a battle could be glorious in the long run, but the battle itself was hell on earth—loud, disorienting, terrifying.

The blue-clad ranks started forward. Nathan trotted along with the other soldiers. There was nothing else he could do. Even if he wanted to turn and run the other way, he couldn't do it because the others were packed in tightly around him, carrying him along like a wave carried a piece of flotsam. And if he could run, one of the officers would surely shoot him down for desertion in the face of the enemy.

Nathan started to cry. He really *was* a coward, he realized. He had mouthed platitudes to Cordelia about right and wrong and standing up for what he believed in, but now he knew the truth. He didn't want to die. He didn't care if the institution of slavery existed for another ten thousand years. All he wanted to do was live!

They had reached the edge of the battlefield by now. As the horrific scene unfolded before them, visible through gaps in the gray smoke that hung in thick clouds over the ground, even the most hardened veterans hesitated and faltered. Men stumbled, some almost fell. Others fell in clumps The advance stopped and started jerkily, prodded on by desperate officers dashing back and forth on horseback. Then, as if from one throat, a great shout welled up from the Union ranks and they surged forward, firing their rifles as they broke into a run toward the Confederate positions.

And they were running, Nathan realized, on the corpses of their fallen comrades.

—⟋⟍—

"DON'T THOSE crazy bastards ever give up?"

No one paid any attention to Titus's question. The other men along the stone wall were too busy firing and reloading and firing into the oncoming wave of Yankee troops.

Titus hadn't really expected an answer, nor did he want one. He was amazed that somehow the Union officers were able to keep their men charging into certain death.

He had been fighting for several hours now, but it seemed longer than that. Everything that had happened to him before today seemed to be fading away into the misty past. His family, the farm, Polly, Ebersole, Mountain Laurel . . . Titus's memories of all of them were dulled to the point that they no longer hurt anymore. It all seemed unreal to him, as if it had happened to someone else and he had just heard stories about it.

His only realities were the Sharps he held in his hands and the death he could deal with it.

A glance toward Fredericksburg told him that still more Union troops were marching out of the town toward the battlefield. Burnside just wasn't going to give up and admit he was whipped, not as long as he had men to send forward as cannon fodder. Titus grinned. He and the other Confederates would just have to oblige old Ambrose.

He lost track of time as the day wore on. It was well after midday, a part of his brain told him, and he hadn't eaten since early that morning. He didn't feel particularly hungry, however. Fighting was like food and drink to him; as long as he had that and air to breathe, even air that was full of powder smoke, he had all he needed to survive.

The Yankees were stubborn. Some of them made it to within a stone's throw of the wall before they were chopped down by rifle fire, falling like weeds before a scythe. Titus kept his head down as he fired, knowing that the enemy wasn't completely toothless. Captain Stevens's death had provided graphic evidence of that. During the afternoon, Titus heard the whine of innumerable Yankee bullets ricocheting around him. Once he even felt one tug at his sleeve.

During a lull in the fighting, after most of the Federal soldiers who were still able to move had pulled back, something on the battlefield caught Titus's attention. He turned his squint-eyed gaze toward it and saw a group of Yankees about two hundred yards out. No more than a dozen of them, they had taken refuge in a small hollow in the ground that gave them scant shelter. In that hellish place, however, any shelter was better than none. They began to pepper the stone wall with shots, causing Titus to duck as a bullet hit the wall near his face and stung his cheek with rock chips. The Yankees were relatively safe from rifle fire, but not from the shelling.

But the cannon fire was dying away now, Titus noted. The Confederate gunners were probably running low on ammunition. At the rate they had poured shells down on the Yankees, Titus wouldn't be a bit surprised if they ran out. That meant the Union troops in the hollow, though pinned down, were safe for the moment.

That stuck in Titus's craw. Those soldiers ought to be running, not holing up so they could continue to put up a fight. As the smoke cleared a little and Titus got a better look at the field's terrain, he suddenly realized that maybe he could do something about that group of Northerners. A small hill rose just behind the hollow where they were hiding, and as Titus's eyes followed the line of the drainage ditch, he saw that it looped behind that hill.

If he and a few other skirmishers could get into the ditch, he told himself, they could sneak up on those Yankees and wipe them out before they knew what hit them. And they could reach the ditch by dashing across the field at the far right end of the

Union lines. The Yankees who were cut off from their fellows wouldn't be able to see them from the hollow.

Titus crouched below the level of the wall and duck-walked along it, motioning for several of the men from the company to follow him. They looked puzzled, but they came anyway. Everyone knew Titus's reputation as a marksman and that he had been promoted to corporal. With the death of Captain Stevens, command of the company had been passed on to a young lieutenant named Frampton, but when Titus looked around for the officer, he didn't see him anywhere. Here in the very front line of the Confederate defense, Titus was as close to a commander as these men had, and he suddenly realized that he liked that feeling.

When he had half a dozen men gathered around him, he raised his voice so as to be heard above the tumult of battle. "Did you see those Yankees hunkered down in that hollow out there?" The other men nodded, and Titus went on, "I think we should go get 'em."

"What the hell are you talkin' about, Brannon?" demanded one of the soldiers. "It'd mean our lives to leave the wall and go out in the open field. Ain't you seen the way we been cuttin' down them Yanks?"

"That's why we're going to stay behind this wall until we can cut across to that ditch and get behind them," Titus explained. "Take a look if you don't believe me. We can do it."

A couple of the men ventured glances over the top of the wall, and when they crouched down again, they both nodded reluctantly. "We could make it, I reckon," one of them said.

"Sure we could. And once we're on that knoll behind them, it'll be like target practice, pickin' 'em off." Titus's hands tightened on the Sharps. "Who's with me?"

"Shouldn't we get orders from an officer?"

Titus laughed harshly. "All the officers are as far in the rear as they can get, boys. It's just us up here, doin' as we see fit."

"I say we go get those Yankees," another man said.

"Brannon's right," agreed another. "It's up to us."

The man who had objected first shook his head. "I think you're crazy, all of you. I ain't goin' out there."

"Then get back to your spot on the wall and at least keep those blue-bellied bastards busy," snapped Titus. "The rest of us'll go do the real work."

For a second, he thought the man was going to take a swing at him, then the soldier just shrugged and said, "You're the one who'll wind up in a hole in the ground." He turned and scurried back to the wall.

"All right," Titus said to the others with a grin, "let's go."

They continued along the sunken road behind the wall with Titus taking the lead. When he reached the end of the wall he peered cautiously around it without straightening up. He could see only a small section of the hollow where the Yankees were pinned down. As he had thought, the knoll blocked the view from there.

A short distance to the left, a road ran through a gap in the ridge and on into Fredericksburg. On the far side of that road were more Union troops, but they had pulled far back, to the outskirts of the town itself. They didn't constitute any real threat, and they had no way of communicating with their fellows trapped in the hollow. Titus grinned. His plan had been hastily formed, but it was coming together just fine.

"Ready, boys?" he said over his shoulder to his companions. When they had all nodded in the affirmative, he came up out of his crouch and shouted, "Come on!"

He broke into a run with no hesitation, heading across the field toward the drainage ditch. The cannons on the ridge were still booming, but none of their fire seemed to be directed toward this part of the battlefield. Titus didn't look back to see if the other skirmishers were following him. He had to trust that they were.

It took him about ten seconds to run the hundred yards to the ditch. Time seemed to slow down as he dashed across the rugged ground, swerving to avoid shell craters and the bodies of dead Union soldiers. Some of them probably weren't even dead, he thought fleetingly, only unconscious.

He didn't stop to check.

When he reached the ditch he barely slowed down before leaping into it. Snow had drifted a little in the bottom of it, so the white stuff cushioned his fall slightly as he sprawled out on his belly. He heard grunts behind him as the other men followed him into the ditch.

Titus lifted his head and looked around. They were all there. He said, "Stay low and follow me." This business of giving orders was easy, he reflected. He supposed that meant he would make a good officer. Better than those fancy-dressed, highfalutin' popinjays in the rear, he told himself.

On hands and knees, being careful to keep the muzzle of the Sharps from getting fouled with dirt, he crawled along the ditch toward the knoll overlooking the trapped Yankees. The other men followed closely behind him. When he judged that they were near their destination, he raised up enough to venture a look. His instincts hadn't played him false; the base of the knoll was right beside them. He jerked his head to indicate to the others that they should follow him, then clambered out of the ditch and started up the slope, moving as quickly as possible now.

The little hill was only about fifteen feet high. That was enough, thought Titus as he threw himself down at the crest and thrust the barrel of his rifle over it. The hollow where the Yankees had sought shelter opened up in front of him. He had a perfect shot. As the other men reached the top of the knoll, Titus opened fire.

His first shot tore through the top of a Yankee's head, blowing away a good-sized chunk of it. More shots rang out from Titus's fellow skirmishers. The blue-clad troopers were already sprawled out on the ground in the hollow, so they couldn't fall as the bullets struck them. But they shuddered with each heavy impact and went limp.

Half the Yankees died in the first volley. Titus finished reloading as the surviving soldiers began to realize what was happening. They started to roll over so they could return the fire coming from above and behind them. Titus put his second bullet through a Yankee's forehead. The man's head snapped back violently, and his back arched up off the ground in a reflexive spasm as he died.

Titus was reaching for another cartridge for the Sharps when something struck the ground in front of him and kicked grit into his eyes. Cursing, blinded, he pawed at his eyes and blinked as fast as he could, trying to clear his vision. Beside him, one of the men who had come with him screamed. Titus heard the whine of bullets in the air and the ugly thudding sound of lead hitting flesh. He jerked around, trying to figure out what in blazes was going on.

He saw at least fifty Yankees charging toward them, no more than twenty yards away.

Reinforcements! Instead of abandoning the men trapped in the hollow, as would have been the sensible thing to do, the other Yankees were trying to save them. Titus felt a wave of horror wash over him as he realized that he and his companions were the ones who were trapped now. The others were being hammered back into the ground by the bullets slamming into them.

He wasn't afraid to die. He knew that. He was just damned sorry that he wasn't going to get to kill any more Northerners.

But he wasn't dead yet, so maybe he could take a few more with him on the road to hell. He dropped the Sharps and snatched up the rifle that had fallen from the hands of the dead man beside him. It had a bayonet attached to it, and even though Titus had never practiced much with one of them, he thought he could manage to jab a few of these onrushing Yankee bastards with it. Shouting his defiance, he charged to meet them and ran straight into what seemed like a wall of orange flame that gouted from the muzzles of their muskets. Grayish white smoke billowed out as well, and still shrieking, Titus disappeared into it, leaving the men who had followed him dead on the ground behind him.

—⸺⸺—

THE IMPATIENCE of the cavalrymen grew worse as the day went on. Mac felt it himself. Though he disliked battle, being an observer was somehow even worse than being in the thick of the combat. He kept his field glasses trained on the area around Hamilton's Crossing, hoping to see some sign of the Stonewall Brigade. For a short time, the Yankees were able to penetrate the Confederate lines there at the intersection, but then they were thrown back. Will might be in the middle of that, Mac thought. If so, at least he was having a chance to contribute to what looked like was going to be a Confederate victory.

Then, late in the afternoon, the cavalry's chance came.

The Confederate batteries on the Union left had been moved to a more advantageous position, leaving the cavalry to cover that flank. A large group of Federal troops that had been attacking the woods in which the Southerners were entrenched gave up at last and began pulling back, leaving their dead and wounded behind. What was at first an orderly retreat changed almost immediately into chaos as some of the Union soldiers peeled off from the main group and fled southeastward.

Fitz Lee saw the Yankees coming toward the cavalry at an angle, and he waved an arm at them and shouted, "Cut them off! Turn them back toward the river!"

The horse soldiers sprang into action, spurring their mounts forward in a gallop. Mac drew his pistol, guiding the stallion easily with his left hand and his knees. He threw a shot over the heads of the fleeing Yankees, hoping to turn them rather than having to kill them.

Seeing that they were on the verge of being ridden down, some of the panicked Union troops became more clear-headed and dropped to their knees to fire a volley at the onrushing

cavalrymen. Mac heard a bullet whine past his ear, and he reluctantly lowered his aim and began firing into the group of blue-
clad soldiers. He saw one of the men go down and was fairly
certain it was his bullet that had struck home.

The Yankees scattered as the Confederate cavalry thundered among them. No man on foot could stand up to a cavalry
charge. One of the troopers tried to jab up at Mac with his bayonet. Mac twisted in the saddle to avoid the thrust, then slammed
the barrel of his pistol down on the top of the man's head. The
Yankee crumpled, unconscious.

As Mac wheeled the stallion around, he spotted several more
Yankees making a mad dash for a thick stand of trees along the
bank of a small stream that ran into Massaponax Creek. Mac
urged the horse into a run, but even with the stallion's great
speed, he saw that he would not be able to intercept the fleeing
soldiers before they reached the trees. Once they were behind
cover, they would be able to turn and put up a fight.

At the moment, however, fighting appeared to be the last
thing on their minds. They were running like frightened rab-
bits. They might not even slow down when they reached the
trees but simply splash on through the brook and keep going.
Mac didn't want to give up yet on either capturing them or forcing them back toward Fredericksburg.

The Yankees threw frightened glances over their shoulders
as they plunged into the woods. Mac was about fifty yards
behind them. The stallion covered that ground quickly. He
hauled back on the reins as he reached the trees, not wanting to
ride blindly into an ambush if the soldiers decided to turn and
fight. Holding his pistol ready in his hand, he sent the stallion
into the trees at a careful walk.

Over the sounds of battle, he suddenly heard a familiar voice
pleading, "Don't kill me! Please, for God's sake, don't kill me!"

Mac frowned. *What in blazes?*

He caught a glimpse of blue and gray through the trees and
undergrowth, and someone yelled, "There!" He knew he had

been spotted as well. Digging his heels into the stallion's flanks, he sent the big horse leaping forward. They broke out of the trees and splashed into the shallow stream.

About ten feet to his right, one of the Yankees spun toward him and fired the rifle he was holding. The bullet went high over Mac's head. Mac squeezed the trigger of his pistol, shooting down at an angle into the Yankee's chest. The soldier was flung backward by the impact of the bullet. He fell next to the legs of a skittishly dancing horse. On the back of that mount, trying to control it, was a Confederate officer.

Mac ignored the officer and concentrated on the remaining two Yankees. Both of them were standing in the brook, trying to draw a bead on him. He whirled the stallion, or maybe the stallion moved on his own, following his own peculiar instincts. Mac wasn't sure which. But when a shot roared out, the bullet missed Mac by several feet. He returned the fire, snapping off two shots. The first missed, but the second tore through the body of the Yankee and sent him spinning off his feet.

That left just one of the Northerners. He had been pointing his rifle toward Mac, but he didn't fire. Mac realized a second later that the weapon must be empty; aiming it like that was a bluff. The Yankee threw the rifle down as Mac drove the stallion toward him. The stallion reared up and lashed out with its hooves, and even though the Yankee flung up his arms in a desperate attempt to protect his head, one of the steel-shod hooves connected with his skull. That cut short the man's scream. The Northerner fell backward, his skull shattered, as the stallion dropped his front legs back into the stream.

Mac was turning toward the officer when an explosion suddenly seemed to go off in his face. He sagged in the saddle and almost fell. Only his instinctive grab for the stallion's mane kept him from toppling to the ground. His face stung where blazing grains of powder had burned his cheeks, and he was deafened by the loudness of the report. Only half-conscious, Mac was vaguely aware of the stallion lunging forward into the other man's horse. The collision almost unseated Mac, but he managed to stay in the saddle once again. Maj. Jason Trahearne was not as lucky. He went flying into the air and landed with a huge splash in the stream. The pistol he had just fired at Mac at almost point-blank range slipped out of his hand and landed on the bank.

Fighting off unconsciousness, Mac slumped on the back of the stallion and tried to take stock of his situation. He realized after a moment that he had not been shot. Somehow, Trahearne had missed. But having the gun go off in his face had come close to blinding Mac and knocking him out. He shook his head as a ringing came into his ears, heralding the return of his hearing.

"Brannon!" Trahearne cried from where he was sitting in the brook. "My God, I thought you were one of the Yankees!"

Mac pushed himself up straighter in the saddle. "Are . . . are you all right, Major?" he asked.

Trahearne scrambled to his feet, clearly uninjured by the fall he had taken. "I'm fine," he said. "What about you, Brannon?"

"I'll be . . . all right . . . Major."

Mac saw Trahearne cast a glance toward the pistol lying on the bank a few feet away. Naked desire played across Trahearne's face. He wanted to lunge for the gun and finish the job he had started. He wanted to kill Mac Brannon.

But Mac was still on horseback and still held his own pistol ready for use. Trahearne was no fool. He wanted Mac dead, but he didn't want to risk his own life in the process.

Mac saw those thoughts as plain as day on Trahearne's face. How it might have ended under different circumstances, he didn't know, because at that moment several more men on horseback pushed out of the trees and rode quickly toward them. "Mac!" Fitz Lee called. Then, more formally, he asked, "Are you wounded, Lieutenant Brannon?"

Mac drew himself up rigidly. Lee's voice had a slightly muffled sound, but most of Mac's hearing had returned. His face still burned, but he could see clearly. "I'm not hurt, General."

Lee looked at Trahearne. "What are you doing in the water, Major?"

"I was thrown from my horse during the fight Lieutenant Brannon and I had with these Yankees," replied Trahearne. He swept a hand toward the three bodies lying sprawled in the stream, then cast a glance at Mac, waiting to see if his story was going to be disputed.

Mac's head hurt. He didn't feel like arguing with Trahearne. He holstered his pistol, since the danger from both the major and the Yankees seemed to be over, and said, "That's right, General."

"Well, it looks like you took care of these Yankees," Lee commented. "Major Trahearne, get mounted up. This little skirmish is over, but the battle continues. We have to hold ourselves in readiness in case we're needed again."

Trahearne caught hold of his mount's reins and swung up into the saddle. He moved stiffly, and he couldn't seem to stop glancing at Mac. Now that his brain was clearer, Mac understood everything that had happened. Lee and the others might believe that both he and Trahearne had pursued the fleeing Yankees into these trees, but the two of them knew the truth. Trahearne had already been here when the three Union soldiers stumbled onto him. Instead of trying to capture or kill them, he had begged for his life instead.

What more could be expected, thought Mac, from a man who had been hiding from the battle?

Then Trahearne, realizing that Mac was aware of his cowardice, had tried to shoot him, no doubt intending to blame his death on the Yankees. That would not only protect Trahearne's reputation, but it would get Mac out of the way as well, so that the major could fulfill his ambition to get his hands on the big silver gray stallion, something that would never come to pass while Mac was alive. Trahearne would have almost certainly gotten away with it if he had not hurried his shot.

In a way, he now held Trahearne's life in his hands, mused Mac. A charge of cowardice in the face of the enemy could end

Trahearne's career. Mac might not be able to make it stick, since it would be his word against Trahearne's, but the accusation would be a permanent stigma.

Tempting though it was, he wasn't going to do anything, Mac decided. Just because Trahearne was ruthless and craven, that was no reason for Mac to follow his example. As long as Trahearne left him alone, he had no interest in ruining Trahearne's career. Mac hoped the major would come to understand that and steer clear of him in the future.

Those thoughts flashed through Mac's mind in a matter of heartbeats, and then he nodded in response to Fitz Lee's last comment. "Yes sir," he said. "I'm ready."

He fell in beside Lee and the other officers as they rode back into the field of battle. Trahearne was somewhere behind them.

Mac didn't look back.

Chapter Twenty-one

I T WAS A RACE against time, Nathan Hatcher thought, between the sun and death.

The sky had been clear all afternoon, when a sensible man might have wished for an overcast so as to hurry darkness and an end the killing. Nathan and the men of his company had been pushed steadily closer and closer to the front, until by late in the day, when the sun was barely over the horizon, they were the next ones in line to charge the stone wall at the base of the ridge.

Lieutenant Baxter rode back and forth nervously in front of them. He had grown more haggard as the day went on. So had many of the other men. From where they were, they could see that the battlefield was covered with blue-clad corpses. In places the bodies were three or four deep where reinforcements had charged over their fallen comrades, only to fall themselves. Men who had been cut down by the Confederate fire but were neither dead nor unconscious added to the din by shrieking and crying and whimpering. The Rebel cannons had fallen completely silent now, and the crackle of rifle fire was not nearly loud enough to drown out the ghastly harmony of pain coming from the wounded men.

Nathan saw quite a few of the soldiers passing around flasks as they fortified their courage with whiskey. Drinking in the ranks wasn't allowed before a battle, but after what everyone had witnessed today, the officers were turning a blind eye to the infraction.

No one offered Nathan a drink. He saw Barcroft take a swig from a small flask, then the corporal sneered at him and drank again. Even now, faced with death as they all were, these Yankees had to rub his nose in the fact that he wasn't really one of them. He could fight beside them, even die beside them, and yet he would never be anything more than a Reb in their eyes.

Nathan licked his lips and glanced at the western horizon. Only a sliver of sun remained to be seen. Already the shadows of dusk were beginning to appear. Surely the Union generals would see that this battle was over and that they had lost. They needed to pull back and save their strength to fight another day.

"Move up!" someone shouted from the rear. "Move up there!"

A courier on horseback raced up to Lieutenant Baxter. They spoke for a moment, then Baxter nodded his head in a spasmodic gesture. He drew his saber and held it over his head. Sweeping it forward, he shouted, "Charge!"

No! This wasn't really happening, Nathan told himself. It was too late. It was getting dark. They couldn't fight now.

The men behind him in the ranks jostled against him, and he had no choice but to move forward. Walking at first, then breaking into a jerky run, the company charged out onto the battlefield. Men began to shout, and Nathan shouted with them, incoherent cries of rage and fear. He was holding his rifle across his chest as he ran. The thought of pointing it toward the Rebels and firing never entered his mind.

A whining sound suddenly filled the air around him, as if someone had disturbed a nest of giant bees. Someone bellowed, "Down! Get down!" Nathan pitched forward onto this face, along with hundreds of the other Union soldiers charging toward the heights. Those who didn't throw themselves to the frozen ground in time were struck by the Confederate volley and stopped short, rebounding and shuddering as if they had just run into a wall. They crumpled, bleeding and dying.

Nathan found himself lying face-down in a pool of blood that had drained from the bodies of the two men flanking him. They had died in an earlier charge, and their blood was thick and sticky and clung to Nathan as he tried to move. He had a terrible vision of that pool growing and tugging him down and swallowing him, his mouth and nose and eyes filled with other men's blood, blinding and choking him until he was dead, too.

He cried and shook uncontrollably, but he stayed where he was, stretched out on the ground underneath the hail of lead that tore through the air above him. He didn't even lift his head to look around. He just squeezed his eyes shut and waited.

Gradually, Nathan became aware that the sounds of gunfire were dying away. He cracked his eyelids open slightly and saw only grayness. Even the blood underneath him was gray now. The sun was gone, and night was falling with a December suddenness. Nathan had no idea how long he had lain there like that among the corpses. At least half an hour, he decided as the gibbering in the back of his brain subsided and he began to think again.

A half-whispered command reached his eyes. "Pull back! Stay low and pull back!"

He didn't care who had issued that order, he was going to follow it. Catching hold of the sodden uniform of one of the men next to him, he started pulling himself around without ever getting up off his belly. When he was pointed back toward Fredericksburg, he began to crawl, pulling himself along with his elbows and pushing with his knees and toes.

He had gone several yards before he realized he had left his rifle behind. Pausing, he lifted his head enough to look back over his shoulder toward where he had come from.

Then, deciding it wasn't worth it, Nathan started crawling again, away from the corpse-strewn battlefield.

———

IT HAD been late in the day before the Stonewall Brigade had pushed forward to take part in the fighting, and by that time the spirit of the Yankees had been thoroughly crushed. Most of the Northerners were fleeing back toward the Rappahannock, and those who stubbornly tried to continue the fight were quickly mowed down by Confederate fire. Will's company hadn't lost a single man, he realized as night began to fall, and they had suffered only a few injuries. As for himself, he hadn't even fired his pistol all day.

He and Darcy Bennett had just finished checking on the men when a figure on horseback came cantering up out of the shadows. Will recognized the big stallion immediately, even in the growing darkness. "Mac!" Will said as his brother swung down from the saddle. "You're all right?"

"Yeah," Mac said as the brothers embraced. "How about you?"

"Not a scratch," Will said. "We missed most of the fight, and by the time we got in on it, the Yankees weren't in much of a mood for it."

"You sound disappointed."

Will shrugged. "I'm glad for my men. None of them were killed." He paused, then added, "What are you doing here?"

"Looking for you," replied Mac. "I thought we might go see if we can find Titus and make sure he's all right."

Will considered for a second, then nodded. "Sounds good to me," he said. "Can the cavalry get by without you for a while?"

Mac grunted. "We're just riding picket duty tonight. The Yankees aren't going to be doing anything except licking their wounds. General Lee's the one who suggested I look up you and Titus."

"All right, then. Just let me get my horse."

A few minutes later, with Will mounted on his dun and Mac on the stallion, they rode along the western edge of the Richmond, Fredericksburg and Potomac Railroad's right-of-way. Veering closer to the hill where Robert E. Lee had maintained his command post all day, they aimed for the dark bulk of Marye's Hill. They had last seen Titus at the stone wall along the southeastern base of the hill.

Darkness had brought an end to the fighting but not to the moans of dying men that came from the field in front of the stone wall. Will grimaced as he heard the horrible sounds. He hoped that when his time came, he would die quickly and cleanly and not linger to shriek out his agony like those men in the cold darkness.

The two riders were challenged by pickets a few times but passed on without hesitation as they approached Marye's Heights. When they neared the stone wall, they left their horses tied to the stump of a tree and walked on foot along the sunken road behind the wall. An officer greeted them and asked what they wanted. "We're looking for Titus Brannon," Will said.

"Don't know him. What company is he in?"

"I believe he said his commanding officer is named Stevens," added Mac.

The man waved a hand toward the wall. "Stevens's bunch is down there a ways. Stevens ain't, though. He's dead." The officer's voice caught a little. "So's General Cobb. None of us thought he was hurt bad. It was just a leg wound. But he bled to death in just a few minutes."

"Sorry," Will muttered. He knew how the man felt. It would be a terrible blow to everyone in the Stonewall Brigade if anything ever happened to Jackson.

The brothers walked on down the road. When they reached the area the officer had indicated, Will called out, "Titus Brannon! Anybody here seen Titus Brannon?"

One of the troopers looked up from where he was slumped on the ground with his back against the wall. "Brannon?" he repeated, ignoring the fact that he was addressing two officers. "You mean that sharpshooter with that big rifle?"

"That's him," Mac replied eagerly. "Where is he?"

"Hell, I reckon." The man jerked a thumb over his shoulder to indicate the battlefield. "Or layin' out there somewhere. It's the same thing."

Will and Mac both stiffened. Will felt his belly clench hard. "What do you mean?" he forced himself to ask.

"I mean Brannon led a bunch of skirmishers out there to ambush some Yankees, only him and the other boys were the ones who got ambushed. Yankee reinforcements came up and wiped 'em out." The soldier shook his head. "He tried to get me to go with 'em. I'm damned glad I didn't. Damn fool never should've tried it."

Without thinking about what he was doing, Will reached down, took hold of the man's coat, and jerked him to his feet. "You son of a bitch!" Will shouted. "That's my brother you're talking about!"

Mac stood numbed with sudden grief. After a moment, he gave a little shake of his head and put a hand on Will's shoulder, gripping hard. "Will!" he said. "That won't help anything."

The soldier hurriedly said, "I'm sorry, Cap'n! I didn't mean nothin'—"

Will shuddered then let go of the man and took a step back. "You're sure about Titus?" he asked in a harsh whisper.

The soldier looked like he didn't really want to answer that question, but he finally said, "We saw it all from the wall, Cap'n. Your brother and the men with him were overrun. What with the smoke and all, that's the last we saw of any of 'em." The man swallowed hard. "I'm sorry, Cap'n. You, too, Lieutenant."

Dully, Will said, "I apologize for jumping you, soldier. That's not the way an officer should act."

"Don't worry about it, sir. I understand, what with losin' your brother and all."

Will turned and looked over the wall toward the battlefield. The thought of Titus lying out there dead or, even worse, alive and suffering was almost more than he could bear. He and Titus had had their differences, of course. Will had disagreed with just about every decision Titus had made over the past couple of years. But Titus was still his brother, and Will loved him. He knew that Mac did, too.

Mac laid a hand on Will's shoulder. "We knew it could happen to any of us. That doesn't make it any easier, but we knew it could happen."

"No," Will said. "It doesn't make it any easier." He thought about how the news would affect the rest of the family, and that only tightened the band that was constricting his chest. He rubbed his jaw, took a deep breath, and said, "We have to go look for him."

"How could we ever find him?"

"Damn it, we have to try," Will blurted out. He started toward the wall.

"Captain!"

The sharp tone of command made Will look around. A heavyset man with a full beard strode toward him. Will came to attention and saluted, as did Mac and the trooper.

"General McLaws, sir," Will said. "Captain William Brannon, Thirty-third Virginia. My brother, Lieutenant Macbeth Brannon, from General Stuart's cavalry."

"It appears you two gentlemen are a bit lost," said Lafayette McLaws. "What are you doing here?"

"Looking for our brother, sir," replied Mac. "This soldier told us he . . . he perished during the battle. We were about to go look for his body."

McLaws shook his head. "Not until morning, gentlemen. General Burnside has not asked for a truce, and we are not going to extend one without a formal request. Tomorrow morning we shall see what the situation is. Until then, we maintain our lines."

"Begging your pardon, General, but we're not talking about abandoning our lines," Will said, anger crackling in his voice. "We're just talking about the two of us taking a torch and going out there to search for our brother's body."

"That's not going to be allowed, Captain, at least until morning," McLaws said firmly. "Now, I suggest the two of you go back to your companies. You have my sincere condolences on the loss of your brother."

Will's teeth grated together. Every part of him wanted to defy the general's orders, except for the small voice in the back of his head that reminded him he was a soldier now. Duty had to come before everything else, even his love for Titus, and duty required him to obey the command of a superior officer. Finally, he was able to jerk his head in a nod and say in a strangled voice, "Yes sir." He turned to Mac. "Let's go."

"And don't go skulking around out there," McLaws called after them. "That's a good way to get shot by our own pickets."

Will knew the general was right. Still, the uncertainly of it all ate at him. From what the soldier had told them about what had happened, it was hard to believe that Titus wasn't dead. But if there was still a sliver of hope . . .

Everyone on both sides of the battle had probably been grateful for nightfall, but now Will felt like he couldn't wait for the morning to come.

—⚬⚬—

THERE WAS no orderly retreat into Fredericksburg by the Union forces. It was a rout, pure and simple. Men crawled on their bellies until they felt that they were out of range of the Rebels' rifle fire, then leaped to their feet and ran frantically back the way they had come, seldom stopping until they reached the relative safety of the town itself.

Nathan found himself stumbling along an alley that was barely lit by the glow from the stars overhead. His strength had almost deserted him, so he stopped and leaned against the wall of one of the buildings to steady himself and rest. His pulse was still hammering inside his skull, and his breath came raggedly, steaming foglike in front of his face in the cold night air.

Once again he had come through a battle alive, he told himself, and he was filled with such relief at that knowledge that he trembled with the depth of what he was feeling. It was true that here at Fredericksburg, just as in Maryland at Antietam Creek, he hadn't contributed at all to the Union effort. So far in his military career, he had been totally useless. Perhaps next time would be different, he told himself.

Next time . . .

Suddenly, Nathan knew he didn't want there to be a next time. He had tried to fight for his beliefs. He honestly had wanted to be a part of the war to preserve the Union, but he knew now he was no soldier.

What could he do? He couldn't desert. He had to find his company and report back in . . .

"Hold it right there, Yank. Don't you move or I'll blow your damned head off. I swear I will."

Nathan caught his breath and flinched back against the wall as the figure loomed out of the dark and came toward him. The faint starlight glinted on the barrel of the pistol pointed at him. Nathan could see that the man was wearing a uniform and an officer's hat. How had the man known that he was thinking about deserting?

And the man had called him *Yank*, Nathan recalled with a shock. The stranger wasn't a Union officer at all. He was a *Confederate*.

Now that he knew what was going on, Nathan heard the man's accent clearly when he spoke again. "You get lost when you ran away from the battle, Yank? I swear, we whaled the tar out o' you boys. Trouble is, it ain't always goin' to be that way. I can see the handwritin' on the wall already."

Nathan had no idea what the man was talking about, so he kept silent.

"I been thinkin' about it," the man went on as he kept the gun pointing at Nathan. "I reckon it's time for this ol' boy to go home. Trouble is, that's over east of here, and I got to go through Yankee lines to do it. As confused as all you Yanks are tonight, though, I don't figure anybody'd pay much attention to one man who acted like he knew where he was goin'." The stranger gestured with the barrel of the pistol. "Get that uniform off, boy. You and me is swappin' outfits."

Nathan felt colder than ever as he realized the man's intentions. He was going to steal Nathan's uniform so that he could pass through the Yankee lines and leave Nathan there garbed in the uniform he had sworn he would never wear: the uniform of a Confederate soldier.

"Wait a minute," Nathan began. "You can't—"

He didn't get out enough words for the stranger to realize that he was a fellow Southerner. Instead, the man grated, "The hell I can't!" and lunged at Nathan, lashing at his head with the pistol barrel.

Instinctively, Nathan ducked the blow and threw himself forward, trying to grapple with the man. Instead, he felt the man's other fist sink into his belly with terrible force. Nathan doubled over in pain and sickness, and something seemed to explode on the back of his head.

He was already unconscious when he fell face-first into the filth of the alley.

—⚍⚎⚍—

NATHAN HAD no idea how long he had been out cold. When he came to, all he was aware of for long moments was how much his head hurt. The pain was a deep, steady throb. Eventually, he realized it was keeping time with his heartbeat.

He rolled over and tried to sit up. That only made him feel more nauseous. He propped himself on an elbow and waited for the feeling to pass. When it finally did, he was able to haul himself upright.

The coat he was wearing seemed too big for him, he realized. He let out a groan. The Confederate deserter could have just stolen his uniform and left him there in his long underwear to freeze to death. Nathan would have almost preferred that to what had actually been done to him. He was wearing the hated Rebel gray, he saw as he pushed himself to his feet and looked down at his body.

A moment of dizziness sent him reeling against a wall, then that passed. He felt sick but a little stronger than when he had first awakened. He forced his legs to move. His brain seemed to be broken into pieces, and one of them sent him staggering toward the Rappahannock in search of whatever was left of his company, just as he had been doing before he encountered the Confederate deserter.

He didn't realize the full implications of what he was wearing until he reeled out of the alley and practically ran into a lieutenant leading a squad of Union soldiers.

The soldiers flung their rifles to their shoulders, and Nathan threw his hands in the air. "Don't shoot!" he cried. "I'm not a Rebel!"

"Hold your fire," the lieutenant snapped at his men. He trained his pistol on Nathan and continued, "Don't move, Reb, or we'll shoot you."

"I'm not a Rebel." Nathan felt a sob coming on and choked it back. "I'm a Union soldier, just like you."

"Mighty funny outfit for a Union soldier to be wearing, don't you think?"

Nathan took a chance and lowered one hand. He plucked at the coat he wore. "Can't you see it's not mine? It's too big. Can't you see that?" he asked desperately.

"I've heard tell that the Rebs are running short on supplies. They have to make do with what they have, whether their uniforms fit or not." The lieutenant, seeing that Nathan wasn't going to put up a fight, reached out and grabbed hold of his collar. He jerked and shoved him out in front of the party of soldiers. "You're our prisoner, Reb. I don't know what you're doing here, but I don't care, either. After what you savages did to us today, you're lucky I don't just shoot you on the spot."

One of the men in the squad spat on the street. "That sounds like a good idea to us, Lieutenant."

Nathan's mind struggled to keep up with the twists of fate that had brought him to this point. He said again, "I tell you I'm not a Confederate soldier. I'm Private Nathan Hatcher from Baxter's company, Tyler's brigade, Humphrey's division of Fifth Corps. If you find Lieutenant Baxter, he'll vouch for me."

Even as he spoke, Nathan wasn't sure Baxter would vouch for the lone Virginian under his command. Wouldn't his sadistic commander think it fitting for him to wind up a prisoner in a gray uniform? That was all too possible, Nathan realized.

"I'm not going to waste my time looking for anybody, mister," the man who had captured him said. "I can see and hear that you're a Reb."

Nathan's eyes closed as his heart sank seemingly all the way to his feet. His Virginia heritage had betrayed him. None of the Yankees would believe that someone with his accent, wearing a Confederate uniform, could be anything other than a Rebel. It was hopeless.

The lieutenant prodded him with the barrel of the pistol. "Get moving, Reb. We've got a few other prisoners. You'll go with them. The war's over for you traitors."

The war . . . over? Those words echoed in Nathan's brain. That was what he had wanted, to be through with the war.

But not like this. Never like this.

The lieutenant sounded positively happy as he added, "Once we get you Rebs in one of our prison camps, you may never see the light of day again."

THE LONG day of December 13, 1862, had been a disaster for the Union forces under Ambrose Burnside. They had lost nearly thirteen thousand men, over twice as many as the Confederates. And yet, that night, at a meeting of Burnside's generals, the only thing discussed was the plan of attack for the next day. It was not until one of their number, Gen. Rush C. Hawkins, made a pencil sketch of the Union and Confederate lines and their relative positions that it became obvious to all the officers that another day of battle would achieve nothing except another defeat and thousands more casualties. Grudgingly, Hawkins was sent to confer with Burnside and break the news to him that none of his generals wanted to continue.

Burnside, assuming that the battle would resume the next morning, was surprised by Hawkins's visit. While pondering the situation, he paced back and forth in his headquarters in a commandeered house until Gen. Joseph Hooker, who was also in the room trying to rest, sat up on his cot and said bluntly, "We've spilled enough blood for now, General."

Burnside agreed. There would be no new attack the next morning or the next day.

The day passed in tense anticipation on the Confederate side, but the Yankees made no move until December 15, when they began crossing back over the Rappahannock on the pontoon bridges that had been so costly for them to build. It took a long time to get their men across the river—but not as long as it had taken them to march into Fredericksburg the first time; so many were left behind to be buried in mass graves on the battlefield itself.

When the Yankees left Fredericksburg, they took a handful of Confederate prisoners with them. Nathan Hatcher was among them, stumbling over the bridge and then along a frozen road as the army moved northward toward the Potomac. Where he would end up, he had no idea.

He stumbled over a rut in the road, tripping and nearly falling. Only the fact that one of the other prisoners reached out quickly and grabbed his arm kept him from pitching forward. As he straightened, Nathan muttered, "Thanks."

"You're welcome, Nathan," a familiar voice said mockingly.

Nathan's head jerked around.

"I thought I recognized you," the man went on. "How'd you wind up here? I heard you joined the Yankee army."

Nathan couldn't speak. All he could do was stare into the haggard, bearded face of Titus Brannon.

Chapter Twenty-two

F OLLOWING THE DEFEAT AT Fredericksburg, the Union
army retreated up the eastern bank of the Rappahannock
only as far as the village of Falmouth, a distance of less than two
miles. Yet it might as well have been two hundred for all the
contact the opposing forces had with each other during the
winter of 1862–63. Each side had had enough for the time being,
and they went into bivouac. The only attempted movement by
either army came in January 1863, when the Yankees, still commanded by Gen. Ambrose Burnside, attempted a flanking
march up the Rappahannock. The maneuver might have succeeded had not the heavens opened and loosed a downpour that
lasted for days, turned all the roads into seemingly bottomless
sinkholes, and completely bogged down the Federal forces.
Defeated again before he had even begun, Burnside returned to
the camps at Falmouth. Within days, Lincoln relieved him of
command of the Army of the Potomac and replaced him with
Joseph Hooker.

"Fighting Joe"—a nickname that Hooker himself was said to
despise—moved quickly to improve the morale of his men.
Eliminating Burnside's unwieldy grand divisions, he reorganized
the army into seven corps, including a corps of cavalry, which
until now had been spread throughout the Union forces, decreas-
ing its effectiveness. Hooker also made drastic improvements in
the army's food, sanitation, and medical care. Within weeks, the
hangover of despair resulting from Burnside's botched attempt
to take Fredericksburg began to be forgotten. Through his skills
as an organizer, Hooker turned the Army of the Potomac into a
force to be reckoned with once more.

It remained to be seen, however, how well he would lead
them in battle.

And on the other side of the Rappahannock, the "victors" of Fredericksburg continued to be undernourished and undersupplied. The only thing the Confederate army had plenty of was fighting spirit.

ARMIES HAD crossed and recrossed this landscape so many times, Will thought as he rode alongside his brother toward the Brannon farm, that it was beginning to look like a completely different place than the beautiful land where he had grown up. Fields had been stripped bare and the ground churned into mud flats that looked as if nothing had ever grown there. Trees had been cut down for firewood. The town of Culpeper itself had a half-deserted look about it when Will and Mac rode through. The South had won more battles than it had lost in this war, but you surely couldn't tell it by looking at northern Virginia, Will reflected.

The turnoff to the farm came into sight. As Will and Mac rode toward the house, Mac commented, "The fields don't look too bad. Henry and Cordelia have done a good job of keeping them up."

Will nodded. The Brannon farm seemed to be in better shape than most of the places they had passed. And as the house and barns and pens themselves came into view, they could see that the buildings looked all right as well. A grim smile tugged at Will's mouth. His mother wasn't just about to let the farm go to pot because of a war.

"I'm not looking forward to this," Mac said quietly.

"Neither am I."

Skeeter came bounding toward them, barking and wagging his stump of a tail. The dog hadn't forgotten them. A moment later, Cordelia came to the front door to see what all the commotion was, and as she saw the two tall, uniformed men swinging down from their horses, she called out their names and ran down from the porch to greet them.

The front door banged behind her. Moments later Henry pushed it open, saying, "What's all the yellin' about—?" Then he let out a whoop as he saw his brothers embracing their sister. He bounded to the ground, ignoring the porch steps, and threw his arms around them all.

Abigail was the last one out of the house. She didn't look particularly surprised to see that her two oldest sons were home. She must have figured from the reactions of Cordelia and Henry that at least one of the prodigals had returned. She waited until Will and Mac had stepped onto the porch before she leaned up to kiss each of them on the cheek. "Welcome home," she said, and Will thought he saw the gleam of tears in her eyes.

"Where's Titus?" Henry asked enthusiastically as he pounded Will on the back. "Where's that old rascal?"

A part of Will wished that he and Mac could have postponed delivering the bad news for a while. But maybe it would be better this way, he told himself. Like yanking a bad tooth, the sooner the pain was over, the better.

Only this pain might not ever be over . . .

Will looked at his mother, and Abigail saw the truth in his eyes. Her hand went to her mouth. "Oh, Lord, no," she breathed.

Cordelia was the next one to understand. She had hold of Mac's arm, and her fingers dug into his flesh. "It's not true, is it, Mac?" she asked desperately.

"What?" demanded Henry. "What are you talkin' about, Cordelia? Why do you all look so glum? It's like— " Suddenly, he paled and in a whisper asked, "Titus?"

"Killed at Fredericksburg," Will said, his voice harsh and flat.

Cordelia let out a sobbing wail and half-collapsed against Mac. He put his arms around her and held on tightly. Henry exclaimed, "No! No, it can't be true!" and tears began to roll down his cheeks.

Abigail said, "What happened?"

"He led some skirmishers out onto the battlefield after a bunch of Yankees who were pinned down," Will explained. "They got trapped themselves when reinforcements came up. Mac and I didn't see it. We were on different parts of the field. But from what we were told, they never had a chance."

Still crying, Henry began to beat his fist against one of the porch posts. No one stopped him.

"Did . . . did he have a Christian burial?" asked Abigail.

Will nodded. "Yes, ma'am." He didn't look at Mac. They knew the truth, but there was no reason anyone else had to. They had never found Titus's body among the thousands that had been strewn on the blood-soaked field. Many of the corpses had been so mutilated that it had been hard to tell if they wore blue or gray, let alone being able to distinguish features. The mostly anonymous dead had been heaped in mass graves, but words had been spoken over each of those burials, so Will felt like what he had told his mother wasn't a complete falsehood. Chances were that Titus had indeed received a Christian burial; they just couldn't prove it.

"Thank the Lord for that," murmured Abigail as she stared down at the porch. She took a deep breath, let it out slowly, and then lifted her head. "Come inside," she said to her children. "You two must be hungry. There's not as much food these days, but we'll make do."

"We brought some rations," Will said, gesturing toward a bag hanging from his saddle. "It's not much, either, but it might help."

"I'll tend to the horses," Mac offered, gently trying to disengage Cordelia's arms as she continued to hold him.

"No, Henry can do that," Abigail said. To her youngest son, she said, "Seè to it."

Henry sniffled and wiped the back of his hand across his nose. "Y-yes ma'am," he managed to say.

Abigail turned toward the door. She shivered and hugged herself as she did so. "It's cold out here," Will heard her say quietly. "We'll build up the fire."

Maybe so, thought Will, but they could never get it hot enough to make up for the chill of losing Titus.

—✦—

WILL AND Mac did not have to report back to their companies for a week. The way both armies were just sitting on opposite sides of the Rappahannock, Will thought he and Mac could have waited until spring to return. Nothing was going to happen before then, at the earliest. But their pass was good for a week, and so a week it would be.

On their third day home, the sound of hoofbeats outside the house drew Will to the porch. He saw a black buggy with fancy silver trim drawing to a halt in front of the house. As he recognized the vehicle and its two occupants, Will felt himself tense. He had been afraid this would happen.

"There ye are, Brannon," Duncan Ebersole said as he replaced his buggy whip in its silver holder. "I heard in town that ye and yer brother were back home." Ebersole stepped down from the buggy and then turned around to help Polly. She didn't budge from her seat, however, so after a moment of standing there with his arms up, Ebersole grunted and stepped back.

Polly wore a dark blue dress. A hat of the same shade was perched on her blonde curls, and a gauzy veil hung from it over her face. She peered intently through the veil at Will and asked, "Is it true, Will? Is what we heard in Culpeper true?"

"I don't know what you heard," Will said harshly. He suspected that he *did* know, but for some contrary reason that he wasn't proud of, he wanted to make Polly say the words.

They came from Ebersole's mouth instead. "They told us that yer brother Titus is dead." Will thought Polly flinched a little as her father spoke.

Slowly, gravely, Will nodded. "It's true," he said, his eyes still on Polly. "Titus was killed at Fredericksburg."

Polly's bosom was rising and falling more rapidly as her breathing sped up. It was difficult to see her face clearly through the veil, but Will thought she had gone even paler than usual. Suddenly, she let out a moan and slumped to the side.

"Damn it!" Ebersole burst out as he leaped to catch her. "She's gone an' fainted!"

Abigail appeared behind Will on the porch. He hadn't heard her come out of the house, but she made her presence known by saying crisply, "I'll thank you not to curse on this property, Mr. Ebersole. Now, bring that poor girl inside. She can lie down on the divan in the parlor."

Ebersole was half in and half out of the buggy, struggling to hold Polly's limp form upright. Will came down from the porch and strode over to the vehicle, saying, "I'll give you a hand."

Ebersole threw a hostile glance at him, and for a second Will thought the planter was going to refuse the offer of help. But then Ebersole moved aside slightly to let Will step up beside him, and together they lifted Polly down from the seat. Will was considerably bigger and stronger than Ebersole, so he got his arms around Polly's shoulders and knees and carried her.

"I never expected th' lass to faint," Ebersole said worriedly.

"She's had a shock," said Will, grunting a little from the effort of carrying Polly up the steps to the porch. She was a slender young woman, but at the moment she was so much dead weight.

Abigail held the door open. Will carried Polly into the house and then turned to go into the parlor. Cordelia came hurrying up the hall from the kitchen. "What's going on?" she asked.

"Polly's fainted," Will said. Carefully, he lowered Polly onto the divan and held her up in a half-sitting position while Cordelia took her hat off and Abigail loosened the collar of her dress. Then he let her lie down.

Ebersole paced back and forth worriedly in the foyer, just outside the entrance to the parlor. "Is she all right?" he asked.

"She will be, I'm sure," Abigail said. "Like Will told you, your daughter has had a severe shock, Mr. Ebersole. She's just learned that her husband is dead."

Ebersole stopped pacing and said, "Husband in name only, and no' even that for much longer. My lawyer's seein' to the divorce."

Will's hands tried to clench into fists. He forced them to relax and said, "There won't be any divorce. Polly is Titus's widow, and there's nothing you can do about that."

Ebersole's mouth was a grim, angry line in his face, but he didn't say anything else. Under the circumstances, it was hard to argue with Will's logic.

Polly moaned again and began to stir. Abigail said to Cordelia, "Fetch a glass of water."

"What she needs is a shot o' whiskey," suggested Ebersole.

"Not in this house."

Ebersole shrugged. Will tended to agree with him for a change. The jolt from a drink of whiskey would probably help Polly right now. She wasn't going to get it, though.

Polly blinked several times, and then her eyes stayed open. She stared up at the people around her, seemingly without seeing them. When her gaze finally focused a little better, she asked, "Is he really dead?"

"Yes," Abigail said. "I'm sorry." Seeing Polly's pain must have brought back some of her own, because tears began to well from her eyes and run silently down her weathered face.

Polly tried to sit up. Abigail helped her and then sat down beside her, putting an arm around the shoulders of this young woman who was still, in Abigail's mind at least, her daughter-in-law. Cordelia brought a cup of water, and Abigail took it and helped Polly drink between sobs. Will stood well back from the divan, uncomfortable in the presence of a crying woman.

Ebersole caught his eye and jerked his head toward the porch. Will followed him outside.

"Tell me what happened, if ye can," Ebersole asked.

"Does it matter? You didn't like Titus, and you didn't want him to be married to your daughter."

"I'll not be denyin' that," said Ebersole.

"And none of us are going to forget what you had your men do to him that night at Mountain Laurel. So don't come over here and pretend that you care, Ebersole. You're not fooling anybody."

Ebersole drew himself up stiffly. "That's Colonel Ebersole to you . . . *Captain.*"

"I don't answer to a colonel of militia," snapped Will. "I serve under a real soldier—Stonewall Jackson."

"Ye damned insolent pup!" Ebersole came a step closer.

"Come on," Will said softly, maliciously. "I'd like that."

His mother would be mad as blazes if he started a brawl on the front porch at a time like this, but Will didn't care. He was fed up with Ebersole, and it was long past time that the arrogant planter was taken down a notch or two.

Ebersole quivered with anger, but he kept himself under control and even moved back a little, putting more space between him and Will. "I'll not be scrappin' with the likes o' you, Brannon," he said. "Out o' respect for my daughter's feelin's, I'll ignore yer insults."

"Wait out here," Will told him. "I'll see how Polly's doing."

Polly's color was a little better when Will entered the parlor. She was holding the cup herself now, and though she was still crying, it was not the uncontrollable sobbing of earlier.

"Your father's worried about you, Polly," Will told her. "I think he wants to take you home."

"I . . . I really should go," Polly said. "This isn't my place . . ."

"Nonsense," Abigail said. "You were married to my son. You're a part of this family whether you like it or not, and you're welcome here, girl."

"Th-thank you." Polly took a sip of the water and then used a handkerchief she clutched in her other hand to dab at her eyes. "You and Cordelia have been so kind to me, Mrs. Brannon, and I don't really deserve it."

"Will's the one who carried you in," Cordelia pointed out.

Polly looked up at him. "Thank you, Will."

He nodded, feeling uncomfortable again.

"I really should go, though," Polly went on. "There are . . . there are things to do . . . arrangements to be made . . ."

"Titus is buried at Fredericksburg," Will told her as gently as possible. "There's nothing you can do, Polly."

"Surely there's something . . ."

Will shook his head.

Polly took a deep breath. "I can mourn him then," she said, almost fiercely. "He and I had our differences, but surely he deserves that much."

"Most folks had differences with Titus," said Will, a mixture of sorrow and fond memories in his voice. "He wasn't the easiest fella in the world to get along with."

Abigail said, "You hush, Will Brannon. That's your brother you're talking about."

"I know, Ma."

Polly looked around. "Where are Mac and Henry?"

"Out working in the fields, trying to get them ready for spring," Cordelia told her.

"Tell them I said hello," Polly said as she came to her feet. She handed the cup to Cordelia and picked up her hat from the end table. She settled it on her head and adjusted the veil, then buttoned her collar. Her eyes were red and puffy from crying, but no more tears came from them.

The front door opened, and Duncan Ebersole called, "Polly? Are ye all right?"

"I'm coming, Father," she responded. She took Abigail's hands and squeezed them for a second, saying, "Thank you, Mrs. Brannon. For a moment, I felt like part of a real family again. Despite the . . . the tragedy, you don't know what a gift that was."

"The hand of the Lord is in everything, Polly. You just remember that and hold to it. It'll comfort you."

"Thank you," Polly said again. She gave Cordelia a brief hug, then looked at Will and said his name politely. He returned her nod and stepped back to let her leave the parlor.

Ebersole was waiting at the door. "Come along, gal," he said. "'Tis time we were gettin' home."

"Yes, I think it is," she said. She let him take her arm, and the two of them went out to the buggy.

Will, Cordelia, and Abigail stepped out onto the porch to watch the buggy roll away down the lane. Cordelia said, "You know, she acted like she really loved Titus."

Will shrugged. "Maybe she did."

"She didn't act like it," said Abigail, "choosing her father over her own husband."

"It's hard to know what goes on in folks' lives," Will said. "I don't reckon we ever know anybody as well as we think we do."

Cordelia leaned against his side and put an arm around his waist. "I know I'm glad you and Mac are home," she said. "I wish you never had to go back."

"So do I," Will said, watching the buggy disappear at the end of the lane. "So do I . . ."

IT WAS harder than Abigail would have believed possible to say good-bye to Will and Mac when the time came for them to return to their duties. In so many ways, Cory was lost to her, had been lost as soon as he had given in to the wanderlust he had inherited from his father. Now Titus was gone, too, struck down by the unholy invaders from the North. The knowledge that the same fate could await her two oldest sons was almost more than she could bear.

"Don't worry about us," Mac had assured her breezily. "We've got so many people praying for us that there must be guardian angels watching over us night and day."

Abigail hoped that was true. She was certainly doing her share of the praying. But a person could always do more, she told herself.

A couple of weeks after the boys had left to return to the army bivouac near Fredericksburg, Abigail was startled to hear hoofbeats outside as she sat embroidering in the parlor. A cold, steady rain was falling, the sort of weather in which no one should be traveling. Cordelia was upstairs, and Henry was out in the barn. Abigail felt a sudden tension grip her. What if a soldier had just ridden up to bring her the news that Will and Mac had been killed? She hadn't heard about any battles, but that didn't mean anything. News traveled slowly and unreliably these days.

Quickly, Abigail put her piecework aside and stood up. She crossed to the window and pulled the curtain back a little, telling herself that her fears were foolish, born only of her grief for Titus. When she saw who was coming up on the porch, she closed her eyes for a second and breathed a sigh of relief. She recognized the tall, brawny figure in the black suit—wet now from the rain—and the black hat with water dripping from its broad brim. She heard him stomping the mud off his boots as she went to the front door and opened it.

"Ben, come in here," she greeted him. "What in the world are you doing out in this weather? It's not fit for man nor beast."

Reverend Benjamin Spanner took off his hat and shook water droplets from it as he grinned at her. "Sometimes I don't quite know which of those two things I am, Abby—man or beast."

She flushed with a mixture of pleasure and embarrassment at the easy familiarity that came from their lips. "You're certainly not a beast," she said. "You're a man, and quite a good one at that."

Spanner came into the foyer. "Right now I'm so wet I feel like shaking like a dog," he said with a chuckle. "I've just been over to the Graham place. Miz Graham's been taken sick."

"Oh, I'm sorry to hear that. Is there anything I can do?"

Spanner shook his head. "I don't reckon. It's a bad case of the grippe. The doc's been out from town to see her, and he gave her some medicine. She's got her sister there to look after her and the little ones, since her husband's off to the war." The trenches in the preacher's cheeks seemed to deepen. "War oughtn't take a man off when his family needs him."

"War takes a great many things," Abigail said softly.

"Aye, that's the truth." Spanner reached out and lightly touched Abigail's arm. "And how are you today?"

"All right, I suppose," Abigail said with a sigh. "Missing Will and Mac. I think it's the weather that's brought on my melancholy."

"A lady as pretty as you should never be melancholy," declared Spanner, making Abigail blush again. "Where are your other children?"

"Why, Henry's out in the barn, working on one of the plows, and Cordelia is upstairs. I can call them . . ."

Spanner's hand tightened slightly on Abigail's arm. "That's not necessary. I just didn't want to shock any youngsters by doing this."

And with that he drew her closer and leaned down to find her mouth with his.

Abigail stiffened with shock. She had never expected the minister to do something like . . . like kissing her! They were friends, of course, even good friends, kindred souls in their search for the Lord's grace. But not this!

She drew back, gasping, one hand pushing against his broad chest. The other hand came up and cracked across his face in a slap. Abigail said, "Oh!"

If Spanner minded being slapped, he gave no sign of it. In fact, he smiled at her. "I reckon I deserved that for taking you by surprise. But you can't say it was *that* much of a surprise, the way we've been getting friendlier and friendlier, and you can't say you didn't enjoy it, either."

"I most certainly can!" exclaimed Abigail. "Enjoy being assaulted? Never!"

"Ah, but that was pleasure I tasted on your lips, Abby."

She opened her mouth to deny the outrageous claim, but then she stopped short and thought about the way *his* mouth had tasted, and the way his hand had held her arm, and the warmth that suddenly had kindled inside her as he kissed her.

"Oh, no," she whispered. "This isn't possible."

"Of course it is," Spanner said, still smiling.

Then, before she could let herself stop to think about what she was doing, Abigail was in his arms, paying no attention to the fact that his suit was soaked. His arms went around her and her face tilted up to his and their lips met again, and for the first time in years, Abigail Brannon felt truly alive again.

It was the most frightening feeling she had ever experienced.

Chapter Twenty-three

B RIG. GEN. FITZHUGH LEE held up his gauntleted left hand, signaling for the riders to halt. The cavalrymen reined their mounts to a stop and sat quietly in their saddles. The breath of men and horses alike steamed in the cold air of late February.

Lee pointed up ahead through the trees that screened the Confederate cavalry. Mac leaned forward in his saddle, looking where the general indicated. He saw movement and flashes of blue uniforms. The smell of woodsmoke was in the air.

"They've made a midday camp," Lee said quietly. "And they have no idea we're here."

Mac nodded in agreement. All morning, Lee's horsemen, some four hundred strong, had been trailing the Union force after finding the tracks of their horses during a patrol. Here along the disputed front between the two forces, it was difficult to tell where the enemy lines were, but Mac was sure they were in Yankee territory because they had crossed the Rappahannock River earlier in the morning. The idea that they were operating behind enemy lines didn't seem to bother Fitz Lee at all.

The Yankees up ahead were cavalrymen, too. Clearly, Lee relished the challenge of pitting his mounted force against that of the Union. He pointed to himself, then to Mac, then swung down out of the saddle. Mac followed suit. They handed the reins of their mounts to another soldier, then stole forward cautiously on foot. The trees didn't provide much cover since most of them were bare at this time of year, but there was undergrowth that also shielded the two men from sight. They came within a hundred yards of the Yankees before Lee crouched behind a bush and gestured for Mac to do the same. From here, they could see the Union camp.

The enemy horsemen had stopped for their noon meal in a large clearing near a church. The whitewashed sanctuary had an air of disuse about it. Like many churches in northern Virginia, it had been abandoned because it was dangerous for civilians to gather anywhere these days. There was no telling when a battle would break out and spill over onto them.

Lee whispered, "How many, do you think?"

Mac was already trying to make a rough count. "Looks like 225, maybe 250," he estimated.

Lee nodded in agreement. "That's how I make it, too. Come on."

The two men withdrew into the woods, and when they rejoined the rest of the cavalry, Lee wasted no time in getting mounted. He drew his saber and called softly, "Let's go, boys. They won't know what hit them."

Mac hoped that would be the case. He unsnapped his holster and drew his pistol as he guided the stallion along the narrow trail behind Fitz Lee.

It was almost inconceivable that four hundred men on horseback could move as quietly through the woods as Lee and his followers did, but as they reached the edge of the trees and looked down into the small valley where the church was, they saw immediately that the Yankees had no idea they were there. Grinning broadly, Lee lifted his saber, then slashed forward and down with it, launching the charge.

The first warning the Union cavalrymen had was the thunder of hoofbeats. They looked up from their campfires to see wave after wave of gray-clad riders bursting out of the trees and racing toward them. The Yankees forgot about their lunch and leaped frantically for their horses, but only a few of them managed to get mounted before the Rebels were among them.

Mac fired at a rider to his right, then swiveled and snapped a shot at a man to his left. Directly in front of him, Lee used his saber to cut down a couple of the Yankees. An irregular volley of pistol fire came from the Confederate horsemen. Some of the

Yankees were trampled under steel-shod hooves, and more fell to sabers and pistols.

Reining the stallion around, Mac plunged back into what was now a confused melee. One of the Union cavalrymen who had lost his gun somehow tried to tackle him and haul him out of the saddle. Mac reversed his pistol and slammed the butt against the man's head. The Yankee's suddenly nerveless fingers lost their grip and slipped off. He fell away to the side.

A moment later, Mac heard Lee bellowing, "Hold your fire! Hold your fire!" The Yankees were giving up, dropping their weapons and thrusting their arms in the air.

Mac looked around and saw that about 150 of the Union cavalrymen were surrendering. Another 50 or so had been either killed or badly wounded in the brief fight, and the rest of the Federal patrol had managed to escape in the confusion. As far as Mac could see, none of the Confederates had been killed. He rode over to rejoin the general as Lee confronted one of the Union officers.

"Who's in command here?" demanded Lee.

"Our commanding officer is Gen. William Averell, sir," responded the prisoner. "But he's not here at the moment. He's on a scouting mission."

"William Averell?" Lee exclaimed. "Why, he and I were the best of friends at West Point!" The general threw back his head and laughed uproariously. "I must leave a note for him. Lieutenant Brannon!"

"Yes sir?" Mac was ready.

"Pen and paper, Lieutenant, if you please."

As Lee's aide, it was part of Mac's duties to write out messages for the general, but Lee insisted on penning this note himself. "I'm asking Averell to return the visit, and to bring some coffee with him when he comes so that we can enjoy a cup while we reminisce."

Mac didn't think there would be much reminiscing going on if Averell did as Lee asked. No doubt the Union general would be furious when he found out that his men had been defeated so handily and taken prisoner. Mac watched as Lee pinned the note to a tree with a broken saber.

"Let's go," Lee ordered when he was finished. "We'll take these men and horses back to camp with us."

The Confederate riders herded the prisoners and the captured horses toward the river. They would have to cross quickly and head back toward Culpeper, where Stuart's cavalry was posted, or else risk being discovered by a larger Yankee force. Mac knew that Lee didn't want to give up his trophies, however.

They forded the Rappahannock and pushed on without incident. When they had covered several more miles, Lee turned to Mac and said with a grin, "Averell's going to be mad as a hornet."

"Yes sir," Mac agreed. He didn't mention something that he had learned as a child.

A maddened hornet was likely to sting.

—◦◦◦—

THE NEWS of Fitz Lee's capture of Averell's men spread quickly, as did the rumors of the boasting note Lee had left behind for his old friend. As Lee had predicted, Averell was furious, as was Joseph Hooker. Hooker called in George Stoneman, the overall commander of the Union cavalry, and ordered him to find a way to put a stop to such daring raids as the one carried out by Lee. Stoneman, facing his first real challenge since being placed in command of the cavalry, was eager to carry out Hooker's orders. Several weeks passed, however, before an opportunity presented itself to do so. Winter was gasping its last breaths, and spring was on the horizon.

Before dawn on the morning on March 17, 1863, Confederate scouts hurried into the camp where pickets were keeping an eye on Kelly's Ford on the Rappahannock River. The scouts brought the grim news that a large force of Yankee cavalry, possibly as many as two thousand men, was on the way to the ford. The drowsy pickets were instantly awake, and they began hasty preparations for the arrival of the enemy. They dug in behind every bit of cover they could find, including trees that had been felled hurriedly. By the time the Union force arrived at the river, led by Averell, the Confederates were ready, and a volley of rifle fire ripped into the first riders to attempt the crossing. Averell pulled back, unwilling to sacrifice any more men in a suicidal effort to cross the river.

Averell was not giving up, however. He had brought along several pieces of light artillery, and he ordered those guns brought up. Soon the cannon were crashing, sending canister and shell screaming across the Rappahannock into the Confederate camp. The Southerners fought back grimly, withstanding the barrage for two hours, but finally it came to be too much. Too many of the pickets had fallen. When the Yankee cavalry charged again across the ford, there weren't enough Confederates to hold them back. The surviving defenders were forced to either flee or be captured or killed. Most died fighting in the rosy dawn light.

But by the time the sun was rising over the trees that lined the borders of the Rappahannock, Averell's cavalry was on the south side of the river, riding steadily toward Culpeper.

MAC LOOKED up in surprise as Fitz Lee burst into his tent not long after a rather skimpy breakfast. "Come on, Mac," the general said excitedly. "We're riding in ten minutes!"

Mac reached for his cap. "Riding where, sir?" he asked as he followed Lee out of the tent.

"Some of our scouts just reported that Averell's cavalry is on this side of the river," Lee explained as he walked quickly toward the pens where the horses were kept. "Our boys tried to stop them at Kelly's Ford, but there were too many. They had horse artillery with them, too. They're coming this direction, but we're going out to meet them before they get here."

"How many?" asked Mac.

Lee turned his head to grin at his aide. "At least two thousand, from what I hear."

Mac's mouth tightened grimly. Lee's cavalry brigade numbered no more than eight hundred men. They would be riding out to meet a force more than twice as large. Yet Lee didn't seem worried, which came as no surprise to Mac. The overwhelming odds would just add to the zest of the situation for Fitz Lee. If he could defeat the Yankees under those circumstances, it would be a glorious victory.

Officers were shouting orders, and men were quickly saddling their mounts. Mac got his saddle on the stallion while an orderly saddled Lee's horse. The two of them mounted at almost the same moment. Lee wheeled his horse and rode to the front of the column that was forming. Mac was right behind him.

Within the ten minutes that Lee had ordered, the brigade was ready to move out. They rode past the long rows of tents where the rest of the Confederate army was bivouacked, and as the soldiers heard the commotion and turned to see what was going on, cheers began to sound. A cavalryman lived for moments such as these, Mac thought as he watched Lee riding proudly past the men. Cheers resounding in his ears, the wind in his face fluttering the ostrich feather in his hat band and the colorful scarf around his neck . . . that was the stuff of life to Lee and Jeb Stuart and the other bold cavaliers who made up the cavalry. Mac felt himself getting swept up in the emotion of the moment. He saw Will standing with the Thirty-third Virginia and wanted to wave to him, but instead Mac sat stiffly in his saddle, his eyes fixed on the back of Lee right in front of him. No matter how Lee might feel about it, this wasn't an excursion, Mac reminded himself. They were riding out to do battle with a force of superior numbers. Not all of them would come back.

Best not to think about that, he told himself. There was no point in dwelling on what might happen.

Lee set a brisk pace during the morning. Scouts ranged out well ahead of the main body, but they kept reporting that they had not encountered the Union forces. Mac could tell that Lee was getting impatient. The general wanted this fight to begin as soon as possible.

It was almost midday when the scouts rode in with the news that Averell's cavalry had proceeded only a mile on this side of the river before stopping near a couple of farms. Lee scowled at the report.

"Averell's found himself a spot he likes, and he's waiting for us to come to him," Lee announced. "Well, we won't disappoint him." He waved the horsemen on.

Soon they came within sight of the Yankee cavalry. The blue-clad riders were lined up on the far side of a large field. Lee reined in to study them through his field glasses, and Mac did the same.

"What do you think, Lieutenant?" Lee asked after a few moments.

Mac answered bluntly, "I think there's a damned lot of them, General. More than two thousand, I'd say."

That response brought another grin from Lee. "Yes, but we know they're all out in the open, not hiding and waiting to ambush us. What we see is what we'll have to deal with." Lee put the glasses back to his eyes and looked intently through them at the Yankees, then suddenly stiffened in his saddle. "Look at him! The rapscallion!"

Mac studied the Yankees through his own glasses and saw one of the officers waving, as if beckoning to the Confederate cavalry. "I reckon that must be General Averell?"

"Inviting us over." Lee shoved his field glasses back in his saddlebag and reached for his saber. "Well, that's one invitation we're damned well going to answer!"

He ripped his saber from its scabbard, brandished it over his head, and bellowed, "Charge!" Then he put the spurs to his mount and sent it leaping forward at a gallop toward the Yankees.

Despite their difference in rank, Lee was Mac's best friend in the cavalry. He dug his heels into the stallion's flanks, and the big silver gray horse lunged ahead, catching up to Lee's horse in a couple of giant strides. Behind them, the rest of the Confederate horsemen charged, yelling and whooping.

Mac expected Averell, with his superior numbers, to sit back and take the defensive, but to his surprise the Yankees charged out into the field, too. The two forces met in the middle of the open ground like two opposing tides slamming into each other.

Bullets whipped through the air around Mac's head, but none of them found him. He was frightened but calm as he lined up shots with his pistol and squeezed them off. He saw one of the Yankees tumble out of his saddle nearby and knew that at least one of his shots had found its target.

There had been plenty of rain during the winter, too much, in fact, so instead of clouds of dust rising from the hooves of the horses, mud sucked at them instead. That slowed the action on both sides. Horses could not maneuver as quickly or as easily. After a couple of minutes of close, savage fighting, the Union and Confederate cavalry began to peel away from each other. Neither side was actually retreating; it was more like a couple of bare-knuckles brawlers pulling back momentarily to warily study each other.

Mac had tried to keep an eye on Lee during the skirmish, but in the confusion the general had eluded him. Now, Mac looked around desperately for Lee, afraid that he might be one of the men who had fallen in the fight. To his relief, he spotted Lee not far away and rode quickly toward him. Lee was still holding his saber. There was blood on it now.

"Over there to that wall, men!" Lee shouted, waving his saber at a low rock wall that divided the field from the next one over. The Confederate cavalry galloped to the wall and leaped their horses over it. Mac caught up with Lee as both men put their mounts over the wall. Lee reined in sharply and turned his horse so he could look toward the Yankees.

Mac did likewise, and he saw Averell was sending his men toward the wall in a charge. Averell had noticed the wall too late to make use of it himself, but maybe his forces could overrun it before the Rebels were ready for them.

"Dismount!" bellowed Lee. "We'll wait for them to come to us this time!"

Actually, no one had waited before, thought Mac. Both sides had been too eager for the combat to begin. Now, after the initial clash was over, strategy began to be more important, especially since the Union forces still far outnumbered their Southern counterparts.

As the troopers swung down from their saddles, men from each squadron were assigned the task of taking care of the horses. The mounts were led back from the wall where they would be safe; their former riders dropped into a crouch behind the low, thick stone barrier. Some of the cavalrymen carried carbines, but most of them had only pistols. They had to wait until the Yankees came in range . . .

Mac knelt on one knee, reloading his pistol. It was a bit nerve-wracking, attempting to do so while hundreds of Yankee cavalrymen were thundering toward him. But his fingers never fumbled, and after a moment he was able to close the fully loaded cylinder and bring the revolver up to brace it on the top of the wall. Without being aware of it, he held his breath as the Yankees came closer and closer.

"Fire!" The command sent a volley of pistol shots crashing into the blue-clad ranks of horsemen. Several of the riders in the lead went down, breaking the momentum of the charge. The Yankees on the flanks tried to veer out even farther in hopes of leaping their horses over the fence and encircling the Confederates, but wickedly accurate fire from both ends of the Southern line turned them back.

Mac, near the center, emptied his pistol for the second time today. Behind him, Lee strode back and forth, calling encouragement to his men. Mac wished the general would get down so that the rock wall would protect him, but Lee remained upright, and somehow the bullets all went around him without touching him. Mac had heard of men who could walk through a rainstorm without getting wet. Fitzhugh Lee obviously was one of those men.

The Yankees withdrew, and Lee called, "Bring up the horses! Quickly, boys, while we've got them on the run!"

Hurriedly, the Confederate cavalrymen mounted, leaped their horses over the wall, and charged after the Northern horsemen. They harried the stragglers, bringing down a few of them, but the main body of Yankees reached the trees on the far side of the field. Rapidly dismounting, the Yankees used the trees as cover and started firing at the onrushing Southerners. Lee was forced to wave his men back before the charge turned into a massacre.

Mac was panting softly as he rode back toward the rock wall. So far this engagement had been a frenzy of action, lurching first one way and then the other. He halfway expected the Yankees to charge again, and sure enough, in less than half an hour, they did. This time they came at the wall from an angle instead of launching a frontal assault, and although the Confederates were able to hold them off for a while, eventually the Federal forces turned the corner on them and pinned them against the wall from the other side, forcing a retreat.

Lee was seething as his troopers regrouped near one of the farmhouses. "Their mounts aren't as fast as ours," he declared. "We'll encircle them."

He gave orders for a quick flanking movement, splitting his men in order to carry it out. Mac frowned worriedly. They were already severely outnumbered; splitting the force didn't seem the best thing for them to be doing right now. In the next hour, though, he saw Lee's daring begin to pay off. Attacked from two directions at once, the Federals seemed sluggish and confused.

The men who had carried out the assault from the side were able to break through the Yankee lines and link up with the rest of the Southern horsemen. Now it was the Yankees who were split, but it wasn't of their own choosing that they found themselves in such a situation.

Averell counterattacked, taking advantage of his superior numbers to do so, and now the Confederates found themselves defending two fronts. Things got worse when the Union gunners came into play. The bursting shells ripped through the Southerners, and Lee had no choice but to order another retreat.

"Damn it!" he cried, smacking one fist into the other palm as he stalked back and forth after dismounting in a stand of trees where he and a small group of his men had withdrawn. "I've never seen the Yankees fight like this before!"

Mac wiped away a trickle of blood on his forehead where a chunk of metal from a bursting shell had opened up a shallow cut. He looked at the red stain on his fingertips and thought about how close he had come to dying, not just that once but a dozen or more times today.

The artillery fire became more sporadic, then stopped entirely. The rattle of gunshots faded away as well. Everyone scattered around this battlefield was taking the opportunity to catch a breath.

Lee looked at his staff officers and snapped, "Casualties?"

"More than sixty men dead so far," one of the men replied. "Another thirty or more out of the fight with wounds."

"We've lost over forty horses," reported another officer.

"It might be time to withdraw, General," the first man suggested.

Lee shook his head. "Not yet. Our own artillery should be arriving soon."

"Actually, it's already here, sir," Mac said. He had spotted the horse-drawn cannon arriving a moment earlier.

"We'll attack again," Lee ordered. "This time, with our artillery covering our charge."

Lee personally supervised the placement of the gun batteries at the edge of a field, then the Confederate barrage began. At the same time, the cavalry charged toward the Yankee line. The bombardment was supposed to distract the Union troops long enough for the gray-clad horsemen to reach them.

Instead, the Federal artillery roared back into the fight, sending shells crashing down around the Confederate batteries. Mac heard the telltale whistle of a shot coming directly toward them and grabbed Lee, flinging both of them to the ground. The shell burst nearby with enough force to shake the earth beneath them.

Lee gave Mac a rueful grin as they picked themselves up. "I'm much obliged to you, Lieutenant," the general said. "We'll have to see what we can do about getting you a battlefield commission. How does Captain Brannon sound? Saving the life of your commanding officer ought to be worth at least that much, don't you think?"

At the moment, Mac didn't give a damn about rank or promotions. He just wanted to defeat the Yankees, but as God was his witness, he couldn't see any way of doing it.

"Everyone to horse!" Lee shouted. "In your saddles, now!"

This was it, Mac sensed as he swung up onto the stallion. The final charge. That was all the Confederate cavalry had left in it. A glance at the sky showed him that the sun was surprisingly low. They had fought at a dead heat all afternoon without even realizing the passage of time.

Lee took the lead, with Mac right behind him. As if recognizing that this moment belonged to the horsemen, all the artillery batteries on both sides of the fight fell silent. The Yankees galloped out to meet the Confederate charge, and once again they came together in a classic encounter of two mounted forces.

Mac fired his pistol until the hammer fell on an empty chamber in the cylinder. He jammed the gun back in its holster and leaned over low to the ground to snatch up a fallen saber. Laying back and forth around him with the blade, he fought with a berserk fury that was totally unlike him. Like many of the other horsemen, the long, futile afternoon had goaded him into a rage that would not be denied.

But despite the furious Confederate attack, the Union line held. Again, there was nothing to do but break off the charge and regroup. Mac wheeled the stallion in response to a shouted order from Lee, and they galloped back to the edge of the field, turning again when they got there to face back toward the Yankees.

Mac looked along the line of horsemen. Their mounts were exhausted, just like the men. Heads drooped. Men wiped blood from haggard faces. For the first time, the Second Virginia Cavalry was experiencing, if not outright defeat, at least something other than victory.

"If they come at us now, we can't stop them," Mac said softly. The general nodded. "I know."

The Yankees had no interest in charging, however. Badly battered themselves, with night coming on, they began to pull back. Company after company withdrew while across the field the Southerners watched with startled eyes. "It's over." The whispered words flew along the line. The battle had ended in a stalemate, but at least it had ended.

Finally, only a small group of Yankees were left in sight. One of them took something from inside his coat and held it up. Lee muttered, "What in blazes?" and whipped out his field glasses.

Mac got his own glasses out in time to see the man on the far side of the field drop whatever he was holding. "That's General Averell, isn't it?" Mac asked.

"Yes, that's him," replied Lee. "What's he doing?"

"I'll find out," Mac heard himself saying. Without thinking about what he was doing, he sent the stallion trotting out into the field. Lee called after him, but Mac ignored the general. Across the way, the last of the Yankees had disappeared.

Mac rode up to the object Averell had dropped. When he saw what it was, he uttered a grim laugh and bent from the saddle to retrieve it. He turned the stallion and rode back to where Lee was waiting.

"What is it?" Lee demanded.

Mac held out the bag full of coffee Averell had left behind. "There's a note attached to it, sir," he said.

Lee snatched the bag out of Mac's hand and opened the note with fingers that trembled with rage. "Dear Fitz—Here's your coffee. Here's your visit," he read. "How do you like it?"

For a second, Lee's face was flushed with rage, and Mac thought the general was going to explode into an apoplectic fit. Then, surprisingly, Lee began to laugh. "There'll be another day," he said. "Averell's not heard the last of the Second Virginia." Then he turned his horse toward Culpeper and said, "Let's go home."

That was the best idea Mac had heard all day.

Chapter Twenty-four

I N APRIL 1863, Abraham Lincoln had paid a visit to the Army of the Potomac at Falmouth. General Hooker received him warmly and regaled the president with several parades and reviews. Lincoln, however, was more interested in what Hooker planned to do about the Confederate army. Hooker, who had recently devised a plan that would finally do justice to his despised nickname of "Fighting Joe," explained to the commander in chief that he intended to make a fast flanking march to the northwest with most of his army, leaving a small part of it in Falmouth to menace Fredericksburg across the river and make the Rebels think it was still his intent to ultimately drive them from their defensive positions there. In the meantime, the greater part of his army would cross the Rappahannock and Rapidan Rivers and concentrate in the vicinity of the crossroads village of Chancellorsville, where they would be ready to attack Robert E. Lee's left flank and rear.

"Lee will have no choice but to retreat toward Richmond across the face of our forces at Falmouth," Hooker explained. "An aggressive attack at that point will crush him."

It was a good plan, Lincoln agreed, but he urged Hooker not to hold back any of his forces when the time came to strike. That had been Burnside's downfall.

And the North could ill afford yet another missed opportunity.

⸻

So FAR, spring had been—as spring usually was in northern Virginia—a mixture of beauty and misery. The clear days were as gorgeous as anyone could ever hope for, crisp and cool and filled

with the scent of wildflowers and rich earth. Then there were
the days when the sky opened and steady downpours drenched
everything. Gradually, as April passed, the rains became less
and the weather was prettier.

Back home, in better days, the fields would have been ready
for planting, Will Brannon thought as he watched his company
drill. All he could do was hope that his mother and Henry and
Cordelia had been able to handle everything that needed to be
done. With rumors flying that the Yankees were on the move,
there was no way he could take the time to ride over to Culpeper and check on things.

He saw a group of cavalry riding in, and a few minutes later
Mac trotted over to the drill field on the stallion. Mac had been
different since the battle at Kelly's Ford more than a month earlier, Will reflected. Always serious and sober, Mac had grown
more solemn than ever, as if something had happened during
that fight that haunted him. He had spoken of the clash a few
times with Will, but he had never gone into great detail.

When Mac was ready to talk about it, he would, Will
decided. Right now, though, Mac looked excited about something else.

"There's news," Mac said as he swung down from the
saddle. "We've picked up some more Yankee stragglers who say
that Hooker has split his army."

Will frowned. "Why would he do that? He's still bound and
determined to run us off from here, isn't he?" Will's eyes cut
toward Marye's Hill, visible in the distance where it overlooked
Fredericksburg. "Burnside wasn't able to do it with the whole
Army of the Potomac. I don't see how Hooker thinks he can
with just part of it."

"We're not at full strength anymore, either," Mac pointed
out.

Will nodded. He knew as well as his brother did that Longstreet's division was somewhere on the Virginia Peninsula.
Robert E. Lee had sent him there to check on rumors of

another Union invasion from that direction, and once Long-street had reported back that the invasion rumors were baseless gossip, Lee had instructed him to remain on the peninsula and gather supplies.

"We'll have to make do with what we've got," Will said with a shrug. "Just like always."

"I reckon." With a wave, Mac took the reins of the stallion and led the big horse after the rest of the cavalry patrol.

Will pondered the news, but not for long. Less than an hour later, excited couriers brought an even fresher report: the Yankees were once again trying to cross the Rappahannock, this time a short distance south of Fredericksburg. Confederate troops were being moved into position to oppose them.

As Will hurriedly assembled his company and told Sgt. Darcy Bennett to get the men ready to march, he spied General Jackson coming out of the house that belonged to the Yerby family, which he had been using for his headquarters. Jackson had been visiting there with his wife, Anna, and their five-month-old daughter, Julia. This was Mrs. Jackson's first visit to her husband in a year, and the first time the general had seen his infant daughter. Jackson looked suitably upset that the Yankees, as inconsiderate as ever, were ruining his family reunion.

Rapidly, the Confederate soldiers marched toward the Rappahannock. When they came within sight of the river, Will saw from the back of his dun that the Federals had already crossed. Through his field glasses, he spotted long lines of blue-clad troops ready for action. For some reason, however, the Yankees had stopped their advance and were just sitting there, waiting as more and more Confederate soldiers filed up to oppose them.

Will lowered his glasses and frowned. Something surely didn't feel right about this, he thought. The Union foray across the river was drawing a lot of attention, but they didn't seem to want to actually *do* anything.

Will's thoughts went back to his days as the sheriff of Culpeper County. He had been involved in plenty of tavern brawls during that time, and he remembered how some fighters always liked to feint, to make their opponent think they were going to do something when they were really about to do something entirely different. He had a feeling that might be what was going on here.

He remembered what Mac had said about large numbers of Yankees moving northwestward. Damn it! he thought. Hooker was trying to set them up for something.

Will wanted to turn around and ride back to Robert E. Lee's headquarters and warn him, but his duty was to stay here with his company. Besides, he told himself, if he could figure out what the Yankees were up to, then so could Lee. The general was a lot smarter when it came to military matters than he was, Will decided.

Still, he wished he knew exactly what was going on there.

MAC REMAINED as quiet and unobtrusive as he could during the meeting. He was a captain now; Fitz Lee had followed through on the promise of a battlefield promotion after the battle of Kelly's Ford. But most of the men in this tent were generals. Mac looked around at Robert E. Lee, T. J. Jackson, and Jeb Stuart and knew there probably wasn't a more impressive collection of military leaders anywhere in the world. Added to them were several of the young firebrands such as Fitz Lee.

More of the cavalry scouts had come in with news. Union forces of varying strengths were converging on the crossroads hamlet called Chancellorsville, some ten miles northwest of Fredericksburg. Some of the Yankees apparently had crossed the Rappahannock far upriver at Kelly's Ford. Other groups of Federals were coming in from the direction of the Germanna and U.S. Fords, which were closer to Chancellorsville. When they all came together, they would form a huge army of at least seventy thousand men, Stuart warned.

Robert E. Lee nodded gravely. "I fear that is exactly what they intend to do, gentlemen," he said. He turned to one of the other officers. "General Anderson, I want you to move your division to Zoan's Church. From there you ought to be able to see what the Yankees are up to."

Maj. Gen. Richard H. Anderson nodded. "Yes sir. It will be our honor to guard the roads."

"Exactly what I intended, General. And keep me advised as to the movements and disposition of the Federal forces."

"Yes sir."

The meeting broke up, and Mac followed Fitz Lee outside. "My uncle is acting with unusual caution," Lee said impatiently. "I think we should hit the Yankees before they hit us."

"What about the ones who crossed the Rappahannock south of here?" asked Mac.

Lee waved a hand. "A diversion, nothing more."

That seemed likely to Mac, too. Ever since Robert E. Lee had assumed command of the Confederate army, he had confounded and defeated the Yankees by doing the unexpected, often at great risk. Mac hoped that the Union forces weren't going to try to turn the table on the commander by using his own tactics against him.

———

THE FEDERAL troops south of Fredericksburg continued to maintain their position during the afternoon. In addition, more troops directly across the river from the town moved around as if they were getting ready to launch a major attack. But still nothing happened. Night fell and passed quietly, with the opposing forces poised for action but not moving.

The next morning was equally uneventful, but around noon, couriers from Anderson came galloping frenziedly into the Confederate camp. Mac was nearby when the men, out of breath from their frantic ride, were ushered up to Robert E. Lee. They snapped to attention, saluted, and one of the men said, "General Anderson's compliments, sir."

"Yes, yes, what word from the general?" asked Lee impatiently.

"Well, sir . . . he said to tell you that there's one hell of a lot of Yankees in the Wilderness."

Mac knew the area well. He had ridden through it on several patrols in the past. The Wilderness more than lived up to its name. Stretching westward for several miles from Chancellorsville, it was a dense thicket of second-growth pine with an underlayer of thorny brush that was almost impassable. Several roads had been hacked through the Wilderness, but if a man had to leave the path, it would be slow going through the woods.

"Did General Anderson estimate the number of troops?" Lee asked.

"He figured there was at least sixty, sixty-five thousand, Gen'ral. Probably more."

Lee took a deep breath and let it out slowly. "That is where the danger lies," he said quietly, as much to himself as to anyone else. He looked around for his orderly. "Summon Generals Jackson, Stuart, McLaws, and Early."

For the second day in a row, a summit meeting was held among the Confederate commanders. Stuart came in first and spoke privately with Lee. By the time the other officers arrived, Lee had drafted a new set of orders.

"Special Orders Number 121, gentlemen," said Lee as he looked around the circle of grim-faced men. "General Jackson?"

"Yes sir?" Jackson responded immediately.

"General Stuart tells me that, according to his scouts, the Federal right is in the air. Therefore, at dawn tomorrow, you will march three of your divisions westward to confront the enemy."

Jackson nodded eagerly. "Yes sir!"

"General Early, your division will remain in place in case General Sedgwick decides to get up any mischief," Lee said, referring to the commander of the Union troops in Fredericksburg.

The irascible Jubal Early nodded his agreement, though somewhat reluctantly. "Whatever you say, General."

Mac thought that Early believed he was being shunted aside, away from the real action to come.

"General McLaws," Lee continued, "leave one brigade on the heights behind Fredericksburg and march the rest of your division to the west, following General Jackson."

"Yes sir." McLaws exchanged a glance with Jackson and Early. "We're going to be dangerously divided, sir, with such a small force here and only forty thousand to oppose Hooker."

Slowly, Lee nodded. "I am aware of that, General," he said, "but it must be victory or death, for defeat would be ruinous."

JACKSON HAD been ordered to march his men west at dawn on May 1, but they were actually on the move earlier than that, heading west along the Old Mine Road by the light of a beautiful spring moon.

Will hoped they hadn't waited too late to move against the Yankees. It looked like his hunch about Hooker trying a feint had been right; otherwise Jackson's foot cavalry wouldn't be racing west now to meet a new Union threat.

The sun rose, heralding a beautiful day. All during the predawn hours of the march, couriers galloped back and forth between Anderson's position at Zoan Church and the advancing divisions under Jackson. Will heard that the Yankees had left the Wilderness and moved on east of Chancellorsville now. Anderson had spread out his men in a defensive line around both Zoan Church and another nearby house of worship known as Tabernacle Church. So much of this war, Will mused, had been fought in the vicinity of one church or another. The sanctity of religion was always swept aside whenever two armies clashed.

The defensive line set up by Anderson came into view around eight o'clock in the morning. Will saw that the troops were busily engaged in digging trenches. That made sense to him, considering the size of the army they would soon be facing. Will was not at all surprised, however, when Jackson abandoned the idea of defense in favor of offense. Taking command, he ordered skirmishers forward.

Within a short time, the rattle of musketry could be heard, and Will knew the leading edge of the Confederate advance had run into the Yankees pushing east from Chancellorsville. Orders came back quickly for the rest of Jackson's men to move up.

Will drew his saber and nodded to Darcy Bennett. "Let's go, Sergeant," he said.

Darcy grinned up at him and then turned to the troops to bellow, "Fix bayonets! Forward march! Come on, boys, let's spank us some Yankees!"

With a chorus of yells, the Confederate soldiers surged forward. Underfed, undersupplied, still showing the ravages of the hard winter they had survived, they forgot all the hardships they had endured. There was fighting to be done, and they were ready.

The Mine Road crossed the abandoned roadbed of an unfinished rail line, wound past Tabernacle Church, then dropped down a gentle slope to cross two more trails known as the Plank Road and the Old Orange Turnpike. Zoan Church sat between those two roads, which roughly paralleled each other and led west to Chancellorsville and the Wilderness. West of Zoan Church between the roads was a thick stand of trees, and clouds of gray powder smoke wreathed their branches. Yankee troops were trying to break out of the trees, but the Confederates under Jackson were pushing them back.

Will pointed down the hill toward the woods with his saber and shouted, "Charge!"

Howling out their determination, the men of his company threw themselves forward into the fight.

Will headed directly toward the trees, trusting that his men would follow him. He saw bright muzzle flashes in the shadows

underneath the branches. Quite a few men, Union and Confederate alike, had fallen in the open ground to the right, between
the Plank Road and the church. Will raced on horseback past
the bodies, aware now that bullets and balls were whipping
through the air around him. As he neared a large tree that stood
beside the road by itself, he reined in and dropped out of the
saddle, leaving the dun there in relative safety. He shifted his
saber from his right hand to his left, drew his pistol, and began
walking deliberately toward the woods.

Several Yankees burst out of the shelter of the trees and ran
toward him. Will fired coolly into their midst, dropping a couple
of them. A bullet kicked up dust at his feet as the remaining
Union soldiers tried to draw a bead on him.

Then, with a Rebel yell, Darcy Bennett bolted past him, followed by several more soldiers of the company. The Yankees
abandoned their position and turned to run back into the woods.
Darcy and the others piled in after them.

Will turned to see the rest of the company entering the
woods as well. He stalked on toward the trees, reloading his
pistol as he went. He reached the edge of the woods and
stepped into the shadows. What sunlight reached the ground
was filtered through the new leaves that clustered thickly on
the branches of the trees, giving everything a greenish cast as if
the men were doing battle underwater. And as if they were
underwater, everything seemed to slow down for Will. He
found a target, fired, twisted, fired again, heard a muffled shout
and wheeled to his left to see one of the Yankees lunging at
him, rifle upraised so that he could drive his bayonet down into
Will's body.

Will lifted his saber and the Yankee ran into it, spitting himself on the blade. Momentum carried him forward, though, and
the tip of his bayonet raked across Will's left hip. Will shoved
the dying man aside and ripped his blade from the Yankee's
body. He stumbled a little from the pain that burned in his hip
from the bayonet gash, but he was able to keep his feet and

shoot another blue-clad attacker. The tide of battle swept on past Will, surging deeper into the woods. He leaned against one of the trees and holstered his pistol, then shoved the saber back in its sheath. He could feel blood trickling warmly down his leg now. He pulled his shirt loose from his trousers, ripped a piece off the bottom of it, and folded the cloth into a compress. He took off his belt, snugged it lower around his hips so that it would hold the compress in place against the wound, then limped forward.

The fighting was fierce over a front that was at least a mile long, stretching from south of the Plank Road to north of the Old Orange Turnpike. The Yankees were steadily retreating westward, though. Will and the rest of his company emerged onto the Plank Road near the point where another trail turned off to the left and led to a foundry known as Catherine Furnace. Hoofbeats behind him made Will stop and look around.

Jackson, campaign cap pulled down tightly on his shaggy head, was riding toward him with several members of his staff. Jackson reined in and called, "How goes the battle, Captain Brannon?"

Will was able to summon up a grin for his commander. "Just fine, General. The Yankees are on the run."

"Of course they are." Jackson looked at the makeshift bandage on Will's hip. "Are you badly injured, Captain?"

"Just a scratch, sir," Will assured him. The wound hurt like blazes, but it was a scratch nonetheless, he told himself.

"Have a care not to let it fester," Jackson told him, then rode on with one arm lifted into the air, as was his custom. The fact that Jackson was heading for the thick of the fighting came as no surprise to Will.

By nightfall, the Union forces had fallen all the way back to Chancellorsville. Robert E. Lee arrived and met with Jackson in a rough camp at the intersection of Plank Road and Furnace Road. Will's company, along with the rest of the Stonewall

Brigade, stacked their rifles and sat down to rest and eat near this makeshift headquarters.

Lee and Jackson conferred privately—and quietly—while sitting on crates of hardtack underneath a tree, not allowing even their staffs to participate in the discussion. Will could see the two men with their heads together, and he wondered what plan they were hatching.

He would find out soon enough, he thought. They all would, probably as early as the next morning.

MAC CAUGHT a few hours of sleep leaning against the trunk of a tree; he was roused long before dawn by Fitz Lee. "We've work to do," Lee said happily, and Mac knew there would be more battle today.

The day before, as Jackson's infantry was driving the Yankees back into Chancellorsville, the cavalry had been busy rounding up any stragglers who tried to flee from the clash. Mac had no idea what their mission was to be today, but he expected to find out shortly.

He was not expecting to see General Jackson talking with Fitz Lee a few minutes later. Nearby, the men of Jackson's command had broken camp and were marching to the southwest. Mac spotted Will riding alongside his company on the dun horse that was his usual mount. Will gave him a grin and a wave, then moved on with his men. Everyone was quiet this morning; the tramp of marching feet was the only sound that could be heard.

"Come along, Captain," Lee said to Mac. "We're going to take a look at the Yankees."

Mac mounted up, seeing as he swung onto the back of the stallion that Jackson was also getting into the saddle. The three of them rode away from the camp.

Their route took them past the foundry, then through the woods of the Wilderness on a small, winding trail. They rode for several miles, heading west and then northwest, until Mac realized they were now far west of Chancellorsville. That meant they were behind enemy lines. Jackson's infantry had been coming that direction, too.

Suddenly, Mac understood what was happening. Robert E. Lee, having already split his army, was dividing it again. Jackson's foot cavalry was performing a flanking march, swinging around to the Federal rear. Mac found himself grinning at the sheer audacity of the maneuver. The Union general, Hooker, had thought to catch the Confederate army in a trap with *his* flanking march up the Rappahannock. Now Jackson was in the process of outflanking Hooker. If it worked, the plan would be sheer brilliance.

But there was still no getting around the fact that the Confederates were outnumbered. It wouldn't be an easy fight, Mac reminded himself.

They reached another intersection, and Lee told Jackson, "This is the Orange Plank Road. It leads east to Chancellorsville."

Jackson nodded. "Then that is where we shall go, gentlemen." The three of them urged their mounts into a trot.

It was midday by the time the riders topped a small hill and came within sight of a large open area just north of the Wilderness. Several hundred yards ahead of them, Mac saw a church and a few houses on the north side of the road. On the south side of the road was a larger building that was probably a tavern. All through the open area, campfires burned as cooks prepared lunch for the Union troops who had gathered there after the previous day's fighting.

Jackson leaned forward in his saddle and observed eagerly, "They have no idea we are here. We shall fall on them in complete surprise." He looked over at Lee. "May I borrow your aide, General?"

"Of course, General," Lee replied.

Jackson turned to Mac. "Captain, I want you to carry word back to Generals Rodes, Colston, and Paxton. Tell them to have our men advance with all due speed. We will attack before the day is out."

Mac acknowledged and glanced at Lee, who nodded his approval. With that, Mac turned the stallion and put it into a gallop, carrying with him the orders that would launch thousands of men into battle.

Chapter Twenty-five

URING THE DAY OF May 2, Hooker received reports from
his scouts that told of fast movement to the west and
northwest by large numbers of Confederate troops. He was
immensely pleased by this news. He had expected Lee to retreat
toward Richmond, but now it appeared they were fleeing in the
other direction, toward Gordonsville. Although such a retreat
would not place the Confederates in a position where Hooker
could utterly smash them, as he had intended, a rout was still a
rout, he reasoned, and as such this campaign would be regarded
as a great Union victory. When he received worried communica-
tions about enemy troop movements from his commanders west
of Chancellorsville, in the vicinity of Dowdall's Tavern, he sent
back messages telling them not to be concerned.

The Rebels, it was clear to Joe Hooker, had given up.

———

WILL COULD smell the smoke from the cooking fires of the
Yankees. They were fixing supper, he thought. But their preparations were about to be interrupted.

It was late in the afternoon of May 2, and everyone was finally
in place as General Jackson wanted them. From the Stonewall
Brigade and part of General Stuart's cavalry on the south end, the
Confederate line stretched northward two full miles, ending with
the rest of the cavalry. From where Will sat on the dun, he could
see Mac on the big silver gray stallion, right up front with Fitz
Lee. The cavalry would lead the attack at this end of the line,
but the Stonewall Brigade was right behind them.

As if feeling his brother's eyes on him, Mac hipped around
in the saddle and gave Will a tired grin. They had spoken briefly
while the lines of battle were forming, and Will knew that Mac

had been up and busy since early that morning, helping Lee and General Jackson scout the enemy's position. Will lifted a finger to the brim of his hat and sketched a salute.

Captain Brannon wishing luck to Captain Brannon, he thought. With good fortune, they would both come through this battle alive.

Moments later, orders to advance came down the line. Slowly and deliberately, the Confederate soldiers moved forward. Will took a deep breath as he put the dun into motion. He smelled bacon and biscuits and coffee. They were that close to the Yankees.

Only a few minutes passed before gunfire began to crackle as Federal pickets were shocked to see thousands of gray-clad figures coming through the woods toward them. With the need for secrecy gone, the Confederate line surged ahead, Rebel yells issuing from countless throats.

The wound on Will's hip throbbed, but he ignored it as he urged his horse toward the enemy. The gash had been cleaned and bandaged by one of the medical officers and had a bulky bandage tied over it. There was nothing else to be done for it. Besides, Will told himself grimly, before the day was over he might suffer much worse injuries. Then he put that thought out of his head as well.

He rode with his pistol drawn instead of his saber. Today, his troops wouldn't need some sword-waving officer to urge them on. In fact, nothing could have held them back. The woods began to fill with the roar of gunfire and the acrid smell of powder smoke.

Just ahead of him, Will saw a group of Yankees trying to form themselves into ranks so that they could fight back as they had been taught. Firing the pistol as fast as he could, Will galloped the dun into them, bowling over a couple of the blue-clad soldiers and gunning down two more. Their fleeting show of resistance broken, the surviving Yankees turned and tried to flee, only to be shot down from behind by Will's company.

The Confederate line swept on and on, driving the Yankees before them. The Union officers, most of them taken completely by surprise, had no chance to rally their men. There was not even a semblance of an orderly retreat. From the first few moments of the attack, the rout was on. Will saw hundreds of Federal troops running wildly through the woods, not caring where they were going as long as it was away from the screaming devils in butternut and gray that pursued them.

"Will!"

Hearing his name being called over the tumult, Will reined in and looked around. He saw Mac riding toward him. Mac's campaign cap was gone, but he seemed to be unhurt. Will grinned as Mac rode up. "What happened to your hat?"

Mac grimaced. "A branch knocked it off. I suppose I'm lucky it wasn't a couple of inches lower. I would have been brained if it had been. Are you all right?"

Will nodded and said, "They didn't put up much of a fight, did they?"

The air was still filled with the sound of gunfire, punctuated by an occasional volley of artillery. "Sounds like they're still fighting to me," said Mac.

Will shook his head. "The battle's over, they just don't know it yet." A thought struck him. "I wish Yancy was here. He'd enjoy seeing the Yankees ran."

Mac started to turn his horse. "I'd better find General Lee. We got separated during the charge, and I want to make certain he's all right."

"Take care, then." Will lifted a hand in farewell as his brother rode off into the gathering dusk.

⚓

BY NIGHTFALL the Yankees had retreated at least two miles toward Chancellorsville. The only things that stopped the Confederate pursuit were darkness and the fact that their advance had been so fast, companies had gotten scattered and separated from their officers. As difficult as it was to move through the Wilderness during the day, it was utterly impossible at night, so the Confederates began to regroup.

A stunned General Hooker sat in his headquarters in the commandeered Chancellor inn and wondered what had happened to his brilliant plan. Though his forces still vastly outnumbered those of the Confederates, he found himself surrounded, with Lee to his east and that devil Jackson to the west. Retreat was an inglorious option, and yet . . .

Sometimes, numbers did little to tell the real story, Hooker reflected bitterly.

⸻

"ATTACK, ATTACK, ATTACK," Jackson said. "It is our watchword, gentlemen."

The general was riding along a narrow path between dark masses of trees that loomed on either side. Full night had fallen, and Mac thought it was about nine o'clock. He and Will rode side by side behind Jackson and several other officers, among them A. P. Hill. A short time earlier, in the camp the Confederates had made once the day's pursuit of the Yankees had ended, the general had expressed his intention of scouting the enemy lines. He had been told by nineteen-year-old David Joseph Kyle, a native of the area and a private in the Ninth Virginia Cavalry, that there was a little-used and little-known trail, known as the Mountain Road, that might enable him to launch an unsuspected night attack against the Federals. Jackson wanted to see it for himself, and he drafted Private Kyle to guide the party.

Fitz Lee had asked Mac to go along with Jackson and bring back word of what they found, and as one of the Stonewall Brigade's officers, Will had volunteered to accompany the small group as well. It was a dark night, and as they rode along, Will hoped they wouldn't stumble into the Federal camp.

Jackson was talkative, exclaiming how the next day would see the Union troops pushed back even farther, when up ahead and to the right of the road, muzzle flashes winked from under the trees and a volley of fire ripped through the peaceful night. "Get down!" Will called to Mac and ducked instinctively as bullets whistled over his head. Someone in the Army of the Potomac, despite its disorganized state, had thought to put out some pickets.

"Ride back the way we came!" roared Jackson as he wheeled his horse around, waving to the other riders to retreat. They put their mounts into a gallop. Will and Mac were near the front of the group. It was difficult to see the road in the cloying darkness, difficult to see even a hand in front of the face. Several minutes passed in the wild ride.

Suddenly, more shots sounded, but these came from in front of them, not behind. Will heard the ugly thud of bullets striking flesh, and someone cried out in pain. One of the horses screamed and floundered, pitching forward and dumping its rider over its head. Another volley rang out as Will and Mac reined in and turned to look behind them. Several saddles had been emptied by the shots, and Will saw to his horror that one of the riderless animals now racing past them was the small sorrel horse that General Jackson had been riding.

"General!" Will cried, while beside him Mac shouted, "Cease fire! Cease fire, damn it! You're shooting into your own men!"

The volleys had indeed come from Confederate pickets. Lt. Joseph Morrison, one of Jackson's aides as well as the general's brother-in-law, rushed past Will and Mac, echoing Mac's pleas to stop shooting. Gradually, the gunfire died away as the Brannon brothers hurried back along the path.

They found a couple of the officers bending over a huddled shape in the road. One of the men looked up and said in a broken voice, "It's General Jackson. He's been hit."

A man Will recognized as General Hill sat in the road beside Jackson and gently lifted him so that the wounded general's head and shoulders rested in his lap. Looking up, Hill barked, "Someone fetch Dr. McGuire and an ambulance!"

"I'll do it," Mac said. He turned the stallion and galloped off toward the Confederate camp.

Will didn't know how badly Jackson was hurt, but the general was conscious, moving around a little and muttering. If anyone could save him, thought Will, it was Hunter McGuire, Jackson's chief surgeon and personal friend. Jackson's adjutant, Capt. James P. Smith, who had not been with the group, came galloping up a moment later and practically flung himself out of his saddle. "My God!" Smith exclaimed. "Is there a litter about?"

Hill shook his head. "I've sent a man for Dr. McGuire and an ambulance, but perhaps we shouldn't wait. We can carry General Jackson in our arms—"

Jackson roused himself, and Will heard him say distinctly, "No, I think I can walk."

Hill looked around at the other men and nodded. They helped Jackson to his feet and put their arms around him to support him as he walked unsteadily along the road. Will had his arm around Jackson's waist, and he could feel the blood soaking into the left side of the general's uniform. Jackson's left arm hung limply, flopping against the back of Will's hand. One of the bullets had broken it, and from the amount of blood that was welling from the wound, Will suspected an artery had been cut, too.

Several men came running up the road with a litter. They were probably from the company that had been placed on guard in the woods, perhaps even some of the men who had fired the shots at Jackson and his companions. Ignoring Jackson's protests that he could walk, he was placed on the litter and carried.

Will wondered where Mac and the doctor and the ambulance were.

To the rear, a Union artillery battery opened up. They had to be firing blindly, just trying to make a show of resistance after the day's humiliation, but the shells burst in the road both in front of and behind the group carrying General Jackson. One of the men holding the litter was cut down by a piece of canister, and as he fell he dropped his end of the litter. Jackson crashed heavily to the ground, falling on top of the litter. He let out an agonized groan as more shells exploded nearby.

General Hill motioned for the men to get off the road. They couldn't carry Jackson to safety as long as the Yankee bombardment went on. Will stretched out on the edge of the road next to the litter, and Captain Smith and Lieutenant Morrison lay on the other side of the general. Whenever Jackson started to try to get up, Smith put an arm across his chest and held him down as gently as possible. Next to them, Will gritted his teeth as the earth shook underneath him from the bursting shells. Fragments from exploding canister rounds whined and skipped around the men and struck sparks from the rocks in the road. The bombardment seemed endless.

Finally, the artillery fire died away. The Confederate officers came out of the woods where they had taken cover, and several men grabbed the handles of Jackson's litter, lifting it and starting toward the camp once more. Will was one of the men carrying the litter. He felt a surge of relief a few minutes later when a shout sounded from up ahead. He recognized Mac's voice.

An ambulance rolled up and stopped. Mac was handling the team of horses. There was no sign of Dr. McGuire, however.

"Let's put him inside," Smith said. "Carry the litter to the rear of the ambulance, boys."

From the woods close by, one of the pickets posted there called out, "Who have you got there?"

Smith answered hastily, "A friend of ours who is wounded," and Will knew the captain didn't want the word spreading through the ranks that Jackson was gravely wounded.

The deception failed, however. Too many high-ranking officers were bustling about for the soldiers to be fooled. One of them cried, "My God, that's Old Jack who's been hit!"

By this time, Will and the other men were lifting the litter into the back of the vehicle. Jackson overheard the exchange, and he said in a low but commanding voice, "When asked, tell the men only that I am a Confederate officer."

"Yes sir," Morrison said. He, along with everyone else, grunted with the effort as the litter was placed in the ambulance.

Jackson was not the only patient. In the dim light of a lantern, Will saw another wounded man stretched out on the hard boards of the ambulance's floor and recognized him as Col. Stapleton Crutchfield, the leading artilleryman in the Second Corps. There was blood on his leg, and despite Jackson's condition, he was immediately worried when he saw his friend.

"Stapleton, are you all right?" Jackson asked.

"General?" gasped Crutchfield through his own pain. "You're injured!"

"Don't worry about me," Stonewall assured him. "I'll be fine, won't I, lads?"

Will saw the glances exchanged between Smith, Morrison, and the other aides who had clambered into the ambulance. "Of course, General," Smith said. It was much too soon to tell, of course, but the amount of blood Jackson had already lost did not bode well.

Will and the other men stepped back as Mac turned the vehicle and started toward the Confederate camp and McGuire's field hospital. He coaxed the team as quickly as he could without jolting the injured passengers too much.

Will watched them go and thought about what a loss to the Confederate army it would be if Jackson were to die from his wounds. The smashing victory won earlier in the day was forgotten. This night, already dark, had just become much darker indeed.

Mac had come across the ambulance carrying Crutchfield and another wounded officer and commandeered it, tying the stallion's reins to the back. The other officer, whose injuries were not serious, had instantly given up his place in the vehicle when he heard that Jackson had been injured.

Now, as Mac held tightly to the reins and guided the team through the night, he could hear Jackson asking for "spirits" in the rear of the ambulance. The general had to be in great pain if he was calling for whiskey. Mac had heard that he preferred to be clear-headed at all times.

He wished that he had been able to find McGuire. The chief surgeon had set up a field hospital near the Old Wilderness Tavern, though. Mac thought surely they would be able to find him there.

After several miles of relatively slow progress through the woods, the ambulance came to a clearing and Dowdall's Tavern. Lieutenant Morrison called out, "That's Reverend Lacy's place. Stop there."

This was hardly the time or place to point out that the lieutenant was giving orders to a captain, thought Mac. He drew back on the reins and brought the ambulance to a halt. "Hello, the house!" he called. "We have wounded men out here!"

Lights were burning inside the tavern. The door opened and several men came out, among them a slender figure that Mac recognized with relief as that of Dr. McGuire. Finally, a stroke of luck on this baleful night.

The surgeon hurried to the rear of the wagon and exclaimed in dismay as he recognized Jackson. Mac heard him say, "I hope you are not badly hurt, General."

Jackson's voice was feeble but calm and coherent as he replied, "I am badly injured, Doctor. I fear I am dying." He hesitated, then continued, "I'm glad you're here. I think the wound in my shoulder is still bleeding."

It was, no doubt of that, thought Mac. The general's uniform was black with the blood. Mac turned his head and watched through the gap in the curtains as McGuire pressed a finger into the gaping wound on Jackson's left arm to stanch the flow of blood from the severed artery.

Jackson's face was ghastly in the lantern light, washed of all color and set in rigid lines of pain. There were also several

378 • *James Reasoner*

scratches on his face from the tree branches that had whipped him when his horse bolted. McGuire glanced up, met Mac's eyes for a moment, and said, "Get this ambulance moving, Captain."

Mac nodded and did exactly that.

Speed was impossible on the rough roads, so it was almost midnight before the ambulance finally reached the field hospital near the tavern. Mac sat on the driver's seat, shoulders slumped in weariness, as Jackson's litter was carefully lifted from the vehicle and carried into the big tent. McGuire was at the general's side, his finger still pressed to the wound to slow the loss of blood, and Lieutenant Morrison was right with him, supporting Jackson's broken arm. Surrounded by Jackson's other aides and several of McGuire's surgeons, the grim-faced group disappeared into the tent.

Captain Smith emerged a few minutes later and came over to the ambulance. He looked up at Mac and said, "You're one of General Stuart's cavalrymen, aren't you, Captain?"

Mac nodded. "That's right."

"You'd better go find him and let him know what has happened tonight. It appears that he's likely to find himself in command of the infantry come morning."

"What about General Hill?" asked Mac with a frown. Hill was Jackson's second-in-command.

Smith inclined his head toward the tent. "I heard in there that General Hill has been wounded, too, though not nearly as badly as General Jackson. Command will go to General Rodes, but to speak frankly, I doubt that he will want it. Rodes is a good man, but not the sort to take charge of an entire corps."

Mac nodded slowly. The fiery A. P. Hill might have been able to replace Jackson, but with Hill out of action, that left Stuart as the natural successor, despite what the chain of command might say. "You're right, Captain," Mac said as he climbed down from the ambulance. He went to the rear of the vehicle and began untying the stallion's reins. "I'll find General Stuart at once."

"Good. I have to get back inside. They'll need men to hold the lanterns while the doctors examine the general's wounds."

Mac swung up into the saddle, forcing his own exhaustion out of his mind. Stuart's headquarters were somewhere to the southeast. It might take him most of the night to find them.

But he had no choice. The news he carried was some of the most important of the war so far.

It was amazing, he thought as he rode off into the night, how the day's stunning victory now had the look of dark defeat.

Chapter Twenty-six

G en. Robert E. Lee, receiving the news of Jackson's tragic accidental shooting, wasted no time in appointing Jeb Stuart to take command of Jackson's corps. Before dawn on May 3, Stuart acted with his usual alacrity.

Will had managed to get only a couple hours of sleep after the events of the previous night. Very early he and the other officers were summoned to a meeting with Stuart. The general had to be as tired as the rest of them, but none of his weariness showed on his face as he explained the plan of attack to them.

"Our scouts report that the enemy has abandoned their forward position on the heights of Hazel Grove," said Stuart. His lips curved in a faint smile. "If he wants to make us this gift, we shall certainly accept it."

"Has Hooker gone mad?" asked Gen. Henry Heth, who was now in command of Hill's division.

"Mad or not, he's doing it," Stuart said. "General, you and your men will take the forefront in the attack to come."

Heth nodded grimly, and Stuart turned to Raleigh Colston. "Your division will form the second rank, General." Without waiting for Colston's acknowledgment of the order, Stuart swung toward Robert Rodes, who would have been in charge of the upcoming battle had he not relinquished command to the cavalry leader.

"General, I know your men suffered the worst of the fighting yesterday," Stuart said gently. "I would not throw them into the breach again were it not necessary."

Rodes nodded. "I understand, General. I assume we will be the third line of attack?"

"That is correct."

"I appreciate that, General," murmured Rodes. At least he and his worn-out troops would not have to lead the way into battle, but no one in the room doubted that before the fight was over, everyone would do his part.

The Stonewall Brigade, including Will and the Thirty-third Virginia, was now under Gen. Elisha Paxton's command. As part of Colston's division, they would be in the second line of troops when the attack began. As the meeting broke up, each of the generals passed on instructions to his subordinates. Will's immediate superior, Col. Abraham Spengler, clapped him on the shoulder as they left Stuart's tent. "We'll soon have the Yankees on the run again," he predicted.

"Yes sir," Will agreed. He might have been more enthusiastic if the wound on his hip hadn't been aching like the devil.

His only chance to talk to Mac had been brief, just a few moments before the meeting. His brother had described the long ambulance ride the night before and the horrible shape Jackson had been in when they arrived at the field hospital.

"I don't know if he'll make it or not," Mac said. "I've never seen a man lose that much blood and live, but I'm not a doctor."

Will thought about Jackson now as he made his way back through the predawn gloom toward his company. There had been no word of Jackson's death, so everyone was hoping that the valiant commander would hang on to life with the same fierce determination with which he had approached everything else. Will had been with Jackson since Manassas, and he found that he could not imagine continuing the fight against the Northern invaders without the general.

Darcy Bennett was waiting for him. The sergeant thrust a cup of hot coffee into his hands. "We about ready to hit them Yankees again, Cap'n?"

"Soon," Will said with a nod of thanks. He sipped the coffee, which was mostly roasted grain, and felt a little stronger.

By 5:30, just as dawn was about to break, the Confederates were in position. The Thirty-third Virginia, along with the rest of the Stonewall Brigade, was aligned just north of the Plank Road, facing east. The morning was foggy, so Will couldn't see much, but he knew that less than a mile to the east was the wooded hill known as Hazel Grove. Just beyond it was the open high ground of Fairview Heights, where the Yankees were concentrated. A short distance to the northeast was the crossroads and the big inn known as Chancellorsville. Tens of thousands of Union soldiers waited out there, no doubt every bit as anxious as Will was at this moment.

Rifle fire crackled in the distance as Confederate skirmishers clashed with the Union forces left on Hazel Grove.

Will stepped up into the saddle and drew his pistol. He looked at Darcy and nodded. The sergeant turned and bellowed to the company, "Move out!"

They started forward, a gray line in a gray dawn. To the north and south of the Plank Road, thousands of soldiers began marching eastward toward the enemy. The march quickly turned into a run, however, as the men's enthusiasm got the best of them. Will heeled his mount into a fast trot as a long Rebel yell split the morning air.

As they charged toward Hazel Grove, the sky lightened more, and Will could see streamers of smoke drifting in the air along the slope of the hill. Artillery boomed, and shells exploded well ahead of Will and his men, throwing dirt so high in the air that it seemed to be raining clods of earth. They continued to charge into the teeth of the bombardment as well as volley after volley from the Yankee sharpshooters. Will heard the flat, ugly, all-too-familiar sound of bullets hotly parting the air near his head.

The first line of the attack under Heth had already reached the base of the hill. The Confederates pushed upward toward the summit, their lines breaking momentarily, then reforming into a solid front. Will knew that each of those breaks represented dozens of men who had fallen to the Yankee defensive fire, but still the attack surged on as fresh troops clambered over the bodies of their fallen comrades, fired, reloaded, climbed higher, fired again, fell, got up, fought on. Many of those who pitched to the ground never pushed themselves to their feet again.

Then Will and his men were at the bottom of the slope. He felt a bullet pluck at his sleeve as he rode higher. The sun was up now, burning the fog away, but the tendrils of fog had been replaced by clouds of powder smoke. Its acrid stench bit at Will's nose and lungs as he shouted encouragement to his men. "Come on, boys, come on!"

The soldiers of the Thirty-third did not need much incitement to action. Yelling and screaming with a roar like one voice, they charged up the hill. Sheets of fire raked through their ranks, but still they kept on.

Will saw men blown apart by artillery blasts, arms and legs flying wildly through the air. He jerked his horse aside as a decapitated corpse stumbled toward him, still on its feet even though a crimson geyser gushed from the hideous hole in its neck where the luckless soldier's head had been a moment earlier. It took several seconds for the poor man's body to realize that it was dead, then it flopped limply to the ground.

When he recalled such sights later—if he survived the battle to recall them at all—Will knew he would be sickened by the bloody horror of it all. For now, though, he was inured to such emotions. He urged his men on, and when he spotted a cluster of retreating Yankees in the bright red-and-blue Zouave garb, he emptied his revolver in their direction and grunted in satisfaction as he saw two of the Union soldiers go down.

Nearby, Darcy Bennett fired his rifle and sent one of the Yankees spinning off his feet, then leaped forward and rammed his bayonet into the back of another fleeing soldier. The man screamed as he went down. Darcy ripped the bayonet free and plunged on up the hill, looking for another Yankee to kill.

The shelling eased somewhat, but the whine and whistle of minié balls continued to fill the air. Suddenly, Will reached the crest of the slope. He saw Rebel gunners turning captured Yankee cannon toward Fairview Heights and Chancellorsville. The deafening roar of shells being fired increased again, but this time most of the fire was directed toward the Union forces.

Colonel Spengler rode by and reined in as he noticed Will. "General Paxton is dead, Captain," he said. "Killed by a rifle shot in the opening minutes of the battle."

Paxton had not been well liked among the men of his command, but still Will felt a pang of sympathy for the man. "What are our orders now, Colonel?"

"Same as always," said Spengler. "Push on and capture Chancellorsville. Rout the enemy."

Will nodded curtly. The fighting at Hazel Grove was almost over. He called for Sergeant Bennett, and when Darcy turned toward him, Will ordered, "Rally the men. We're bound for Chancellorsville!"

Darcy wiped the back of his hand across his face and smeared blood on his features as he grinned at Will and responded, "Yes sir, Cap'n!"

THE EARLY morning attack lasted several hours, and the fighting was desperate as the Federal troops tried to hold their ground. Gradually, they were pushed closer and closer to Chancellorsville itself, where the impressive, red-brick inn still served as Hooker's headquarters.

Confederate artillery began to reach the structure, and Hooker himself was put out of action for a time from the concussion of an exploding shell. Dazed by his injury, Hooker chose not to relinquish command.

With the Yankees embattled from the west, Lee then struck with his remaining forces from the east, sending the divisions under Richard Anderson and Lafayette McLaws racing westward along the turnpike toward Chancellorsville. The end was in sight.

THE CAVALRY had been held in reserve during the first waves of the attack, but as the morning went on, Stuart sent more and more of his men forward. Mac had listened anxiously to the firing in the distance and watched the smoke rising into the sky. He couldn't help but wonder if Will was still all right.

It was a great relief to him when the order finally came sending Fitz Lee's cavalrymen forward toward the front lines of the battle. "Reports indicate that our boys are closing in on Chancellorsville itself," Stuart said to Lee as they conferred briefly. "I want you to find out just how close we are."

Lee nodded and waved for Mac to join him as he turned and rode toward the east. "About time, eh, Mac?" Lee said when they were out of earshot of Stuart.

"One thing, General," Mac said. "When we find out the situation, I don't want to be the one to gallop back to General Stuart with the report."

Lee stared over at him for a second and said, "Why, that's damned impertinent for a captain to be dictating assignments to a general. You just don't want to leave the field of battle once you get there."

"I follow my commander's example, sir."

Lee squinted at him then laughed. "Indeed you do! Let's go!"

They kicked their horses into a gallop.

The Confederates secured the high ground at Hazel Grove and moved their own artillery into position there as well as putting captured Federal batteries to good use. Shells poured into Fairview Heights, and the woods around Chancellorsville were on fire. Black clouds billowed into the air on both sides of the Plank Road as Lee's cavalry pounded along it. Mac no longer knew if the day was sunny or cloudy. The thick smoke created an overcast of its own, a flame-tinged gloom that he imagined must be very much like the atmosphere of Hades itself.

As they drew closer to the crossroads, a rider came racing toward them. The soldier stopped short and saluted, his face a grimy mask, his eyes wide. "Message from General Lee for General Stuart, sir!" he said.

Fitz Lee jerked a thumb over his shoulder. "Back that way about half a mile, son," he said. "But tell me, how's my Uncle Bob?"

The trooper's eyes widened even more. "Uncle Bob, sir?"

"I'm Fitzhugh Lee."

The messenger swallowed and said, "General Lee is fine, sir. His forces are quite near Chancellorsville to the east, and the Yankees have started a general retreat to the north."

"Glad to hear it," Lee said. "Now, go on, son." He waved the messenger on toward the west, then turned to Mac. "That report should satisfy Beauty, and now we can all stay and join in the fight."

"Yes sir," Mac agreed.

They rode on and shortly reached the top of a long down-slope that led to the crossroads and the Chancellor inn. To the north, bunches of blue-clad men were visible through the gaps in the smoke as they stumbled toward the Rappahannock. The Federal retreat was in full swing.

Lee drew his saber, lifted it over his head, and called out, "Ahead, boys, let's send the Yankees home!"

With a shout, the cavalry swarmed down the road toward the burning house.

—————

THE STONEWALL Brigade, without its namesake but still filled with his spirit, was in the thick of the fighting as the Northern-ers were driven back across Fairview Heights. Will dismounted and led charge after charge against the fading defensive lines of the Yankees. Sometime during the morning, without his notic-ing, the wound on his hip broke open and blood stained the leg of his uniform trousers. But he did not suffer any other wounds, despite heavy losses in his company. A Yankee bullet struck Darcy Bennett in the left arm, but that wasn't enough to stop the big sergeant from fighting. He cut a swath through a fading wall of Yankees, crushing skulls with the butt of his rifle and disemboweling men with his bayonet. Will was right beside him, slashing with the saber in his left hand and firing his pistol at point-blank range into the Yankees who lunged at him.

Late in the morning, as the Federal forces continued their steady retreat to the north, artillery set fire to the Chancellor inn. Leaning exhaustedly on his sword as he stood at the edge of the road, Will watched the clouds of black smoke billowing up and knew the battle was done. Outnumbered, outgunned, with every advantage against them, the Confederate army had defeated the Yankees with speed, daring, and sheer grit.

Hearing hoofbeats, Will turned and saw his brother riding toward him. Mac reined in the stallion, dismounted, and threw his arms around him. They pounded each other's back, overjoyed to see that the other had lived through another battle.

"You're hurt!" Mac exclaimed when he looked down and saw the blood on Will's leg.

Will shook his head. "It's nothing. An old wound."

An old wound, he thought. Suffered the day before. Already, that battle seemed far, far in the past. Each day was an eternity in war, he realized, because each day might be the last.

But not today. Today, he and his brother were alive, and they and their fellow Confederates had emerged victorious, and Will was content to stand and watch the burning building as the flames leaped and roared and the sparks danced high into the sky.

A cheer suddenly went up, and the brothers turned to look toward the east. Troops from Anderson's and McLaws's divisions were pouring into the clearing around the house. The rattle of muskets and rifles filled the air, and cannon roared and shells burst. But through the din of battle came the cheering, crescendoing as a ramrod-straight figure on a familiar gray horse rode to the head of the troops.

"General Lee," Mac whispered almost reverentially.

It was indeed Robert E. Lee, thought Will, and he felt a tightening of his throat as emotion threatened to overwhelm him. Against the hellish backdrop of the burning forest, Lee rode, and the men he had sent into that hell cheered him on. Feeble shouts emanated from the wounded, but full-throated roars of admiration and appreciation thundered from the able-bodied. Mac lifted his saber, and Will raised his empty pistol above his head as they added their voices to the tumult. Will had never seen anything like it.

He suspected that he never would again.

Chapter Twenty-seven

C aptain Brannon!"

Mac stiffened in his saddle as he saw Robert E. Lee and Jeb Stuart riding toward him. It was Stuart who had called out to him.

Will had gone to check on his company, but Mac was astride the big stallion near the Chancellor inn. The structure was still burning, but the flames had died down considerably. So had the sounds of battle. Rifle fire still popped to the north, where the retreating Yankees were being harried along by Confederates. The artillery was mostly silent.

The ground around Chancellorsville was littered with bodies, both Confederate and Union. Wounded men cried out for aid, and surgeons and orderlies hurried from place to place, doing what they could for the men who could still be helped.

Mac saw the pain in Lee's eyes as the general reviewed the results of the battle. But Lee was a soldier above all, and duty made him turn his gaze forward instead of dwelling on what had been lost.

As the two generals rode up to Mac and reined in, Lee reached inside his coat and brought out a folded piece of paper sealed with wax. Extending it to Mac, he said, "General Stuart tells me you are familiar with the whereabouts of General Jackson, Captain."

Mac took the paper without hesitation. "Yes sir."

"I'd like for you to deliver that dispatch to him."

"It would be an honor, sir."

"And then come back and let us know how the general is faring," added Stuart.

Mac nodded. "Of course, sir." He didn't have to ask if the two generals wanted this done right away. He saluted, wheeled the stallion around, and rode quickly along the Plank Road to the west, between the burned-out sections of the forest in the Wilderness and on the road toward the Lacy home.

Though the road was clogged with ambulances, supply wagons, and Yankee prisoners, Mac was able to wind his way through the traffic and a short time later reached the field hospital where he had left Stonewall Jackson the night before. He didn't know if the general was there or not, but if Jackson had been moved surely someone could tell him where he had been taken.

As soon as Mac spotted Lt. Joseph Morrison on a stool just outside the hospital tent, he knew that Jackson had not been moved. The lieutenant would never be far from Jackson's side.

Morrison looked up, saw Mac, got to his feet, and saluted. "Captain," he said. "Can I help you?"

Mac swung down from the saddle, saluted, and said, "I have a dispatch for General Jackson from General Robert E. Lee."

"The general is resting inside, sir."

Mac nodded his thanks and pushed through the entrance flap. Morrison followed him. Mac saw the general on a cot with Dr. McGuire and Captain Smith at his side. The faces of both men were haggard with strain, but clearly they had no intention of seeking a respite from their vigil.

Jackson himself was awake and seemed alert, though he was still quite pale. Mac felt a tinge of horror as he noticed that the general's left arm was gone, amputated just a few inches below the shoulder. What was left was swathed in bandages.

Mac saluted and announced, "A dispatch from General Lee, sir."

"Thank you, Captain," said Jackson, his voice a shadow of its former booming self. "Captain Smith, please read it to me."

"Yes sir," Smith replied, accepting the paper from Mac and breaking the seal. For a moment, the captain seemed overcome with emotion, but he collected himself and read the message in a firm voice.

"'Headquarters, May 3, 1863. General Thomas J. Jackson, Commanding Corps: General: I have just received your note, informing me that you were wounded. I cannot express my regret at the occurrence. Could I have directed events, I should have chosen for the good of the country to be disabled in your stead. I congratulate you upon the victory, which is due to your skill and energy. Very respectfully, your obedient servant, R. E. Lee, General.'"

There was a hush in the tent when Smith finished. Mac felt the same wave of emotion that had washed over him when Lee rode into the clearing at Chancellorsville. After a long moment, Jackson turned his head, clearly gripped with feelings of his own.

"General Lee is very kind," he said, "but he should give the praise to God."

No one argued with the general.

Mac caught Morrison's eye and angled his head toward the tent's entrance. The lieutenant followed him outside. When the two men had walked several paces away from the tent, Mac explained quietly, "General Lee and General Stuart asked for a report on the general's condition, Lieutenant. Could you ask Dr. McGuire if I might be able to see him for that information?"

"I can ask, sir," Morrison replied, "but I don't know if the doctor will leave the general's side. He has not since he first met the ambulance last night."

Morrison ducked back into the tent while Mac waited. After a few minutes, Hunter McGuire came out. He stopped and allowed his shoulders to slump in weariness as he let the canvas flap fall shut behind him, and a shaky hand came up to rest over his eyes for a few seconds. Then the slender physician straightened, took a noticeably deep breath, and walked over to Mac.

"Lieutenant Morrison says you need to speak to me, Captain."

"General Lee and General Stuart have requested a report on General Jackson's condition, Doctor."

McGuire nodded. "Of course. Naturally they would want to know. General Jackson is doing well for a man who has been so grievously wounded." The doctor's voice was clipped, direct and businesslike, as he went on. "He suffered three major injuries. A bullet penetrated the palm of his right hand, broke two bones, and lodged just under the skin on the back of the hand. It has been removed and the wound dressed. There was also a long wound on the left forearm where a ball entered the outside of the arm just below the elbow, passed through, and exited the inside of the arm just above the wrist. The most serious wound, however, was in the upper left arm, some three inches below the shoulder. The ball that struck the general there broke the bone and severed an artery, causing a significant loss of blood. The general had instructed me when we reached the hospital to do whatever I thought necessary in his behalf, so with the agreement and aid of the other surgeons, I amputated the left arm above the wound. The operation was simple and without complications or extensive additional blood loss."

Though McGuire's voice was strong, he swayed slightly as he described his patient, and Mac thought he might have to take the doctor's arm to steady him. McGuire gathered his strength, though, took another breath, and folded his arms across his chest.

"Thank you, Doctor," Mac told him. "What are the general's chances?"

McGuire shook his head. "It's too soon to say, Captain. Such serious injuries might have already killed another man who was less determined to live. But I suppose I am guardedly optimistic that Providence will smile upon the general."

"Can I tell that to General Lee and General Stuart?"

"By all means," said McGuire.

"Thank you, sir." Mac turned toward the stallion, beginning to order his thoughts for his report to Stuart and Lee.

"Captain," McGuire suddenly added, "as soon as possible, I'd like to move General Jackson to a safer location where he can be better cared for. If, of course, General Lee concurs."

Mac nodded. "I will tell him, sir." He mounted up and rode toward Chancellorsville. Behind him, McGuire turned and walked slowly back into the hospital tent.

—◦◦〜〜◦◦—

THE YANKEES, however, were not quite through. Hooker had sent word to General Sedgwick in Fredericksburg on May 2, ordering him to break through the Confederate defenses under Jubal Early and come to his aid at Chancellorsville. Sedgwick proceeded cautiously, though, not launching an attack on Marye's Heights until near midmorning on May 3.

The fighting was brutal, requiring four charges by John Newton's division before breaching the line of Southern defenders behind the stone wall at the foot of the heights. Bloody corpses were stacked high on both sides of the wall by then.

Once the Yankees had broken through, Early split his forces, sending most of them south so that the Federals would not be able to flank, encircle, and destroy them. A smaller force under Gen. Cadmus Wilcox retreated west toward Chancellorsville, fighting a delaying action so that Sedgwick could not easily come to Hooker's aid.

But despite the best efforts of Wilcox and his men, help was on the way to Hooker, whether Fighting Joe knew it or not.

—◦◦〜〜◦◦—

THE BANDAGE around Darcy Bennett's left arm was bloodstained, but the burly sergeant's face bore a broad grin as he sat on a fallen log and cleaned his rifle.

"Whipped 'em good, didn't we, Cap'n?" he asked Will, who was looking over what remained of the company. Half a dozen men had been killed in the fighting, and at least another score had suffered wounds serious enough to put them out of action for a while.

"We were lucky, you could say," Will said grimly. "They either didn't know that they outnumbered us almost two to one, or Hooker didn't have the guts to try to take advantage of it."

"Either way, they was the ones runnin' at the end," Darcy pointed out.

Will had to smile faintly. He couldn't argue with that.

He looked around as a rider galloped past. Anyone moving that fast had to be on an important errand. Curious, Will followed the trooper toward the temporary headquarters that had been set up on the grounds of Chancellorsville. The building itself was a smoldering hulk, with a few tendrils of smoke still rising from the blackened debris.

Several other officers gathered to hear the report being made to Robert E. Lee and Jeb Stuart. Will looked for Mac but didn't see him. He knew from a brief conversation with Fitz Lee that Mac had been sent to find General Jackson with a dispatch. Will supposed his brother had not as yet returned.

His jaw tightened as he heard that Sedgwick was marching on the Confederates from Fredericksburg. Lee and Stuart were equally grim-faced.

"I hate to do it to men who have already fought so valiantly and suffered so many losses today," murmured Lee, "but Sedgwick must be stopped."

Stuart nodded. "General Jackson's corps will be up to the challenge, General."

Lee frowned in thought for a moment, then shook his head and said, "I'm sending General Anderson and General McLaws to deal with this, General. General Jackson's men—your men now—bore the bulk of the fighting both yesterday and this morning. I want them to continue pressing Hooker toward the Rappahannock. If he regroups and launches a counterattack, that could be disastrous for our cause."

Will thought Stuart looked reluctant to accept Lee's decision, but he nodded and accepted the task.

Will drifted back toward his company. The rest of the Stonewall Brigade might not be heading east to meet this new threat, but he had already decided that he and his men would go along with Anderson and McLaws. If Sedgwick roared in unstopped, the Confederate victory would be compromised. Worse, it might even turn into defeat.

"Get the men ready to move, Sergeant!" Will snapped as he came up to his men.

Darcy smiled eagerly. "More fightin'?"

"Maybe," said Will. "We'll know soon."

Anderson's and McLaws's divisions moved out shortly thereafter, heading east, and if anyone wondered why a company of the Thirty-third Virginia was going with them, no one said anything. Will knew he might catch hell for this later from Colonel Spengler or even General Lee, but as he rode alongside his men, he looked forward to the battle.

That was a little worrisome, he mused. Here he was, worn-out from two days of fighting, his wounded leg freshly rebandaged and aching like blazes, his company at half-strength or a little less. And yet he was hurrying toward another fight instead of taking advantage of the opportunity to rest. Had he grown so hardened by war that there was nothing left inside him but the desire to kill the enemy?

He rubbed the back of his hand across his mouth and told himself it wasn't that way at all. The sooner the invaders were driven back where they belonged, the sooner the war would be over and the killing would stop. That was why the battles had to be fought and won, so that the war would end.

The sound of firing diminished behind the marching men then gradually increased in front of them as they approached this new battleground. Most of it was rifle fire, as not much artillery was involved in this fight.

A colonel unknown to Will rode by, calling out, "Move up quickly, men! Wilcox is making a stand at Salem Church!"

Will remembered the little church that sat beside the turnpike where another road joined it from the south. Like everything else in this area, it was surrounded by thick woods. Only the area along the turnpike and around the church itself had been cleared.

The weary troopers broke into a run along the road, forcing leaden leg muscles to work overtime once more. A Rebel yell rolled through the line of men, energizing them with the emotions it stirred. Will heeled the dun into a trot to keep up with his company.

Clouds of smoke began to cast a gray pall over their surroundings as the Confederates approached Salem Church. The little house of worship itself then came into view, and the line of men in butternut and gray surged forward. As they reached the church, the first rank dropped to a knee and fired a volley at the Union line less than a hundred yards away. Cheers came from the church as the men holed up inside realized that help had arrived.

Will dropped from the saddle and sent the dun galloping toward the rear with a slap on its rump. He drew his pistol and fired into the mass of Yankees who were within range of the short gun. The familiar whine of bullets sang in his ears.

Again and again the tide of blue surged toward the church, and again and again it was turned back. As the final charge broke, Will waved his men forward and drew his saber. The Confederates who had held the church launched a charge of their own, smashing into the retreating Federals and hurrying them on their way. For Will it was more brutal, hand-to-hand fighting, slashing back and forth with his saber and running through any blue-clad figure that loomed up in front of him. It was his third such fight in less than two days, and when the Confederates finally pulled back, he looked at the blood smeared on the blade of his saber and felt a coldness inside. War was truly butcher's work, he thought.

The afternoon had passed in battle, and night was coming on. It was Sunday evening, Will realized.

And this Sabbath day had been anything but holy.

―――

On May 4, in a maneuver hatched by Robert E. Lee, Jubal Early swung his regrouped forces back toward Fredericksburg and recaptured Marye's Heights, putting him at the back of Sedgwick and the Union corps that had been stopped cold the day before at Salem Church. Sedgwick, realizing the perilous situation in which he found himself and knowing by now that Hooker had been driven away from Chancellorsville, did the sensible thing and began retreating toward the Rappahannock himself. Lee's attempts to move enough men into position to crush Sedgwick were delayed by miscommunication, and Sedgwick slipped out of the potential trap during the night of May 4.

Hooker had already made his escape, and by the morning of May 5, virtually all of the Union army was once again north of the Rappahannock. Hooker's grand scheme had resulted in an ignominious defeat instead of the glorious triumph he had predicted so confidently.

The Confederate victory, however, had come at a high cost.

MAC RODE the stallion alongside the gently swaying ambulance. Robert E. Lee had agreed with Hunter McGuire's suggestion that Jackson be moved to a safer place to begin his recuperation. The general himself had selected the destination, the home of the Thomas Coleman Chandler family near Guinea Station, some ten miles south of Fredericksburg. The Chandlers were old friends and more than happy to have the general stay with them while he recovered from his injuries. So, on the morning of May 4, while Lee was trying unsuccessfully to surround and destroy Sedgwick's corps, the ambulance carrying Jackson had set out from the field hospital. Mac was part of the small detail assigned to see that the general reached Guinea Station safely. Fitz Lee had grumbled a little about having his aide so frequently borrowed, but he certainly wasn't going to argue with orders that came from "Uncle Bob" and Jeb Stuart.

And those orders were plain. Mac was to stay with Jackson's party until it was certain the general would recover. As soon as

McGuire was convinced of that, Mac would carry the word back to Lee and Stuart.

Mac wouldn't let himself think about the other possibility: that he might have to carry sadder news back to the generals.

Jed Hotchkiss, the civilian cartographer who, as a member of Jackson's staff, had mapped out most of his campaigns, had selected the route the ambulance would follow. With an eye toward both safety and comfort, Hotchkiss had sent the little caravan by the smoothest roads, which was also the quickest way. The route led past Todd's Tavern and Spotsylvania Court House.

McGuire, Captain Smith, and Chaplain Tucker Lacy were riding in the ambulance with the general, and Mac could hear Jackson talking animatedly with them. The general seemed much stronger now, leading Mac to hope that Dr. McGuire's guardedly optimistic prognosis would turn out to be correct.

He grinned as the ambulance passed small clusters of Confederate soldiers trudging along the road. Word of Jackson's moving had somehow gotten around, and many of the men knew who was in the ambulance. Cheers went up from them as the wagon rolled past. Ill-fed, in torn and tattered uniforms, exhausted from days of marching and fighting, these comrades from many battles found the energy to let out a shout or two for their beloved commander.

No matter what the outcome of the war, thought Mac, the Yankees would never conquer the Southern heart.

The Chandler mansion, Fairfield, was already full of wounded men, the Jackson party discovered when it reached Guinea Station late that afternoon. The family had prepared a small outbuilding that had served as the plantation's office, however. It had two bedchambers, and Jackson's litter was carried through a small anteroom into the one on the right. The general's wound still bled from time to time, and a crimson smear appeared on the jacket of one of the litter bearers. Clearly, the man didn't mind. To bear the blood of Stonewall Jackson would be a badge of honor.

As he stood in the anteroom while McGuire settled Jackson in and examined his wounds, Mac heard the general ask, "How long until I can take the field again, Doctor?"

"That depends on the speed of your recovery, General," McGuire said dryly. "Right now, I would not venture a guess. I will say, however, that the journey here seems to have done no harm."

"Excellent. I shall have to learn to ride into battle without one arm upraised, but I suppose I can manage that."

Mac smiled and shook his head. He had heard from Will and then seen for himself Jackson's habit of riding around with one arm raised. Like the general said, he would have to get used to not doing that now. Jackson's left arm, in fact, had been buried in a field near the hospital tent where it had been amputated.

For the next two days, Jackson lay in the bed in the little cottage and discussed battle tactics and religion with McGuire, Smith, and the other men keeping vigil with him. Mac spoke to the doctor a couple of times outside of Jackson's hearing, and McGuire assured him that the general's condition was indeed improving as much as it appeared to be.

"I think it would be safe now for you to return to General Lee and General Stuart, Captain, and carry the good news to them," McGuire told him.

Mac nodded. "Thanks, Doctor. I'll start back first thing in the morning."

By the morning of May 7, however, there had been a setback. Jackson's breathing had grown labored during the night, and he suffered from nausea. McGuire had felt confident enough in the general's condition to snatch a few hours of sleep, and when Jackson began to feel ill, he ordered that McGuire should not be awakened.

Mac knew something was wrong as soon as he stepped into the building that morning to say good-bye and inquire if there was any message the general wanted to send to Lee and Stuart. He saw the worried faces of the men in the anteroom, and when

McGuire emerged from Jackson's bedchamber a few minutes later, the surgeon's face was grave.

"General Jackson has developed pneumonia," he announced in a quiet voice. "There is little that can be done . . . but we will do what we can and trust in the Lord for the rest."

Pneumonia. Mac heard the word and turned to go outside and unsaddle his horse. He would not be riding back to Lee and Stuart today.

Drugged and in the grip of a fever, Jackson spent the next two days slipping in and out of consciousness. The general's wife, Anna, arrived, having been summoned from Richmond, and Jackson rallied somewhat when he saw her, recognizing her when he had failed at times to recognize the men around him, men who had been with him for so long, through so much. Anna offered to bring their young daughter, Julia, into the room for a visit. Through the open doorway, Mac heard the general's weak voice reply, "Not yet, dearest. Wait until I feel better."

That day was not going to come, thought Mac. What had looked so promising a few days earlier had rapidly changed. The hoped-for recuperation had become a deathwatch instead.

On Sunday morning, May 10, Mac was sitting on a stool in front of the cottage, smoking his pipe, when the canter of hoofbeats drew his attention. He came to his feet as he saw a familiar dun approaching.

"Will!" Mac exclaimed as his brother reined in and dismounted. "What are you doing here?"

"Fitz Lee told me where you were," he said, "so I decided to ride down and see you. The army's been given some time to rest up before we go chasing Yankees again."

"It's good to see you," Mac said as he clasped Will's hand. "How's your leg?"

Will shrugged. "Tolerable. By the time the war's over, I reckon I'll be so shot up I'll limp the rest of my life."

So far Mac had been just about untouched in battle. But that was just like Will, to be where the flying lead was the thickest.

Mac felt a sudden tightening in his chest as he looked at Will. A man's luck could only last for so long.

Will nodded toward the cottage. "How's Old Jack?"

Mac shook his head, and Will's expression grew grim as he explained. "He has pneumonia. He's not going to make it."

Quietly, but with every bit of feeling in his heart, Will said, "Damn. He was the best of us, Mac. The very best."

Mac nodded but didn't say anything. There was nothing left to say.

They sat and smoked and talked quietly as the day went on. A nurse brought the infant Julia from the Chandler house and handed her to Anna Jackson at the door. While the bittersweet visit was going on inside, McGuire stepped out. He looked more haggard than Mac had ever seen him.

In a hoarse voice, the doctor said, "I have told Mrs. Jackson that her husband cannot survive the day, and she has told him."

"What did he say?" asked Mac.

A ghost of a smile touched the doctor's lips. "He told her not to worry, that he might yet get well. He never gives up. And yet, in his heart, I think he knows the truth." McGuire looked at Mac. "I'm surprised you're still here, Captain."

"I'll stay until the end," Mac said, his voice sounding hollow even to his own ears.

That afternoon, Mac and Will were in the anteroom when McGuire offered Jackson some brandy. The general, lucid at the moment, refused. "It will only delay my departure and do no good," he said. "I want to preserve my mind, if possible, to the last."

The last could not be long in coming now, thought Mac. Jackson's breathing was shallow and rapid, each breath more choked than the last as the congestion in his lungs stole away his life bit by bit. Mac turned and looked out the doorway. From here he could see the tents of the nearby camp, and he knew that each of the men was aware of what was happening in the cottage. Probably thousands of prayers were going up to heaven right now on behalf of the general, but they would do no good. The hush of death hung over the estate.

"Tell Major Hawkes to send forward provisions to the men!"

The command came in a loud, strong voice. Next to Mac, Will jerked. As a member of the general's corps, he had heard that voice lifted in command numberless times.

"Order A. P. Hill to prepare for action! Pass the infantry to the front!"

The general's mind was on the battlefield once more, back home. Perhaps he heard the rattle of muskets, the roar of the cannon, the tinny music of bullet-dented bugles, the shouts of the men he was leading into battle. Tears rolled down Mac's cheeks as he seemed to hear those same sounds filling the tiny cabin. Everyone was in tears now, and silence settled over the place as the clamor of battle—real or only imagined, Mac could never say—faded away.

Then Jackson's voice came again—clear, aware, even cheerful. "Let us cross over the river, and rest beneath the shade of the trees."

The man known as Stonewall was gone, and the Confederacy would never be the same.

JAMES REASONER is a veteran writer of historical fiction. Author of several volumes in the Wagons West series, he has also written Westward, Expedition, and Outpost, a frontier trilogy set in the years before the Lewis and Clark expedition. Reasoner lives near Azle, Texas.

Jacket design: Bob Bubnis/Booksetters

Cover painting: Before the Storm by Don Troiani, www.historicalartprints.com